Praise for *When*

Filled with intrigue, heartache, love, *Tomorrow Came* had me hooked from the beginning. Regency genre held me captive with this unique story of the siblings Heath and Nan. Following their journey through the years in England had me crying and cheering for them. I can't wait to read her next book!

— Kimberley Woodhouse, bestselling author of award-winning
Secrets of the Canyon Series and *Bridge of Gold*

Hannah Linder dazzles with a timeless voice. I predict she'll become a staple in the Regency fiction genre.

— Caroline George, award-winning author of *Dearest Josephine*

Hannah Linder takes you back into the past where you just want to stay and be best friends with all of her characters.

— Lynette Eason, bestselling and award-winning romantic suspense author

Hannah Linder is one of Christian fiction's newest young writers that can easily stand alongside bestselling authors of Regency romances. Ms. Linder has a firm grasp on the historical nuances of the era, with quick and witty dialogue reminiscent of Austen's novels.

— Rita Gerlach, celebrated author of historical fiction

WHEN TOMORROW CAME

HANNAH LINDER

BARBOUR
PUBLISHING

DEDICATION
To my dear Granddaddy, with infinite love

PROLOGUE

*A*ll these years." His mouth dried as an acrid taste climbed his throat. He held her eyes, expecting there'd be precious tears, that in this moment—as he asked for her hand in marriage—she'd be looking at him with flashes of pleasure. With surprise. With that faint, thrilling glint of desire that kept him dreaming all the night.

Never had he imagined this.

With a reckless laugh, she twisted her hand away from his fingers. "What sort of fool do you think me, boy?"

Boy. The jab cut deeper than he was prepared for. So different from the familiar endearments, the loving way she'd always breathed his name before. *Boy?*

He moved closer, but she backed away, farther down the path. Closer to the roses he'd trimmed for her, and the lilacs he'd picked for her, and the peonies he'd tucked into her hair.

But they were dead now. Every flower was dead.

All these years. The words circled in the pit of his stomach. *All these years.*

"Lord Vickridge promises to have a statue made in my likeness, if I permit him to court me. Mr. Maffatt vows to take me to the theatre every night during my next season in London." A smile. A mocking clasp to her chest. "And the elusive Mr. Hemphenstall, who is rarely known to bestow his favor upon anyone, visited my father only a fortnight ago and seemed more than willing to forgo his trip abroad to spend his time, and money, on me." The eyes that had always teased him became cold. Somewhere in their pull, in their chill, the life and heart drained out of him. "Pray, what have you to offer me?"

Nothing. Before, he might have said love. He might have imagined it would be enough. Might have taken pride in the heart he handed to her.

But there was no heart left.

No love, no feeling, no life.

All these years.

He sprinted away from her so fast the garden, the world, became a blur. Blackness wrapped deathlike fingers around his stunned soul. He clutched his ears. Choked out air. Wished to heaven the sound of her inhuman laughter would stop ringing in his ears.

But it didn't. Maybe it never would.

All these years, I've been a fool.

CHAPTER 1

London's East End
March 1801

*I*mpulse made Heath Duncan's hands slick, made his young muscles tighten with the urge to sprint away. But he remained still like the cobblestones and merely swept a careful glance around him.

People milled by, arrayed in colors as drab and worn as the murky sky. The hum of words mingled with the steady clomp of a horse, the creaking wheels of a hackney, and the faraway shrill of a woman's hue and cry.

One second passed.

Then two.

From three feet away, the apron-clad baker exchanged another loaf of bread for two halfpence. "'Ere ye go, fellow, and 'ave a good day."

"Can I 'ave it wrapped?"

"For sure, ye can." The baker shifted, reached for something on the other end of his table—

Now. Heath grabbed the loaf. Heart pounding, he brushed past shoulders and stared ahead, as if an imperative errand urged him on.

"Thief!"

Panic drove him faster.

"Him! That's him!" the baker's raspy voice called. "Stop that thief!"

The streets narrowed, the crowd grew, and the cobblestone became jagged, as if with every intention of stopping him. Wind tore the cap from his head.

"Thief! Thief!"

Dodging around a woman and her bushel, Heath jerked around the corner bookstore and darted down an empty, shadowed alleyway.

Please, please. Half-frantic prayers made a helter-skelter race in his mind.

Shouldn't he be used to it by now?

He didn't know. Didn't know if he'd ever be.

At the alley's end, he cut around a second curve and navigated toward Lought Street, where he spared a glance over his shoulder.

Nothing.

He dragged his sleeve across his wet forehead. Needed to slow down, play the part of the errand boy again. Then again, who would think *him* an errand boy?

He didn't even have shoes. Hardly had arms and legs, either. Just a lot of skin on bones, with dirt so thick that he imagined it was the only thing that kept him warm at nights.

I have bread. Not much else, but he had bread. They wouldn't go hungry tonight. He wouldn't have to watch her hollow, desperate eyes go dim again, wouldn't have to listen as she lay on her side and dry-heaved, wouldn't have to grasp a thin hand that was starting to feel like bones only lightly covered with skin.

At least not tonight.

Another curve landed him on Cocksedge Road, where evening shadows invaded as quickly as the cool fog.

Just a few more minutes. Two or three at the most, then Nan would have something to smile about again.

Something drifted across the air, a sound that had no place in a dirty street. Soft, lulling, and familiar. Heath froze until the words finally penetrated his shock.

Nan. He sprinted across the street, following the song as if it were a paunchy gentleman with short pockets. When he neared, no one crowded around her. No one even stopped. They merely passed by, as those who crush a flower without ever realizing the glorious scent enhanced their day.

Midsentence, her song fell away. "Heath."

He grasped her hand, peeled back her fingers. One farthing.

"Heath, I'm sorry."

A reprimand tried to surface, but he had no strength. Instead, he grabbed her elbow and tugged her back into the alley she shouldn't have left. Mud, always mud. The stench of it became swallowed in every breath, absorbed in every rag of clothing.

God, I can't do this.

When they reached the empty crate, he yanked off the blanket and motioned her in. They squeezed in next to each other, close enough that their knees were forced to their chests, before he dropped the blanket back down.

Then silence.

Tears appeared, just as he'd known, in six-year-old eyes that were empty and starved. "Did you—"

He pulled open his coat, slipped out the loaf.

Her laughter was half whimper as she tore it in two, handed him the rest, and took ravenous bites.

Can't, God.

"Good." She brushed crumbs away. "This is good, Heath."

He nodded. Held it in his hands, but couldn't eat. Why couldn't he bring himself to eat?

"You had trouble?"

Shook his head.

"No one caught you?"

Had they? Strange, how all the days were starting to blend together like a nightmare. He should have known they couldn't make it alone. Should've never tried in the first place. Should've stayed where Nan didn't have to go hungry, even if—

"Heath? Did they?"

"No." The first word raked past his dry throat. "No, they didn't."

"You're angry with me?"

"No."

"I'm sorry."

"I know."

"I won't sing again."

How many times had she said that? Didn't she know the danger she was in? How easily a stranger could cart her away?

No, she didn't know. Too young, too innocent. He was wrong to expect it of her, wrong to leave her here alone, wrong to make a crate her home.

"Eat it, Heath—"

"We're going back."

"What?"

"We're going back to the Bobber."

Silence again for longer than he'd expected.

Then her chin rose with a tremor. "No."

"We have no choice."

"No."

"We can't keep on like this."

"I won't go back!" The scream vibrated the frail crate walls. "I won't go back for nothing, Heath, not nothing. I won't let her hit you like that."

"It doesn't matter."

"I hate her."

"I know, but—"

"She'll kill you if we ever go back. She'll beat you over and over, just like that time you helped the rector with his goat." Tears trailed through the grime. She shook her head. "You wouldn't wake up. I thought you were. . .thought she. . ."

Heath leaned backward. Sounds of her sobs made him sick, achy. *God, what to do?*

No voice answered. Again. He was tempted to forget everything the rector had ever taught him, but then what would he have left?

"Heath?"

"Yes?"

"When's Papa coming back?"

"Today or tomorrow." Why did she ask the same question every day? And heaven help him, why did he always have the same answer?

"I wish he was here."

"I know."

"I'll never go back to the Bobber."

"We have to."

"I won't."

"You must."

"You can't make me."

"If I have to—"

"No!" In one swift movement, she lunged past the threadbare blanket.

Heath rolled out, scampered to his feet. "Nan, wait!"

Matted hair billowed behind her as she splashed through the mud.

"Nan!" He raced forward as she left the alley behind and hurled into the street. "Nan!"

A deafening scream stopped him. Horse hooves had crashed into flesh and cobblestone. He was rocked by the high-pitched groan and curse of a driver atop a carriage.

Heath's feet caved under him. *Nan.* Blur, all a blur. *God, no. Please, no. I beg of You.*

She wasn't hurt. She was all right. Papa was coming home. Today or tomorrow. They would never have to go back to the Bobber. Never, ever again.

Tell me it's so, God.

His vision cleared when he didn't want it to, afraid of what he might see. *Nan, my Nan.*

In the stilled street, a middle-aged gentleman flung aside his topper to hoist Heath's sister into his arms. The man's voice rose with orders, then the driver hurried to open the carriage door.

Seconds later, the wheels carried her away.

And Heath had no idea what to do.

Glass circles made the eyes staring at her seem bigger. Nan Duncan wished they wouldn't look at her. She wished they were not so close. She didn't know anyone who wore spectacles. What would Heath say?

Soft, empty, sleepy space enveloped her. Then waves, almost like the sea. Was that a ship?

Oh, she wished it were a ship. She wished it were Papa's. She wished he were coming home. *"My little Nan, is that you?"* His voice carried over the dreamy waters. *"Nan?"*

Then another voice, one that made the ship go away, one that made the warm waters turn to ice. *"You little beggar! Your* père *is never coming back."*

He was. Today or tomorrow. Heath said so.

"Where is your brother?"

The rectory, she hoped, but she'd never tell.

"Where?" A hard slap, plunging her deeper into the cold. *"Where is the little rat. . .little beggar. . .where. . ."*

Nan's limbs jerked. She seemed wet all over, but something cool brushed away the moisture. No more sea. No more ship. No more Madame Le Sueur's fury and the Bobber.

Heath? She tried to rise, but nimble hands ushered her back down.

"There, there, child." The eyes again. The spectacles. "There is no need to try to move."

Panic stabbed as she noticed clean walls with pictures, four green bed curtains, and a face she'd never seen before.

A smile creased clean, smooth skin. "I shall have you know it is morning, little one. Did you know you slept through a great raucous?"

She couldn't answer.

"You did, indeed." The man set aside his cloth and finally tugged the spectacles from his nose. "It seems the ornery side of a mouse was revealed today, as the little varmint scampered halfway up the innkeeper's dress. Are you certain you heard no screaming?"

Her tongue didn't want to move, so she shook her head.

"I say, that is strange. I was frightened out of my wits—though you must vow not to repeat the confession. I cannot have all of London thinking me the coward, now can I?"

She glanced about the room again, this time with tears. *Heath?*

"Oh, listen to me, won't you? Here I am talking about a great scare, and here you are half in one yourself." He drew the covers closer to her neck. "The name is Mr. Fredrick Stanhope, and I am the unfortunate fellow whom you collided with on Cocksedge Road. Just now, you are at an inn I often frequent, and the doctor has already confirmed that—beyond a poor bruised leg—you are quite on the mend. I am deeply sorry for my carriage's role in your distress."

"H–Heath?"

"Who?"

"Heath." She swallowed. "He's my brother."

"Oh yes, of course. If you tell me the address, I shall send for him at once, along with anyone else you wish to see." He waited. "Can you not think of it, dear?"

Should she tell him of the crate?

"Of course you cannot, given what you've been through. I shall bring in some soup and cocoa, and we shall both think better after that." With a slight, gentle pat to her cheek, the stranger turned and walked away.

Nighttime came with greater cruelty than ever before. Even the crate called to him, with its thin cloth—hardly even a blanket anymore—and rotten boards.

But he couldn't go back there. Not now. For the second night in a row, he must remain where he was. He must watch the white-painted door. He must remain alert for the moment Nan was tossed back out.

Why had they waited so long? By this time, whatever pity the gentleman must have had was doubtless worn as thin as the crate's covering.

Unless she couldn't be moved.

Slow, poisonous fear entered his veins. He shifted on the ground and stiffened his back against the faded brick wall. *"The Lord thy God will shield thee, my son."* The rector's words rang like a lullaby. *"Pray to Him and He shall answer."*

The rector's gracious smile, his soft touch to Heath's shoulder, his ever-whispered words of God and faith—that is what had pulled Heath through. Always bruised. But the rector had never scolded him. Always hungry, but the rector had always ushered him inside for bread. Always fearful, but the rector had never failed to soothe him with a coaxing laugh.

Until the man had taken another parish.

Then the rectory had been left empty.

Now Heath had nowhere to go when he hurt, when Madame La Sueur came at him again, when he wanted to die for the pain.

Some shield. The words left a dry, wretched taste in his mouth. *God, forgive me.*

After all, he still had Nan.

He hoped.

The inside of the carriage was big. Bigger than the crate even. She wished she had a carriage of her own. She wished she could live here, where the seats were warm and soft, where the walls kept away the cold wind.

All too quickly, the movement stopped.

"Here already, my dear." As soon as the door opened, Mr. Stanhope vaulted to the ground, then reached for her. "Are you in much pain?"

She inched across the seat until his hands lifted her.

"That's a fine girl." He settled her tight against him, as if he didn't notice her dress was soiled, as if it didn't matter that she smelled of alley mud.

"Any pain now?" he asked again.

Was there? She didn't think so. For two days in a row, she hadn't been hungry—and that was the only pain she hated. "No, it don't hurt."

"Jolly good. Driver, wait for me here, won't you? We shall only be a minute." His eyes resettled on her. "All right, where to, dear? Consider me your own personal carriage. How is that?"

She pointed down the alley. "This way."

"This way it is." With a hum on his lips, Mr. Stanhope strolled forward and around the mud holes. She wondered if he liked to sing too. Sometimes she remembered Papa singing, with his pipe pressed between bearded lips, and his eyes crinkled in the firelight.

Heath never sang, though. Not ever.

"There, Mr. Stanhope."

Mr. Stanhope halted two steps from the crate. "There what, child?"

"There's my..." The sentence quivered as slightly as the blanket in the faint breeze.

Mr. Stanhope's eyes remained fastened on the object. His smile sank a little, then his shoulders sagged. "Oh, I see, Miss Duncan."

"Heath isn't here."

"He lives here too, does he?"

"Yes, sir."

"Where do you think he has gone?"

"He'll be back."

"Think so?"

"Yes," she said. "He gets us food. I'll just be waiting for him. I always wait for him."

"By yourself?"

She nodded.

With one hand, Mr. Stanhope lifted the crate blanket. "I suppose there is nothing to do but say our goodbyes, hmm?"

"I wish Heath could see you."

He leaned her inside. "Fine fellow, is he?"

"Oh, yes. He's tall."

"Taller than me?"

"No. Heath is only twelve. You're all grown."

"Grown, am I? Do try not to mention it to Mrs. Stanhope, should you ever meet her. I have the dear woman convinced I am a young dandy, and she loves me all the more for it."

She smiled.

"Say, say, now. What are you thinking?" He smoothed her dress back over her knees. "Smiling like that, you must be thinking something."

"Nothing."

"Oh, come now."

"Just that. . ." Her chin dipped to her chest. She couldn't look at him. "You're so very nice, and you took care of me and you. . ."

"And I what, child?"

"Gave me so much to eat." Tears welled, even when she wished they'd go away.

Behind the spectacles, Mr. Stanhope's did the same. She couldn't imagine why.

"Dash it all," he murmured, pulling her back from the crate. "I cannot very well leave you here, now can I?"

"But Heath—"

"We shall leave him a note to come for you at the inn. How does that sound?" Without waiting for a response, he trotted back through the mud and left her crate behind him.

꧁꧂

The paper was so white against the grime of his hands. He read it twice—first with quick, desperate glances, then slower, as the reality filtered through.

What is this? Heath crumpled the letter in his fist. Why would the man do that?

No one else even cared to hear her sing. At the Bobber, lodgers always shoved her aside or made her carry their valises, serve their port, or fetch another dice for hazard.

Why should a stranger do all this?

Heath tossed the paper and sprinted away from the alley. He'd followed the carriage. He'd watched the way the man had carried her, watched the sweet glow in Nan's eyes—that faint, seldom glint of comfort.

Comfort Heath couldn't give her. Couldn't ever give her.

As long as he'll have her, she can stay. He wouldn't go to the inn. He wouldn't take her away from such a haven, not even for a moment.

Because soon enough, the gentleman would turn her out.

Heath would be waiting.

Then they'd return to the Bobber, if that's all they could count on.

Nan waited and waited and waited, but Heath never came. First one day, then two days, then three days, then four.

Mr. Stanhope said she shouldn't rise from bed, but she did anyway. As soon as he left the room, she'd limp to the window and stare down into the street.

Not like Cocksedge Road. Instead of ragpickers, she noted ladies with pretty bonnets. Instead of smoke and dirt, the buildings all had flowers, even fancy curtains in some of the windows. Instead of beggars and fishermen, the streets were filled with matching horses and carriages.

But she wanted Cocksedge Road. She wanted her crate. She wanted Heath.

Where are you? She pressed shaking fingers against the cool glass. *Please come for me, Heath. Please let him come, God.*

The fifth day, Mr. Stanhope swept into her room with a package. A present, he said. Had she ever had one before?

She couldn't remember. She tore away the paper and found a dress that had no holes or dirt or patches. But even after she put it on, fear hurt her stomach more than hunger ever had.

Something had happened, something terrible. Why had she not listened?

She should have stayed in her crate and never sang. She should have listened when Heath wanted to return to the Bobber. She should have stayed close to him, shouldn't have run, should have remained close enough to him that the carriage wouldn't have hurt her. . .

Heath, I'm sorry. Empty, broken words. No one here to listen. No one here to say it would be all right again. No one to promise her when Papa was coming home.

Today or tomorrow, today or tomorrow, today or tomorrow. Over and over again, until she almost believed them. *Heath, why won't you come?* She pressed her hands into wet eyes. *Why won't you come?*

"Now see here. I've been all day in Lord Wain's office, watching him imbibe brandy and talk of Parliament nonsense, with nothing to keep my sanity but the pleasant hope of a smiling face. And when I should finally escape, what do you think I should come home to?" Mr. Stanhope doffed his beaver hat as he advanced toward the bed. "Indeed, I should rather endure his lordship than a face as dismal as yours, Miss Duncan. Whatever is the matter?"

Nan didn't look up. She knew she should look at him, knew she should answer, knew she ought to make the tears ride back down her throat.

But even when she told them to, they didn't listen.

Mr. Stanhope must have known. The bed creaked as he settled next to her, then his large hand enveloped hers. "It is the days you have been counting, is it not, my dear?"

Pain pulled her hand from his grasp. She looked away, frantic. "I want Heath."

"As I am certain he wants you." His hand grasped hers again. It was Papa's, she told herself, only she knew it wasn't true. He wasn't Papa. She didn't want his hand. She wanted Heath's because Heath always took care of her, always made everything all right, always prayed when she was scared.

"My, my, are those more tears?"

"I want. . .Heath."

"I know."

"Why won't he come for me? Why won't he?"

"He will."

"When?"

"Most likely today or—"

"No!" She didn't want to hear. She hated the lie. She hated waiting for today or tomorrow. "No, no. I want Heath." She pushed the man back.

"There, there, dear. If I could give him to you, heaven knows I would."

The pillow drank her tears, just like Heath's shirt.

"But you need not worry. I have been looking. I shall not abandon you, child."

Papa had. Heath too.

"If he does not appear in the next four days, I shall take you with me to Dorrington Hall. A balm it is for weary souls, my dear. Green grass, rolling terrain, a thousand trees all in loveliest bloom. I am most confident you shall be happy. Did I tell you I have a son near your brother's age?"

"H–Heath." Heat burned across her chest. "What about Heath?"

"I shall continue looking for him myself. If he is nowhere to be found, we shall leave another note." Mr. Stanhope's eyes gleamed behind the spectacles. "And like as not, we'll have no more than arrived at Dorrington Hall when your brother shall be hurrying after us."

Light drizzles fell from a fearsome noon sky, cold enough to make his flesh rise in bumps, dastardly enough to make the streets slick under his feet.

But he kept running, ever running.

Ahead, the carriage made another turn. Slower now than before. Was the driver remorseful that he had injured a little street waif less than a fortnight ago?

Prickles of excitement darted Heath into breakneck speed. Just a few more moments. He knew where the carriage was headed, had known as soon as the gentleman carried Nan from the inn.

Grateful. He wiped more moisture from his face, as the carriage cut off toward Cocksedge Road. *Grateful she was fed, taken care of.*

For ten days, he hadn't carried life and death on his shoulders. He hadn't watched her hurt, hadn't suffered the failure of another sunset with empty stomachs.

Even so, he'd never known ten days to last so long. Why did it feel like years?

A grin started as he stepped around a rippling puddle. In the first haze of dawn, he'd nabbed a fresh chunk of cheese from a sailor who'd gotten more occupied with a mug of ale. All day long, Heath's mouth had watered and his stomach had tightened with a cold longing for just a nibble.

But he'd saved the whole of it.

Oh, to see Nan's face! Mayhap he'd ask her to sing for it, the little songbird. Nothing in the world like the rich, childlike music that had so often calmed him in the deadest night—

"'Ey, there, sonny. Watch yerself, won't ye?" Body odor and the bare shoulder of a weighty strumpet smacked him off balance.

Heath's bottom slammed wet cobbles, but he scrambled back to his feet. The carriage was just reaching the alley—

"Bad form, ye know." A podgy hand snatched his coat. Seams ripped. "Ain't ye goin' to say nothin'?"

Heath wriggled from her. He groaned with the snapping sound of more thread. "Please, I—"

"Fie, get off'n yer little throne, beggar. Ye're no better 'an the likes o' me."

One final lunge. The shoulder of his coat tore open, but he hastened far enough away that only the woman's vile oaths could reach him. Cold, damp air invaded where his shirt was not thick enough to protect. Madwoman. Why couldn't she have left him alone?

As he neared, the *clomp, clomp, clomp* of horse and carriage was already moving away.

He gave one more pat to the cheese—at least the madwoman hadn't bothered that—and dashed into the dank alley. Quieter than he would have thought. Why had he half expected Nan to be singing?

As he neared the crate, something odd quivered the corners of his soul. Strange, how uncanny and still it seemed as if. . .

Heath bent before the blanket. Cold, numb fingers brushed it back.

No, God.

Empty space stared back at him.

And a note.

CHAPTER 2

Dorrington Hall
Somerset, England

*C*oarse rope burned the palm of Gilbert Stanhope's hands as his foot finally caught the top of the stable window. Halfway up already. Just a few more feet and—

"How ye doin', Master Stanhope?"

"Do not talk to me."

"Eh, what's that?"

The heels of Gilbert's shoes made a scraping sound against the brick. "I said"—he grinned and pulled himself higher—"do not *talk* to me. Can you not see I am a bit occupied?"

The servant boy, Loftus, must have at last moseyed away, for the incessant questions settled into blissful silence.

Almost there. A thrill rippled through every muscle as he yanked himself inches from the rooftop. One hand dropped the rope just in time to catch the ledge. The other clung to the rope, as his leg swung up—

"Gilbert!"

The cracking bellow jolted his hand from the ledge. Then his leg. *No.* Hissing air, his mother's shrill scream; then the raspy grunt from his own throat as both hands finally secured the rope.

His body dangled back and forth, like the rocking of a Scots pine in an autumn breeze.

"Heaven help us, Gilbert, whatever are you doing?"

He laughed. "Nothing at all, Mamma."

"Nothing, indeed! Have you no thought of what could have happened? Why, I nearly watched you tumble to your death!"

As if in scolding, his sister's infant cry rose from their mother's arms. Only three months old, and already she was against him.

"Now come down this instant, Gilbert."

"Say what?"

"Come down!"

"Stay up here, you say? Ah, you're a gem, Mamma. For that I shall give you a kiss and—"

"Really, Son, no more jesting. Now do as you're told before I go and write your father another letter—"

"Mrs. Stanhope!" From somewhere below, untimely Loftus returned with more of his shouting. Why must the old chap always shout, anyway? And couldn't he see it was no time to be a bother with his superior hanging from a rooftop?

"Yes, yes, whatever is it? Are you the one who talked Gilbert into such a scheme? I shouldn't be surprised at all. Gilbert, what have I told you about playing with the servants?" She paused for only a breath. "Come on, down with you, Son! Now Loftus, whatever is so important?"

"Just that the carriage, madam. It's coming through the gates."

"Whose carriage, pray? I do wish you would get straight to the point instead of always meandering about a matter as if you had all the time in the world."

"Sorry, Mrs. Stanhope. I'll do better, I will."

"Well then?"

"Papa." From his heights, Gilbert spotted the familiar carriage easing toward the house with dust billowing in its wake. He let out a whoop. "Papa's home!"

"Are you sure?" asked Mamma.

Even the baby squealed.

"Never mind that. Just climb down here and do not get excited. A pitiful homecoming that would be, if you were to fall to your death."

Gilbert slid down the rope, past the stable window, and landed with ease on two firm feet. "See? Unharmed again. Now may I have that kiss?"

"You shall have more than a kiss when your father hears of this. Now make yourself presentable and—oh, here, you hold Charlotte while I freshen up." After shoving the baby into his arms, Mamma scurried back to the manor house through the courtyard entrance.

Baby Sister stared up at him, for all the world looking like a smaller image of himself. Same blue eyes, same unruly brown curls, same fair skin much too prone to burn during playtime outdoors.

"Here." Gilbert outstretched her to Loftus. "Be a good chap and take her, won't you?"

"Not me." The little coward backed away with his hands up. "All to yourself,

Master Stanhope."

"Lucky sort, I am." Situating her to the shoulder, Gilbert darted for the manor's northward side, fast enough that he was waiting at the massive front steps when the carriage drew to a stop.

His father hopped out with a smile large enough to cover the whole of his face. "Well, Son, what have you there?"

An amused snort. "What do you think it is?"

"Oh, come now, we've long since stopped calling her an 'it,' haven't we?" Rather than approaching with his customary hug, he turned back to the carriage instead. "All right, child. No need to be daunted now." With the words, Gilbert's father drew out a small figure from within.

Dressed in a clean, buttoned gown, with glistening auburn hair tied away from her face, one might have mistaken the girl for a servant or even a village child.

But the shoes gave her away.

They were small, filthy, with holes big enough that some of her toes peeked through. Was that a bandage wrapped about her leg?

She smoothed her dress down before he could tell.

"See here, Nan. This is my Gilbert I told you of. Nearly fourteen. The little one is Miss Charlotte, not yet four months."

"And already as devious as you please," Gilbert said.

With a cold, distant stare, the street girl's eyes slanted to his. "How do you do?"

He bowed slightly. "Fine, thank you."

"Well." His father removed his hat. "Where is Mrs. Stanhope gone off to? I had rather hoped she would be here to greet me."

As if on cue, the mahogany front doors flew open, and she floated down the stone steps in a different gown from earlier. "Fredrick!" With cheeks unusually flushed, she hurried into her husband's arms. "A short trip, indeed. I shall never believe that again. Whatever took so long? We expected you four days ago."

"Apologies, my dear." He nodded to the child. "Allow me to introduce Miss Nan Duncan, our honored guest for as long as she shall have us."

Gilbert stepped forward with a flicker of annoyance. "How long, Papa?"

"Who can know?"

"If you were going to bring home an urchin, Papa, could you not have brought home a boy?"

"Gilbert!" His mother spared a warm smile to the child, even wrapped an arm around her scraggy shoulder. "You are more than welcome here, my dear, I assure you."

One by one, they turned to the stone steps in the hum of conversation. First a footman, with his father's bags in tow. Then Papa, who ascended hand in hand with Mamma.

Then the urchin lastly, with a limp that made every step seem laborious. Only once did she glance back.

If her eyes had been cold before, they were fire now.

The hearth crackled with sounds that were soft and melancholy. In the firelight, Mamma's face creased with frowns. "Who is she, Fredrick?"

Gilbert's breath hitched in waiting. From behind the damask chair, where he lay undetected, he saw Papa light a cigar and puff.

Shouldn't be here, of course, but he'd learned so very little about the girl at dinner that he could bear the suspense no longer. After all, if she was to be a new Dorrington resident, didn't he have the right?

"That I hardly know," Papa said at last, exhaling the scent of cheroot. "Beyond her name, she has told me nothing."

"Where did you find her?"

"Half beneath my carriage."

More silence, as Mamma cast a fretful glance back into the hearth. "I've never seen a child so painfully thin. She is near starved, you know."

"I know."

"Did you see her poor feet? Beneath those wretched shoes were only dirt and bruises."

"I do not doubt."

"Has she no one at all? No family?"

"Only a brother."

"Where is he?"

"By George if I know. I went looking for the lad a dozen times or so, even waited there at the little crate they inhabited."

"Crate? And he never came?"

"Never. Probably saw the chance to be rid of her, if you ask me. Of course, we could never relay as much to poor Nan."

"No, of course not. Never." As if in some sort of mood, Mamma rose from her chair and settled onto the Persian rug before her husband. Her hands grasped his, and her whisper crackled like the flames. "You did right to bring her here, my dear."

"Yes. I rather imagined you would say so."

The Bobber stood in the darkness, its outline shrunken and withered. The windows glowed. Sounds drifted into the air, with discordant tunes and the occasional slurred laughter of drunken men.

She'll never have to go back. Heath's bare feet remained planted in dewy grass. He watched as a shadow passed over the window, a man he'd never seen before, and he slouched against the glass as if his legs wouldn't hold him up.

She won't go hungry. One step closer. *She won't live in the crate. She won't have to sing for anyone.* Three steps from the door, he reached for the note in his pocket, fingered the soft paper, and told himself to do what it asked.

But he couldn't.

God, I want to.

Couldn't.

Let me get her.

No, couldn't ever.

I'll die alone.

Silence answered his silent cries to heaven.

With numb limbs, he approached the door he hated. He pushed the knob, then passed from soft grass to rough boards.

The blur of dirty fishermen, shabby gamblers, and scantly clothed trollops all sped before his eyes like a nightmare.

One he'd lived before.

In silence, he slipped to the splintery wall and followed it toward a door—

A man's hand snatched his collar. "Well, wot do ye know 'bout that. The little brat is got tired of his pig's feed, hain't ye?"

Heath didn't shrink away. Only nodded.

"Someone, go get the Frenchy." The man jerked Heath toward a corner table, kicked out a chair, and thrust him into it. Then he sat across from him with a grin. "Now this is something I's gots to see. A mad Frenchy is a right humorous Frenchy, eh wot?"

Heath circled his hands around the chair. Sweat poured. His stomach cramped as he turned his mouth into his coat and heaved nothing.

A moment fled.

Then two.

By and by, the man across from him passed out with his face in the table—which meant there was still time to run.

But he couldn't run. Too weary, too hungry, too lifeless.

So he sat and waited until sleep persuaded his eyelids to close, and his pain dissolved into dark pits of blessed oblivion—

"Where is your *sœur*, your smelly little sister?"

Panic shuddered his chest even before he opened his eyes. He rose from the chair, swallowed past a lump. "She is g–gone, Madame."

"Dead?"

Did it matter?

"Answer me, boy."

"No."

"Coming back?"

He shook his head.

The woman's dark, crazed eyes glared at him. "Then why did you?"

He nearly wilted.

"Why did you come back? You think because your *père* left you here, I will take care of you always?"

"Please, I—"

"I tried so many years, but you are worthless. You want the streets, you stay on the streets!" Her hard, cold hand seized his ear. Fingernails dug into tender flesh. Blood trickled as she slung open the rattling door. "Now go!"

He grasped her arm. "Please, Madame, I'm so hungry—"

"*Oui*, but you should have thought of this before you left."

"Anything, please, but I—"

"You will get nothing from me. Not again." With one vicious swing, she whacked him outside. She started to slam the door, then froze as if with thought. "Except maybe this." She reached into her sagging blouse and yanked out a small letter, tossed it down at him. "For all the good it will do you." The door crashed shut.

Heath grabbed the letter without looking at it. He pulled himself to his feet, stumbled into the darkness, fell beside a tree too small to lean on.

God, let it end. He wept so loud the night seemed to echo his pain. *Please let it end for me.*

He didn't deserve anything good. Not like Nan, with her sweet voice and eager eyes. She would be happy because God wanted her to be happy. She would have a family because she was worthy of one.

Never in his life had he been worthy. He caused his father to leave, the madame to hit him, his sister to run away from him.

Why won't it end? Grief clawed away the last of his strength. *Have mercy and let it end, my God.*

But it never ended, yet one more prayer unanswered, and all night long he lay and trembled.

Not until morning transformed the sky and he'd pushed himself from the ground did Heath finally glance at the letter.

He read the name, scarcely believing.

The rector.

CHAPTER 3

For two days, Gilbert had only seen the child at the table. She never looked at anyone. She only sat—as pale as she was skeletal—and ate so little he wondered if his mother had been wrong. If she had truly gone without, why would she not eat?

On the third day, she entered the breakfast room as early as he had. With the sight of him, a deathly pallor crossed her cheeks. She retreated two steps.

"Don't go." Gilbert bolted from his chair. "Papa shall be down soon, and he shall be glad to see you."

She hesitated.

"Oh, come now. I shall even prepare your plate. What shall you have?"

Her eyes darted to the sideboard. "I can get it myself."

"I would like to help you."

"I don't need you."

"Very well." Gilbert sank back into his chair as she limped to the sideboard. Her stance was rigid. Auburn curls reached halfway down her back.

She bothered him, the little creature. For several nights, her impish shadow had invaded his dreams and her eyes had haunted him, like a ghost he'd once seen in a childhood storybook.

Papa should have never brought her. He didn't like her. Didn't want her here. Never seen anyone so strange—and yet it was more than that, somehow.

Sadness.

As she turned with her plate, the realization made Gilbert's insides tighten. Yes, it was her sadness that bothered him most—because try as he might, he could not stop it from infecting him too.

"You do not like me very much, do you?" he asked.

Her face flushed with anger, and she hurled back French.

"What?"

She repeated herself.

"I heard you, but what does it mean?"

"You don't know French?"

"No." Gilbert brought his fork down into a sausage. "By no fault of my tutor."

Instead of responding, she took another bite of plum cake, chewed for a bit, then swallowed it down with a sip of milk. Dainty little thing, even for a street urchin.

"Well then?" Gilbert ripped away his napkin. "If you are angered about what I said to Papa about a boy—"

"I don't care what you say!" Fury whipped into an unsteady voice. "I don't like you." She jerked back her chair. "I wish I never saw you. I wish I had my. . .my. . ." A sob claimed her last words as she darted toward the door.

Gilbert flung after her. "Miss Duncan!"

Three steps shy of the stairs, her leg crumbled beneath her. She smacked the polished floor, her moan mingling with the sharp crack of bone.

Gilbert slid to his knees next to her. "Miss Duncan." He rolled her over. "Miss Duncan?"

"What is the meaning of this?" From behind, his father's tone rose in panic. "Gil, what happened?"

"She was angry, Papa. She started running and fell and I. . ."

"There, there, Son. Move over." His father swept the girl into his arms. "She is out cold. Go fetch your mother and send a servant for the apothecary."

"Yes, sir." Gilbert sprinted up the stairs to his mother's bedchamber through a blur. "Mamma? Mamma, come quick!"

She answered the door with little Charlotte in her arms. "My heavens, whatever is the matter?"

"There has been an accident. . .the girl."

"What happened?"

"She fell. . .her leg."

"Oh my." She shifted the sleeping bundle into his arms. Only when she'd hurried a few paces down the hall did he catch her faint murmur, "God, be with her."

'Twas a prayer he echoed himself. For no matter how much she bothered him, he had no wish to see harm come to her. Especially harm that was his fault.

❧

By the third knock, the familiar voice drifted through sturdy oak wood. "Come in, come in."

Gilbert pushed his way inside, rolling down one of his sleeves.

"Well, what have you been doing?" His father turned from a shelf of books, one volume in his hand. "You look a mite out of sorts."

"Just riding Briar again."

"You be careful with that horse. He has more verve in his bones than good sense."

"I'm careful." Gilbert plopped into a chair by the unlit hearth as his father thumbed through old pages with seeming interest.

From above the desk, the bracket clock twanged the hour, before settling back into a constant *tick-tock, tick-tock, tick-tock.*

"All right." The book snapped shut. "What is it?"

Gilbert focused on his sleeve, a small rip. "I, uh, saw the apothecary leave."

"Just so."

"He was here a long time."

"Yes." His father moved behind his desk and sat in a chair that groaned. "I'm afraid he left us with less than encouraging news."

"Such as what?"

"She has quite broken her leg."

Air built inside of his chest, forcing his eyes back to the rip. He poked a finger through the hole. "Will she walk?"

"Likely, yes. The apothecary has done all he can, and the rest depends vastly on her own ability to heal."

Another tick. Another tock.

"Son?"

Slowly, his eyes raised to meet an older, bluer likeness of his own. "Yes?"

"By no accounts was any of this your fault, you know. I shall not have you bearing guilt over the matter."

"I upset her."

"She was upset already."

"I made her cry."

"Her tears were not for you nor because of you." From behind the desk, his father arose and approached Gilbert's chair. The man's strong grip squeezed his shoulder. "Now let us not talk of this any longer. Concerning little Nan, I ask but one thing of you."

"Yes, Papa?"

"Be kind to her. Whether she stays for one day more or all her life, be kind to her." A tighter squeeze. "Can you do that, Son?"

"Yes, Papa." A strange, almost fearsome pride fluttered through him. This was a task Papa needed of him. Maybe the little girl needed of him too. If everyone else at Dorrington Hall should be welcoming to the child, shouldn't he?

He met his father's eyes again and nodded. "I shall."

❦

Again, she was not allowed to leave the bed. This time, she didn't try. There was no reason to look out the window. There were no people out there, no alley with an empty crate, no Heath waiting for her.

There was nothing. Just hills, so many hills.

When's Papa coming back? In the silence, she mouthed the words.

Four mean, lonely walls stared back at her.

"When's Papa coming back?" Aloud this time, as if from some hidden place, Heath would step around the mirror or crawl out from under the chair or. . .

He's not coming back. She glared down at her legs and wished they had the strength to run away. *There is no today. No tomorrow.*

Because they weren't coming back for her.

Neither of them.

❦

"All right, he is bringing her down." In the candlelight and evening shadows, Mamma's face was warm with anticipation. "Temperance, will you go and get the cake, please?"

With a quick bow, the little maid slipped away to do her bidding.

"And Gilbert, won't you please get up from the floor? With the baby too, of all things. I should think you will never learn to become a genteel person."

"Come now, she likes it, Mamma. See?" He pulled her away from the rug, but her tiny fingers clung to the golden fringe. "Little imp, she is."

"Really, Gilbert. No nonsense now. Up, up."

He had no more than swung to his feet—with Charlotte in his grasp—when the drawing room doors parted.

His father entered with a tiny, almost ghostly little being in his arms. "I told you everyone should be waiting for you, did I not?"

Glistening, timid eyes roamed to all of their faces before they quickened back to the buttons on Papa's tailcoat.

"Oh yes," Mamma said. "We have all been looking forward to seeing you again, my dear. Now Fredrick, place her here on the chaise lounge where she shall have more than enough space."

Strained silence endured for moments longer than it should have. Then Papa, ever faithful to entertain, launched into a lively tale of the mill he'd attended in Sussex last season.

Not even his enthusiastic reenactment, the hearty laughs, or the Banbury cake

Temperance returned with could persuade the child's lips into a smile.

Gilbert sat in his chair, bouncing Charlotte on his knee until her cackles stretched into yawns.

"Shall I take her, dear?" Mamma asked.

"No, not yet." On any other evening, he would have returned the little elf to Mamma. He would walk to the window and stretch. He would watch Papa light another cigar and ask, as he often did, when he himself would be old enough to smoke.

But tonight, his greatest diversion was the babe growing tired in his arms. Little Charlotte's fussing kept him from joining the conversation, kept him from looking at the urchin, kept him from colliding with her gaze by accident.

What must she think of him? What did he think of her?

He could not tell. She spoke so little, smiled never, changed expressions only when she thought herself unobserved.

Be kind to her. His father's words resurfaced. Why was he so afraid to? She seemed hostile, set against him. Or was she against them all?

Without meaning to, his eyes fell to her leg. A small ounce of guilt pricked him, as tiny as a thorn to the finger, yet painful enough to become a bother.

Yes, he should be kind to her. He *would* be kind to her. After all, she was very young and alone and frightened. Unapproachable, perhaps, but still very frightened.

When his parents turned their conversation to each other, Gilbert crept from his chair to the lounge. "May I?"

Her lips pressed. A mere nod.

He sat close to her with hopes that the baby's snores would soften her face of stone. Never a girl yet who would not swoon at the sight of a wee one. "Do you like her?" He pressed the baby closer.

Heat crawled along the pale cheeks. Then a shrug.

"She likes to play with the rug, you know. Quite the ornery little thing. Should you like to hold her?"

Nan shook her head quickly.

"Don't be afraid. She always sleeps with her mouth open like that. Watch this." He jiggled her chin with his finger. Still, his sister slept on. "See? You cannot even wake her. Here—"

"No." Quivering voice, yet steel lined her words. "I don't want to hold her."

Gilbert froze. Stared at her.

From across the room, Papa must have seen, because he hurried over and eased Nan back into his arms. "I think it has been quite the evening for all of us. Ready to retire to your chamber, Miss Duncan?"

Her nod was frantic. "Yes."

When Papa had swept her from the drawing room, Gilbert sank lower into the lounge and sighed. If nothing else, he was trying.

'Twould be much easier if the girl would try back.

❧

The walking was endless. Rain, then mud. Rain, then mud. Rain, then mud all over again, until the chill spread into his bones.

Sometimes a wagon would stop along the road. Heath would climb into the back, burrow himself under hay that was soft and damp, and imagine the rocking was only Papa's ship.

But too quickly, the hay was gone. He was on his feet again, trudging through mud, drenched in rain.

At night, he would venture away from the road. Sometimes he climbed into a tree. Other times he crept into barns that were quiet with cattle moans and heavy breathing.

But always, no matter where he was, he would draw the letter back out of his pocket. He would open it, smooth it, read it all over again:

> *Dear Heath,*
>
> *If this letter ever reaches you, I shall know that Providence led me to write it. My pities, my prayers, and my heart went out to you, as I learned only yestereve that you and young Nan had disappeared from the Bobber.*
>
> *Should I have known you had such plans, I would have taken the both of you with me to my new parish many months prior. My only reason for not doing so was my hesitancy to remove you from the home your father chose, for should he ever return, that is doubtless where he'd go.*
>
> *Please know, my child, that if you ever must find me, I am in Chanfest, Kent, at the St. Jericho Church. May the grace of God be with you eternally.*
>
> *Yours,*
> *Mr. Mayhew*

By now, the parchment was stained, the ink splotched with moisture. How long would it be? How long had it been already? Rain, mud. Rain, mud. Rain, mud. When had he eaten last?

The farmer with the bowl of mutton. The traveler who'd tossed bread out the

34

window of his curricle. Then the peddler day before who'd shared his meal of venison. Or was that the day before that?

He didn't know and there was no one to tell him. He only stumbled farther, coughing until his chest burned, watching for a church tower with every hill he crested.

Heaven help him, if he wasn't close, he'd die.

Or maybe he was dying already.

CHAPTER 4

*E*very day, Mr. Stanhope came back to Nan's room. At first he would sit in the chair by her bed, then poke at her leg a bit, then tell her all sorts of stories that made her smile.

She didn't want to smile. Not ever again. But she couldn't seem to help herself.

Then he'd take her into his arms, with his cheek against hers, and say, "What say you to an evening of fun, little one?"

She never answered, but he always carried her downstairs anyway. Sometimes he'd place her back on the lounge, where Mrs. Stanhope would sit beside her and read her books. Other times, he'd walk her outside to the stables, where Gilbert would show her every horse and where they lived.

She pretended she didn't like horses. She never touched them when he asked her to or fed them when he handed her a bit of oats. She only hugged Mr. Stanhope's neck and looked away, time and time again.

Days came and went, each one so alike, until it almost seemed familiar. Mr. Stanhope always came for her, just like Heath had always returned to the crate. Mrs. Stanhope always read to her, and her eyes were soft and nice. Even little Charlotte, who had been pressed into her arms more than once, always wore a smile.

But Gilbert was different. She didn't like him. He was terrible to wish she was a boy, and even though he tried to be nice, she still remembered what he'd said.

He didn't want her here.

For that, she would never like him.

"Where to, then?"

"Chanfest, sir."

"Aye? 'Tis a bit o' luck shinin' on ye then. Headin' to Chanfest meself."

Luck? The irony slapped Heath in the face. As another wagon wheel dipped in the road, Heath grasped the seat and shuddered. "How far?"

"Two days or so, I'll wager."

"Two?"

"What I said, hain't it?" A grunt, then a chuckle. "Ye can be ridin' with me all the way, if ye 'ave the mind to."

"Thank you, sir."

"Though I can't rightly see wot the deuce ye want in Chanfest. Hain't a decent place for a dodger like yerself. Not enough pockets to pick—if ye know what I mean."

Shame made his skin clammy and heated. Or was it the fever?

"Ye hear me, lad? I said there hain't no future for ye there."

Dizzy, so dizzy. Why did the wagon keep moving in circles?

"All right, lad, into the back with ye."

Heath blinked, shivered again. "What?"

"I said into the back o' the wagon. Ye're a sick dodger, if e'er I saw one, and I surely don't be wantin' no dead gooses to bother with."

Heath had stumbled over the seat, dropped into a pile of damp-smelling sacks, and half drifted to sleep before the man muttered, "Hain't nothin' at all in Chanfest, fool lad. Not nothin' at all."

But the man was wrong. Something *was* at Chanfest.

The last of his hope.

❧

"Who's there?" Nan's legs dangled on the edge of the bed, her gaze fixed on the door.

For the second time, it creaked open another notch. Still, no answer.

A slight giggle escaped, as Nan waited for Mr. Stanhope to fling the door open and plunge inside. He was funny. He didn't sing like Papa or comfort her like Heath—but he did make her laugh.

But when it finally eased open, it wasn't Mr. Stanhope who stood in the doorway. Instead, it was a girl. Hadn't Nan seen her before?

She was pretty and wore clean dresses. Nan did now too. She never had before, though. Not at the Bobber. Or even before that, when it was just her and Heath and Papa.

Sadness swept over her, but she tried not to think of them.

"I'm Temperance, miss." A quick curtsy. "I'm ten already, and Mrs. Stanhope says I'm old enough because my mother was, and her mother before that, and—"

"Old enough?"

"Yes, miss."

"What're you old enough for?"

"To be your lady's maid, of course."

"I'm not a lady."

"Neither am I."

"Then why do you want to be one?"

"I don't. I mean, well, of course I do. I always have. My mother was, and her mother, and her mother too."

"I don't have a mother." Sadness again.

The girl's blue, rounded eyes lifted with shock. "Oh, Miss Duncan, I'm ever so sorry. I never should have spoken about my mother. I promise I shall never do it again. I won't even speak of my father. Will that make you happy?"

Nan didn't know what to say, so she pointed to the cane partly hidden behind the girl's dress. "You can't walk either?"

"Me? Oh, no. I mean, yes, I can walk very fine, Miss Duncan. Loftus says I run almost as fast as him sometimes—he works at the stables, you know—but I don't pay him any mind because he only says it because he likes me so." Temperance came forward and presented the thin, gilded cane. "Mr. Stanhope said I should give this to you. Should you like to try it?"

Nan eased her best foot down before slowly sinking her other to the soft rug. Pain made her clutch the cane with tears. "It hurts."

"Oh, dear. Is there anything I can do? I can do most anything, you know. That's what a lady's maid is for."

Nan looped her free arm around the girl's shoulder. She was nice too. Just like Mrs. Stanhope. "We can walk to the stairs."

"All that way?"

"Maybe Mr. Stanhope will be surprised. Then he won't have to carry me."

"He likes to carry you. Everyone has such good things to say about you—well, everyone but Master Gilbert, that is."

Her grip tightened on the cane. "What does he say?"

"Nothing at all, miss. I daresay, nothing at all."

Go away. Probing hands hurt Heath. Every muscle tightened in waiting, but the blow never came. *Please—*

"You answer me now or I'll just be leavin' ye right here."

The words sliced into his consciousness. Heavy lids squinted open to a face too close to see clearly.

"That's better now. Ne'er could stand to talk to a bloke what wouldn't look me in the eye." The man edged back a mite. "Now, ye best be tellin' me where to, if there is a place, 'cause I got to be on my way."

The church. He moved his tongue across cracked lips. "Th–the. . ."

"Speak up, now."

"The. . .church."

"Pshaw." The man hoisted Heath's arm around his shoulder. "Ye would 'ave to say the one place I done swore ne'er to go to."

Heath's knees buckled as they hit ground, but the man kept him steady. Hazy everywhere, almost like London. "Where. . .where am I?"

"Chanfest, o' course. Where you think?"

"But two days. . .you said it'd be two days."

"So it was. Ye know, I must be a mite saintly at heart, 'cause I done listened to you moan and groan the whole way and ne'er once dropped ye out."

Thank you. The words built in his throat, but he wasn't sure if they ever made it out. The man helped him across the street toward the church. Distant birds disturbed the morning silence, and the songs put him faintly in mind of Nan's.

At her name, the last of his strength threatened to dissolve.

"Just a step or two more. Don't ye be givin' out on me now, lad, or I'll be forsakin' ye yet. Just see if I don't."

I won't. The promise swelled, as his bleary eyes lifted to the stone church. Gray, rising fog enshrouded the building. Almost in greeting, rays of sunshine poked through like tiny celestial fingers beckoning him home.

"All right, lad, but I won't be goin' with ye no farther. Like I said, on me mother's grave, I done sweared to ne'er come inside a church again—and I hain't willin' to dishonor meself now."

Thank you. Again, no voice.

The man retreated back into fog that engulfed him.

God, please. Every step led Heath closer, until at last his bare feet climbed the dewy, upward steps. Thousands upon thousands of them, but he couldn't give up now.

At the door, he pounded both fists. The weak sound echoed into silence. Why was no one coming? The rector. . .wasn't he here?

He must be here. He *was* here. God would not lead him this far only to—

Heath crumbled against the door. Weeping writhed his aching shoulders, but he made no sound. *Please, please.* More pounding. *Please come. Please—*

"Child?"

Heath turned and stared down the stone steps as the man climbed them slowly with familiar ease.

"I was tending Polly." The rector bent next to Heath with a voice that chased away a thousand demons. "You remember, do you not, child? The goat who was always invading the garden patch?"

Heath fell into the rector's arms. More sobs came, and this time, he didn't try to stifle them.

The rector said nothing after that. For a long time, he merely held Heath and rocked him back and forth. The motion was consistent, safe, the first moment of comfort Heath had known in so long.

Then the rector gathered him up. With strength mindful of Heath's weakness, the man carried Heath into a small rectory and lowered him into a bed with drawn coverlets—almost as if the rector had been waiting for him.

Perhaps he had.

Heath's soul soared.

Of course he had.

With every week that passed, the ghost of a girl began to change. The terrorized, hungry shadows melted into features that were soft and glowing. Her smiles became more frequent, her laughs much happier—and once or twice, when she suspected no one was near, Gilbert detected the youthful sound of her singing.

She was adjusting very well.

To everyone, that is, except him.

Gilbert had done as Papa had asked. He'd been kind. He'd treated her cordially, helped as often as she would allow, and returned every glance with a smile.

But dash it all, he had his pride too. How long could he go on bothering with the little chit when she apparently despised him?

Enough was enough. Perhaps he had insulted her, but if a chap couldn't make one mistake, what hope had he?

None at all.

For as long as Nan Duncan remained at Dorrington Hall, Gilbert was doomed to fill the role of her despicable enemy—but he would do so from afar. No more would he give her chances to frown at his smiles, shrink away from his hand, or turn her face from his words.

With that resolve, a new set of days unfolded around them. April crept into May, then May into June, until all the mornings were warm and sunny.

On one such day, he rose early enough that the breakfast room would be empty, polished off a plate, then scampered out of doors to take Briar for a trot. The hills took him far out of sight, deep into familiar realms, alongside trees that clapped and swayed.

When he reached a flattened valley, he slackened the reins enough to let Briar have his pleasure. Hooves pounded. Air whistled. With exhilarating, reckless speed, the horse charged on through sweet-smelling air, as if a wicked gnome were on his heels.

Sweet mercy, not even climbing roofs or hiding the tutor's quizzing glass could be such sport.

One hour sped into two, and by the time he returned to the stables, the late morning sun had replaced the early one.

"That's not true."

Gilbert froze outside the stable door.

On the other side, someone grunted. "Ye are a stupid one, hain't ye? Just a good thing ye're a crippled one too, else ye'd be a houseless waif again. Why do ye think Mr. Stanhope brought ye here in the first place?"

"He likes me."

"His conscience, ye mean—"

Gilbert yanked open the double stable doors, pulled Briar inside.

From two stalls away, Loftus's wide-set eyes swung over. His mouth gaped without words as he shuffled away from the figure he'd been towering over.

Gilbert flung aside leather reins. "What are you doing?"

"N–nothing." Another retreating step. "Nothing, Master Stanhope, just gettin' ready to—"

"Apologize."

Silence.

Then defiance raised the boy's chin an inch higher. "Now just ye wait, Master Stanhope. I know me place and e'erything, but she's just a—"

"Apologize."

"But she—"

"Apologize, Loftus, before I make you do it."

"Yer papa will make me do it, ye mean. Not you."

Irritation flared. "You saying I can't?"

"We'll ne'er know. If ye weren't nothin' but a servant, like as me, I'd whup ye quick, I would."

Already, Gilbert was shrugging off his tailcoat, rolling up his sleeves. "Then I'm a servant."

"Ye'd tell on me, for sure."

"Never." Edging closer.

"How do I know?"

"You have my word." Closer still, until Gilbert finally raised his fists and grinned. "Ready?"

"But Master Stanhope—"

Gilbert swung, catching the boy's jaw. A returning fist whizzed past Gilbert, but he ducked in time to tackle Loftus's legs.

They smacked the ground, rolled, grunted as one blow followed another. *Whack.*

Colors danced just long enough for Loftus to slip on top. *Whack, whack.*

Gilbert flung his hands free and sent his knuckles into the other boy's nose. Blood sprayed.

Whack, whack, whack.

One punch for another, until Gilbert's mouth tasted coppery and his muscles started to ache.

Loftus scooted backward first, whimpering with raspy breaths. "Leave off, will ye. . .Master Stanhope?"

Gilbert dragged himself up. "I daresay we've just begun."

"No more. . .can't take no more."

"See here, fellow. You did say you were going to whup me, did you not?" When Loftus only glowered, Gilbert reached for his hand and hauled him up. He brushed the straw from his shoulders. "All right, we shall say no more about it."

Loftus nodded, started past him—

"Ah, ah." Gilbert snagged his elbow. "One more thing."

"What?"

For the first time, Gilbert's eyes wandered back to the corner, where little Nan stood as still as a painting. A solemn, frightened painting, at that.

"Apologize," he said again, "and never trouble Miss Duncan again."

"Sorry." The word exited half mumble, half scowl—before Loftus jerked free and dashed out the stable doors.

In his absence, a strange quiet fell.

Gilbert didn't look at her, only returned to where Briar was waiting, grabbed the reins, and led his horse to an empty stall. He pulled off the saddle. *Fine mess I'm in.* As soon as he entered the house, he had no doubt but that his mother would be there, waiting for an explanation he couldn't give. *If I told her I—*

"I'm sorry."

He paused, turned.

Nan stood at the stall's entrance, no taller than the walls on either side of her. "I'm sorry," she said again. "I am."

"No need." Gilbert hung the saddle, grabbed a brush. He waited for the slight patter of little feet to fade into stillness.

But she never moved.

Except closer.

Gilbert remained still, though he was tempted to squeeze into the corner. What was she doing, little chit? If she was going to hate him, she might as well keep her distance.

"It hurts?"

"What?"

"Your lip." Brown eyes peered up at him. "And your cheek."

"Oh." Gilbert drew a hand across his mouth, frowned at the sight of blood. "No, it doesn't hurt. But you had better return indoors—"

"Come lower."

"Huh?"

Her finger motioned him downward. "Real close."

Dash it all, what was she up to? Even so, he knelt to her level and watched with wariness as she lifted the hem of her dress.

She swished it across his cheek. Patted softly. Rubbed painlessly. "There." The first smile she'd ever bestowed on him. "No more blood on you."

Should he thank her?

"I always help Heath. Sometimes he don't wake up, though."

"Your brother?"

Her head bobbed. Tears appeared, then disappeared as quickly as a cloud obscures the moon. "But that was at the Bobber. I don't have to go back there, not ever."

Gilbert rose. What to say?

At his silence, her face scrunched together. She shuffled backward, rubbed her eyes—

"Here now." Gilbert followed her out into the open, caught her arm, and knelt back before her. "Why the tears? I should think you would be very happy."

"I'm not happy."

"Why shouldn't you be?"

"Loftus was right."

"Doubtful. Poor chap, he's never right. What did he say?"

"He said. . .Mr. Stanhope didn't want me here. Or Mrs. Stanhope, either."

"What a lot of rubbish. Can you not see they adore you?"

"But you don't want me here." Tears leaked free in glistening rivers. "I know you don't."

Guilt made a small nip at his chest. For a second or two, he merely looked at her. Then he dropped his hands and sighed with exaggeration. "Behaved badly again, haven't I?"

She stared at him.

"I'm always behaving badly. Just look here what I've done today. Chances are, if I were not getting into trouble, I would have nothing at all to do with myself."

A hint of a smile surfaced. "I get in trouble too. Heath gets mad."

"Everyone gets mad at me. Have you ever seen my dear mamma when she's in a state? If it were not so unfortunate for me, it would be funny."

She laughed, a delicate sound, and it thawed his ill opinion of her.

"Now, Miss Duncan." He grasped her hand and pulled her back to the stall. "Have you ever had the honor of grooming such a handsome horse?"

She shook her head.

"Should you like to?"

A nod.

"Very well." He fetched her a stool and lifted her up, planted the brush in her hand, and guided her strokes down the animal's back.

For a long time, he stayed and helped her, talking and laughing, flipping the horse's mane one way to another. When at last she was ready to return indoors, she left her cane some forgotten place on the stable floors.

And took his hand instead.

CHAPTER 5

Dorrington Hall
September 1807, six years later

*G*oodness, Nan. Can you not play something a trifle less dismal?"

Without looking up, Nan glided her fingers the length of the pianoforte, hit the final notes, then dropped her hands to her lap. This was dreadful. *Gilbert* was dreadful. How could he do this to her?

Frustration built inside her chest and made her sigh. "I can only play happy songs when I am happy."

"I see." Mr. Stanhope's eyes flicked to the longcase clock on the other side of the room. "Though I daresay, if a birthday cannot make you happy, what can?"

She turned back to the keys again, but Mr. Stanhope captured her hand.

"Now no more of that. Come into the drawing room and talk to poor Charlotte, for if someone does not entertain her, I fear she shall turn into one of those trinkets people are always stuffing in shelves."

"But I must practice."

"You may practice another day." He pulled her up and looped her arm in his. "Besides, mourning away in the music room shall not make him come any faster."

"But he promised!"

"So he did." They left the music room in silence and navigated along pristine, empty corridors. "But you must remember our dear Gilbert is not ours alone anymore."

"What do you mean?"

"He cannot run about and play backgammon for the rest of his life, now can he? As much as we would like to keep him at Dorrington Hall, he must eventually adopt a world of his own."

"How terrible."

"Come now. You are only sulking because he has not arrived for your birthday. Yet he shall be home not five minutes and you will be bickering with him."

Amusement tickled through her despite a second sigh. "It shall be his fault."

"So you always say." He parted the drawing room doors, and Nan took her place beside Charlotte, who made herself a nuisance by bothering the ringlets of Nan's hair.

This was *very* dreadful. For the umpteenth time, she searched the room for a clock. The ticking hands heightened her dismay. *My twelve years have met a bitter disappointment, indeed.*

❧

This was the one place in the world where everything was still. Only the evening shadows stirred, dancing and scurrying from the stained-glass windows as silently as the sun sinks to night.

Heath dipped his brush back into soapy water. *"Papa, why is she screaming?"*

"Hush, Heath."

"Is she going to die?"

"No, she will not die." Faint, indistinct—but he remembered Papa standing, walking across the room, and entering the room of screams.

With both hands, Heath scrubbed the brush along wide, grainy floorboards. Forward, back. Forward, back. Soap mingling with last Sunday's dry dust.

"I want to see Mamma."

Days had gone by, or had it been but hours?

Papa had stood on the threshold. No more screams. Just a bloody, half-wrapped creature in his arms, who lay as still as sleep.

"Papa?"

Never a word. Just a raging, hollowed look. He'd come forward and pressed the creature into Heath's chest, stared at it a minute, then left the cottage.

Heath hadn't wanted to enter the room, not the room of screams, not when it was so silent.

But he'd clutched the babe and crept in anyway.

Mamma was in the bed again. She'd been there a lot lately. Almost every day. She'd been tired, she said. Always tired. Something was wrong with her tummy, something that would give him a sister, something that made her cry.

"Mamma?" He'd crept to the bedside so he wouldn't wake her. *"Mamma, we have a baby now."*

He waited for her to smile. She would be happy because she'd waited for so long. They all had.

But she remained still, with cheeks that were white as the bedclothes, with legs that were tangled and splotched with dark blood.

"Mamma, are you dead?" He'd touched her hand. Cold, clammy, limp. *"Mamma—"*

"There you are."

Heath jerked.

The rector's shadow passed over the soapy floor. "I have been sitting at the table waiting for you, my son."

"I'm sorry." Heath dumped the brush back into the bucket, stood. "I had forgotten."

"Forgotten to eat?"

Warmth erased a portion of his nightmares. "It will not happen again," he said, lifting a smile. "I'll finish in here as soon as we're done."

"Never mind. I ate without you before the mutton grew colder." The rector took the bucket and brush. "You go and eat, my son, and I will finish in the church."

"No, sir, let me do it—"

"You work very hard. Let an old saint have his small part in the Lord's work, will you?"

"You make it sound like an honor, sir."

"It is."

Heath nodded, tried to smile, started away—

"My son?"

He stopped short of the church doors. "Yes, sir?"

"Whatever troubles you this day, the Lord thy God would like to know. He may not always change it, but He certainly showers it with grace."

A knot sprang to Heath's throat. Couldn't answer, but he knew he didn't have to. As he passed through the massive church doors, a small prayer sprung within him. *Wherever she is, Lord, let the day of her birth be happy.*

That was all he wanted.

All he'd ever wanted.

Why did all the world—or Dorrington Hall, that is—retire at such an early hour? Eleven was not so very late, after all.

"Thank you, Murray. Take care of the carriage, won't you?"

"Yes sir, Master Stanhope. I shall also deliver your luggage upstairs."

"All but this." Gilbert reached back into the dark carriage and plucked a small package from the seat. "For Nan."

The servant flashed a smile. "Yes, sir."

If she will speak to me. With a rueful twinge, Gilbert jogged up the steps, slipped inside, and walked as soundlessly across marble as his pumps would allow.

"Fredrick, is that you?"

Gilbert turned to where a glowing candle brightened the foyer doorway. He approached with a grin. "No, Mamma. Take a better look."

"Gilbert. How wonderful!" She leaned in for a kiss to his cheek. "However was your stay with the Onslows?"

"Tolerable."

"Only that?"

"Well, there were stimulating games of whist."

"Oh dear. Is that all you did?"

"What did you expect?"

"Lady Onslow does have three daughters, you know."

"Does she? I hadn't noticed."

His mother harrumphed. "Listen to you, nonsensical boy. If you are not grown by nineteen, I have little hopes you ever will."

"Not to worry. There will come a day." He glanced toward the doorway. "I don't suppose Nan would forgive me if I woke her, would she?"

"She will not forgive you if you do not. Why do you make such ill-thought promises to the poor thing? You knew it would be impossible to arrive in time."

"Was she terribly miserable?"

"Never mind that now." She slipped him the candle. "Go up and see her before she cries herself to sleep."

Gilbert exited the foyer to the stairwell and hurried up two flights of winding steps. When he reached her door, he tapped lightly enough to prevent Charlotte being disturbed from across the hall.

No answer.

Poor thing. Had she already fallen asleep?

As carefully as he could, he eased open the door and slipped into darkness, bringing the glow with him.

There she lay, the sweetest little child he'd ever seen, so angelic in slumber that he wondered if it were the same Nan he knew.

As if she sensed him, bright eyes burst open. "Gil!"

"Shhh, now. If you wake Charlotte, I'll not be the one to persuade her there are no goblins in her chamber."

"Maybe there are."

"You would contradict me, wouldn't you?"

An impish, happy smile transformed her features. "You smell funny."

"Hmm, really?"

"Like a lady."

"That's what comes of dancing with so many of them. Speaking of which"—he drew the present in front of her—"there were quite a few who had something like this."

"What is it?"

"Look and see."

She tore away the wrapping and let the tiny gold pendant fall into her fingers. A small diamond glistened in her palm. "It is so lovely."

"You might have to grow a mite before you can wear it."

"Why can't I wear it now?"

"Such a thing is for a lady. Twelve isn't all that, you know."

"Can't I try it? Please?"

"All right, give it here." He unlatched the back and slipped it around her neck.

She pulled the diamond in front of her nightgown, then flung her arms around his neck. "Oh, thank you, Gil. I never had a more wonderful birthday. Not ever!"

"Enough of all that." He pulled her away with a laugh. "But at least I have redeemed myself."

"Yes. I was so very angry toward you."

"Here I thought you were sleeping sweetly—and all the time, you were doubtless thinking of every wretched thing you would say to me as soon as I arrived. Am I right?"

A faint giggle. "Closely enough."

"That's what I thought." He pushed her back into her pillow with one hand, messed her curls, then told her to unhook the pendant before she went to sleep.

"Can I not keep it on awhile longer, Gil? Please?"

"Just for a while, I suppose."

"When can I wear it always?"

"When you are a lady, little Nan."

"And when will I be that?"

"Soon enough." He smiled as he retreated to the door. "Good night and happy birthday to you."

"Good night."

And he shut the door quietly behind him.

CHAPTER 6

May 1811, four years later

Nan?" The door thudded. First once, slowly—then a second time, with a wobbly jerk. "Nan, open up."

"No."

"Come now, I mean it."

"No." Dread twisted along her throat like vines to the stable walls.

The door banged again. "Temperance, are you in there? Do be of some assistance and unlock this door before I get angry and knock it down myself."

From across the room, the maid shot Nan a look, but she stayed in her corner. Dear, faithful soul.

"There, you see, Gil?" Nan eased sweating palms down the satin of her new gown. "You shall never get in, so you might as well go away."

"And what shall I tell Papa?"

"I am ill."

"You sound well enough to me. Besides, you were all color this morning at breakfast."

"That was just the trouble."

"What?"

"Breakfast. It set most disagreeably with me, and I have been weak and languid ever since."

"Rubbish. Now sick or not, I shall not have you curse Papa with mortification and scandal. The guests shall be arriving soon, and you cannot have a coming out while remaining in your bedchamber."

"He is right—"

"Oh hush, Temperance." Nan jabbed the key in the door, jerked it, and flung open the door. She glared at the despicable, grinning creature on the other side.

"I positively loathe you, Gil."

"May I come in?"

With a faint nod, she whirled to her dressing table and allowed Temperance to resume adorning her hair with a chaplet.

Gilbert towered next to her. "Is it the guests?"

"No."

"The young dandies?"

"No."

"The dancing?"

Her eyes lifted to his through the mirror. "I do not know why there should be a ball all for my sake. You know I shall make a perfect fool of myself."

"That's not so. I've watched you with the caper merchant—"

"No caper merchant can teach away a limp."

"It is so slight no one shall notice—and I myself think it makes you dance even more lovely."

"You are only being kind."

"And you are only being severe." He glanced down at the surface of her dressing table, then reached for whatever had caught his eye. "Mayhap this will cheer you."

The tiny, cold pendant pressed into her hand.

"Now put it on and recover quickly from your dreadful illness," he said. "All the world will be waiting downstairs."

Heath closed the door behind him and wiped cool moisture from his face. The small, damp room held lingering scents of the evening rain, and a ragged curtain swayed in the open window. But even with its chill, the fresh air was welcome for it frightened away the stifling odors of death.

"Where is she?" The baritone of the rector's voice seemed to spill serenity into every nook and cranny and every eager face.

"In here, sir," said the mother, as she eased open a battered door. "And I'm rightly beholdin' to you for comin'."

"Where I am needed, there shall I go. But was the doctor not called for?"

"Our Jenny don't be needin' a doctor, sir." Hollow, stricken gaze. "Not now."

Heath's chest squeezed as he helped the rector off with his coat, then his hat.

"Do all you can out here, Heath."

"Yes, sir."

"Do not forget to pray."

"I shan't."

With moist, somber eyes, the rector followed the mother into the darkness of another tiny room. The door clicked shut behind them.

Be with him, God. Heath claimed a chair when it was offered, refused a cigar from the father, and returned a slight smile to the two little girls across the room.

But as the eventide lengthened, it was the door their eyes kept returning to, part in dread and part in desperate hope. Hope the rector had given them.

And God.

Heath folded his hands together, squeezed them, trying to quell the nervous dread running through him. He remembered too well what death felt like.

But when Mamma had been in the room of screams, there'd been no kind rector to come and pray and sit by her bedside. They'd been alone.

One day, Heath would fill that void. Like the rector, he would visit thatched cottages, whisper prayers in dank rooms, and give hope in places where it seemed too dark.

He would be to someone else, someday, what the rector had been to him.

The entrance doors stared at her, strangely in likeness to the growling, widening mouth of a lion. A lion prepared to swallow her.

I cannot do this, God. Cowardly emotions drew her two steps backward. Why in heaven's name had Mr. Stanhope not listened to her?

"I wish to see you do well, my dear," he'd said. *"Married well, even."*

"I have no hopes for a marriage."

"Of course you have."

"No, truly. I would much rather live out my own quiet life, however I please, without the inconvenience of a husband."

"Love shall one day persuade you. And in the meantime, I mean to see you have every opportunity."

But opportunity, as he so gracefully put it, would only render her unwanted suitors, a lot of senseless prattle and dancing—the latter of which, despite what Gilbert said, was among her lesser qualities.

From beyond the doors, Nan caught bright flashes of colors, feather plumes, and glistening chandeliers. Music leaked out into the halls. Had she ever seen Dorrington Hall in such a state?

And all for her.

It was baffling—and overwhelming.

"What a rogue you are, Aylmer." A trilling laugh, approaching footsteps. "Next time you take Charles's barouche out for a drive, do act as if a bit of sense embodies you, hmm?"

Nan froze as the couple turned the corner.

Both paused—the lady with a curtsy, the gentleman with a widening stare.

"If your escort has abandoned, miss," he said with a belated bow, "you must allow us to accompany you into the ballroom."

"Really, Aylmer, you are such the simpleton! Can you not see this is our young hostess?"

"Miss Duncan?"

"Yes." A breath eased out as his hand captured hers. Her appreciation of gloves grew immensely with the following kiss.

"Allow me to make introductions, Miss Duncan. I am Lord Aylmer Humphries, and this is my sister, Lady Julia Humphries, though I'm certain you've already met. You must forgive me for not recognizing you, but I have been on a lengthy grand tour. I have only just returned this week."

A forced smile curved Nan's lips. "I am very pleased to meet you."

"Shall we go inside?"

With her consenting nod, the tall gentleman took her elbow and guided her through the doors she had so dreaded.

"Is that a sugar sculpture, Miss Duncan?" Her ladyship pressed close. "What a masterpiece."

"The true masterpiece," said her brother, "is not the sculptures, if I may be so bold."

Was he insinuating Nan?

She didn't have time to ponder the question, for another gentleman approached with the same height and dark, characteristic curls as Lord Hump or Humphries—or whoever he said he was.

"Ah, this is my elder brother, Miss Duncan, the Marquess of Somerset—otherwise known as Lord Somerset. Charles, do make acquaintances with the handsomest lady present, although if you try to steal her, expect our brotherly relations to be hindered."

"I would not think of it." The marquess's bow was quick, stiff, his eyes devoid of interest. "If you will excuse me?" Without waiting for a response, he navigated away and disappeared into an ocean of dresses, tailcoats, and ostrich feathers.

If only I could disappear so easily.

"I was most in earnest, Miss Duncan, when I threatened Charles. I do not wish to seem presumptuous, by any means, but could I persuade you to join the set?"

She glanced at the dancers already stepping into formation with ease and confidence and—

"Miss Duncan?"

"Yes." A sigh escaped, faint enough to be undetected, as she offered him her hand. "Yes, I would be very delighted, my lord."

❧

"Look at her." Mr. Stanhope's gaze followed the white and green of Nan's satin dress, as she was swept away to another partner. "Just shy of sixteen, yet the loveliest of all creatures."

Gilbert handed his father a glass of lemonade. "You do realize she was unprepared for this."

"So are all young ladies."

"Did you know she—"

"Yes, I know all about her sudden, fabricated sickness. But you know as well as I do, she must adapt to the ways of the world at some time or another. Why she is so set against it, I shall never understand."

"That is her way, Papa."

"What?"

"To be incomprehensible."

A chuckle, a raise of his glass. "Truer words were never spoken. But give her time—and a handsome gentleman—and she shall be marching into the courts of society and matrimony with all the rest. Her bloodlines may raise a question or two, but the dowry I've provided should be grand enough that any such concerns should be overlooked."

"Mayhap so." Gilbert stared at Nan—the flushed cheeks, the bright and timid eyes, the lips lifted with a childish sort of bewilderment. "But talk of matrimony might be doing it too much brown."

"How so?"

"Why, after all, she is only but a slip of a girl—"

"There you are, Mr. Stanhope." A large, silk-turbaned woman made an invasion, followed by her shorter, hairless husband. "You do remember me, don't you, Mr. Stanhope? Why of course you do, for you did dance with me once, many years ago, at her ladyship's ball. Did you know her offspring are in attendance tonight, even the one who has so long been abroad? Of course you would. After all, you did invite them, didn't you?"

"Yes, well—"

"Listen to me being all mawkish. I daresay, I am always thinking back to better times. But all that aside, allow me to introduce my husband, Mr. Fortescue, who is a fourth cousin twice removed to the Regent himself—"

Gilbert made a hasty bow and excused himself before a catastrophic change of topic could entangle him. He'd attended more than one event with Mrs. Fortescue, and given a bit too much ratafia, she could be most monopolizing. Let his father suffer this one. After all, he *had* invited them.

Easing his way around the ballroom's perimeter, Gilbert revisited a table of refreshments. He had just grabbed a fruit when—

Nan.

Her foot slipped, and she careened forward.

A gentleman swept her into his arms. As if with some sort of authority, he pulled her away from the dance and never removed his hands from her. Good heavens, did he not think Nan could stand on her own? And wasn't that the fellow who had dangled after her all evening?

Ridiculous calf-lover. Could he not see she was a child, coming out or not?

Tossing his fruit back to the table, Gilbert weaved through chattering couples until he was close enough to snag Nan's gaze.

Pleading tears welled, as pitiful as he'd ever seen.

The gentleman must have asked her something, for she tore her eyes away from Gilbert and bobbed a nod.

Quickly, with another unnecessary press to her arm, the gentleman scurried away.

"Oh, Gil." As soon as he neared, she turned her back to everyone present. Tears began to slip. "Did you see me? I would have tumbled had he not—"

"Yes, yes, I saw all of that." Gilbert handed her a handkerchief. "Hurry up and dry yourself before you make matters worse."

"You don't understand!"

"Shhh." He leaned closer. "Do you want everyone to peer at you?"

"Gil, I—"

"Never mind." He took her arm. "Come along and we shall take a stroll outside. But do keep your chin up, eh?"

"But Lord Humphries went to fetch me a glass of lemonade—"

"Oh, dash him. He can drink it himself."

She didn't protest, only did as he instructed and kept her head high as they ambled toward the white veranda doors.

Sharp music, high-pitched voices, and the constant thump of dancing slippers all gave way to a low, soothing drone.

Nan hurried to the edge of the rain-scented garden, found a seat on the iron bench. "You might have rescued me a mite sooner."

"Rescued you? I thought you were enjoying yourself."

"How could you say that?"

"Lord Humphries *was* rather attentive."

"Stifling, you mean."

"Didn't you care for him at all?"

"No." With more tears, she slipped her hand to her leg and rubbed. "And of all the horrid things for me to do, I had to go and stumble into his arms."

"I am certain he did not mind." Gilbert knelt and inspected the leg. "Hurt badly?"

"Only my dignity."

A laugh rumbled out. "Poor Nan. Has anything about this day been good for you?"

"Only this." Two fingers touched the pendant, as he settled onto the bench next to her. "I can scarcely stop looking at it."

"Listen to you."

"Truly, Gilbert." Round, eager eyes found his. "Don't you know I have waited every day for you to let me wear it?"

"Why so?"

"Don't you remember?"

He laughed again. "You are prodding, Nan."

"Then let me prod. Do something nice for once. Tell me plainly, and I shall be happy."

"Happy?"

"Yes."

"And no more tears?"

"No more tears."

"All right." Gilbert stood, grasped one of her hands, and raised an imaginary sword in the other. "I, Gilbert Stanhope, do hereby knight you as a grown"—he lowered the sword to her shoulder—"sophisticated, formal, and lovely lady in every sense."

Her laugh made a pleasant echo into the night as she clapped both hands. "And henceforth, you may never call me your little Nan."

"Now that I cannot promise." He pulled her to her feet and faced her in the right direction. "Back into the battle, my knight, and do not let the dragon Lord Humphries defeat you."

"You need not worry of that—nor of any other dragons."

"Promises like that shall make Papa a liar."

"What?"

"Never mind. Run along, and if you fall again, just hurry back up."

"I will." She took two steps toward the veranda, then whirled back around quickly. "Thank you, Gil." Her lips landed on his cheek. "I shall be the bravest knight I can."

❧

A creak invaded the warm layers of sleep, pulling Heath back into a room that was dark and quiet.

Then a light spilled forth. With soft orange glow, it highlighted the rector's face as he shut the chamber door behind him. "How late is it?"

The two little girls must have fallen asleep, for only the father stirred in the darkness. "Past four, sir," the father said.

Heath rose and waited as the rector lowered the candle to the worn table.

"We won't be needed here any longer, my good man." His voice stung the silence a moment. "Your daughter was not as eager for heaven as you imagined."

An incoherent noise, then the father drew closer. "Wh–what?"

"I said Jenny was not eager for heaven, at least not yet. It seems the Almighty thinks she'll be of better use on grass and soil than clouds and gold."

Tight, massive shoulders wilted with sounds that were too happy to be sobs. "Thanks be to God." The father's hands clasped the rector's. "Thanks be to God for your prayers, sir. For all our prayers."

"You had better go to her."

"Yes, sir. Thank you, sir. Thank you." And he disappeared behind the creaking chamber door, leaving behind a glorious aura of joy.

Heath fetched the coat, the worn hat, and the Bible they never failed to bring with them. Without words, the two left the small abode into a night that was moist and cool.

The streets were barren, undisturbed. Brilliant stars winked and glowed in the velvety sky.

Heath stifled a yawn with his fist.

"You are weary, my son?"

"No, sir."

"It has been a long night."

"For you especially."

"Perhaps in flesh. But my soul, it is. . .it is. . ."

"Sir?"

The rector jerked, then gasped. His Bible thumped the wet cobblestone.

"Rector." Terror sliced through Heath as he groped for the man's coat, held his arms, and tried to keep him up.

But he fell anyway. They sank together on cruel, damp street stones.

"Rector, what is wrong?"

Gripping his own chest, choking in air.

"Rector. . .please. What is it?"

Mouth gaped, wider, wider, wider. One breath in, but it took so long for another to come back out.

"God, no." Senseless, maddening fear clamped Heath's throat. "God. . .God, please." So close to the church, to the rectory. He'd carry him there, drag him there, anything. He'd be all right. The doctor would come. People would pray, just as so many had prayed for little Jenny. . .

But slowly, unseeingly, the warm eyes began to wander away. The lips slackened without the rasp of breath. The body stilled beneath the frayed, woolen coat.

No. Heath released the fabric. He sat still, numb, with eyes that darted back and forth between a dead face and a starlit sky.

God, why?

⚜

"The most wonderful, beautiful thing has happened to you, and yet you sit as still as the Earl of Cheshire hanging over your head."

Nan glanced up at the ancient painting, then resumed her unfolding of the letter. "Temperance, this is neither a beautiful thing nor a wonderful thing, so never say so again."

"But do you know who Lord Humphries is?"

"Of course I do."

"If the Dowager Marchioness of Somerset's *son* cast eyes upon me—though of course such a thing would never happen, for what is an abigail anyway, even if I weren't already promised to Loftus? But if such a thing did happen, I undoubtedly would not just glimpse at the letter as if it were commonplace. Why, he practically danced with no other at your ball when he could have had—"

"Anyone. Yes, I know." Nan scanned the contents of the letter.

"Well?"

"Well what?"

"Miss Duncan, do not leave me in suspense! What did he say?"

"Let's see. . .he hopes I am doing well."

"That is good."

"And he most enjoyed my company."

"An obvious point."

"And he. . ." Nan squinted at the black, neat script before she crumpled the letter.

Temperance hovered over the writing desk with a gasp. "And what?"

"He wishes to see me."

"Oh, heavens! What a delight!"

With neither smile nor frown, Nan reached for her quill, dipped the tip in ink, and laid out a blank paper. She wrote quickly, then folded it as she rose from the desk. "Will you seal this for me, Temperance?"

"Yes, of course, but shouldn't you like to read it to me first? I am terribly good at finding mistakes, Miss Duncan, and am also very good at—"

"I am sure you would not enjoy the contents."

"Miss Duncan, you don't mean you. . .that you. . ."

"Yes, I refused him." Nan started for the door, throwing over her shoulder, "But do not worry. I did so as kindly as possible."

Shadows, dark and long, lay across the grave in endless shapes. Some were tall, broad, like the struggling farmer whom the rector had given his goat. Others were slight and maidenly, like Jenny and her mother, who held hands within their cloaks.

Then Heath's. His stood alone, even when all the others went away, until another nightfall came to claim his shadow.

God? Reckless, empty question. Over and over, until his limbs shook with the weight, with the horror. *My God, why?*

He wanted to get on his knees. He wanted to run his hands through the soil. Fresh, earthy soil. The rector would have wished to plant seeds in ground so rich.

"This is the Almighty's happiness, my child." Patting the dirt with old, dirt-stained hands. *"He sits up in heaven and smiles every time something grows."*

But nothing was growing now.

God wore no smile.

Because the ground reeked of death, and the dirt shrouded a lifeless coffin, and no more gardens would be cultivated by a rector's loving hands.

Why must he leave? Pain kicked in every place it hurt, until the bleeding made him weak, the bruising made him tremble. No tears, though. Couldn't cry. Not even when the constable had finally come, or when the doctor had probed the rector's chest, or when the funeral procession had marched the Chanfest streets.

Why must he leave when he's all I had left? For the thousandth time in his life, there was no answer. No voice rang from heaven. No angel swept down to end the nightmare.

He ought to curse it. Curse it all. Where had Christ been at the cottage when the screams came from the bedchamber? Where had He been when Papa had left for sea, when Madame Le Sueur had hit him, when they'd gone hungry in the streets?

And Nan. Her name racked him with memories he longed to shrink from.

Where had He been when Nan had been taken from him?

A throb pierced his head, his chest. *Where are You now?*

But when the darkness was invaded by morning, and when his shadow reappeared above the grave, he never cursed God as he'd wanted to. He never asked any more questions. He never crumpled onto the grave and wept.

Instead, he put the hat back on his head and walked away. The rectory waited for him. The trees were green and swaying, the windows open and quiet, the sun warm and blazing.

He entered the potting shed first, grabbed a handful of cornflower seeds, and shut the door quietly behind him. He bent to his knees in garden dirt.

One seed at a time, he planted. Painful, but he planted. Aching, but he planted. Desolate, but he planted.

I'm making God smile, Rector. He covered the last seeds with dirt. *I'm making Him smile for the both of us.* Whatever happened, Heath would stay true. He would do the things the rector had taught him. He would go on visiting the sick, and scrubbing the church floors, and praying with the ones too broken to pray for themselves.

He would be the man to the world that the rector had been to him.

CHAPTER 7

Chanfest
Kent, England
July 1813, two years later

$\mathscr{I}$t's about time the likes o' you showed your face."

Heath entered the sweltering kitchen, tossed off his hat, and carried his string of fish to the table.

The housekeeper pulled on a stained pinafore. "Out gallivanting to the docks, and poor ol' me left to handle all your bleeding house callers."

Heath glanced up in question.

"Yes, you heard me right. The new rector arrived more than an hour ago—already settled into his chamber and moving his books into the study." She rolled up her sleeves, grabbed the newly caught fish. "Though I don't mind saying, I ne'er bothered telling him to make hisself at home since all the others only stayed long enough for the bishop to remove 'em. Third replacement in two years, and I'm getting rightly tired o' all the fuss. Ne'er signed up for so much changing and such." She paused for the space of a breath. "Anyway, go and see the other gent I left waiting in the parlor."

"Other gent?"

"That's what I said, ain't it?"

"Who's he?"

"How should I know? Scroungy-looking codger, though, by all accounts."

Heath quit the kitchen and weaved his way through narrow, stifling halls. Why had no one built more windows in this house?

Perhaps the heat is what drove all the rectors to such unfavorable behavior.

When he reached the parlor, Heath eased open a door that whined in protest as if swollen from the heat.

Across the room, a hunched figure faced the open window. Sunlight and dust motes framed a body clothed in a tattered coat, continental hat, and articles that were patched.

Heath cleared his throat. "Sir?"

The man's shoulders stiffened.

Heath took a step closer. "Forgive me if I kept you waiting. The new rector just arrived this morning, so if you have business with him, you may stay for supper."

With movements slow and hesitant, the figure finally turned. Gray, messy whiskers. Wrinkled, weather-browned skin. Strange, liquid eyes. . .

Eyes he knew.

Pain mingled with a surge of excitement as his chest barreled a thousand words. None of them surfaced. None of them made sense. None of them made it past his lips.

"You are your mother's child." Odd, how familiar the voice sounded even after all these years. "I'd forgotten her face until just now."

Sweat filmed Heath's palms. Why couldn't he talk?

As if plagued with the same inability, the old man nodded. He drew his hands from his pockets—one knotty and dirty, the other a dull metal hook. "Lost this in the Arabian Seas."

More silence.

"Fell out of a rowboat and let a bloody shark sink his teeth into me—"

"How did you find me?"

"The Bobber. The madam told me where you had gone."

"And Nan?" Heath's throat nearly closed. "Did she tell you of Nan?"

"Isn't she here?"

He shook his head.

"Is she—"

"A family took her in."

"How long ago?"

How many years had it been? He shrugged.

Pain curled his father's whiskered lips. "The two of you—you should have never left the Bobber. I sent plenty of funds, funds to see Nan in pretty dresses and you in good learning." He crossed the room with tears, stood before Heath with brows twisted in agony. "Why, Son? Why didn't you wait for me? Why didn't you keep her safe?"

"I tried."

"Did you?"

"I couldn't watch her suffer. . .wasn't enough food."

"Food? But the funds—"

"There were no funds!" Heath's hands shook so hard he couldn't make a fist. He took a step back, raked in air, swallowed hard. "There were no funds, Papa, not that we ever saw. And we left the Bobber because. . .because of the madam."

"But she knew your mother. She promised to care for you."

"It is over, Papa."

"But Nan—"

"Nan is safe now." The words dried his mouth. "Safe and happy—and had she stayed with me, she would have perished in the streets."

In a stunned silence, Papa sank into a worn damask chair, the same one the rector had always occupied with his Bible. "So this is what has become of you." Raspy, despondent words, as his only hand lifted to cover his eyes. "So this is what has become of my children."

What had he expected?

One chamber away, Papa was situated in the only spare room. Sometimes Heath thought he detected noises, soft snores. Or did he imagine them?

God, help me. Awake, he faced the wooden ceiling, staring at dents and cracks so hard his eyes burned. *Why is he here?*

All through supper, Papa had sat across from him. Heavy breathing was all he contributed to the meal. He seldom looked up, but when he did, guilt and unease lingered in his eyes.

Stranger. Pressure built in Heath's chest as the realization knifed through. *He's nothing more than a stranger.*

How many times had he longed for the day they'd meet again? How many times had he told the rector how big his papa was, how strong his papa was, how mighty his papa was?

But he wasn't.

He was a haggard old man with one hand instead of two—and Heath didn't know whether to love the stranger or abhor him.

When morning finally came, Heath dressed in his finest breeches and tailcoat, washed his face, and took his Bible downstairs.

The new rector must have already hurried down and left, because the remains of his plate still sat at the breakfast table, along with partially readable sermon notes.

"Eggs and ham, then?"

Heath nodded to the housekeeper. She'd no more than returned with his plate when another figure entered the room—a figure who chased away Heath's appetite.

"Reckon that'll be two," said the housekeeper, and she bustled away again, leaving silence in her wake.

The chair legs scraped wood as Papa pulled it from the table. "Sleep good?"

A nod.

"Good." The man sat across from him. "Nice bed. Haven't slept in one since the *Fräulein Clare* ported at Devonshire."

Heath nodded again, speared ham with his fork.

"Fine garments you're wearing."

"It's the Lord's day."

"Oh. The rector teach you that?"

"Yes, sir."

"What else he teach you?"

With her usual morning grumbles, the housekeeper swept back in and lowered a steaming plate, along with a glass of water. "Anything more? I won't be coming back in. Other things to do, you know."

"This is fine. Thank you kindly, ma'am." Papa turned his attention back to Heath. "Madame Le Sueur told me of the rector's letter, that she gave it to you. That's how I found you. But when I was passing through town, I heard the old man died two years back." He shrugged. "I'm sorry about that. Would have liked to meet the man who took in my boy."

"Thank you."

"I suppose that's why you stay."

"What?"

"Here." His father swept a half-mocking hand toward the window, where a view of the church was visible through the dust. "In a. . .rectory."

"I like it here."

"Doing what?"

"Helping."

"Who?"

"Villagers, the church—"

"You can't give all your life to that rector, even if he did take you in." Papa's hand flattened on the table. "You need to know a trade. Life on a deck could teach you more."

The church steeple tolled with echoing power.

"I learned to be a man out in the seas."

Dong, dong.

"Learned how to fight, how to stand tall."

Dong, dong.

"Good to have a son again. . .someone I can teach what I know."

Heath jerked from his chair. "Church will be starting."

"That I can hear."

"Are you coming?"

"No." The wrinkled face turned back to the plate of eggs. "No, you go on without me. Do as that rector would have had you do."

Heath started for the door—

"And Son?"

He stiffened at the word. The rector had always made it sound approving. Why did it seem so foreign and empty on his own papa's lips?

"When you return, we will talk."

Again, all he managed was a nod.

Then he fled into the sanctuary of his church.

It was only a matter of time before the noise was discovered. *Thud, thud, thud.* Softly at first, but growing louder every second until—

Oh no.

From the other side of the aisle, the Dowager Marchioness of Somerset craned her neck so slightly that no one else would have noticed.

Except for Nan.

The threatening, flashing eyes caused her heartbeat to match the annoying pattern of Charlotte's slipper against the wooden pew. Why must the woman be so patronizing?

From beside her, Gilbert must have finally noticed, for he leaned over to Mr. Stanhope, whispered something, then straightened.

Mr. Stanhope, however, was much too captivated by the vicar's sermon. He only nodded in agreement to something said from the pulpit, then stared at his Bible.

Oh, this is dreadful. Nan's cheeks burned. Others were flicking glances their way. Were they to meet with ruin on a Sunday so lovely as this?

Not if she had anything to say about it. Something must be done. And now—before the vicar silenced his entire sermon to stare, just as he'd done when Wydenshire's cobbler had drifted off into a snore.

Nan nudged Gilbert's knee, signaling with her eyes. *Try again.*

In answer, he turned back to Mr. Stanhope, who instead of ignoring his son, sent him only a disapproving glare.

Dear mercy, if only Mrs. Stanhope were here. She would have never allowed unruly, reckless Charlotte to disrupt the service like this.

Thud, thud, thud.

Nan bent low before she had a chance to reason out the consequences. "Charlotte." Desperate, breathless whisper.

The twelve-year-old persistently whacked her foot against the pew.

"Charlotte!"

The thudding stopped.

The preaching stopped.

Everything stopped.

With burning in her cheeks, Nan forced herself back upright. If she had been brave, she would have looked all the congregants in the eye and done something brilliant—like smile or nod or *something*, at least.

But she only closed her eyes, as if in repentant prayer.

With a few disapproving comments from the vicar, the sermon fell to an abrupt end, one last song was sung, and the congregation began to disperse.

"Going to sit there all day, Nan, or are you going to let us out?"

"Never speak to me again, Gil."

"Me?"

"Yes, you."

"I cannot imagine what I did."

"It is what you did *not* do that most infuriates me."

"I shall defend myself later. You had better rise and face the dragon again."

A groan filled her throat, but as she could not bear any more embarrassment in one day, she turned toward the aisle with a smile. "Lord Humphries."

"Miss Duncan." A quick bow, followed by another condescending glint from his mother, the dowager marchioness.

"My, but yours are feeling spritely this morning, are they not?" the dowager asked.

"Yes, my lady," Nan said.

"How shall that preoccupied girl adapt to the ways of society if she cannot behave herself for the length of one small sermon?"

"I am certain it shall not happen again."

"I should hope not. I was most distracted. Not to mention your little outburst."

"Mother—"

"Shh, Aylmer, and say good day. Now come along."

With a begrudging smile, Lord Humphries bowed a second time, wished her a pleasant afternoon, then followed his mother, sister, and brother from the church.

From behind, Gilbert patted her shoulder. "Nicely done, little Nan. Although I cannot determine if you rescued yourself from his lordship—or if her ladyship did it for you."

"How can you laugh when my pride has just been so unjustly slaughtered?"

"I am not laughing."

"I do not know why her ladyship despises me so, when I have given no encouragement in the least to her son."

"Doubtless mere precaution."

Nan huffed. "She needn't worry. I shall not entertain him now any more than I did two years ago. Come along." When they'd reached the aisle, she nabbed Charlotte's hand with theatrical aggression. "Let us return home before the dragon decides to return and more disaster befalls me."

"We're leaving here, and we're going to find Nan."

Heath stood at the foot of the hearth, a stale afternoon breeze rushing in from the window. Every muscle tensed. Leave the rectory? The church?

"You should have done it a long time ago." His father pulled a scratched pipe from his whiskered lips. "A girl needs to be with her family, her own blood."

"It was impossible."

"Well, it ain't now."

Sweat formed at his hairline. "Papa, we can't."

"Why not?"

"Because she's protected, provided for. If we go now, it could ruin her—"

"She can decide for herself." His father rose. "She *will* decide for herself. I don't care who she's living with. Any daughter of mine will be proud of the Duncan name—and anything that comes with it."

"But—"

"It's bloody time you be taking pride in it too, Son. Come from a good breed of Scottish highlanders, we do, and not a one of them ever threw their lives away to no church."

"I like it here."

"Fine. You can come back to it if you want." His father sank back into the chair with a hard puff to his pipe. Smoke billowed. "But you're going to take me to Nan first."

Unease raced through Heath as fast as his deepening breaths. He belonged here. His purpose was here. Living in the rectory. Helping in the church. Serving the people, just as he'd promised God and the rector. Could he leave? Was it right to leave?

Papa's unwavering gaze cut through him.

"Fine." Heath would go—but he was coming back.

71

CHAPTER 8

*T*he knock came just raucously enough that Gilbert needn't guess who stood on the other side of the door. Annoyance built into a sigh. "Come in, Charlotte."

The study door swung open, and in she swept—with reckless curls and a spencer jacket missing two buttons. "What are you doing?"

"Working, if you please."

"On what?"

"Nothing you need worry about."

"Can I help?"

"No."

"Boring ol' ledgers again, I see. If I had my way, every book would be thrown into the hearth and burned."

"Just let Mamma catch you talking that way."

"I can't help it. All anyone wants to do is bury their noses in books and more books. Just a lot of dust and bother, if you ask me."

"Yes, well, they aren't my fascination either, but we all must deal with unpleasantries." He dipped his quill into a cut-glass inkwell. "Don't you have something to do?"

"No."

"A book to read or something?"

A pout settled around her lips as she slumped into a wingback. "That's not funny, Gil."

"Isn't it?"

"Can't we just do something?"

"Like what?"

"I don't know. Riding or something?"

"Maybe Nan—"

"I already asked her."

"Then Papa—"

"Gone to the village."

Another sigh. "I anticipate the day Mamma returns from Aunt Lydia's. A fortnight is much longer than I realized." Gilbert flipped his ledger shut, scooted from his desk, and strode for the door. "All right, let us have our little ride."

"Oh, thank you, Gil!"

"But you must promise to leave me be afterward. I have a dreadful amount to do, so you must entertain yourself with other poor victims. Agreed?"

She squeezed in front of him. "Agreed." With skipping steps, she hurried through the house in her rumpled pink dress. Good gracious, hadn't she worn that yesterday?

Little vixen.

When they reached the stables, Gilbert flung open the doors with a bang. Loftus was nowhere to be seen, so he entered Briar's stall and saddled the animal himself. He was just going for Charlotte's pony when—

"Master Gilbert?"

Temperance hurried in with a perplexed, reddening expression. "Master Gilbert, I fear you are needed greatly indoors."

"Why? What is it?"

"Miss Duncan, sir. She's in a most exaggerated state, if you know what I mean, crying and carrying on the way she does."

"Whatever for?"

"It seems her ladyship did something most unexpected—in her letter, I mean—and I'd be rightly at sixes and sevens if I didn't know her son was the one behind it."

"What did it say?"

"Her ladyship wishes to visit Dorrington Hall, she does. And on the morrow, if you can believe it."

"No wonder Nan is frenzied. With Mamma gone too, of all the times." He glanced back to Charlotte, who was already forming another distinct frown. "Charlotte, give me but a moment to pacify Nan and then we shall have our ride. All right?"

She flopped herself onto a wobbly stool. "Letters are no better than books."

"I think, at the moment, Nan might agree with you." With a quick wink in her direction, Gilbert hurried after Temperance for the house.

"I want to go alone."

From across the uneven, gritty floorboards of the Wydenshire inn, his father's eyes met his. In all the days they'd traveled together, Heath had told him little. He'd listened to the stories of the seven seas, the tales of exotic islands, the nostalgic praise of life atop the mast. Sometimes, as they camped along a rutted road, his father would take out a bottle of rum and drink away the long night hours. He'd cry sometimes. Other times, he'd sit close to Heath and press his good hand on Heath's shoulder, squeeze hard for a moment or two. "Good to have a son again," he'd say. "You and Nan. . .you're the only pride I got left."

But in all those days, his father's eyes had never looked at him as they did now. Stark, panicked, even degraded—and it made him uneasy.

"Yes," Papa finally said, wiping his mouth, pulling off his hat. "You go alone. You ought to."

"I'll be back soon."

"Yes."

"I'll tell her you're here."

"Good."

A lump formed in Heath's throat, big enough to make breathing a chore. He grabbed his coat, turned for the door—

"Son?"

He halted halfway through the doorway.

"Do you suppose. . .suppose she'll be coming to see me?"

"I don't know." A sniffle came from behind him. "I don't know if she'll see me." After all, he'd never come back for her all those years ago. Had she forgiven him in the time they'd been apart?

Or hated him?

Of all the untimely, preposterous, ridiculous things to do. It didn't make sense. Of all the places the Dowager Marchioness of Somerset should wish to dine, Dorrington Hall should have been among the least.

Nonsensical woman. Wasn't she afraid for her son? That a girl beneath English peerage should at last give way to him?

From behind, the two drawing room doors squeaked open. "Let me see that." Gilbert crossed the room and snatched the letter from her hands. He scanned the words as one brow rose in puzzlement. "By George."

"Please say something more helpful."

"I don't know what to say." He handed back the letter, his calm flicking more irritation through her panic. "Though it does seem a mite peculiar."

"Peculiar? It is the positive end of me."

"Now, Nan. Let us try to keep our wits, eh?"

"For two years, she has been coldly severe and Lord Humphries just the opposite. Every encounter stresses my nerves, and to think I shall now have to entertain them for a private dinner—"

"There are worse things, you know."

"I can think of none."

"Temperance was right."

"About what?"

"You are in a state."

"Leave me alone, Gil. I must devise some sort of plan of endurance, and I only have one day and night to do it." Heat racing along her skin, she tossed herself onto the chaise lounge and fanned her cheeks with one hand. Her stomach churned. "Why would she do such a thing?"

"Perhaps she has changed her mind."

"What?" Upright again. "You do not mean to say she fathoms Lord Humphries and I. . .surely she would not be so very foolish."

"Perhaps, given his unconventional admiration of you, she does not find the thought foolish at all. Rich or not, all mammas like to see their children attain their desires. Besides, you must give the unfortunate chap one thing—he's determined."

"And exhausting."

"Perhaps one day he shall win you yet."

She scowled and bit her lip against angry words when Gil laughed at her. Why must he always make light of everything?

Pulling gloves from his pocket, he persuaded her into a ride with him and Charlotte—who, he mentioned, had been left sulking on a three-legged stool. Nan might as well accompany them. Perhaps the cool air would drive away her distress—or the heat at the very least.

"She shall be most relieved when Mamma returns," he said, on the way out of doors.

"I even more so. Her ladyship's letter might have been so much easier to bear if Mrs. Stanhope were here to run the house."

"You worry far too much."

"Only when given opportunity."

"Is that all you have to say for yourself?" He pulled open the stable doors, followed her inside, then hesitated. "That's odd."

"What?"

"I left Briar saddled and ready, but it seems. . ." Another pause, longer this time, as his eyes swept the length of the stables. "Charlotte?"

No answer.

"Charlotte, are you here?"

With undoing dread, Nan followed his gaze to the empty stool—and Briar's empty stall. What had the foolish girl done now? Were they to meet with two dilemmas in one day?

With every ridge he crested, Heath watched for that first, startling sight of Dorrington Hall. There'd be windows so many he couldn't count them. There'd be stairs and balconies and white statues, just as he'd pictured over and over again.

Every time he'd wanted to run to her, he'd counted the windows. Every time he'd wanted to bring her to the rectory, he'd think of the mighty stairs, the statues, the splendor. Every time he'd been so alone, longed for just one more familiar song, he'd envisioned the balconies—and how safe it might have felt to look down from one.

Nan was standing there, he'd always told himself. She didn't cry anymore. Never shivered in alley crates. Never wore rags that hung from a thinning frame, or sang on muddy street sides, or wept because there was no more left to eat.

He'd done right to leave her alone. He'd done right to forsake her. He'd done right to give her a chance to escape. Perhaps her only chance.

Would to heaven she would understand that.

Beneath him, his chestnut roan swung her head.

"Whoa, Golda."

A snort, then the ears lifted.

"Hear something?" He patted the damp hide, looking left to right. Flower-dotted grass, a mossy fence, a dry and stony gully—

Pink.

The flash of color caught his attention, where a glistening steed pranced in sight. Whether the animal was truly large or the rider only small, Heath could not tell—but they raced down the hillside in wild, careless speed.

Messy ringlets flapped in the wind, the pink billowed, then the girl's squinted eyes finally collided with his.

A child?

She jerked on the reins.

Heath urged Golda forward, but he wasn't fast enough.

The steed reared. Once, then twice, as the girl lost contact with the saddle. Her grip must have been deathlike, because when the horse lunged toward the gully, she was carried off with him.

Heath's heels kicked hard. Faster, faster, galloping. Still not close enough. Why didn't she jump?

With demon speed, the child's horse bolted along the edge. Should the dirt shift, should the hooves falter—

Please, Lord. Wind whipped Heath's face as he came within feet. Nearer, nearer, nearer still until he could almost reach out and snatch her.

"Here!" His shout mingled with pounding hooves, her panicked whimper. Both hands groped for her and hefted, but the giant steed reared again. *No, no.* Toppling to the ground, rolling to the gully's edge.

Hooves. Pounding. Hooves. Thunder. Hooves again.

Then nothing.

He lay still on dirt and grass, his legs tangled around pink fabric and half boots. *Child?* His throat worked for air. "Ch–child?"

A slow movement, a wiggle of one black boot.

Heath pushed himself up, grabbed her arms. "Are you all right?"

She stared at him, blinking faster than necessary, eyes wider than half crowns. She took one look at the gully, then another up ahead, where two galloping horses sprinted away. "Gil will be angry." Rounded features scrunched. Then a sob. "Briar will n–never come b–back and Gil shall murder me."

"Where do you live?"

"Dorrington Hall."

Relief tunneled through his tension. "Can you stand?"

She shook her head, still weeping, and made no move to rise.

Brushing off his breeches, Heath strode a few feet away and whistled. In answer, faithful Golda turned her heels and hurried back to the familiar, piercing sound. "Good girl." Heath patted the foamy neck, tugged the reins back to the distraught adolescent, and hoisted her atop the saddle. "Just hold tight." When he'd climbed next to her, he guided the reins back for Dorrington Hall. "You'll be home very soon."

A consolation for the girl, an uncertainty for himself.

She should have gone with him. She shouldn't have agreed to stay behind in the event Charlotte could make it back on her own.

Because they both knew she couldn't. Not with her riding skills.

Or lack thereof.

Nan crossed the stable for the third time, brushed dust from a saddle seldom used, and ran her hand down the length of a bridle. Leather mingled with horseflesh and hay, and the scent brought back a sea of memories. Hiding in the hay loft, braiding Briar's mane, following Gilbert as he moved from stall to stall. Why had she so long forgotten the joy of this place?

She ought to ride more often. She ought to play more often too, lady or not. Oh, why had she not occupied Charlotte today when she'd begged for a companion? Would it have been so insufferable to amuse the child?

Poor thing, she was not like Gilbert and Nan had been. They'd always had each other. But Charlotte was so desperately lonesome, so very set apart in years and mind from the rest of them.

Which was no excuse, of course, for taking off on Gilbert's steed. How could she be so heedless?

The faint pound of hooves announced a rider.

Nan lunged for the stable doors, threw them open one at a time. If Gilbert was back so soon, then Charlotte mustn't have ventured very far, after all.

But it wasn't Gilbert.

Sun burned her eyes, as she watched the horse saunter toward the house. The stranger dismounted slowly, then pulled down an unkempt Charlotte and led her to the stairs.

Thank heavens. Just wait until Mr. Stanhope and Gil got a hold of her for this. Nan started forward.

And froze.

Something strange and cold forced her to retreat. One step, two steps, until her back hit the rough brick of the stable wall.

It's him.

With slow, familiar movements, the stranger helped Charlotte up the last step. He tapped the brass door knocker with a hand she remembered. He placed his arm around the girl, just as he'd always done to her. He pulled off his hat when the door finally opened, like the days when he'd begged for coins because there was nothing else to steal.

God, please.

Farther and farther she shrank, until she'd crept into the stable doorway.

The maid must have ushered Charlotte inside, because he stood alone now, with his hat back on. He turned.

She wanted to dash away, escape his eyes.

But they found her anyway.

She couldn't do this. Panic hurled her back into the stables. She raced as far as she could go, to a wall with one window, whose dusty glass was scratched by an outside branch. Pressure stacked in her chest like logs heaped inside a hearth.

God, please, I'm so afraid—

A creak.

She knew the sound, because many times she had crept inside the stables to startle Gilbert, only to be discovered by that traitorous board.

For once, the warning was for her.

Please, please. Frantic thoughts, but she didn't know why. Only knew she couldn't face him. Couldn't turn around and look at him, the face she'd so long wept for, the eyes she'd nearly forgotten. Were they brown like hers? Or were they blue like Papa's?

She didn't know. Couldn't remember anything. Not anymore.

Another creak. Then, huskily, "Nan."

The sound undid her, flung her deeper into webs of confusion, memories, longing. Without meaning to, she pivoted.

The eyes were waiting, just as she'd known, and there were tears in the blue and gray. "Should I leave?"

"No."

Another step forward. So much taller than she'd remembered, with muscles instead of mere bones, with sunlight on cheeks that used to be sallow. Same blond, ragged hair. Same sharp, cleft chin. Same sad, quiet eyes. How had she ever forgotten them?

"I'm sorry for coming this way. . .for coming at all."

Hurt jolted her.

"I don't want to ruin things for you. Not ever." He looked away, perhaps so she would not notice that one of the tears fell loose. "But I wanted you to know that. . .that our papa is returned."

"Returned?"

"He is waiting at an inn in the village. The Simon and Cat."

"And he. . ." Her voice dissolved. "He. . .wants to see me?"

"If you wish it."

"When?"

"Today or—"

"Tomorrow." Deep, shaking. "Yes, I know."

There was silence, an unspoken cry of lost years and endless questions. Then he turned, hurried for the stable doors.

"Heath, wait." She raced for him, stepped between him and the open threshold. Everything ached, begged for answers, but she didn't know how to ask them. "Please just. . .wait."

A vein bulged in his forehead. He blinked twice, lost more tears, then swallowed her into his arms. He held her for several heartbeats before he writhed from her touch. "Forgive me, Nan."

He exited the stable before she could assure him she already had.

"What have you to say for yourself?"

With ringlets still damp and cheeks freshly scrubbed, Charlotte stared at Gil from her place at the dinner table. "It was just an accident."

"Accident? I suppose you accidentally stumbled upon Briar's back?"

"Now, Gil." Mr. Stanhope half grinned as he forked a morsel of partridge. "It is all done and repented for, so sit down and eat your supper."

"Repented for, indeed." Gilbert pulled out his chair, sank down, and loosened the sweaty cravat from his neck. His blood still boiled. "But I shall have you know, Sister, that I spent the better part of this day hunting the earth for you. After I found Briar halfway to Wydenshire, I nearly lost my head with worry."

"I'm not a baby, Gil. I can ride."

"Not well and not a horse like Briar. He is used to me alone—and even I can hardly handle him at times." Gilbert dished out partridge, mashed turnips, potatoes, and a piece of apricot cake. The warm mixture of scents grumbled his stomach. He'd missed a meal because of her. "Why the deuce did you not ride your pony?"

"Briar was already saddled. Besides, he was tired of waiting too."

"Heaven have mercy, Charlotte, if Mamma does not return soon to care for you, we shall all go insane. My childhood mischief was miniscule compared to your little incidents."

"Not so, Gil." A slight chuckle from his father. "You forget much. You and Nan were a pair of rapscallions, to be sure."

"Where is she, anyway? Still despairing over the dowager's letter?"

"I don't know anything about a letter," said Mr. Stanhope. "But she retired early with the plea she felt unwell."

"I fail to understand why she allows herself to be so exasperated. It's not as if her ladyship—or even Lord Humphries—can do any true harm." Gilbert downed the rest of his dinner, left half the cake uneaten, and finally returned the cunning, apologetic grin Charlotte kept throwing his way. Little imp. "Excuse me, Papa, but I'm going to go see to Briar again. Poor horse raced himself into quite a lather this afternoon."

"Fine. Oh, and Gil?"

"Yes, Papa?"

"Will you see to Nan first? I suppose it is only a daft man's qualms, but she did seem strangely pale this last hour."

"I suppose. But I still say it is only her dashed nerves." With a sigh, Gilbert quit the dining room and bounded up the stairs. He knocked four times before opening her bedchamber door. "Too sick for dinner, eh?"

Solemn, moist eyes stared back at him.

"Not that I blame you." Gilbert pushed the door open wider and leaned against the frame. "I was ready to never eat again when I thought poor Charlotte had been thrown. Now I am ready to throw her myself. When did she return?"

"Not long. . .after you left."

"Why the devil did you not ride after me?"

"I just. . ." The sentence lingered. "I just do not feel well, Gil."

He tried to keep the smile from his lips, lest she anger at him. "Tomorrow it shall all be over, and you may quit all this fretting."

"I know."

"A bit of discomfort, perhaps, but I am certain you shall do and say all the right things. You always do."

"I hope so." Tears flashed. "Desperately, I hope so."

CHAPTER 9

A tiny flame danced from the pewter candlestick, casting light across the four sheltering walls of her bedchamber. Sometimes, the light made forms. Slight, shadowy—but forms nonetheless, like the constant rolling of the sea or the wobble of a ship struggling to stay afloat.

Oh, how she'd longed to be on that ship. Away from the Bobber, with its tainted plaster walls and its stench of drunken men. Away from the madam and the terror of her fists. Away from the streets. The hunger. The crate.

Dear heavens, how many times had she groped for Heath's promise, his whisper of what today or tomorrow might bring them?

She never really believed it would come.

Until now.

Angst wrestled with fear, then fear with rage, then rage with an empty sadness. What to feel? What to think?

Part of her longed for more tears, something that would unleash the torrent of emotion. If not tears of pain, then tears of joy?

She didn't know. Didn't understand. For long hours she sat before a closed window until the candle dwindled to darkness, deep and blinding.

Tomorrow was almost here.

After years of living for some faraway future, she'd finally surrendered to the present. Dorrington Hall had been her refuge, her salvation from a childhood marred with woe. She was becoming the woman she was meant to be, in the place she was meant to be.

But the past was drawing her back. Heath's promise was ready to be fulfilled. Tomorrow, she'd meet the man she could only remember by his songs.

Songs she'd long ago failed to sing.

❧

Nan stood before her full-length mirror, a spasm of panic unfolding as quickly as the dawn outside. The plain lavender gown fell to her ankles, where black half boots peeped out beneath a simple hem. She'd located an old straw bonnet, unadorned enough to cause little attraction in the early morning streets of Wydenshire. She could only hope she was not recognized. What havoc the gossipmongers would wreak if she were spied without chaperone—and visiting the inn, no less.

After finding her cloak and draping it about her shoulders, Nan escaped her bedchamber to the quiet, undisturbed halls. In less than an hour, Temperance would be bustling down this same corridor, intent on waking her mistress with a cheerful smile. What would she say to find Nan gone?

Guilt nudged Nan's stomach, but there could be no help for it. Temperance was far too overwrought. She could no sooner seal a secret than lead Wellington's troops into French battlefields.

When she reached downstairs, she broke into a run, flew through the unlit hallways, and bounded through the foyer without seeing a soul.

The morning air was dark, foggy, biting. Faint color streaked the sky overhead on her way to the stables.

"Up and about it early, aren't ye, Miss Duncan?" From a lantern-lit corner, Loftus sat on a workbench and eased a rag across Gilbert's saddle. "Need somethin' prepared?"

"The gig please."

"The gig?"

"You heard me, Loftus, now make haste."

A mild oath followed—a disrespect he would've never shown to a Stanhope— then he set the saddle aside and moseyed to do her bidding. "A'right, Miss Duncan." He waited until she'd climbed in before he handed over the reins. "Here's yer gig and ribbons, though I can't see why ye'd be wantin' it so early in the mornin'."

"That is none of your concern."

"No matter. I'll just be askin' Temperance. She tells me e'erythin' anyway, ye know."

"Well, she won't be telling you about this because she doesn't know about it." Nan pulled her cloak tighter against the chill. "And neither should anyone else. Understood?"

"Not really." A riling grin. "But whate'er ye say."

Nan frowned, then made a quick nod for him to open the stable doors. As soon as they parted, she whipped the reins and rolled out into the dense morning fog.

What if he told?

She'd never ventured off on her own before, never left without telling a soul, never done something that would render worry in a family she treasured.

But now she had another family to think of too.

Her own.

Winding road stretched before her. The countryside was dull and sleepy, quiet as a sea-covered grave. All too soon, the rising fog was intermingled with darker puffs of smoke lifting from countless Wydenshire chimneys. Was she there already?

Nan guided her gig to the western side of the giant-stoned church. At least if the gig and mare were recognized, her motives could not be questioned.

Please, God. A vicious throb drove nails through her temples as she slipped unseen down a barren street. She tugged her cloak tighter. *Please help me.* Help her what? Face the man she'd waited a lifetime for? Speak to the papa who had held her every happiness in his hands but had failed to give it to her?

And what of Heath?

So much she wanted to say, needed to hear, longed to understand. But after all these years, did any of it even matter?

Below the swinging sign, whose faded yellow paint read THE SIMON AND CAT, she paused and glanced both ways. No one noticed her.

She stepped into a small, low-ceilinged taproom scented with nauseating wafts of coffee, ale, and unwashed bodies. Along one wall, a crude bar held a man on top of it and another slumped against it from the floor, both unconscious. Two empty tankards littered the floor.

Clutching fists beneath her cloak, Nan hurried to where a stooped, sleepy-eyed man sat before a hearth, his apron signifying him as the proprietor. "Sir?"

A bleary gaze lifted. "Hmm?"

"I am looking for a Mister. . .Duncan."

"This ain't no brothel, chit. Respectable establishment. . .that's wot this is."

"I assure you, sir, my reasons in coming are of the utmost innocence." Her throat dried. "And importance."

"Likely."

"Please, I just—"

"Listen, chit, ain't a decent reason for a lady to come a-callin' alone in wee mornin' hours." He stoked the fire with an iron poker. "Best you be movin' kindly along."

"But you see, I—"

"You heard me!" A quick movement, then the man's hand snaked around her elbow. "Little trollop, ought to see you to the door meself—"

"Wait!" Her boots grounded against his tugging. "Mister Duncan. . .he is my bl–blood relation."

"Eh?"

"Yes." Her arms slithered from the man's grip. "So you see, there is nothing untoward in my visit, and you are at risk of no disreputableness in your inn. Now may I see him?"

The man's eyes widened as if considering her words. With a slight curse, he nodded. "Fine. Up the stairs, room eight. An' mind you, don't be stayin' too long."

"I won't." Nan hastened toward a splintery door, eased it open, and climbed a flight of stairs that creaked and moaned. She was just rounding the curve when—

A well-dressed man collided with her, flattening her against the wall of the narrow stairway.

A grunt, deep and throaty, then the gentleman backed away as if the touch of her had soured him. "Out of my way."

"Forgive me, I. . ." Her sentence fell apart as the cloaked figure tore down the stairs. Something about him, his shoulders, the husky quality of his voice. . .

But the door slammed before she could remember where she'd seen him before.

Help me please, God. When she reached the top of the stairs, the hallway was faded, quiet, disconcerting. She passed along wooden planks until she reached a doorway that froze her.

Room number eight.

"What do you mean she is gone?"

Gilbert clicked the study door shut behind him, unease stitching across his chest. "Just what I said. Temperance has been crying for over two hours."

"Two hours? Why didn't you tell me?"

"I thought perhaps she'd taken a walk. Maybe even a ride."

"Alone?"

Gilbert approached a chair, pulled his hat into his hands, and faced Papa. "I do not know. In any event, I just checked the stables."

"And?"

"Loftus says she took the gig."

"The gig." His father pulled a hand down his face. "That makes little sense. What time did she leave?"

"Early, it seems—and from Loftus's account, in hopes of secrecy."

"Nan never keeps secrets."

"Apparently one." Flashes of her face last night, the quick tears. Why hadn't he paid heed to them? Should he have pressed her?

Tap, tap. The knocking diverted his thoughts.

Mr. Stanhope rose. "Come in."

A young footman swung open the door and stood in rigid position. "A carriage arriving, Mr. Stanhope."

"Who is it?"

"We believe it to be Mrs. Stanhope, sir."

"Jolly good." His father scooted around his desk and motioned for Gilbert to follow. "Let us go and greet your mother. If anyone knows what is to be done about Nan, it will undoubtedly be her."

"Papa?"

Mr. Stanhope paused midway through the door. "Yes?"

"What is to be done about her ladyship?"

"That, my son," he said, with a slow grin, "is also a matter for your dear mother."

Gilbert frowned. Was that what this was all about? Was Nan so set against entertaining her ladyship that she would disappear for the day?

He was different. Smaller, more worn, like a broken seashell cracked and dulled by a million unforgiving waves. Hard lines engraved his face. Age defined his yellow, crinkled eyes. Pain flattened the chapped lips.

Not at all like the papa she had envisioned.

Heath slid the door closed behind her. The click sounded with finality. Closing her in. Suffocating her.

No one spoke.

Tension vibrated as steadily as each weak, trembling heartbeat. How long would this silence go on? Looking, but never speaking. Crying, but never weeping. Hoping, but never knowing for what.

Then Heath edged closer, his fingers knit with hers. How strong the grip, how familiar, lending strength when she had none of her own.

"My." Papa spoke the solitary word, part whisper and part sigh.

Nan's knees threatened as the old man approached.

He stood closer than she would have expected, face-to-face, looking betwixt her and Heath.

Then he touched her cheek with a withered hand. A hook framed Heath's. "Look at you. . .my children." Pulling them closer, hugging them into his neck. "My children, my children, my children."

And the room came alive with the strange, remarkable sounds of all their cries.

For all the color and delight of the dishes spread out before her, the Dowager Marchioness of Somerset bore unmistaken displeasure on her tight face. "Surely this is not all present."

Gilbert glanced at both Papa and Mamma before finally returning to the dowager. "Yes, my lady."

"There must be a grave mistake."

"I do not think so."

"Oh yes, there is." She laid both veiny hands upon the gleaming table. "I wrote a very specific letter to Miss Duncan, and I know for certain it was delivered. Now where is she?"

"Her absence is to all of our regret," said Mrs. Stanhope, with the sort of tone that might soothe a child. "We offer sincere apologies."

"I see." The dowager sniffed. "Well, Aylmer, you can see what comes of my trying to pacify you. At least now you cannot blame me for undesired results."

"Mother." Lord Humphries flushed a deep, vibrant shade. "If Miss Duncan could not arrive, I do not doubt it was for great reason."

"Yes." This came from his sister, seated left of him, who brightened with an all-too-cheerful smile. "Might I comment on the exquisite roast, Mrs. Stanhope? Every dish, in fact. It all appears cooked to perfection."

"Thank you, Lady Humphries," said Mrs. Stanhope. "You are too kind."

"Yes, Julia." The dowager's sharp, low whisper could be heard by all occupants of the dining room. "You are much too kind, indeed."

Gilbert leaned back into his chair and tightened a fist around his fork. 'Twould be a long evening.

Just wait until he got ahold of Nan.

The gig's wheels made slow, soothing sounds as they turned over gravel. Evening shadows danced across the horizon in hues of deep purple and blue.

"Now what?" The murmur, one she'd been asking herself all the day, finally came to life.

Heath leaned forward and managed the reins, eyes intent on the road ahead, as if in it could be found their answers. "I don't know."

The daytime hours had sped away, as unreal as anything she'd ever known. They'd wept, held each other, spoken of the past for the first time in so many years.

They'd told Papa everything.

Some Papa already knew, some he didn't. Twice, he had broken with sobs. Once, he'd cursed God. A hundred times over, he'd blamed himself.

But in the end, he shrank into a shell. A quiet, sad, mournful shell—and he'd stared at them oddly, as if their faces were those of ghosts.

By the fall of evening, he'd ordered Heath to return Nan where she belonged. He didn't say if he would see her again. Or if he wanted to.

As the quiet journey home led them deep into familiar countryside, she tried to unravel the hurting strings of confusion.

"I don't know what he wants." Heath's shoulders sagged. "From either of us."

"And you?"

He turned to her in question.

"What do you want of him?"

"I don't know. It is too late for much."

"But not too late for everything."

Heath clenched his jaw. She'd noticed it fleetingly throughout the day—faint glimpses of resentment, a certain tension between father and son.

Nan's throat burned. "Will you return to the rectory?"

"He doesn't want me to."

"*I* don't want you to."

Softness crept along Heath's face. No smile, though. Not even the hint of one. When was the last time she'd seen him smile? Before the Bobber? Could she even remember that long ago?

Hurt washed to shore, bringing with it wave after wave of desperation. She slipped her arm into his and leaned into him, clinging as one might hold to a lifeline. "Heath, I'm so afraid."

"Please don't be."

"I cannot lose you. . .cannot lose either of you. Papa. . .he is so strange and so very sad. I want to help him. I want to be close to him. For all he's done, I still cannot help loving him and I. . ." More tears. Oh, how many could one cry in a mere day? "I cannot help but wish. . .we could all be together again."

"Would to heaven that were possible."

"Why can't it be?"

"I would die before I would jeopardize you. I think, in the end, that is why Papa wanted you returned."

Nan's chest quivered. "Then you do not think he will see me again? And you will. . .you will return to wherever it is you came from and never think of me again?"

The gig yanked to a stop. He turned to her, the last of sunlight illuminating an expression so fierce it might have been fatal. "I have never forgotten you."

"Nor I you."

"Whatever I do is for your good."

"Then stay here...both of you. My reputation is of little matter, and if it hinders me from what I desire most, then let it be ruined."

A battle raged across his expression, but the darkness fell before she comprehended which side won. He hurried the gig back into motion, and the long road of silence drew them back to the moonlit grounds of Dorrington Hall.

When he'd helped her from the gig, he untied his horse from the back and mounted in one swift movement.

"Heath, wait." She neared the animal's side and stared up at him. "Promise I shall see you again."

A faint nod.

"You will talk to Papa?"

He hesitated, but in the end another nod followed.

"Thank you." She reached up, locked hands, squeezed. "God would not have brought us today and tomorrow, Heath, if He did not mean for us to keep it."

He pressed her hand once more and rode away.

"That is far enough."

"I thought the house would be abed."

"Did you?"

"Yes."

"I, for one, could not sleep." Gilbert approached the base of the stairs, his beeswax candle throwing yellow light to where Nan still stood frozen halfway up. Irritation mounted with the realization she was safe and unharmed—and a dashed coward for abandoning them. "Come back here, and if you argue, I shall carry you down myself."

"I am tired."

"Now, Nan."

"We can discuss it in the morning."

"We shall discuss it now. Or wouldn't you care to hear how we managed with your guests? Mamma was just returned from a lengthy trip and had not ample time to even take a breath before she was forced with the responsibility of preparing the house. Pray, was enduring the dashed dragon so grim that you would suffer us with such worry? I daresay, Nan, that was less kind than what Charlotte—"

"Enough, Gil!" She whirled with anger he hadn't expected, her eyes wild and glowing. "Leave me alone, I say!" She ascended quickly, disappearing beyond the candle's reach.

Gilbert bounded after her. He snatched her arm before she reached the top of the stairs, pulled her down to where their heights became equal.

"I said leave me be—"

"Get ahold of yourself. Dash it all, you behave as if I were some stranger. A threatening one, at that."

"You have no right to—"

"Speak with you? Inquire where you have been all the day? I always thought that you were fonder of me than that."

As swiftly as the words were breathed, her expression crashed. A new, more vulnerable one rearranged her face. "I am."

"Then tell me where you went today."

"I cannot."

"Why?"

She looked away, nibbled the bottom of her lip.

And barreled tension through his stomach. "Nan. . .please."

With pain, her eyes edged back to his. "My father, my brother."

"What about them?"

"They are back." Her breath shattered with the words. "Gil, they are back."

By the time Heath returned, the Simon and Cat's taproom had loudened considerably. Ten or so men gathered around the bar, raising toasts in grubby tankards and ignoring threats from an ill-humored proprietor.

Heath was headed for the stairs when a voice rose above the rest, "To the *Lady Vallantine*, the ship I would've married had she been o' flesh and bone."

Coarse laughs erupted. A loud clink of tankards.

Heath's mouth soured as he watched Papa lean heavily against the rough wooden bar.

"And to my hook, mates." He raised the dull metal until it caught the light of a nearby wall sconce. "Anyone of you tangles with me and I'll. . .I'll swipe you with it." With the swing of his hook, several heads ducked and another round of laughs rippled throughout the room.

Heath moved forward and wrapped a hand around his father's hunching shoulder. "Papa."

He turned, eyes filmy and strained. "Son." Humor crashed hard. "Son. . .this is my son, boys. Someone, get a drink for him. . .for my son."

Heath ignored the foamy tankard someone slid his way. He pulled Papa from the bar, yanked out a wooden chair, and helped him into the seat. "We need to talk."

A raspy laugh, but the sound soon trickled into a grunt. "Talk is not worth a halfpenny, boy. Action. . .now that'll get you places in life."

"About Nan."

"Eh?"

"You know what this could cost her. Her future, her hopes of a marriage—"

"Get me my drink." Cold, cutting. "If you were any kind of a man, you'd down one yourself."

Repulsion needled every inch of Heath's chest. He bent next to Papa and tried not to waver before the eyes. "It must be decided. For all of us."

"You don't think I know that?"

"Yes, sir, but—"

"I didn't come all this way to turn back now. My daughter is a Duncan—and ain't no one going to tell me to forsake my own."

"I'm not asking that. But there must be a way."

"There is." His father wiped a small drizzle of ale from the corner of his mouth. "There is always a way. And I always find it."

Heath wished that were true. That he could believe the words.

But Papa had made promises before.

CHAPTER 10

"*Y*ou cannot be serious."

Gilbert slid in next to Nan at the breakfast table, handed her a cup of strong-scented cocoa, and nodded for the second time. "Serious indeed. Want a fruit?"

"I do!" Charlotte reached across the table without the slightest heed for manners. If Mr. or Mrs. Stanhope had been present, the offense would have been scolded.

However, Nan was in no temperament to administer correction—and Gilbert didn't seem to notice.

Nan clenched her fingers around the warm cup. "And who, may I ask, came up with this nonsensical scheme?"

"Although you fully anticipate laying the blame on me," said Gilbert, "I am sorry to inform you it was Mamma's. But do not worry. She has every intention of accompanying you."

Nan smacked her cup back onto the tablecloth, chocolate sloshing, heat springing to her cheeks. "It is not going so much that irks me, but the thought of apologizing to *her ladyship*—"

"I hate apologizing too." Charlotte licked a foamy brown ring from her upper lip. "But no one listens to me."

As if in testament to her words, neither Nan nor Gilbert acknowledged Charlotte. Instead, Nan raised her eyes to Gilbert in bewilderment. Words threatened to spill, questions she'd been alone with all night long. *Have you told them? What did they say?*

He seemed to sense her thoughts, although he only smiled and continued his meal. Centuries passed before Charlotte finally finished her peach, toast, and cocoa. Even then, she lingered, pouting about the frilly dress her mother had returned with and the unfavorable book her tutor had assigned her.

At last, she grew bored of indifferent responses and ambled away with grumblings.

"Well?" Nan scooted out of her chair to face him. "Did you?"

"Did I what?"

"Gil, don't you dare tease when I—"

"No." His eyes sobered. "It is not my secret to tell."

"But you think I should."

"Don't you?"

Exasperation pulled her back into her chair. "More than anything. I only hesitate because. . .well. . ."

"Well what?"

"Heath."

"What about him?"

"It is just that he has sacrificed so much, forfeited a lifetime. . .all so I could have this." She swept her gaze around the room, the bright wallpaper, the gleaming sideboard, the sparkling chandelier that shone with all the radiance of a morning sun. "He fears what might happen if my true heritage is known."

"We have never lied to anyone."

"I know."

"People have always known you were not a Stanhope, and with the dowry Papa has put up for you, it has never hindered your options. I daresay, Lord Humphries seems quite oblivious to the mystery of your bloodlines."

"They are not my worries. I only fear hurting Heath and—"

"There you are, Nan." Mrs. Stanhope swept into the room, her smile so natural it was evident she had heard none of the conversation. "Are you prepared to leave for the dowager's? I was hoping to get a good start, dear, if it is all the same to you."

"Yes." Nan spared Gilbert one last look and groaned within herself. "I am as ready as I shall ever be."

Trepidation formed along the pit of Heath's stomach as Dorrington Hall drew near. Daylight elevated the manor house to a different level of magnificence. Huge, age-old stones formed the three-story structure. Balconies—just as he'd known—jutted into the air with blooming vines accenting the white railings. At the base of the front stairs, two stone cherubs lifted their faces heavenward, arms raised as if in welcome while their feet melted into splendorous grass.

Not the largest house, perhaps. Maybe, outside of Chanfest's small village, he'd beheld bigger and wealthier abodes.

But there was a calm, gentle sense of contentment about this place. It seemed to possess the same cheer of Nan's songs, or the same delight of the rector's smile, or the same wonder of a church bell's chimes.

Maybe that was what frightened him. The thought of tearing Nan away, uprooting her again. And for what? What could their papa—by this time, a total stranger—possibly give her but more hurt?

Even so, he urged his horse forward. Supposing there to be a servants' entry along the house, he dismounted and led his horse to the back. A door was ajar, with kitchen smells wafting out into the warm air.

"Good girl, Golda." He looped the animal's reins around a small shrubbery, gave her neck a quick pat, and turned for the door—

"What else do ye want me to say?" From inside, the raised male voice halted Heath in his tracks. "Don't act as if I just trampled all yer dreams, girl. It's not as if I was a-hurtin' you purposely, huh?"

"You have slaughtered everything." A female voice. "Every hope I have ever had, every chance of any happiness, and you have—"

"See, that's just it. If you ain't chatterin' on, ye're blubberin' about this or the other thing. Ye can't very well blame a body for wantin' free of the likes of ye—"

"Loftus, you cannot mean this. No, you certainly cannot mean to say that I...that you..."

Heath shuffled back a few feet. Heat crept along his cheeks at the thought of intruding on such private ground, but would it be any better to run away?

Before he could decide, the man's tone rose an octave. "Let's not be fools, eh, Temp? Ye ne'er loved the likes of me any more than I loved you. 'Tis a game we've played for too long."

"But that girl, that beautiful girl from the village with the gold ha—"

"If it weren't her, it would've been someone else. Can't you see what I'm bloody well tryin' to tell ye? Can't ye get it through yer stupid, flighty head?"

A sniffling sound, whispers too low to hear.

"What's the bloody use?" An unsavory string of words, then the door came crashing open.

Heath jolted as a young man rushed out into the yard.

He cast one fierce glance Heath's way, scowled, then sprinted from the house as if it carried a disease.

Should Heath leave? Perhaps the visit with Nan should wait. Or perhaps he should find another entrance, one that would not disturb the poor girl who—

He glanced to the doorway again.

Lost and sagging in the threshold stood a young woman. Her dress was dark linen, her skin alabaster, her hair as black as a midnight sky. Wispy ringlets framed cheeks that were already blushing. "My goodness, you must have heard everything."

The words rendered him speechless. What to say?

Smearing her cheeks with the back of her hand, she stepped down into the grass. "Not that it matters. By eventide, all of Dorrington Hall—and probably half of Wydenshire—shall know of my helpless state. All I ever wanted in life was a suitable match, a happy match. I always supposed that for an abigail, Loftus was the greatest I might afford. It seems not even he will have me, though."

An uncomfortable pause ensued.

More tears gathered.

Heath shifted, wiped a sheen of moisture from his forehead. For lack of any response, he pivoted—

"Wait. You can't go on account of me." She hurried to him, sniffling. "The answer will undoubtedly be no to whatever you want to ask, but I can't deny you the privilege of at least asking. My mother always said a question never did any harm to anyone, least of all a poor man."

He cleared his throat, took a long glance left and right of him. "If this is a bad time—"

"It is a terrible time. It is the worst day of my life, but there isn't a thing either of us can do about it. Now if you're looking for work, I don't think there's anything at all unless you hope to become a footman. Mr. Hill just recently fell off his horse, see, and can't do anything but lay in bed and groan all day. If Mr. Stanhope weren't such a kind sort, I don't doubt Mr. Hill would be houseless by now. But you hardly seem the footman type, for they usually have a look about them. Isn't that strange? I always thought stable boys had a look about them too." A cloud dampened her expression, and without saying anything else, her eyes lifted to his expectantly.

"Yes, miss." Heath hesitated. "I mean, no, miss. I'm not a footman."

"Then what are you?"

He didn't quite know the answer to that himself. "I, uh, was hoping to inquire after Miss Duncan."

"That's very strange. I never dreamed you should ask after Miss Duncan. Do you know her, then?"

"Yes."

"What an oddity when I know all of her acquaintances by heart. Who did you say you were?" When he hesitated, she said, "It doesn't matter. She is gone calling with Mrs. Stanhope to see the Dowager Marchioness of Somerset, and who knows when they shall return?"

"I see."

"I'm deeply sorry I could not be of more help."

"And I am deeply sorry, miss, for taking up your time." Heath bent slightly in a bow. "Good day, miss."

"Temperance."

"Pardon?"

"Temperance—my name." She retreated back into the doorway. "And if you wish to call again, Miss Duncan will be in tomorrow. Who shall I tell her to expect?"

He left the question unanswered, tipped his hat, and hurried back to where Golda waited for him. His body relaxed in the saddle as he exited Dorrington Hall's iron gates. The man Loftus had been right in at least one of his points. He certainly didn't seem to love the maiden. And judging by her swift recovery, the maiden didn't love him.

But any man who would make a woman cry that way, in terms so cruel, did not deserve her. Poor pity to the next girl he entangled with.

Heath squinted against the sun, the warmth dampening his shirt with sweat. Nan had been to see a marchioness? Yet another reminder she had risen above her station.

He did not wish to pull her back down to cheap inns and dirty beds and the shame of a drunken sailor. She deserved more than that. More than anything they could ever give her.

Hopefully, Papa knew.

On any other day, Nan's courage would have been depleted long before she reached the dowager's doorstep. The events of last night, however, brought her current visit into a whole new perspective.

Mrs. Stanhope must have noticed, because she leaned over to whisper, "I am quite proud of you, Nan, for I envisioned you much less composed. Have you changed so very much in the short time I was away?"

Nan had no time to answer, for the large, white-paneled doors opened.

After they requested to see her ladyship, the butler made a formal bow and instructed them to follow him. He led them through an enormous great hall, down several corridors, and into a parlor so bright that the colors were nearly overwhelming.

"If you will care to wait, Miss Duncan, Mrs. Stanhope," said the butler.

Both nodded and took seats on adjacent sofas.

"Isn't it all lovely?" Mrs. Stanhope scanned the length of the room—everything from the murals on the wall, to the open hearth, to the vibrant Turkish rug and matching draperies.

"I suppose so."

"La, such lack of enthusiasm, my dear. Doesn't anything impress you?"

"I suppose—" The parlor doors opened again.

In floral waistcoat and perfect cravat, the dragon entered with his trademark grin in place. "Ah, what is this?" He bowed twice—first to her, then to Mrs. Stanhope. "I do hope you did not travel all this way because of last night."

"Yes, actually." Mrs. Stanhope rose, her slanting glance a signal for Nan to do the same. "Will her ladyship not be joining us?"

"Indisposed, I fear, with a gruesome headache. Please accept apologies on her behalf."

"Of course."

Lord Humphries's gaze traveled her way. He truly wasn't lacking, by any means, in general attraction. His features were pleasant, boyish, and his voice possessed an uncommon sweetness. Why was it, then, that his attentions always made her hurry for an escape?

Nan folded her gloved hands in front of her. "My lord, I fear I did you a great injustice."

"Bah, nothing of the sort."

"No, please. I must explain. You see, I never meant—"

"Quite enough, Miss Duncan. I shall hear no more of this. Although I must confess to great delight in your visit, it truly was not necessary. Nor is an explanation."

Warmth nudged away a portion of her dislike. "Your understanding is very commendable, my lord."

"Think no more of it. Although, if I may take advantage of some of your time, a stroll out of doors would be most gratifying. Would you mind?"

Mind? Yes, a bit—but surprisingly less than she would have expected. Considering he was a dragon, that is. With a smile, she nodded. "Of course."

"Splendid, Miss Duncan. I have no doubts but that you will vastly adore the gardens here at Bletherton Manor. Mother takes great pride in their overseeing, as I am sure you will find." He approached, offered his arm, and extended the offer to Mrs. Stanhope. Thus, they exited into the great outdoors with her hand nestled against the smooth fabric of his arm. She would resolve to enjoy herself at least this once. Not in returned affection, but in gratitude.

After all, he had avoided her an apology with her ladyship.

The scent of cheroot rose into the air, just as it did every evening, in a way that had long since become a comfort to Nan.

Across the drawing room, Mrs. Stanhope was seated on the lounge with her needlework. Charlotte lingered at the unlit hearth, never seated because of her boundless energy. Gilbert sat next to the window with his chin perched on his fist.

And Mr. Stanhope. Dear, beloved Mr. Stanhope was settled in his usual chair, smoking his long cigar, chuckling softly over a bit of news Mrs. Stanhope had just related.

Nan didn't wish to disturb such a scene.

But she must.

Rising, she drew enough resolve to slip into the center of their circle. "I must have a word, please."

"Don't tell me. I already know. Leave the room—"

"No, Charlotte." Nan snagged the girl's elbow before she could depart. "This is something all should hear."

Mr. Stanhope leaned forward. "Upon my word, Nan, do not look so woebegone. Surely this news of yours cannot be so very bad."

"It is not bad at all."

Gilbert rose from his chair. The simple act bolstered her strength.

"I wish to make it known that...my papa and brother have arrived in Wydenshire."

Mrs. Stanhope lowered her needlework.

Charlotte sank into a chair.

Even Mr. Stanhope, for all his usual calm, yanked the cigar from his ruddy lips. "What?"

"It is true." Emotion clogged Nan's throat. "Heath...he was the one who found Charlotte, who brought her back."

"*He* is your brother?" Charlotte's mouth gaped. "Truly?"

"Yes." Yet even as she answered, Nan kept her eyes fixed on Mr. Stanhope. "Did you know that all those years ago Heath knew you had taken me home?" A small laugh, fragile enough that tears softened the sound. "He had the letter...all this time."

"Then why, my dear?" Mr. Stanhope rose too. Crossed the distance. Took both her hands in his warm and soothing grip. "Why in this world did he never come for you?"

"He feared what might become of us."

"But he could have stayed here, and he could have—"

"Please, it doesn't matter." Her shoulders wilted as pain swallowed her. She didn't want to hear what might have been. "None of it matters now. He has returned. The both of them have, and for the first time, we can be together again."

A stillness fell upon the room. Thick, startling, lengthy.

Then Gilbert stepped closer, voicing in quiet words, "You don't mean to say that if they were to depart. . .you would go with them?"

She swayed her eyes to his, then back to Mr. Stanhope's. Both were bright with tears.

"I should never like to leave." Her thumbs caressed the veiny skin of Mr. Stanhope's hands. "I should never like to leave or be left by anyone. Not ever again."

CHAPTER 11

$\mathscr{I}$n all the world, there was nothing as lovely as Miss Duncan's voice.

From a chair tucked out of the way, Temperance tapped her finger in perfect timing to the music. The tune was familiar, modish, dynamic. One could easily get lost in such a whirl, lost enough to forget uncouth stable boys and stabbing rejections.

Even if she had seen the rejection coming.

A deep stir rose in the pit of her stomach, unbearable enough that she might never eat again. *Stupid. Flighty.* She slid her eyes shut. *Chattering. Blubbering.*

She wondered if the village girl, the one whose hair was gold and copper, had talked too much. Had she fluttered her eyelashes at Loftus instead of her lips? Was that what had turned his heart? Or had it happened long before that?

Oh, the questions. How she wished they all had answers. Then again, did she really want them to? For what if Loftus was right? What if the fault was her own?

All her life, people had tried to tell her. *Quell your tongue, do not carry on, try to contain yourself.*

By this time, she should have mastered the art. One would have thought, after years spent in her mistress's company, that she would have adopted some of Miss Duncan's amiable, genteel ways.

But she hadn't.

And everything Loftus had said was likely true. Could her predicament grow any worse? Could anything more dreadful have happened?

The loss of their future together, of Loftus himself, was not the true grief. But a life fated to lowly service as an unfavorable ape leader, a pitiful spinster? That was the catastrophe. The heartache. The ruin.

Without warning, the door opened, halting both Miss Duncan's singing and Temperance's melancholy thoughts.

"A visitor to see you, miss," said the footman.

"Who is it?"

"An anonymous caller, I fear. Shall you see him in the drawing room?"

"I shall be right there."

"Very good, miss." The footman whisked back away, leaving the door open behind him.

Nan brushed down her olive-striped gown, tightened her sash, and glanced at her reflection in a hanging mirror. "How odd. Who do you suppose?"

A quick image returned—a handsome stranger dressed plainly, with flaxen hair and quiet tongue. How she envied him that!

"Temperance?"

She started. "Oh—yes, miss?"

"You are not feeling unwell again, are you?"

"Oh no, miss. You cannot think I am so under Loftus's spell that a broken engagement could injure my health. I am simply thoughtful today, more so than normal." She followed Miss Duncan into the corridor scented with linseed oil and fresh roses from a vase. "There was a small matter I wished to tell you, but with all the events of yesterday, I was much too distraught to remember. A man came by—a strange sort—and who do you imagine he was asking for?"

"Who?"

"Why, you of course, Miss Duncan. I'd never seen him before. Not even once. And come to think of it, he was rightly considerate, although I fear I exposed him to my worst side all in the space of a few moments. . ."

They had reached the drawing room, and the footman was already waiting to draw back the doors.

Temperance had taken just two short steps into the room, still in Miss Duncan's shadow, when she caught sight of the anonymous visitor.

"Heath!"

How startling it was—watching her mistress rush into the arms of this tall, rugged guest. Good heavens, was this some sort of secret love tryst?

But the endearment seemed almost fraternal, as Miss Duncan tucked her arm inside the man's, turned, and gleamed. "Temperance, I should like to introduce you to my brother, Heath—the one I used to talk of so much."

A flame soared up Temperance's neck as she curtsied. "Very pleased, sir."

He nodded, then turned back to Miss Duncan. "Papa would like to see you. Can you come?"

"Of course."

"How soon?"

"Just as long as it will take to don my pelisse."

Temperance started for the door. "I shall fetch it, miss—"

"No, please. Charlotte darted away with it only hours ago, and I know just where she has hidden it." Miss Duncan flitted from the room.

Temperance was left alone.

With the man.

Heat rose up her neck again, this time spreading to her cheeks and ears.

Hands behind his back, Miss Duncan's brother studied his boots. Did he dread another rapid conversation, as yesterday? Or was he only shy?

"I am very sorry, Mr. Duncan," she said. "You must think me quite the prattling fool."

He lifted pale eyes. Curious, soft—but certainly not unkind. "I don't think that at all, Miss Temperance."

Her name. Why did it sound so different from his lips?

A silence followed, one she ought to fill with something. Why couldn't she think? *My sakes, what is wrong with me?*

Perhaps Miss Duncan was right. She was falling ill.

As if on cue, her mistress came hurrying back. "I am ready." She took his arm again, and they moved for the door.

Temperance retreated out of their way.

Mr. Duncan paused at the door with a quick glance in her direction. "Goodbye, Miss Temperance."

An earthquake couldn't have shaken a word from her. She managed a nod, another curtsy, then stood still as stone while the pair quitted the room.

She must be gravely ill, indeed.

"This is not the way to the village."

As their mounts clip-clopped over an arched bridge, Heath nodded up ahead. "See those trees?"

A small cluster of hawthorns and whitebeams formed a secluded grove, the foliage nearly hiding the distant figure and his horse. Relief tunneled through anxiety. Thank heavens. She was to avoid another visit to the seedy, less than reputable inn—and the accusing innkeeper who called her a trollop.

Hunched and garbed in frayed tailcoat and breeches, Papa leaned against a hawthorn and breathed smoke from his pipe as they approached.

Strange, how such a small thing could bring back a world of memories. Curled on his lap, head against his chest, listening to whispered songs...

103

"Let me help you." Heath had already dismounted, and he swung her off her horse.

"There she is. Come here, girl, and let me take another look at you."

She moved closer to the tree and stood amid leaf-shaped shadows that danced in the breeze. "Hello, Papa."

"Sit down, girl. Right next to me."

She sank beside him, close enough that she inhaled his tobacco smoke. "You wanted to see me?"

"Heath, you take a ride, hear? I'll have a word with my daughter alone."

Heath's eyes were careful, hesitant, as if one signal from her would keep him close. But at her nod, he led his horse away.

"Now we can have our time, can't we?" Red-rimmed eyes turned to her. Studying. Memorizing. Deciding almost, but on what she wasn't sure. "Don't suppose you know much about your mother, do you?"

"No, sir. Very little."

"Och, she was a lass. I was naught but a blacksmith's apprentice at the time, strolling into the Bobber for a dram of ale—and there she stood. Part child and part woman, she was, but I couldn't take my eyes off her. Two days later, I married her."

A shiver crept the length of Nan's spine. She'd never imagined her mother in the vile, filthy rooms of the Bobber. Had she stayed there of her own choice? Or had she been prisoner, just as her children would become?

"Wish I could say we were happy, the two of us. What we had. . .well, it was the first love in my life that didn't turn around and bite me. Felt good and clean, it did. Like it would last forever." The edges of his lips hardened. "But not even love could live off the little food we had, the dirt in those stinking flats, the cold nights and burning days. Sometimes I'd just sit and watch her in those years after Heath was born—watch how she'd stare at fancy ladies and their dresses, wanting but never asking. Watch how she'd shrink a little with each day, how she'd grow quieter and quieter, how she'd slip deep inside herself until no one could reach her. Not even me."

"I'm sorry." How shallow the words, but what else could she say?

Papa shook his head. "She didn't die giving birth to you, Nan Duncan. She was dead long afore that."

"I'm so sorry, Papa."

"I know." He grabbed her hand, leaned closer, a breath away. Fierceness shot through his pupils like glowing, smothering coals. "Girl, this is what I want from you. . .and you listen good to me, hear?"

Disquiet unfurled and wetted her palms as she nodded.

"You're going to marry well. You're going to give your mother the one thing I never could. You're going to give it to me too. You're not going to go hungry or want for things or—"

"Papa, please—"

"No!" Both hook and hand landed on her shoulders. Pulled her closer still. "You *must* listen. I'm going to stay here in Wydenshire. I'm going to take me a cottage and ain't no one going to know who I am."

"Yes, but—"

"You can come and see me. We'll be close, just a ride away from being together again. Ain't no devil's ship to keep us apart no more." His brows quivered. "Heath told me 'bout the marchioness you went a-visiting. I done heard the talk—talk about her eligible sons, talk about the one who has his heart on you."

She pulled in a slow breath. "Papa, I don't have my heart cast on him."

"Ain't you heard nothing I just told you?"

"Yes, but—"

"Love ain't something to fall in your lap. You have to go out, grab it by the stem, pick it off the bloody tree. You may not fancy to this bloke right off, but given half a chance, couldn't it be?"

Heat warmed her cheeks at his cursing. Her heart tripped faster. "I—I don't know."

"'Course you don't. Not yet." He patted her cheek. "But you will, Nan. You will."

"And if I don't?"

"Then I'll be as miserable. . .as desolate and dead as your mother was."

The words pierced with the cruelty of a jagged blade. "Papa, you ask too much."

"Too much for a broken old man? Is it so wrong to wish his daughter married well? Comfortable?"

"I'm sorry." She withdrew and scrambled to her feet. Tears spilled before she had any hope of stopping them, but she dashed them away with the back of her hand. "I wish. . .I wish I could make you happy."

"You can."

"Not this way."

He too pushed to his feet. His hand flattened against his chest, rubbed for a second or two. "If you cannot love him, so be it. But if this man, this son of a marchioness, has any chance of winning your love, will you let him? Will you at least try—if not for my sake, if not for your own, then for your mother's?"

The question hung as unsteadily as the hawthorn branches wavering in the breeze.

"Yes." There could be no sin in that, could there? She had to work up the courage to voice the next words. "I shall try."

Heath listened from the other side of room eight as raspy breathing lifted, then fell in rhythm. Almost as if Papa had to fight for each breath.

But then again, he always had been a fighter. A rough one. A giant hero in a world of tiny creatures, capable of most anything in the world.

Except the things that mattered.

Heath ripped off the scratchy counterpane, swung his legs out of bed, and pulled on thin boots. He left the room as silently as possible. Not that it mattered. Even if Papa had been awake, the evening ale had dulled his senses.

Heath slipped down black stairs and felt his way to the unlatched door of the quiet inn. He stepped outside, where the empty streets looked much like Chanfest, where the distant shapes of buildings and windows seemed almost like the rectory. He breathed in air scented of horse dung and chimney smoke and cool night.

God, why did You take him? Shouldn't pray the prayer so often. The rector wouldn't want him to. Mayhap it was a sin to question the Almighty about the intricate ways of death and man.

But it came all the same, like a festered wound that ever oozed, hurting long past the injury itself. *God, give me peace. I want to make You smile, the both of you.*

And he would. He'd return to the rectory and live his life fulfilling a promise. More than a promise. A desire. A zeal. A need inside of him to please God and serve with a heart like the rector—

A noise, sharp and shrill against the night. "Egad, who the deuce are you?" Coming from the other side of the inn, followed by a spout of curses. "See here, fellow, is this some kind of—"

A scream. Deep. Throaty. Agonized.

Heath plunged around the inn's brick corner, ran for the sounds—

"Stop right there."

Heath halted just as his boots bumped something on the ground. Something soft. Like flesh.

"Wrong time to be prowlin' the streets, me cove." The shadow swayed, as indistinct as George III on a shilling rubbed smooth. "Wot say you just turn 'round and face the wall, eh?"

Every nerve sharpened, Heath didn't move.

"You a deaf bloke or wot? I said—"

Head first, Heath dove. He caught the man's middle, tackled him as cold metal met his arm. Pain flared.

No, no.

He groped through the darkness, seized the deadly wrist. Squeezed, squeezed. Heaven help him squeeze...

Metal clanked against the cobbles.

Heath rolled on top of the man. He caught one punch before throwing several of his own.

"Stop!" A spray of the man's spittle and blood splattered Heath's face. "Stop, you blackguard...you're...you're bashin' me face in!"

Heath's fingers curled around the man's oilskin coat. He staggered to his feet, yanked the stranger up with him, and slammed his back against the grimy inn wall.

Furious eyes stared back at him. "Now wot?"

Heath hauled him back out of the alley. He glanced both ways down the dark street. "Move." First, he'd find the constable. Then bring back help for the body in the alley.

Then stop the blood leaking from his left arm.

Pressing the wound to his side, he nudged the offender forward, their boots scuffing cobbles. A burn sizzled through him, reaching deeper than was comfortable. He'd been out of control. For a few moments, with the man trapped beneath him, his body had shaken and his fists had pounded so fast and hard there was no stopping them.

Flashings of the madam blinked in the darkness. His arms shielding his face. The blows striking him anyway. The need to stop her, to end the pain—but not being strong enough.

He shuddered the memories away and flexed his hands.

He would not lose control of himself again.

CHAPTER 12

"Whatever is the matter with you?"

Charlotte trudged in front of Nan's easel, her frown pronounced by the way she cupped her jaw. Ever dramatic, this one. "I. . .av. . .too. . .ache."

"What?"

Charlotte dropped her hands in aggravation. "I have a *toothache*."

"So that's where you went." Smiling, Nan dipped her paintbrush into an overcast shade of blue. "I wondered what would take you and Mrs. Stanhope out so early. Back to the apothecary for more clove essence, hmm?"

"Yes."

"If you would refrain from so many jellies and scones and things, you wouldn't have such problems."

"I know. Everything good for me I cannot have." She circled to the other side of the easel and peered at the painting. "What is it?"

"The courtyard, of course. See there, that's the fountain."

"Oh." A shrug. "Guess who I saw?"

"At the apothecary?"

"Uh-huh."

"Who?"

"Your brother. He was hurt, I think, because Mr. Puttock took him in the back so he could take off his shirt. There was blood on it."

Nan stilled her brush, breath hitching. No, not blood. Please not blood. His nose, his forehead, his lips—where the madam's ladle had bashed more cuts. *"Heath, wake up."* Grabbing him, shaking arms that wouldn't move. *"Heath, please wake up!"*

"Nan?"

The palette slipped from the palm of her hand and toppled to the ground. Shiny blue, brown, and gray seeped into the courtyard grass. And red. Red like blood. Heath's blood.

"What's the matter with you?" Charlotte retrieved the palette and outstretched her arm so the paints wouldn't drip on her dress. "Now they are all quite smeared—"

"How long was he there?"

"What?"

"Heath—how long was he in the back?"

"I don't know. Mrs. Puttock gave Mamma the clove essence, and we left before he did."

"Here." Nan thrust the dripping paintbrush toward Charlotte. "Have someone take in my easel, won't you?"

"Where are you going?"

"Just do as I ask." With a sickness clawing her stomach, Nan scurried across the courtyard, weaved around the fountain, and slipped back inside. She needed her gloves, a bonnet, her reticule—and Temperance. Oh dear, where was Temperance when she was needed?

"There you are, Nan." Mr. Stanhope hailed her just before she reached the stairway. "I was about to send a servant out to search the grounds. Painting, were you?"

She glanced down at her colorfully stained pinafore. "Yes, but—"

"No matter. Just take it off quickly and come with me."

"I cannot. I was just going into the village—"

"That shall all have to wait." A hesitant smile, one she knew well enough to dread. "You have a guest."

"So you are the one." The magistrate sat behind a rosewood desk, his large hands steepled in front of him. His nose twitched. "Name?"

"Heath Duncan, sir."

"I see. Occupation?"

"At current, none."

"I see." Sharp, age-worn eyes peered at Heath—much longer than they should have. What was the matter with the man? Did he think *Heath* had committed murder, then hauled an innocent off the streets and blamed him instead?

"Why are you here?"

"Sir?"

"Do not be daft, Mr. Duncan. I asked a very simple question, and I expect an answer in return. Why are you in Wydenshire with no apparent livelihood?"

Tightness rippled across Heath's shoulders. What could he say? That he'd come for his sister—one whose name must remain unspoken?

The magistrate's wrinkled lips twisted. Amusement and disgust seemed to vie for control before he leaned back in his chair and snorted. "Not going to answer, I see. And I'm supposed to cart off a man to gaol on the word of a vagabond—"

"Sir, I am not the one who killed a man."

"Of that I am aware." With one hand, the magistrate reached behind him and tugged a floral bellpull on the wall.

His study door opened, and a manservant entered and bowed. "Mr. Goody?"

"Send in the prisoner."

"Certainly, sir." The door opened wider, and three others marched in, the middle of which wore chains.

In daylight, the man from the alley appeared much smaller and thinner. Shocks of greasy hair dangled in front of his eyes, and his cheeks were narrow and bruised. His tongue slipped from one corner of his busted lip to the other. "Glad to see you, me cove."

Heath held the stare. He'd done much damage to the man's face. He should have stopped sooner. Should not have battered him with so many blows.

"Nice to know what you look like so's I can 'member when I come back to carve a demon in your bloody face—"

The magistrate rose and clapped his hands a couple of times. "Let us save the theatrics for later." He swiveled toward Heath. "Now, Mr. Duncan, do enlighten us on the events of last night."

Sweat dampened Heath's palms. "I heard a scream."

"Ah, a scream. Man or woman?"

"Man."

"Correct. The body in the alley was a Mr. Acker, resident of who knows where and lodger of the Simon and Cat as of three days ago. Do you know him?"

"No, sir."

"I see. Neither do the rest of us—except, of course, Mr. Coombs here. In any event, do proceed, Mr. Duncan."

"After the scream, I ran into the alley. A man was there, came after me with a knife—"

"Liar!" The prisoner lurched, but the two guards held him back. "Bloody liar, I say! Shut the devil up!"

"You, sir," said Mr. Goody, "shall have the decency to remain silent. Heaven knows you haven't the decency for anything else. Continue, Mr. Duncan."

"We fought, and I hauled him to Constable Hearne."

"A man of many words." With a slight grin and a rub to his chin, Mr. Goody returned to his desk. "Well, Mr. Coombs? If you've anything to say for yourself, I suggest you do so now."

"I didn't do it." The words seethed through blackened teeth. "I didn't kill no bloke in no alley."

"Then you must have seen who did. After all, if you didn't kill him, you must have been aware that—"

"He did it!" Cursing, writhing, rattling his manacles. "I swear. . .I swear this blackguard Duncan did the killing!"

Heath glanced at the magistrate, blood flow gaining speed, but Mr. Goody only smiled. "Rest assured, Mr. Duncan, your word—however much I might distrust it—has considerably more validation than that of current company. And thus"—he clasped his hands and faced both men—"I am sending you, Mr. Coombs, to HM Shepton Mallet Prison, where you shall await trial. Mr. Duncan, you shall act as witness. Understood?"

Coombs flung his head back, unleashing a demon sound.

"Take him away, men," the magistrate said.

"I'll get you, Duncan." Coombs reached out and groped for Heath despite the distance. "I swear on life and death, I'll get you. I'll kill you. I'll destroy you. . ."

Heath clenched his jaw while the men dragged the prisoner away. More threads of anger tangled inside him, each one stringing the madam's obscenities and punishing shouts closer to his heart. They morphed into the stranger's threats. "I'll be your end. . .your bloody end. . ."

Even when they'd yanked him outside, the roars still drifted through closed windows and quiet walls. "I'll see your carcass into the graveyard, Duncan. If it's the last thing I do."

❧

He smelled of a strange mix of bay rum and peppermint comfits. Every smile was perfect. Every word melodic and complimenting. Every movement fluid in a way that was too elegant to be unpracticed.

Love him?

Yesterday, she would have said impossible. Today, she almost hoped she could. If it would make her father stay, if it would make him happy, proud of his little Nan—

"I appreciate deeply, Miss Duncan, your willingness to entertain me."

"Not at all, Lord Humphries." She didn't tense when he took her hand, didn't allow her smile to falter when his lips touched her knuckles, though thoughts of Heath still nagged her brain. Why had the man come at such a terrible time? And worst of all, why had Mr. Stanhope insisted she see him—despite her need to hurry to Heath?

She drew in air. "Won't you be seated?"

"Thank you, I shall." He motioned toward a chair. "But only after you."

La, such gentility. Perhaps if Gil could adopt such manners, he would not be unwed at five and twenty.

Once seated, Lord Humphries inquired after each member of the Stanhope household.

"They are all well, thank you."

"How perfectly wonderful."

"And yours?"

"Splendid as well. Julia, as you might have expected, has recently become affianced to Lord Kettlewell of Maisley House. A very agreeable match for everyone involved. Mother is most pleased."

"I would think so, only I wonder if. . ." Her fingernails pinched into her palms. Dare she broach such a question?

"Only what, Miss Duncan?"

"Oh—nothing."

"Please. You must bear your heart to me with any matter, little or great. What would you ask?"

"I only wondered. . ." The whisper lost power until she had to start again. "I only wondered if your mother is pleased with your lack of attachment."

"Do you mean to say, my lovely dear, my *choice* of attachment?" His cheeks flamed. "For surely, you cannot think I am unattached—at least not in matters of the heart."

Old fears begged her to look away. New courage kept her eyes fixed on the gentleman before her. "Sir, what would her ladyship think of such an unconventional match?"

"You speak of us."

"Yes."

"You must know that garners hope."

"Not intentionally, my lord. I only wish to be candid and discuss the matter as rationally as possible, all matters considered."

"Including my mother."

"Yes."

"And you?"

"Sir?"

"What of the matter of you? That is, I must admit, what I most desire to discuss."

Nan's sigh filled the room with all the answers she couldn't say.

Lord Humphries seemed to understand. "I see, Miss Duncan. And please know, I am aware that you are indifferent to me. Were you any other way, perhaps I would not have pursued you so ardently."

"Then you must know such a pursuit is futile."

"On the contrary."

"But your mother—"

"Is wrapped about my finger, as she always has been. Advantages of being the youngest." He leaned forward, the scent of peppermint floating toward her. "And you, my lovely Miss Duncan, need only give me a chance. I shall ask no more from you until you wish it."

She knew he awaited an answer. An inkling of hope. A small chance—just like Papa. What right had she to deny them that?

"My lord, I can make no promises."

"None are expected."

"You must know I have never wished to wed, and if ever I should, it would be for love alone."

"Agreed."

On weak legs, she rose, a swirl of dread mingling with a nudge of resolve. "Very well, my lord."

He sprung to his feet.

"You may court me for the present, but my heart will have to decide on the future."

⁂

Heath pulled a rickety chair by the window in their room, rolled up his sleeve, and unwound the bandage around his left arm. The minty scent of loosestrife powder and coppery blood lifted. Still burning and throbbing, the cut ran ragged through pink, swollen flesh.

Yet more scars.

As if he hadn't enough.

Grabbing a linen from the inn's stand, Heath eased it across the cut. Red seeped into the white fabric, spreading along the threads—

Knock, knock, knock.

Had Papa returned already? A pint of ale must have lured him from the afternoon's heat and his quest for a cottage. "Come in."

The door eased open, and two figures swept in, both in dresses of bright colors, both with eyes as wide as moons.

Heath dropped the linen. Stood. Swallowed hard, as he glanced from Nan to her blushing maid. "What are you doing here?"

The maid scuttled back out the door.

Nan stood firm. "I had to come." Her gaze swayed to his arm. "Heath. . .what happened?"

He turned away, grabbed up his bandage. "I will be out in a minute."

"Let me help you."

"Nan, really I can—"

"Shhh." Already, she was next to him, gentle fingers guiding him back into the chair. "We are not so changed we can no longer help each other. What happened?"

"A man." He winced. "Not too tight."

"Do not tell me how to act the doctor," she said. "Remember, I have done it before. The man what?"

"We fought."

"When?"

"Last night. Caught him in a killing. . .on his way to gaol now."

"You make it sound so simple."

"It was."

"Who was killed?"

"A fellow named Acker. No one seems to know him."

"And Papa? Where was he for all this?"

A shrug. "Don't know. He was gone this morning. Left a note he'd be finding a cottage."

Nan bent down before him, eyes soft and childlike, tearful as he ever remembered. "I am so very sorry you were hurt last night, Heath—but I am infinitely grateful it was not worse. I do not think I could bear it if something happened, if anything happened, to ruin all of this."

"All of this?"

"The cottage. Papa staying. The three of us being together after so many years."

A sinking feeling rushed through him. "That means the world to you, doesn't it?"

"Yes."

But it shouldn't. Not with Papa the way he was. Not with how easily everything could fall apart and change. What did she really imagine they could be—the three of them—after all these years?

Sighing, he captured her hand as he'd done in bygone days. How little and trusting she still seemed in his grip. "Then we will beg of God's mercies that nothing ruins it."

Was her entire life to be nothing but one foolishness after another?

Not that Temperance could blame a soul. Every misfortune was her own blunder. Talking too much, dreaming too often, forgetting things, and. . .barging into a gentleman's chamber unannounced.

Temperance paced across the same worn floorboards—enough times that even amid her mental scolding, she detected the one creaking board and avoided it.

Was that how people treated her? Stepping around her, hurrying in another direction just to escape her nonsense?

Of course they did.

Mr. Duncan would be no different.

A thousand thoughts of condemnation fell upon her as heavy and choking as a woolen death shroud. She never should have accompanied Miss Duncan up the stairs. Never should have stood next to her at the eighth door. Never ever should have marched right into the bedchamber, the bedchamber of a red-blooded man.

Could she ever look at the fellow again? And blessed day, how would she survive if he decided to speak with her? Ludicrous thought, that one. If he ever spotted her again, it would doubtless be too soon.

"Who the dickens are you?"

Temperance whirled.

From the other end of the narrow hall, a sun-bronzed old man strode forward, scowling beneath untamed whiskers. "That's room eight, you know, and you ain't got no business there. Get out of here."

"Oh, sir, you don't understand. I have every right to be here. I mean, well, I have to be here."

"What?"

"I'm an abigail—Miss Duncan's abigail, that is. She's inside, should you like to see her."

"Inviting me in my own room, are you?" The man grabbed the knob, muttering something about the privacy of a cottage, and slipped his way inside. Was that boorish fellow Miss Duncan's father?

Words lifted inside, too low to understand. Then the unthinkable occurred. The door swung open.

And out came Miss Duncan's brother. Alone.

A galaxy of panic formed in her stomach, while shooting stars burned their way into her chest. Sweet heavens, but he was handsome.

He looked at her with a pair of solemn, powerful, cobalt eyes. How easily they might have bewitched her, if only she allowed herself to dream.

But she couldn't. Disappointment was far too excruciating, an agony she would not soon bear again.

"I am sorry you were left alone, Miss Temperance." His lips twitched ever so slightly, though with smile or frown she could not tell. "We can go downstairs, if you wish."

We? Did he really think to accompany her?

"Papa." He tilted his head back to the door. "He wishes a private word with my sister."

"Oh—oh, I see."

His brows raised in waiting until she finally gathered her senses enough to nod. The following process was simple, normal.

He offered his arm.

She looped hers with his.

But however commonplace it should have been, unfamiliar jolts chilled the length of her spine. Perfect nonsense, of course. Her imagination, doubtless. A foolish heart at play again. Oh, what was she doing?

"Here, watch your step." He swayed her away from a cracked stair board. A knight in shining armor if ever she'd seen one—for surely, in her frenzied state of mind, she would have tripped on the board and toppled to kingdom come.

When they reached the taproom of the inn, Mr. Duncan's gaze turned with caution to the other side of the room.

Men were already gathered around the bar, drinks swishing, mild oaths lifting.

"This way." He led her toward a corner table, pulled out her chair, and saw her safely seated before he joined her. "I'm sorry there isn't a better place."

"I don't mind. Not at all, really. I so rarely leave Dorrington Hall that even the commonest surrounding is a welcome change. Is that terrible of me?"

His mouth twitched again. "No. I don't think so."

"You probably wouldn't say so if you did. Most people like candor, but I receive it so often that I much more prefer someone who is discreet. I don't suppose anyone wants to be scolded all of the time, even if it is for their own good. Are you discreet, Mr. Duncan?"

He seemed at a loss.

Temperance's spirits plummeted. Again, she had failed. "I had better go see to Miss Duncan—"

"Don't go."

"Very kind of you, sir, but I have bothered you quite enough." She flung from her chair, but he reached out and caught her.

"You didn't bother me." So sweet she could almost imagine he was genuine. "Please stay."

"Really, I cannot. If I had any hope of quelling my tongue, I would visit as long as you pleased—but you see, such a feat would be impossible, as I would only end up exasperating the both of us."

"Not me."

"Pardon?"

"I said you would not exasperate me, Miss Temperance." Then it happened, the first curve of his lips she didn't have to guess over. Amusement, kindness, and a bashful sort of charm—all displayed in one slow, startling smile.

She sank back into her seat without another word.

All through dinner, Nan had been quiet. Twirling her spoon about her white soup, casting languid glances about the dinner table, answering questions with just enough smile to keep anyone from prodding.

My, she was always the puzzlement. One minute a timid little dove, the next a swooping heron. Would anyone ever understand such a creature?

When the meal was finished, Gilbert followed the rest of the family into the drawing room.

Nan didn't join them.

For a while, the evening wore on with as much pleasantness as it ever did. Same satisfying scents, same drone of conversation, same fussing and ridiculousness from Charlotte.

Still, how strange it all felt with one of them missing.

"I say." Gilbert stood. "What's the matter with Nan anyway?"

"The matter with her?" His mother shrugged. "Why, I didn't know anything."

From behind rounded spectacles, Papa's eyes smiled in amusement. "Do not fret over Nan, my son."

"Why not?"

"She must be forgiven her solemn mood. After all, she was forced to entertain Lord Humphries—and before noon, I daresay."

"Dreadful indeed." Gilbert chuckled, started across the room—

"Where are you going?"

"I shall be back. A little nonsense from me shall bring her back into better spirits." He left the drawing room, departed the house through a servant exit, and jogged along the perimeter of the stone-walled courtyard.

He didn't have to guess where she'd be. He went straight to the massive English walnut tree whose heavy green branches proffered shade to the courtyard grounds.

Gilbert grinned.

Amid the foliage and three feet up, two blue slippers dangled back and forth. Right he'd been. Not that his prognostics were any great feat. After all, hadn't they climbed this tree a hundred times? Didn't she always come here when something was amiss?

"Gil, is that you?" Surprised, exasperated.

He stepped to his left until he gained a view of her face. "A bit old to be playing up there, aren't you?"

"I shall do as I please."

"You always do."

A sigh, but no rebuttal. No more fight than that? This was a rare disposition, for sure. The dragon must have breathed great fire today.

He shrugged off his tailcoat, unknotted his cravat, and reached for the lowest branch.

"What are you doing?"

"If you can play, so can I."

"Gil, stop it this instant. I shall not have you invading me."

"From what I remember, this was my fortress."

"What?"

"Ah, yes." The higher he climbed, the more familiar all the branches became to him. "Yours was over in the stable loft, if my memory serves me. I believe you called it the Castle of Gypsies. Remember when you wished to become one?"

"Yes. And you were a stalwart pirate with but one eye."

"A very good one, at that."

"I should hope, with as many times as you abducted me."

"Oh come. Did I not always set you free again?" By this time, he had reached the branch they so often occupied in younger years—and her eyes finally cast upon him with a growing touch of warmth.

As if from habit, they fell into silence, a silence too comfortable to need disturbance.

Land stretched out before them, covered in dusk and treetops, with the sky a deepening shade of pink and blue. It seemed, if he looked close enough and listened hard enough, he could still see the pirate ship in the sea of trees, could still hear the jangling gypsies with the song of the wind.

"Gil, I'm afraid."

The words struck a dissonant tune. He took in her profile—the somber features, the glowing eyes, the hesitant lips. "Why?"

"I don't know."

"Is it Lord Hump—"

"No." Defense cut him off. "No, it is not him."

"Then what?"

Silence. Her sigh came and went, then she swayed her slippers back and forth again. "Did you know Papa has found a cottage?"

"Then he will stay?"

"Yes. They both will."

"You are happy?"

"Oh yes. Never more happy, Gil."

"Then why—"

"I don't know." She faced him, imploring, until he grasped her hand on impulse. Her heartbeat thrummed against his fingers. "I don't know, only that I fear something terrible might go wrong."

"Why should it?"

"It shouldn't."

"Then why worry?"

She tugged her hand free. Emptiness swelled through him at the loss of the touch. Strange, that.

"You're right, of course," she said. "I shouldn't worry. I won't worry. Not on account of a mere strange feeling."

"You must know that feelings are not to be trusted. We can no more lay store in them than we can become pirates or gypsies."

A breeze swept through, rustled a hundred leaves, and played and danced with the auburn tendrils of Nan's hair. Her whisper came like music. "You are ever saying just what I need. I always feel the better for it. Do you promise to always console me?"

"Forever, if you wish it." Something passed between them. He didn't know what. But it ran in her eyes and stirred at his heart—this promise of forever—with a ring that was true, honest, and right.

She belonged to him, his little Nan.

Always would.

Though as she swept a lock of hair behind her ear, and her sigh escaped, and a smile chased away the last crease of worry from her smooth brow. . .

He looked away with a new sensation working through him. She was not so little anymore.

CHAPTER 13

Nan never imagined it would be like this. Choosing a dress to match the jonquil waistcoat Lord Humphries often wore, bidding Temperance to redo her hair for the umpteenth time, standing before her mirror with the wide eyes of a nervous ladylove.

But she wasn't nervous.

And she didn't love him.

"There, Miss Duncan. Now, if you don't make haste and say it is lovely, I shall be utterly overwhelmed with my own inadequacy and will doubtless never have confidence again."

"Please, Temperance. Must you be so excitable?" Nan parted a thick curl with her fingers, patted the strands back in place, then angled her head. "Well, by her ladyship's standards, it is probably frightfully lacking."

"Will she attend the picnic too?"

"The letter did not say, but one can never be too cautious."

"True enough."

From the other side of the room, a knock sounded on the door, then Gilbert's voice. "Nan, the coach is arrived and ready to leave."

"Already?"

"What do you mean *already*? You've had all morning to prepare, you know."

"Yes, I know. Temperance—where is my reticule? Never mind, here it is." She snatched the strings of her reticule, grabbed her bonnet on the way to the door, and hurried out into the hall.

Gil stood waiting, grinning. "You seem to be making the best of an undesirable circumstance."

She strode past him before he could read her face. Never remarked. Never even breathed a sigh.

121

Because she wasn't going to battle with the dragon.

Not this time.

Instead, she was preparing to surrender.

"Who're the likes o' you?"

Heath stood before Dorrington Hall's kitchen entrance, his eyes holding those of a squat, red-cheeked maid who leaned out the doorway.

With one hand, she swathed her apron across her forehead. "Come on, I've not got all bloomin' day, you know. If you've come to beg for scraps, you can just be—"

"No, miss." He took one step closer, the inferiority of approaching a manor so large again prickling over him. "I was hoping for a visit with Miss Duncan."

"You?"

If she thought him scroungy now, she should have seen him thirteen years ago.

A throaty grunt. "You can be headin' back to wherever it is you came from 'cause she ain't here." The door swung—

Heath lodged his foot in the crack. "Then Miss Temperance."

"What about her?"

"I would have a word with her. That is, if she is willing."

The maid scowled, and ripping off her apron, she flung the door wide open. "All right, come in—but mind you don't be gettin' no dirt on me clean floors. Keep your hands to yourself too. Catch you thievin' and I'll clobber you with a frying pan, I will." She bustled out of the kitchen, and Heath took a chair by the hearth, where a massive cauldron fumed and boiled with a taunting smell.

Had he eaten today?

Couldn't remember. Too busy following Papa to the tiny cottage, moving their meager things inside, scrubbing away the dirt and cobwebs—just as he'd always done at the church. God hasten the day he could go back there. Maybe he'd bring Nan too. Let her sit in the linseed-scented pew boxes, meet all the lowly, simple villagers, and visit the grave of the greatest man Heath had ever known—

"Mr. Duncan."

The hushed voice jerked him to his feet. "Miss Temperance."

In she swept with a clumsy, happy sort of grace—her lips stretched in smile, her eyes glittering and eager, her cheeks an amusing shade of pink. Was she blushing?

The strange thought raised his hairs in alarm. And pleasure.

"I suppose you've already met with the unfavorable news, haven't you?"

He lifted a brow.

"About Miss Duncan, I mean," she said. "How dreadful that you came all this way only to meet with bitter disappointment. If I had any inkling of when she might return, I would bid you to sit and wait, but I fear a great many hours might pass before she is home. Is it terribly urgent?"

He hesitated.

"Your visit, I mean, with Miss Duncan. Not that I mean to pry, of course. You must forgive me if I seem. . ." A quick sigh left lips that were already faltering. "I am sorry, sir, your sister is not here."

"No matter." Heath waited, but Miss Temperance must have been afraid of speaking too much, for she stood before him and said nothing at all. "Your family is well?" His odd question struck the air like an inharmonious note.

She didn't seem to notice. "They are all in the best of health—a family attribute, I think, as I have never been ill more than a day in all my life."

More silence.

Heat swirled about the room, much more so than before, as if the red-cheeked maid had crept behind him and stirred the hearth's coals and embers. Indeed, had she showered them over his head? He resisted the urge to loosen his collar—or better yet, take a quick bow and exit the house.

But for reasons unknown, he remained planted. His mind scrambled a thousand different directions, hurrying for anything solid to say, grasping for a bit of conversation to end the silence. Then, with a slow glance to her face, "Is Mr. Hill still abed?"

"Mr. Hill? Why, no. How kind of you to remember. He is back in his livery and wig and no worse for the wear, I daresay."

"Then I, uh, suppose a position is no longer wanted."

"A position? Here at Dorrington?"

He nodded.

"Oh, there must be something!" Perplexity dampened her expression, but then another look shone through—and she was smiling all over again. "Of course. How could I have forgotten? Only two nights prior, I heard Mr. Stanhope tell Loftus he would soon be stable master. Then we shall be in desperate need of a stable hand. Do you know horses well, Mr. Duncan? But then of course you would. How silly of me to forget. After all, you did rescue little Charlotte from that wild brute of a horse, did you not?"

"Well I—"

"And you mustn't worry, for Mr. Stanhope is sure to happily place you under his employ. I shall do my best to have a word with him this evening if you like. Should that please you?"

Please him?

He didn't know what to think, what to say. He rarely did in her presence. "Yes, Miss Temperance. I am beholden."

"Perhaps to God and others, but never to me." Delight and merriment rang in her voice like music, followed by a laugh that seemed more celestial than earthly. "Good day, Mr. Duncan. You will come back soon?"

"Tomorrow, perhaps."

"There is no better day than tomorrow, and by any good fortune, I shall have news of your new position. And Mr. Duncan?" She had already backed toward the doorway from which she had entered, but she paused and stared after him. "Do you suppose you shall like it here at Dorrington Hall?"

He nodded, a smile leaking out.

"I'm glad." She dashed away with all the enthusiasm of a jovial troubadour.

With quick steps, Heath exited the way he'd come and swung himself on Golda. Even away from the kitchen's sweltering hearth, his hands were damp with sweat. What was wrong with him? Why had he asked after her in the first place?

After all, he'd had no intentions of inquiring after a position. Even today, as he'd helped his father with the cottage, they'd discussed more than a few jobs he might seek in the quiet village streets.

For Nan's sake. The words pushed through his confusion. *That's the reason I made such an absurd inquiry.*

Even so, all the way back to the cottage, a certain sound invaded his memory. A voice soft and fresh, a laugh soothing and kind, a silence so strange and breathless.

And it had nothing to do with Nan at all.

❧

She was encouraging him.

From the other side of the neatly spread blanket, Gilbert sat with his back against a lone tree, tapping a twig against his palm. It wasn't true, couldn't possibly be. Of any other maiden in the world, he might have believed such a thing.

But not Nan.

And by George, not with the dragon.

"See here what you have done?" With a smile that lacked any restraint, Nan scooted an inch or two closer to Lord Humphries, brushed a bit of plum pudding from his cravat, and never so much as flinched when his face drew close to hers.

"My dear, you are a creature divine," he said.

"All for removing a bit of pudding?"

"Grant me one more favor, and you shall be queen of the world. Would you like that?"

"Queendom or your favor?"

"Both."

"For the first, I would not care for it at all. I could not bear the thought of so many depending on me."

"And the latter?"

"You must tell me what it is, and then I shall decide."

Gilbert's twig snapped between his fingers. He shoved to his feet before the ridiculous fellow—and Nan, for that matter—could make any greater fools of themselves. "I say, anyone game for a stroll?"

From their position along the left corner of the blanket, Lady Julia and her betrothed glanced up without expression. Both declined in unison and continued to pick grapes from a hand-painted bowl.

Lord Charles Somerset, who sat alone with a bottle of claret and a book, simply lowered the volume and frowned. "Anyone who walks in such heat is uncommonly beetle-headed. Must be hot as down under out here."

Pleasant fellow.

"Now, Brother." This came from Lord Humphries as he came to his feet and pulled Nan along with him. "Do let us keep glad spirits, eh?"

"The deuce with glad spirits—but if you must stroll, then hurry up and do so. I have more important matters to attend to than squandering time in this devil's oven."

"Very well." Lord Humphries eased Nan's arm into the crook of his elbow. "Shall we go, my dear?"

Gilbert waited for it, watched carefully for her hand to slip free, for her eyes to harden with a flash of defiance and hesitancy.

But she only smiled, even chuckled for a second or two—and off they started on a stroll of their own.

Of all the strange, outrageous things. What in the name of sanity did she think she was doing? Didn't she realize that, minute by minute, she was tossing away years of discouragement? That the dragon, as tenacious as he was, would never let her be now?

And all this time he'd pitied her.

Hah.

Reckless irritation hurled through his chest as hot and burning as the afternoon sunbeams. He supposed he ought to follow the two. After all, the walk had been his suggestion.

But his temperament was beginning to match the doleful marquess's, so he decided against it and cut toward the coach instead.

The marquess's horse, tied beneath a shady sycamore maple, glanced up and snorted. Smart fellow, that Lord Somerset. If Gilbert had been half as smart, he would have brought his own horse and departed this very moment.

But as it was, the rest of them had ridden together in the coach. A hot, sweltering, unbearable coach—where Nan had spoken and laughed all the way with a man she supposedly despised.

Just wait until he got her alone. He half hoped she'd give some excellent explanation that would make sense of today's doings, that would unpuzzle the strange behavior and flirtation. But what could she possibly say? What reason could there be?

From atop the coach, the driver's chin jabbed his chest for the second time in a row. Heavy breathing and an occasional snore drifted through the air loud enough that if her ladyship had been present, she would have shouted her servant from his slumber.

Might as well let him sleep, poor fellow. What harm was there in that?

As he passed from sunlight to shade, Gilbert took the handle of the coach and eased the door open. He lifted one foot inside—

And froze.

The navy velvet cushions of the carriage were slashed open. One window was cracked, weblike, smudged with dirty fingerprints.

And a knife.

Gilbert lifted himself inside and removed the weapon from the carriage wall, a tiny paper falling into his hands.

He ripped it open and studied the inky, crude drawing. A shield flanked by ribbons. A mangled bear looming from the top. Two swords clashing together behind the head.

'Twas a crest he'd seen often. Everyone had. Even today, it was engraved pridefully on the door of this very coach—in honor not only of her ladyship and her children, but of every ancestor who had ever died with such noble blood in their veins.

How the lot of them would have fainted now.

For whoever had reproduced this crest had taken great care to make every detail precise—except for one. The mighty, righteous head of the giant bear was torn in half. Drops rained from the gash as if in blood.

"What are you doing?"

Gilbert spun, sank hard into one of the gashed seats, and tightened his fist around the drawing. "Something has happened."

"I thank you for stating the obvious, sir." The marquess took one step closer to the open coach door. He held out his gloved hand. "Now may I have that paper?"

"I'm mighty surprised at ye, Temp."

One of her hands froze along the leafy stem of a delphinium. An odd pain surged through her stomach, coupled with a dread that was new and old. She didn't turn. "I'm most surprised too. I should think with such a remarkable position as stable master forthcoming, you would have better things to do than visit a lowly garden."

Loftus walked closer, crunching through growth instead of following the garden path. Ever heedless, he was. Didn't he know such tiny plants needed care instead of cruelty? That one tender bruise could destroy a whole flower of beauty?

"I honestly thought ye'd ne'er go anywhere without me—but here ye are, bravin' the deuced garden all on yer own with not a soul to talk to. Or have ye nattered the petals off these poor blooms?"

She plucked one and thrust it into her basket. Should have known he would have some unkind thing to say. Hadn't he always been like that? Even in his romance, those rare moments of meaningless sweetness, hadn't there been condemnation?

But such days were over and finished. A fool she might have been, but no more. That was one good thing about her. She was never stupid twice.

"Oh dear, have I made ye mad now?" He caught her elbow and turned her to face him. "Almost pretty, ye are, when ye're blushin' like that and fever-eyed."

"Loftus, please." She shrugged away from him. "I've plenty to do and can't be bothered. I want to pick flowers for Miss Duncan, and I'll never get them ready if I don't make haste." She crept away and resumed picking the delphiniums. Cowardly hands, if ever she saw any, for they trembled with each bloom she plucked. "Besides, your village lass would look unfavorably upon you if she knew you. . .you. . ."

"What?" Mirth filled the word. "Knew I was out here pesterin' the likes of Temperance the abigail? You are right. A serious rival you make, indeed." His laughter trilled with mockery, but she only marched farther down the garden path without defense.

Halfway to the gate, he called out to her, "Temp?"

She turned quickly enough that some of her blue-and-white delphiniums floated to the ground. "Say what you will, and then I have something I wish to say."

"Then by all means, have at it first."

"I had every intention of marrying you because you made me believe such a match was both of our wishes. Even from a child, you marked me as your own. I never questioned your heart, and I never stopped to examine mine."

His eyes widened.

"But you changed that for both of us, and I am infinitely grateful now. I fear such a union would have led to both of our despair. And now, if you please, I should like to be left alone. As you seem to despise my talking so much, you will be pleased to know we need never converse again." She nearly looked away and wilted beneath his eyes of growing shock.

Then his mouth snapped shut. "Cook must've been right."

"About what?"

A hint of disappointment creased Loftus's forehead. "Ye must've been unnatural happy when that Duncan fellow stopped by. Unnatural happy, indeed."

There was something about his face—or rather, his eyes—that seemed so much the schoolboy. An absurd thought, of course. Lord Humphries was nearly three years Nan's senior.

Yet even so, hidden along all of his charms and just beneath his decorous ways, she could not help but think of him as a nervous youth.

"You are glad you came, are you not?" The question accompanied a smile, yet the voice rang with uncertainty.

"Of course." She didn't take time to analyze the honesty of her answer. She had chosen to be here, and therefore she was glad. Emotion had not a thing to do with it.

"Good, my darling. You must know this has been the most pleasant afternoon of my life."

His whole life?

He must have perceived her doubt, for he took her hand and pressed it to his chest. "What must I do to convince you?"

A smile tugged her lips. "Is my being convinced so very important, my lord?"

"Vastly important—and to prove it, I shall propose a carriage ride day after tomorrow."

"So soon?"

"I would have said in the morning had I not feared being presumptuous." His hand tightened around hers. Gentle, possessive, endearing—but even still, she felt a faint urge to pull away.

Instead, she surrendered her other hand to his grasp. "Then a carriage ride it shall be, my lord, though I do hope you shall not find my company intolerably dull."

"Never say such a thing. You are enchantment itself."

For a second, a small stir of pleasure warmed through her indifference. She groped for that pleasure, held on to it, determined to keep it for as long as it should last. Slowly, faintly, as if crossing a bridge one shaky board at a time, perhaps she would reach the side she hoped for. The side Papa hoped for. The side her mother would have hoped for. Oh, why could it not have been simple? Why had such a great feat been asked of her?

Perhaps she thought of marriage too sacredly. She had never truly entertained matrimonial thoughts—not because she would not have enjoyed a marriage, but because she had never imagined the magic of true love ever really befalling her. Too many wed on nothing more than practical arrangements and frivolous attraction. What sort of happiness was there in that?

None.

Such a match was an injustice to both husband and wife—and that is why, no matter what Papa and Lord Humphries longed for, she would not succumb unless her heart agreed.

Unless she loved him.

"We have strolled quite enough now, my darling, and certainly too far from the others. I can no longer hear my sister laughing about the latest on-dit. Do you suppose they've all fallen asleep?"

"What sport we shall make of them if they have."

"Is this a mischievous side to the lovely Miss Duncan? And all this time, I imagined you shy and unassuming."

"Oh, well. . ." She turned. *Gil.*

He waited outside a cluster of trees, with the scene of the picnic a few yards behind him. Shimmers of sunlight played in his short brown waves and reflected in eyes that were narrow, uncommonly serious. "Walking without chaperone, Nan?"

She blinked, stiffened.

Lord Humphries, usually the exemplar of grace, took one step forward and frowned. "I assure you, Mr. Stanhope, that Miss Duncan was not compromised in any way. We only barely wandered from sight of the others."

Gil's gaze settled back to Nan in a way that made her stomach twinge with discomfort. What was the matter with him anyway?

"Come along, Nan," he said at last. "We are returning home immediately."

"But have you forgotten we discussed a game of shuttlecock? Surely you do not expect the rest of the party to depart when—"

"That is just what he means, Miss Duncan." Lord Somerset stepped around a tree branch and joined them. He speared a gaze to his brother. "Aylmer, if you had not insisted on promoting that slumbering wastrel to driver, none of this would have happened."

"None of what? What goes on?"

The marquess scowled, lifted a small drawing into the air. "See for yourself."

Nan let out a small gasp. What in heaven's name was that?

Tension jittered through his legs, until almost unconsciously, Gilbert's foot tapped up and down upon the carriage floor.

No one spoke.

Lady Julia cast a worried frown out the broken window. Beside her, Lord Kettlewell plucked a gloved finger at one of the cushion's tears.

And Nan. She sat more still than the rest, very quiet, composed save for a slight redness of her cheeks. What was she thinking?

Be hanged if he knew. He hoped it was remorse that made her color up—not that Lord Humphries, even with his carriage sabotaged and his heritage insulted, was still staring at her like a mawkish fool.

None too quickly, the iron gates of Dorrington Hall opened up to them. Swift goodbyes were mumbled, then Gilbert leaped out and swung Nan to safety before the dragon had a chance to do the job himself.

Nan watched in strange silence until the carriage passed beyond the wrought iron gates. She turned—

"Where are you going?" Gilbert pulled her back.

Still, she didn't look at him. "Inside. Where do you think?"

"So you're not going to say anything?"

"What would you have me say?"

He laughed, humorless and empty. "Have you say? Are you in earnest? Why, you practically made a cake of yourself when you—"

"When I what?" She ripped from his hold. "Because I do not remember doing anything so wretched, and if you are referring to my treatment of Lord Humphries, then you might as well get used to it."

A blow landed in his stomach, stole his breath. "What are you saying?"

"I should think it would be obvious."

"Say it."

"Why?"

"Say it, Nan."

Her cheeks flamed for the second time, her chin raised, and distinct moisture filmed her soft brown eyes. "I have given Lord Humphries my consent for a courtship. Perhaps I should have done so a long time ago."

"I don't understand."

"You do not have to."

"You cannot be serious. You know you do not care for him, could not ever care for such a dragon of a man, so why would you—"

"Do not call him that." She backed away, evening breeze spilling curls about her anxious face. "I mean it." Farther. "I mean it, I. . .I. . ." And with a gasp that sounded half sob, she swiveled around and fled for the house.

Courtship. The single word inhabited the air, tainted even the ground he stood on. He told himself not to be angry. He had no right to be. He told himself not to alarm, for weren't all girls prone to nonsense and romance?

But something deep inside of him, in the places he hardly understood himself, began to unravel.

And he'd never thought of the dragon so wickedly in his life.

CHAPTER 14

Mr. Duncan had arrived.

What a puzzlement that everything seemed so different, that the walls of Dorrington Hall were suddenly thrust into light and beauty. Every room—every vase and drapery and furniture—took on a new glow, a quality of splendor. Did the air taste different too?

Temperance couldn't tell, couldn't seem to get enough of it in her lungs.

"Mr. Stanhope shall see you now, if you will follow me." Mr. Hill's voice echoed down the passageway, then footsteps made happy music on marble floors.

Temperance ducked out of sight. The study door creaked shut, and she knew Heath Duncan was standing before a man who determined his present fate.

And hers.

Ah, but she longed to listen. How easily she might slip back into the hall, pass by the door, and hesitate long enough to hear.

But she had better not. Naughtiness was rarely rewarded—and even if she could hear, what difference would it make?

She would know soon enough.

"There you be." From another entrance, a lower maid eased the door back shut with her foot whilst toting a soapy bucket in both hands. "What you be doing in here?"

Temperance glanced about her. The saloon. How to explain this one?

But the maid only shrugged and deposited her bucket, then peeled back the Turkish rug for cleaning. "You're a strange one, for sure, Miss Temperance. Do you ever have your wits about you? I think not. If you did, you'd be knowing your lady is been looking everywhere for you."

"For me? Right now?"

"Surely is. Had to help her on with her stays myself, I did. Where you been all morning, anyway?"

"Was she terribly urgent to find me—Miss Duncan, I mean?"

Before the maid could answer, a sound came from the hall, followed by one set of footfalls.

Temperance dashed from the saloon before she had a chance to stop herself. Then, just as quickly, she halted.

Dressed in a gray woolen coat, Heath Duncan turned. Soft, steady eyes met hers more purposefully than they ever had before, and a new look passed across his face. She couldn't decipher such an expression, but with any imagination at all, she would have marked it as a flash of pleasure. "Miss Temperance."

"Well?"

Her frankness must have surprised him. He grinned. "You must have been very convincing."

"Do not talk in circles, I beg of you. I hate guesswork of any kind, because more often than not, I interpret everything wrong. So tell me plainly—did all go well?"

"Yes, very well."

"Then Mr. Stanhope said you are needed?"

"Yes."

"At the stables?"

His eyes laughed, followed by another quiet "Yes."

A spasm of joy unleashed like a cool shower of spring rain. She would have said more, but the study door opened again, and Mr. Stanhope stepped between them.

With one amused glance, he turned her way. "Temperance, I recall our Nan being in desperate search of you. Do you think you might go and put her to rest, by any chance?"

"Oh yes, Mr. Stanhope. I shall do so right away. I would have done so sooner, but all morning I've been. . ." Her neck burned as she chanced one last look in Heath's direction. "I. . .I shall go find her now." With a fast, perhaps less than gracious curtsy, she slipped back into the saloon, flung past the maid, and hurried out the other door.

The bedchamber door stood half-open as if careless Charlotte had exited in a whirl and forgotten to pull it shut behind her.

In the open space, Gil crisscrossed on the Axminster carpet. Nan had known he would be here. All through breakfast, Charlotte had begged and sulked for Gilbert to assemble her new toy theatre.

"Come now, Charlotte. Can't you have Mamma assist you?"

In answer, Charlotte had tugged her lips into a well-versed pout. "But she shan't do it well. You know that. The whole thing would be ruined!"

Thus, he sat alone in the hot bedchamber of his sister, fiddling with cardboard and glue and tinsel-print characters. He didn't look up when she entered, just muttered, "Whatever happened to your promise of helping me, hmm? I knew you would run off and desert me."

When she didn't answer, he glanced up. Sweat wetted the ends of his dark hair, and he must have long since ripped off his coat, for he wore only shirtsleeves and neckcloth. "Oh, it's you." Flat voice, even as his eyes hurried back to the thin cardboard. "You walk as lightly as Charlotte, you know."

"Are you mad?"

The question didn't so much as falter him. "No, I am not mad."

"You have not spoken to me all day."

"You seemed more content alone."

She dipped to her knees beside him, tugged the sticky cardboard from his fingers. "Please look at me, won't you? I know I have been terrible, but do not punish me like this. If you are angry about yesterday—"

"I am not angry. I told you that." He looked at her with a different expression than she expected. Disappointment. It caused every organ in her body to shrivel and ache. "Hand me that sheet, won't you?"

"Gil, I'm sorry."

"The sheet, Nan."

She snatched the printed sheet and pressed it toward him. "I really am. I behaved so unkindly to you yesterday when you had every right to question—"

"This is not about me." He dropped the sheet, the cardboard, everything, hands fisted on his knees. "If you're doing this for the money, the title—"

"No. How could you say that?"

"What else should I say? One does not go from loathing a fellow to wooing him without some form of motive."

"I am not wooing Lord Humphries."

"No?"

"No. He is wooing me." Nan pushed to her feet. "And furthermore, I cannot believe you think me so mercenary as to stoop to such 'motives,' as you call them. You must know I would never ever marry unless I loved that man in entirety."

"And you think Lord Humphries could be such a man?"

"Is there any reason he shouldn't?"

Gilbert's jaw tightened, and his eyes flashed with a lividness she very seldom witnessed. Then, in a voice of total calm, he said, "If you see Charlotte downstairs,

135

tell her she had better find the wire if she wishes me to complete her characters."

Nan nodded. With tears stacking her throat, she hurried from the room. He was dreadful to accuse her that way and dreadful to judge her. She certainly didn't owe him an explanation.

But she wished, just the same, he had asked for one.

The world of eventide descended, bringing with it all the lively music of night bugs and the rich scent of cooling air.

Nan's horse stayed very close to his. The drum of its hoofbeats mingled with Golda's and formed a lulling, muffled tune.

"Sing, Nan."

As if drawn from a well pool of thoughts, her eyes swung to his in quick surprise. "Sing?"

Heath smiled, nodded. "One of the old songs."

"The old songs." She echoed the words as if they stirred bittersweet happiness. Then, with a shy smile of her own, her voice leaked out into the night. How sweet, how childlike she sounded, even after all these years.

Every word entered his soul. Comforted him. Relieved him after so many silent, anguished nights. *God, thank You.*

When at last the song had ended, Papa's cottage was already in view, partly hidden behind the arms of a giant English oak. The thatched roof was slumped, the walls covered in drooping vines, the windows without shutter or glass. Why was it that the old cottage seemed so much like the man who now lived inside?

But even if the place had been a bit decrepit, Nan seemed not to notice. Her sigh was eager, contented. "Isn't it lovely? And to think the both of you shall be this close. . .close enough to visit anytime I wish. If only it could have always been this way."

A faint pain accompanied the thought, but it lasted only long enough to irritate him. He dismounted and led both of their horses to the small barn, with Nan following at his heels as she'd always done as a child.

"I'm very glad you took the position at Dorrington, you know."

"Are you?"

"Surprised a little, but very glad. Why did you not say a word?"

"I only knew myself yesterday."

"Oh?"

He swung Golda's saddle across a flimsy stall. If she asked him anything more, he would walk away without saying anything. After all, what could he say? That the woman—or girl, really—who he had met only a few times had affected him? That unacquainted as they were, she had made him alter his plans?

No, he couldn't say such a thing. Shouldn't even think it, really. Who was he that a woman so sweet and happy as Temperance should care for him? Life seemed to radiate from her. Exuberance pranced in every laugh, delight in every smile, joy in every fleck of her eyes.

All the things he lacked.

With Golda in her stall and Nan's horse tied, Heath took Nan's arm and led her back through the tall-grassed yard, through a splintery gate, and up the stone path. He pushed the knob.

Locked.

"What's the matter?"

"Don't know." He tried again. "Papa?"

No answer.

"Papa, can you hear me?"

Noises, low and scratchy, then something crashed like the shrill explosion of glass.

"Step back." Heath eased her behind him. "Papa!"

A gurgling response, one he was beginning to know. The door thudded with Papa's weight. "That you, boy?"

Nan's eyes rushed to Heath's in question.

"That you. . .Son?"

"Yes, Papa." With one hand, Heath tugged Nan farther away. Should have known better than to bring her here this way, unannounced, not knowing if Papa had—

"Heath, stop it, please. What are you doing?"

"I'm taking you home."

"I don't want to go. I want to see Papa. What's the matter with him? Something broke inside, and the door—"

"It does not matter. Please come."

She slipped free of him. "I have every right to be here. Just as much as you."

"I will not have you see him this way." His statement stilled her. "Neither would he."

A pallor stole over her cheeks. She glanced toward the cottage. "Perhaps. . .you are right."

"Let me take you home."

"No, I shall go myself."

"Nan, let me—"

"I can manage on my own. The distance is not far." Sighing, she marched through the dusk, fetched her horse, and rode away without a parting wave.

Then the door eased open.

A red-faced man peered out, half-dressed, his whiskers uncombed and scruffy. "Found the key, I did." One hand raised a bottle, while his hook dangled the rusty key. "Found it on the floor. . .just lying there on the floor. You put it there?"

"No, sir."

"You didn't, eh?"

"No."

"Come 'ere, boy. Face me like a man, you bloody fool." He stumbled forward, dropped the bottle, grabbed Heath's neck. "Better learn to fight. . .take care of yourself, boy. Ain't no one in this world is going t' help you. . .not no one, hear?"

Disgust made every muscle rigid, but Heath didn't back away and didn't answer.

"Bah, you fool. You weak, stupid fool." With a slurred curse, he ripped away from Heath, stumbled back through the broken glass, and slammed the door.

"Miss Duncan, is that you?" From the other side of the bedchamber, Temperance's figure stood erect in soft candlelight.

"Yes, do not alarm." Nan eased the door shut behind her. "I wonder that you are yet awake. What are you doing?"

"A bit of mending to your redingote. I have been putting it off for ages and decided—seeing as how I could not sleep—I might as well make use of myself. But what of you? Did I not understand that you were to spend this night with your papa?"

"Yes."

"But it is so late. Whatever are you doing back?"

"Papa was not. . ." A dreadful, persistent knot swelled in her throat. She hardly knew why. Hadn't she known he was no pious man of scruples? That even though he had returned, nothing would be as perfect as she had imagined?

But a small part of her soul throbbed with familiar disappointment—the same she'd felt all those years, waiting for a ship that never came.

"He what, Miss Duncan?" Temperance moved closer, the brown redingote laid across one arm, her eyes luminous and seeking in the candlelight. "Pray, do you feel well? You appear terribly lost and pale tonight, and your hair is in much disarray. Have you been riding alone?"

"I needed time to think."

"Miss Duncan, that might have been very dangerous."

"I know—but there is no need to fret, for I am returned safely. Now will you please help me off with this dress?"

With nimble fingers and a comforting drone of conversation, Temperance helped her off with her attire and into a cotton night shift. Then, as she pulled back the bed curtains, she asked, "Has your papa said something to upset you greatly?"

"No, he said nothing."

"Then perhaps. . .your brother?"

"No." Unwilling to satisfy Temperance's curiosity—or perhaps accept her genuine concern, whichever it was—Nan slipped into bed and turned the bed linens over her shoulder. Thoughts burned like fire—Papa's slurred voice, Heath's anxiety to pull her away, the cold reality that the loving father she desperately needed was a man with needs himself.

The same fear returned. The same deep, cold, unsettling quiver that wouldn't go away, that ebbed away at her frail joy.

Because something wasn't right. Something she didn't understand. Something that was going to take away what she'd waited so long for.

I only want us to be together, God. Was that so much to beg for? To be with the brother she loved and the papa she'd spent a lifetime aching for? *Please.*

From across the chamber, Temperance's candlelight swept closer. "Miss Duncan?"

"Yes?"

"I don't mean to disturb you, but I just recalled the note I was to give you."

"Note?"

"From Master Gilbert. I cannot imagine what it would say, and you must know I thought very wickedly about peeking. I didn't, of course. Should you like for me to read it now?"

"Yes, please do."

Her maid fumbled to smooth it out. "Very short, I daresay. Master Gilbert never was the sort to indulge in letter writing, was he? But let me not get distracted. He says, 'Dearest Nan, you must forgive me for today. You are a dreadful little imp, but never mercenary, and I was a fool to say such a thing. Perhaps tomorrow you shall let me make it up to you, for it has been far too long since we have taken one of our rides across the countryside.'" Temperance lowered the note and started to place it upon the bed stand—

"No, give it here." Nan reached for the paper, curled her fingers around it, and bid her maid a quick good night.

Once the room was quiet, she pressed it close to her chest in the darkness. For the thousandth time in her life, his words brought a wealth of comfort until all of her worries and fears so softly flitted away.

She fell asleep with the soothing thought of riding the countryside.

❧

"Ye don't be knowin' too much 'bout horseflesh, do ye?" From the carriage house doorway, Loftus hooked both arms in front of his dirt-smeared shirt.

Heath lowered a hoof, stood straight. "Some."

"Well, we have a blacksmith for what ye're thinkin', so just be leavin' that half breed alone, hear?" He thrust out his chest as if in fulsome show of his authority. "Now go o'er there, find yerself a bloomin' bucket, and start scrubbing down these stalls. Mr. Stanhope—he don't like no dirty walls an' I can't say as I blame him."

Heath followed the man's nod toward a line of buckets and lifted the largest. "And the well?"

"Out back."

"Thank you."

Loftus answered with a throaty grunt, as if he would not deign to respond more completely.

Bucket in hand, Heath left the stables through a back door, cut across well-trimmed grass, and hooked his bucket to the well rope.

From somewhere close, pleasant smells drifted his way. Lilies, zinnias, apple blossoms, and—

Something else.

A smell unique, gentle and flowery, yet so unlike anything he'd ever detected in the rector's garden.

He turned.

With black ringlets dangling alongside blushing cheeks, there she stood—grinning as if she'd expected him to be here, swaying slightly with a bucket of her own. "You too?"

"Yes." He reached for her bucket. "May I?"

She surrendered it easily enough, then leaned against the edge of the stone well as he lowered his first. He detected every one of her breaths. Soft, patterned, yet quick with excitement, it seemed—and he wondered if he could be the cause.

The thought hitched his own breathing.

"I love wells, I think," she said. "I never really thought of it before, but now that I'm here, I think they are really quite splendid. One could spend forever gazing down into such a pleasant hole of water. See how blue it appears in the morning light?"

With a hard tug, he hauled the bucket upward again and trained his lips to keep from smiling. What a fool he must seem to her, never knowing what to say, never seeing things the way she did.

She didn't seem to mind. Her smile cast fully upon him, and if anything appeared blue in the morning light, it was her eyes and not the well water. "I don't normally fetch water," she said.

"No?"

She shook her head without further explanation, but her smile widened and brightened until one of his own sprang forth.

How unspeakable it felt, this air between them. Seconds passed, whether one or a hundred he could not tell. He studied every curve of her face, the shape of her cheeks and slope of her jaw, the dark lashes of her eyes. Not that he meant to. With any strength, he would have shoved another bucket into the well and looked far away.

But weakness came more easily. Maybe if he stared long enough, the memory would stay vivid throughout the day, then to the close of night when he lay restless in his bed. Why did she feel like a breeze to him? He was scorched and tired, always tired—but she was cool, invigorating, a breeze like he'd never known.

Perhaps she was only playing. Maybe her attentions were only in jest. Likely as not, today's smile, upon the morrow, would be bestowed on another more worthy.

Game or not, she was sparking something new in him. For this moment, he felt happy.

Her eyes lowered first, as shy as his for once. "I had better hurry back inside, for if not, I shall soon be discovered for stealing the scullery maid's chore. Not that she will mind, I'd wager, but I am desperately loath to conjure up an explanation. One would think, by this time, I would be much better at talking my way out of things—yet it seems when it is most important, my tongue always lets me down."

He started to sling down her bucket, but her hand caught his.

"No, please don't." She drew it away from him empty. "If I return the bucket unfilled, I may never have to explain at all." Like a dream, she slipped away, the grass barely trodden where her footsteps had been.

In her wake, the air still tasted of flowers. Nice scents, familiar scents—but it lacked something vital he'd just learned to appreciate.

The scent of a maiden.

And a pretty one, at that.

Gilbert had hurried through his morning routine with a different kind of urgency. He took breakfast alone in the predawn hours. He hastened down to the stables with instructions to saddle mounts, then went to his study and fumbled without interest through endless paperwork. He even located the characters for Charlotte's paper theatre and resumed attaching the wires.

But his mind was elsewhere. Thoughts lingered somewhere between yesterday's note and the enthusing possibility of a ride with Nan. How long had it been?

They used to ride most every day. Never too dangerously, never too recklessly—for Nan's limp had always made her a rather timid, incapable creature in all things adventurous. But they were pleasant rides, mayhap the best of times, and how sweet it would be to revisit them.

Without knock or warning, Nan entered the study complete in her riding habit and jockey bonnet, looking for all the world like a sweet-tempered fairy. Would she ever lose that look? That rich glow of youth and honesty and earnestness?

He shoved the characters back to his desk. "I take it I am forgiven?"

"In every sense." Her gaze gleamed. "And me?"

"What about you?"

"Am I forgiven as well?"

"I don't recall what you did"—he came around the desk and grabbed his frock coat—"but if there is cause for pardon, it is yours. Are we ready?"

"Quite."

"Good. Loftus should have the horses prepared and waiting." Taking her arm, he led the way. "Speaking of stables, I passed some time with your brother this morning."

She glanced at him, smiling. "Truly?"

"Yes, indeed. Splendid fellow. Did you know you bear the same nose?"

"You think?"

"The only resemblance I could find."

"Papa says Heath took after our mother while I took after him." They passed through the main door, descended the broad stone steps. "What did you talk about?"

"You mostly."

She started to answer, but something gave her pause and snagged her eyes. Gilbert followed her gaze.

A shiny barouche with painted yellow wheels passed the wrought iron gate. Even if he hadn't noticed the crest on both sides, the fancy coachman sitting high upon his box seat would have given the visitor away.

"Lord Humphries." Nan spoke the name with a disconcerting lack of surprise. Almost as if she'd known.

Ire flamed anew, whether at Nan or the dragon he didn't know. He freed his arm from hers. "I suppose you knew about this."

"I had forgotten—"

"And I furthermore suppose you are going to go off with him in that thing. Is that right?"

"Well—yes, of course I am. We can go riding anytime, and I did promise his lordship my time. You would not have me break my word, would you?"

"I would not have you giving promises to such a man in the first place."

There.

He'd done it again.

The tenderness of her face dissolved, and when she spoke again, her tone nearly lashed him. "You might as well leave off apologizing if you intend to continue this insufferable nonsense. I am going with Lord Humphries, and there is not a thing you can do about it." Tossing down her riding crop, which she apparently would have no need for, she marched for the barouche that had pulled to a halt.

The dragon made swift time in assisting her up, the coachman closed the crested door, and then they were off again without so much as a look or a goodbye.

Gilbert retrieved the riding crop. He sliced the air once, twice, then a third vicious time. What a dashed fool she was making of herself. She'd never behaved like this, never flirted or entertained suitors or gone on carriage rides with eligible young men...

Gilbert's chest constricted. Had he thought this day would never come? And why did it enrage him so much that it had?

Three factors kept Nan inside the barouche. One, she'd given her word. Two, Papa. Three, her stubborn pride.

But three reasons or not, nothing could have been more tempting than to pry her hand from his lordship's glove, fling open the door, and leap to the blessed safety of the roadside.

Oh, why did he have to come today? She tried not to entertain the thought that at this very moment, she might have been nudging her horse to keep up with Briar's unmatchable strides, letting her hair go to the wind, and laughing at Gil's stories and nonsense.

Instead, she had left him alone. Hurt him somehow or betrayed him, though she didn't know why.

She'd make it up to him, apologize all over again, and win back the smile she depended on like air and water. Almost instinctively, she clasped the tiny pendant at her neck. Smooth, round, precious. Why had she behaved so crossly? But then again, why had he? They had always fussed with each other to some degree, but never like this.

This was different.

And altogether distressing.

"Such quiet must indicate grave thoughts. Any chance I might invade them?"

Nan tried to focus. "I am afraid not, my lord. They are much too trifling."

"Grave and trifle—now I am curious. May I guess?"

A bit annoyed but also thankful for the diversion from her own melancholy, she nodded. "By all means."

"You are in a dilemma. A great choice was landed upon you, one which you made in haste—and now you are naturally unsettled with the fear that you made the wrong one. How am I so far?"

"I daresay you are something of a wizard. But what was the choice?"

"Dare I speak it aloud?"

"Please do."

"The one I cannot be sure of, but as for the choice you made, you are wearing it."

"Pardon?"

"Your attire, of course. With a mother and sister, you cannot think me unwise as to the vexations of the female sex, my darling. But if it's any consolation, I think the riding habit you are wearing was indeed the right pick. It becomes you marvelously."

Was he in earnest?

Here she had almost been intrigued, almost found him witty and amusing. Shouldn't she have foreseen an answer so trivial and bothersome?

Before she could formulate a response, a flash of black and red appeared around the road's bend. A horse, lathered and pounding. A gentleman, without hat and leaning forward, as if for more speed—

"Watch out!" Lord Humphries bellowed as the coachman jerked back the reins. A groan, hooves scraping on gravel and dirt, the barouche sliding to a desperate halt.

Then the lone rider.

"Charles." Lord Humphries stood and faced his brother just as the marquess raced his horse next to the carriage door. "What are you trying to do by bolting around that curve like—"

"Something has happened."

"What?"

"Something has happened, I say, and if you were not off roaming about in this stupid carriage, you would know what goes on." With dark, furious eyes, the marquess's gaze fell upon her. Hot, accusing, loathsome. With a muttered oath, he snapped his attention back to his younger brother. "Out of the carriage this instant. Take my horse and make haste for home."

"But Miss Duncan—"

"I have needs in town and will take her home myself—but you must not argue.

Mother is in a state and wants for you alone, though I shall never know why. You are never any help in matters of importance." Cursing, he swung from his saddle and replaced his brother in the barouche.

Lord Humphries turned back, however, before mounting. "Miss Duncan, I hope you do not mind the change in plans?"

"No, of course not."

"I shall make it up to you any way I can, and you may expect word from me sooner than later." He appeared as if he might have said more, but the marquess motioned to the coachman, and the barouche lurched forward.

Not until they had turned back toward Dorrington Hall and Lord Humphries had galloped by with a wave did Nan's nerves begin to tighten.

She didn't move, not an inch, for fear she might bump the sleeve of a man whose mere silence was frightening. On average days, the marquess was cool, detached, arrogant. Now, he was all but on fire.

And she didn't want to risk being singed by any of his flames.

As if sensing her thoughts were of him, he spoke without facing her. "Permit me to be honest with you."

Not a question, really, but she nodded anyway.

"I have advised my brother to end this outlandish match. While Mother cares largely about our precious bloodlines—which she is apparently willing to compromise for his sake—I, on the other hand, must view the situation as it is."

"And what is it, my lord?"

"A ridiculous disaster. And as you permitted me to speak frankly, I must continue in saying that you are the last woman I should ever deem fit for Aylmer—or any other peerage."

Her cheeks stung. "And why, my lord, do I meet with such vengeful disapproval?"

"For many reasons."

"Such as?"

"Your birth, for one. Although Wydenshire may well assume you are some distant cousin of the Stanhopes, I myself could not be satisfied with such mystery. Do you care to enlighten me?"

"No."

"I did not think so."

"And the other reasons?"

"You have no great dowry."

Great enough for most. "And the other?"

"Must I continue?"

"Yes, please. I am very interested in hearing the rest."

"Then I shall be as candid as possible, Miss Duncan. I do not like you. You are insincere where my brother is concerned, you are much too reserved in social assemblies, and you walk—forgive me for mentioning it—with a painfully noticeable limp. I fear you would bring disgrace upon all our heads, a calamity which I do not intend to watch unfold. Have I made myself clear?"

"Quite, my lord."

"Excellent." As if ridding himself of an unpleasant affair, he dusted off his gloves and turned his face the other direction.

So much for not getting burnt. Why ever had she dubbed Lord Humphries as the dragon, when his brother was the one so natural at breathing fire?

Yet she couldn't be angry. Instead, she sat in perfect silence, taking her gaze to countryside that was bright and open. If the opinion of a marquess had meant anything to her, she might have been injured. If said man had possessed any hold on her, she might have been daunted.

But as it was, the marquess and his words bore no great effect on her.

Except one.

She would pursue Lord Humphries and open her heart as wide as the portals would stretch. By any luck at all, she'd fall in love with him, even marry him.

Because it was her choice.

Papa wanted her to.

And no one had the right to stop her from loving the man who already seemed to love her.

Heath drew to a stop in the stable doorway.

A small, purple-clad figure appeared for a second, half-hidden behind Golda and her stall, then disappeared again with a giggle. "Hold still now, girl. Do you want to make me mess up?"

With quiet steps, Heath approached.

The child stepped out into the open, tugged a ribbon from her springy curls, and tied it around a small braid on Golda's tail. "There. I shall bet you never looked so fine in all your. . ." The sentence trailed away as quickly as the girl's eyes snapped up. They rounded at Heath for a long time before she spoke. "What are you doing here?"

A small smile crooked his lips. "Getting ready to go home."

"Well, I wasn't doing anything wrong." Defense made her young chin lift a notch. "I'm allowed to play with the horses, you know. Papa said so."

"I see."

"Do you know who I am?" The girl's arms folded across her chest. "I'm Charlotte Stanhope. You probably remember me because I was the one on Gilbert's horse—when he ran away with me. That's him over there." She motioned toward another stall. "His name is Briar."

Heath nodded, rubbed a hand down Golda's back.

"Want to know what *her* name is?" Charlotte drew closer. Just beneath him, looking up with childlike eyes. "Her name is Lady of the Bright Stars. I just met her today. Want to know why I call her that?"

"Why?"

"Because these little speckles on her legs. Don't they look like stars?"

Heath glanced down and grinned. "A little."

"I braided her mane too. And her tail."

"Looks good."

"Thank you."

With one hand, Heath hefted his saddle from a peg and slung it across Golda's back, aware that he was under great scrutiny from the little bystander.

His actions must have angered her, for she huffed loudly enough to be heard. "Why are you doing that?"

"What?"

"Putting a saddle on Lady of the Bright Stars."

"Well"—he flung the stirrup to the other side and tightened the cinch—"I guess because she belongs to me, and I was kind of counting on her taking me home now."

"Belongs to *you*?"

He nodded.

"But I thought. . .you mean she isn't. . ." The words dissolved into a sigh, a disheartened pout. "Now I shan't be able to play with her at all. I never get to do anything I want to do." She padded after him toward the stable doors. "Mr. Duncan?"

"Yes?"

"What is her real name, anyway?"

"I call her Golda." Amusement stretched through him. "But I don't think she'd mind too much if you called her the other."

"You mean I can? I can still call her what I want?"

A nod.

"And I can still play with her in the day?"

Another nod.

"And I can even braid her mane if I want to?"

His final nod accompanied a grin. Then, without saying anything, he tugged

Golda outside and mounted.

He would have ridden away had Charlotte not come bounding after him. She stared up with newfound admiration and a bright, almost comical look of excitement. "Mr. Duncan?"

"Yes?"

"I think we ought to be friends. After all, we both like Lady of the Bright Stars quite a lot—and you did save my life."

He wasn't certain how to answer, so he did what he was best at and simply nodded. And as he rode to Papa's cottage, a comforting song of peace drummed at his heart. He was almost glad Papa had found him. Though he would return to the rectory, he was grateful that providence had led him to Dorrington Hall for this short time.

Because his life didn't feel quite so empty.

And for the first time since the funeral, he had more than the rector's memory to make him feel accepted and alive.

"What does it say?"

Nan bit back a smile. "Temperance, you really ought to practice reserve. You are far too curious and have all the makings of a village gossipmonger."

With an aghast drop of her jaw, Temperance hurried next to Nan, where she sat motionless on the pianoforte stool. "Miss Duncan, you must never say such a thing again! I should never ever be so horrid as to spread rumors and hurtful chatter. Tell me now, and I shall never ask after another letter again."

Despite her efforts to constrain it, Nan's laugh came chuckling out. "Ask all you wish. Here—read it if you want." She passed the letter into her maid's eager hands.

"Apologies for the abrupt end to your carriage ride. . .regretful he did not write sooner. . .wishes you to visit Bletherton Manor at your earliest convenience to console his sister?" Temperance lowered the letter. "Whatever is the matter with Lady Julia?"

"That is just it. I don't know." Nan rose from the pianoforte and left Temperance with instructions to store the letter with her others. She'd been keeping all of them of late. After all, if she were to marry Lord Humphries, wouldn't they be tokens she would cherish forever? Even if she didn't cherish them now?

Earlier in the day, Gilbert had mentioned something about fixing the longcase clock in the second-floor hall. Whether he could fix it or not was yet to be seen, but when she climbed the two flights of stairs, he was hard at work.

At her approach, he released the brass pendulum and smiled. It lacked luster and never quite reached his eyes.

Funny, but in the two days since her aborted carriage ride, neither she nor Gil had spoken much. They had been polite, smiled a bit here and there, and even played a game of whist once.

But the air was heavy with tension.

Short of never seeing Lord Humphries again, she didn't know how to make that tension go away.

"Is it working?"

At her question, he rose and eased the key lock door shut. "Afraid not. Much more complicated than I anticipated." He unrolled his sleeves one at a time. "What are you doing up here? Come to help me?"

"Hardly." She grinned slowly at first, as if to test his response.

He didn't smile back.

"No." She looked away. "I came for a different reason."

"Oh?"

"I received a letter and am needed at Bletherton Manor."

He started for the stairs. "Can Lord Humphries not come and take you himself?"

"I'm sure he would—but it is his sister, from what I understand, who most needs my presence."

On the third stair down, he turned and glanced back with a questioning, half-cynical look. "Lady Julia needs *you*, Nan?"

"Yes. What is wrong with that?"

"Nothing. I just did not realize you two had become so very intimate."

"Well, we—"

"What's the matter with her anyway?"

Nan tried to keep up with his fast descent on newly polished steps. "I don't know exactly. The letter sounds urgent, though, so I was hoping you might take me there today."

"Me?" He stopped and turned to her, frowning. She was certain he would refuse, when he sighed and continued faster down the stairs, saying over his shoulder, "All right. I shall prepare the gig."

Surprise flared along with a bit of pleasure. Was he finally accepting her choice?

By the time Gilbert had the gig pulled outside, Nan was sweeping down the stone steps and rushing toward him. She wore a new dress—probably a gown she'd been saving for Lord Humphries. Dark blue, satiny, a great contrast to the creamy fichu she was still tucking into place.

"Sorry it took me so long."

"It didn't." He caught her waist. As he lifted, one of her hands rested on his shoulder, brushed his neck without gloves. . .

A jolt thrilled his stomach. Quick, insane, undoing. He released her so hurriedly that she blinked. But she couldn't possibly have known. He didn't know himself.

He backed away, walked around the rear of the gig, and hesitated before joining her in such a tiny space. This was absurdity. Utter nonsense.

Sweat filmed his palms because he didn't know what was happening, why his abdomen still stirred from her touch, why he couldn't make himself climb in next to a girl he'd spent most of his life with.

Nan was everything to him, but she wasn't this. He shook his head free of cobwebs and climbed next to her, groaning in his chest.

Because when her elbow brushed his, it happened again. His heart stuttered. In heaven's name, what was wrong with him?

CHAPTER 15

$\mathcal{D}$arling, I cannot express how grateful I am that you are here." The moment she arrived, Lord Humphries's hands had swallowed hers, and he'd even been bold enough to press a quick kiss to her cheek.

Nan didn't glance Gilbert's way. What did it matter if he had seen? The entire ride here, he had not so much as breathed a word to her, obvious signs of his lingering anger.

Let him fume and pout. He was getting more and more like Charlotte every day.

Apparently forgotten by Lord Humphries—and purposely ignored by Nan—the two left him alone in the anteroom and made quick haste to the morning room.

"She is just inside," said Lord Humphries before he pulled open the silver-knobbed doors. "Indeed, she has not come out in hours. Even Mother cannot soothe her."

She would have inquired further as to the cause of Julia's distress, but he swung open the doors and sent her in alone before she had the chance.

The room engulfed her with vibrant colors of red, gold, and green. Faint flower scents lifted from various painted vases, and even though the Grecian-style drapes were all shut, the room still possessed a lavish hint of cheer.

From the striped settee by the window, Julia sat like the empty armor of a battle-wearied knight. Her eyes were red, swollen, concentrated on some unknown object. The hair usually perfectly arranged was limp, draping down her slumped shoulders in testament to her misery.

Nan almost backed away. Perhaps she would have had Lady Julia not met her gaze.

"There will be no wedding." The words struck the air with panic and hurt. For the first time, Nan noticed the letter still crumpled in the woman's pale hand. "I suppose you know what this means for me, don't you?"

Nan sidled forward and sat beside her. "The letter. . .it is from Lord Kettlewell?"

"Yes."

"But, my lady, you were both so very happy—"

"Happy?" Julia's tone quivered. "We were of equal station, Miss Duncan, and we were companionable and alike—but we were not happy." Tears escaped like dew drops sliding down rigid stems. "I never once imagined we were."

"I don't understand."

"It is very simple. We were prepared to wed on nothing more than mere logic, as such a matrimony would benefit us both in many respects."

"Then what has changed?"

"The benefits."

"Pardon?"

"The benefits, Miss Duncan—because after what has happened, marriage to me could only result in scandal and outrage."

"But what has happened?"

"You must remember. You were there for the first event. Do you not recall that ghastly note that was placed in our carriage the day of the picnic?"

A shiver passed along Nan's backbone. "I remember."

"That was only the beginning. The day after, a fire was set to the gazebo in our garden. It burned to a crisp and destroyed half our plants before it was discovered. Then, two days ago, Mother's magpie cat—the one she always takes to bed with her—was found slaughtered and left in her bed linens. It is almost as if"—she clasped Nan's hands with a cold, desperate touch—"whoever is doing this wants not only to taunt us but to destroy us. But why? Who could possibly wish to do us such harm when we have never been anything but generous to all of society...to all of humanity?"

Empathy pulsed at Nan's heart. "My lady, I don't know."

"Already, I am robbed of Lord Kettlewell and his promise. Who knows if I shall ever be affianced again? Who would want me? Who would possibly wish to unite with a family of such bizarre tragedies...such horrible, terrifying tragedies?" She jerked her hands away and cupped her mouth before a sob could leak out. "I am so frightened. I am so very, very frightened."

Gilbert stood close to the dragon. He held his eyes—held them like his life depended on it, for to look away now would have demolished his manhood.

As for Lord Humphries, he seemed perfectly willing to oblige. A bit clueless, perhaps, but he held Gilbert's stare with every bit as much stamina.

Until her ladyship walked in.

"Aylmer, what are you doing here in the anteroom when I called for you over ten minutes ago?"

"Mother, my *guests* have arrived." He spoke the word with a curious sound, as his eyes swung back to Gilbert. "And on that note, can I offer you tea, sir?"

"No." He regretted his tone for her ladyship's sake, so he tried again with a light smile. "No, I must decline, but thank you."

"You cannot stand here by the door like a wooden hall tree, Mr. Stanhope. You will have tea with us. Come along." She marched back through the door, neither her words nor her air offering any choice but to follow.

Lord Humphries motioned him first, so at least he did not have to walk in the dashed man's shadow the length of the way. The sooner he got out of this house, the better. Neither the people nor the grandeur interested him in the least. What in heaven's name did Nan see in any of this?

He wouldn't think of Nan. Couldn't think of her.

Not yet.

Not until he could make sense of this madness and unravel the questions that jabbed so hard they hurt. How was that possible? How was any of this possible?

"Sit down, Mr. Stanhope—not in that chair. Over there." The dowager flipped her wrist toward a wingback chair next to Aylmer's. "Yes, that will do nicely. Where is that unpredictable housekeeper? So exasperating, the service these days. Mrs. Gregory!"

In a bustle, a wiry little woman entered with a silver tray of tea, crustless sandwiches, and seedcakes. "A'ready prepared for you, my lady. I was just a-waiting for you to be—"

"Do not ramble with senseless excuses, Mrs. Gregory. Where are the lemons?"

"Forgive me, my lady." A curtsy. "I'll be fetching them. I'll be right back. I'll hurry." She dashed away in an embarrassed fluster.

Gilbert reached for a cup and tray. "A bit severe on your staff, are you not, my lady?"

Lord Humphries straightened. "I shall ask you to show respect—"

"Enough, Aylmer." His mother cocked her head, focused her rheumy eyes on Gilbert. "I like a man who can speak his mind. I rarely listen to anyone else."

"But Mother—"

"Enough!" Then, lowering her voice, "Mr. Stanhope, you are right. I am temperamental of late and often take it out on those nearest me. We have been under, shall we say, a new sort of strain these last days."

"Oh?"

"My daughter, as you might have noticed, has taken matters the worst."

"Then I offer my condolences."

"For what good it will do, which is none, I thank you." She glanced back at the silver tray. "Take a sandwich, Mr. Stanhope."

"Thank you, but—"

"I said, Mr. Stanhope, take a sandwich. You shall like it splendidly, and if you don't, you may have fisticuffs with our cook. I am sure she deserves it most of the time." Pouring a cup of tea herself, she raised it to her lips, then lowered it again. "Mrs. Gregory, Mrs. Gregory—the pitiful, dawdling woman. Doesn't she know by this time that I cannot take tea without lemons? Aylmer, go and fetch her at once."

As much as Gilbert was glad for Lord Humphries's absence, he was left to the excruciating company of the dowager marchioness. She asked far too many questions—pointed questions. Why had he never been married? Who had he cast his sights upon? When was the last time he'd visited Bath or London? And heaven have mercy, but did he notice how astonishingly low Miss Onslow had worn her neckline at church last Sunday?

For the most part, he avoided questions with a bite of sandwich or a sip of tea. Indeed, by the time Nan entered the room with the butler, he'd drank two cups and already had a piercing headache.

Her ladyship lifted a direct look at Nan. "I trust you were able to offer some comfort to my daughter?"

"I cannot own to doing much, my lady, but Lady Julia has retired to her bedchamber. I believe she is feeling less dreadful."

"That's the trouble with Julia. She never says how she really feels. In truth, she is probably in a worse state than when you arrived."

Nan didn't so much as frown, only glanced to Gilbert with her shoulders back. Why on earth was she spinning? "Are you prepared to return home, Gil? We shall be expected soon."

"Very true." He stood—perhaps too quickly because his legs buckled beneath him. He crashed back into the chair. Gasped, heaved. Turned his face the other direction and vomited.

"Gil!" Nan's voice, very close to him, but his eyes couldn't seem to focus.

Mercy, was he falling asleep?

No, not asleep. Spinning, though. Round and round, up and over, down and down, down, down. . .

His body struck the floor, stunning him, jarring away the darkness for a few fleeting seconds. Nan was crying. Why was she crying?

"Somebody, help me. . .he's fainted!"

No. With one hand, he pushed himself upward. "I'm all right." Weak, even to his own ears. What was wrong with him? "I'm. . ." Another gag, then he retched again.

"Lord Humphries. . .lift him, won't you?"

He tried to protest, but it did no good. The darkness carried him away before the dragon's claws ever touched him.

"Miss Duncan, please." A hand circled her arm, tightened, started to tug. "Step aside and let the servants handle him."

Handle him. As if Gilbert Stanhope were nothing more than a trinket to be moved to another shelf or a tapestry to be hung on a different wall or a—

"Nan." The use of her forename jolted her, struck through some of the panic long enough to make her rise.

Lord Humphries drew her back. "Take him to one of the guest chambers on the east wing, men. Careful you do not jostle him."

Jostle him. Her chest hammered. *No, please do not jostle him.*

Even when the manservants circled him, lifted him, he didn't stir. His head dangled. Eyes remained shut. How long had they been like that?

"Let me go." She pulled against the hold on her.

The servants passed through the doorway, disappeared.

"My lord, let me go—"

"Miss Duncan, do not take on hysterics." Her ladyship, for the first time, finally pushed from her chair. "You are forgetting yourself entirely. Sit down and *calm* down, if you please."

"But I want to—"

"Nan, Mother is right." Lord Humphries caught her shoulders, trapping her. "We have already sent for the apothecary, and there is very little you can do."

"I want to be with him."

"But it would only further upset you, my darling—"

"The only thing further upsetting me is your hands. Now will you please let me go?"

At the words, her ladyship inhaled a lungful of air, and Lord Humphries reddened by three shades. With an awkward apology, he walked away from her. "Of course, Miss Duncan. Forgive me. I was only attempting to calm you."

With gathering tears, she fled through the same doorway the servants had exited. Big, empty, glittering halls. How thudding and severe fell her footfalls on marble so pristine.

God, what is wrong?

She mounted mahogany stairs when a maid pointed her in the right direction. Up, up, up—but it took much longer than it ever should have.

Please, God.

She halted in a carpeted hall, approached the only door swung wide open. Three servants slipped out, no expression, finished with one duty and off to the next.

Then Nan entered.

He lay still upon a four-poster bed, an elderly maid already hovering close—but at the sight of Nan, she retreated to a corner chair and said nothing.

"Gil?"

His eyes adjusted on her, hazy, uncertain.

She pressed close to the bed and grasped his hand. "Gil, you are awake?"

"Yes." Strange, how his voice could sound so normal when his face appeared so wan. "Yes, awake."

"What is wrong?"

"Don't. . .know."

"Is there pain?"

"Burning."

"Where?"

"Mouth. . .throat. Everything so. . .blurry and. . .and. . ."

"And what?"

Stared at her, stared hard.

"Gil?"

First, it was just a twitch, a faint jerk of his chest. Then his arms began to shake, his legs, everywhere.

"Gil!" Her scream summoned the maid to her side. They seized his arms. "Gil, please."

Convulsing, half breathing, teeth jarring in a deathlike rhythm of pain. Just as quickly, though, the writhing ceased. He lay limp as before. Didn't move, hardly breathed.

Just looked at her.

"In the name of mercy, what is the matter with him?" She lifted his hand to her chest, squeezed with the same devilish fear as when Heath would not wake up. "What is the matter?"

She hadn't expected an answer, but a voice from close by whispered anyway. "I 'ave not seen this in a long time, miss." The old maid reached out and mopped sweat from Gilbert's brow. "An' I had 'oped not to see it again."

"What? Tell me, please. Why is he so ill?"

"Not ill, miss." A disheartened sigh. "Poisoned."

Mr. Puttock was slow. Everything about him, from the perpetual rise of his scraggly brows to the movement of his hands as he reached into a bag and fished out a bottle. He swished the reddish-brown liquid several times before he finally glanced up. "Give him plenty of wine and ten or so drops of this laudanum throughout the remainder of the day."

Nan clasped her hands. "Then he shall be all right?"

"Undoubtedly. He is resting now."

"But what is the matter with him?"

With another raise of his brows, he handed the laudanum to Nan. Hesitated. Frowned. "Camphor."

From beside Nan, Lord Humphries went rigid.

Her ladyship, who sat in her plush chair with untouched lemons still waiting on their tray, did not so much as blink. "Impossible. You and that ludicrous upstairs maid are both mistaken—or in some kind of cohorts to ruin me. Which is it, Mr. Puttock?"

Unruffled by the accusation, Mr. Puttock shrugged. "Neither, my lady. I have simply given you the truth of the matter." He grabbed his bag, turned to leave—

"Just a moment, Mr. Puttock." The dowager's voice cracked like lightning. "Do not dare turn your back and leave without first offering some sort of explanation."

"I should think that would be your department, my lady, as you were the man's hostess."

"*I* did not poison him."

"I did not say you did."

"You insolent fool! I cannot have you walking out of here and telling all of Wydenshire my guest was nearly murdered. What am I to think of all this?"

"I would suggest directing your line of thought to what the man ate or drank since arriving."

"Tea and sandwiches," said Lord Humphries. He glanced at the tray. "I ate a sandwich myself and never suffered."

"How many cups?"

"Pardon?"

"How many cups did young Stanhope drink?"

Her ladyship sniffed. "No more than three, I am certain. Surely you do not think—"

"I think so indeed, my lady, and were I you, I would stop fretting over gossip and consider that this poison might have been meant for you."

She gasped.

"Furthermore, whoever stirred camphor into your tea had no intentions of killing anyone."

"What nonsense! Mr. Stanhope was nearly dying not five minutes later."

"Which proves my point."

"How so?"

"The blackguard who did this would have no guarantee as to how many cups would be drunk. If he had wished to kill, he would have added sufficient amount that one cup would do the job."

Lord Humphries pulled back the teapot lid, stared down as if incredulous. "Then what purpose could he have had?"

"I can see only one."

"Which is?"

"To make you all sick." Mr. Puttock planted his hat on his head, raised his brows once more. "Very sick, indeed."

The same fear Nan had witnessed in Julia's eyes gnawed deep inside her. She didn't know why this was happening to her ladyship and this household. She didn't know who could wish them such pain.

She only knew Gilbert should not be a part of it.

He could not die.

CHAPTER 16

$\mathcal{I}$'m going back to the Bobber."

Heath's knife stilled halfway into a chunk of bread. Why the pub's name still affected him he didn't know, but he glanced up with a pang of unease.

Papa sat across the table, his hook digging scratches into the grainy wood. "I'm going back to see Madame Le Sueur."

"Why?"

"Why?" Papa echoed the question, slurred, as if nothing could have been more outrageous. "What do you mean *why*, boy?"

"No reason for it."

"There's every bloody reason."

Heath eased the knife through the bread and tossed his father half. "There is nothing to be gained by going back now—"

"You woman." His father jerked up. "You should have gone a long time ago. You should have done something about that witch, taught her a lesson for them things she done to you, to my little Nan."

Heath's throat tightened.

"But no...you just sit there. Is that what the rector taught you? To be a woman?" When Heath didn't answer, he swore with a breath that reeked of ale. "You don't know nothing, boy, about this cursed world."

"Papa—"

"Leave me be." He ambled for the door, grabbed his tattered hat from a rusty peg. "Tell my daughter I'll be seeing her when I get back. Tell my son he better start acting like the Duncan clan he came from."

"Or what, Papa?"

"Or I don't have no son." He slammed the door, rattling the cottage walls behind him.

159

Heath ran his fingers through his hair. Papa was everything the rector was not. And everything Heath never wanted to be.

This was not something Miss Duncan would do. Or any refined lady, for that matter. Why was it that Temperance thought up the worst plans of all time?

No, that was not true. Hadn't Nero set Rome on fire and played upon his fiddle as it burned? Hadn't Mary Queen of Scots been accused of murdering her husband—only to then marry the other murder suspect?

Not very wise, that. In any event, it was a consolation to think of others' failures when her own loomed so heavily in her mind.

With one hand shading her eyes from morning sunlight, Temperance swung her wicker basket with the other. The motion helped alleviate her nerves, if nothing else. She was close now. Still far enough away to change her mind but close all the same. How worn and sagging the thatched roof appeared from this distance. The old cottage, so long empty, appeared no happier than before it was inhabited.

Indeed, it almost appeared sadder for the change.

But that was nonsense, of course. After all, what do walls and roofs and windows know of emotion?

Temperance halted.

Something ahead, a distant figure upon a horse, made a turn onto the road. Perhaps she had not come early enough. Heath was leaving for Dorrington Hall already.

And in a hurry too.

The animal galloped down the straight stretch, dust flaring behind like gathering storm clouds. Did he always ride so?

Yet the figure hardly seemed to be Heath at all. Where Heath was tall and broad of shoulder, the figure upon the mount was thin, hunched, and aged. The nearer he drew, the more she recognized the wizened face of the elder Mr. Duncan.

"Out of the way!"

The gravelly warning shook her, shattered her scrutiny, and for a moment she could not move. Then she lunged off the road.

Whoosh.

The beast and rider zipped by, and the cloud of dust billowed around her in a suffocating shroud.

She wiped at her dress, coughed. Goodness, where had she slung her basket?

"Oh dear." This she spoke aloud, for she had not slung her basket at all. She had dropped it in the middle of the road, where it now lay broken, scattered, and wretchedly unrecognizable.

Were all her days to be one mishap after another? Couldn't she do anything without catastrophe?

She couldn't go to the cottage now if she wanted to. She couldn't knock on Heath's door as she'd planned, smile brightly enough that he would smile back, and persuade him to accept the food she'd been so sure he'd love.

More horse hooves sounded behind her.

Oh please, do not let it be him. But the thought or prayer or whatever it was had no bearing, because when she turned around, Heath Duncan stopped his mount before her.

"I fear I have made a great disaster of everything." Her excuse trembled as it left her lips. "Miss Duncan has remained at Bletherton Manor, as Master Gilbert was not well, so I was left with nothing at all to do and no one to attend to."

Heath dismounted, saying nothing.

"And Miss Charlotte has been telling Mr. Stanhope such marvelous tales of your horse. Indeed, he was so grateful that you allow Miss Charlotte to pet and fuss over the animal that he agreed you should have a day to do whatever you wish. So you see, you really do not have to go to Dorrington Hall at all today."

He glanced at the remains of wicker and sugar biscuits and mangled cloth.

"Oh—and the basket. Miss Duncan always loved these biscuits so much, see, that I thought you might enjoy them as well. Cook said I might have them. They always throw out the extra anyway." With a shiver of discomfiture and shame, she raised her eyes to his.

He was smiling. "I do like sugar biscuits."

"You do?"

"There used to be a rector—he would give them to Nan and me sometimes when we were children."

"And you have not had them since?"

"Not since the rector's. . .passing." His expression shifted, the distinct mark of pain and longing and tender veneration.

How sweet it would be to learn more. To talk with him, to tell him everything, to dissect every word he said in return. She'd do anything to learn his secrets. Anything to understand him. Anything to love him.

But that was a fool's thought. Perhaps everything she'd done had been foolish. Seeking him out, smiling so often, coming here. One couldn't simply decide to fall in love, to wish for another's heart, and make a marriage turn out in the end. Somehow, in some strange and unknown way, it had to happen all on its own.

And he had to want it too.

Pain wiggled deep into places already too attached, too full of care. Why had she done this to herself? Too dangerous, too risky, too many chances he was another Loftus who would not want her in the end—or perhaps did not want her even now.

She took a step back. "It would be best for me to return now, Mr. Duncan, and I am sorry for the disappointment of no sugar biscuits."

"It was kind of you anyway."

She made a swift curtsy. Turned and started down the road on legs that felt awkward and with arms that had no basket to swing—

"Miss Temperance?"

She stopped, glanced back.

He was quiet for a moment. Was it the sunlight that made his cheeks seem so warm?

"Perhaps you might stay?"

Stay? She had expected a goodbye of sorts, words of brief gratitude, a mention of seeing her again on the morrow. But to *stay?*

The sunlight must have been hotter because his cheeks grew pinker. "I've no basket, but perhaps we might partake of milk, cheese, and bread."

"Oh, could we? A picnic of sorts?"

"If you wish."

"In a field perhaps? Or mayhap under some lovely tree?"

A brilliant grin, a treasure so rich and blinding she felt unworthy of it. "In a field *and* under a tree, if you wish it, Miss Temperance." He stepped forward and opened his hand.

She slipped her own into the warm, strong grasp. And wondered if, for once, she had done something right after all.

Surely this was a dream. The room was pale and accented with gold, while wall murals depicted celestial clouds and unclothed seraphs floating about with massive wings. Heaven, perhaps?

Nan slumped in a wingback chair, asleep like an angel. Auburn ringlets framed her cheeks like little vortexes of fire.

Little. The word burrowed deep into Gilbert's memory. The frightened little urchin with filthy shoes who alighted from Papa's carriage. That sad, hungry look that made him so uncomfortable at first. The delight of the very first smile she ever bestowed upon him, and the warm excitement in knowing he was finally at liberty to help her.

But in the end, she had helped him.

Been his companion.

His reason for coming home after parties that were long and taxing, balls that only annoyed him, outings that never elated.

All along, it had been Nan—his playmate, his confidant, his lifeblood, the only soul in the world who understood him in fullness. *Dear God, how could I have not known?*

His chest throbbed. He watched her slumber, and every long-hidden thrill raced across a heart so long unaware.

But the joy died. Died because he knew the truth. Because he knew Nan. Because no matter how the world had changed for him, it had not changed for her.

Almost to taunt him, she stirred. Her breath drew in softly, then sleepy eyes lifted and sought his face. "Gil." How quickly she approached him. With hands that bore no hesitancy, sweet fingers grasped his cheeks. "Tell me how you feel."

No, couldn't do that. He hardly knew himself.

"Gil?"

"I feel well."

"Truly?"

"Yes. . .truly. Is there water?"

She brought a small glass to his lips. The cool liquid eased down his throat and chased away the lingering burning.

"Enough?"

He nodded, guided her hand away, and scooted up. "How long have I been here?"

"Since yesterday. Do you remember?"

"A little. I was sick."

"Very—but not what you think." She leaned close, closer than he was prepared for, and his pulse maddened. "You were poisoned."

Poisoned. But it didn't matter, because he loved her. Because he needed her. Because he'd shattered something familiar and built something new in its place. When did it begin? At the tree? When she'd promised the dragon a courtship? When she'd abandoned their riding plans?

Or years before that?

"Did you hear me?"

"Yes."

"Isn't it dreadful?"

"Yes."

"There are strange things happening, things that cannot be explained."

"I know, Nan."

She paused. Brows came together as if she perceived something off-kilter but couldn't comprehend what. Then she scooted off the bed. "You had better rest quiet now. I shall tell her ladyship you are awake." She leaned down and left a kiss upon his cheek. "And I must tell you, I was never so frightened in all my life. Were something to happen to you, I think I would perish."

If only she knew something *had* happened to him. That in some respects, she had lost him already.

Nothing could ever be the same again.

Nan walked along corridors that were soundless, brushing her finger below the ancient portraits of solemn-looking faces. They all bore a likeness to her ladyship. With relatives so lofty and rich, it was no wonder the dowager took such pride in them. Who in the world would want to threaten an old woman's standing like this?

True, the dowager was not of the kindest demeanor. But weren't all the peerage of England a bit high in the instep? Who would want to hurt her this way—hurt all of them this way?

Nan sighed. Gilbert had not seemed interested in the unknown danger. Indeed, he had scarcely changed expression when she mentioned the word *poison*.

Maybe he didn't feel as well as he claimed. A day more in bed, perhaps, would return him to good health and jovial spirits.

She reached the stairs and descended the first flight, then turned—

A man slammed into her. He grunted, caught her from a tumble, then withdrew from her touch with a frown. "Do you ever heed where you are going, Miss Duncan?"

Nan glanced up into the marquess's pinched face, his direct eyes. "My apologies, my lord."

"Accepted. How fares Stanhope?"

"As well as can be expected."

"You act as if I were the cause of this."

"No, my lord—I am just surprised at your concern. I have never witnessed you to have any before. Not in any matter, really."

"How observant. You fascinate me. Anything else about myself you should like to insult?"

"No. I might ask the same of you."

"Do not bother. I never wait for an invitation." With a faint bow, he brushed past her and stomped around the corner as a child in some sort of tantrum.

Nan sighed away her small frustration. Was there ever a more miserable man? One would think, with all his wealth and prestige, he could manage a bit more optimism.

It was not until she had reached the bottom of the stairs and passed through another hall that an odd emotion struck her. One that tugged hard at a cord of familiarity and reoccurrence. One that brought her back to the Simon and Cat on the night she had first visited Papa, when a stranger had collided with her on the stairwell...

"*Out of my way.*" That voice. "*Do you ever heed where you are going, Miss Duncan? Do you ever heed where you are going? Do you ever heed?*"

A prickle of disquiet made her pause in the hallway and glance back in question.

No, it could not have been the Honorable Marquess of Somerset. Not in a place such as the Simon and Cat. The idea itself was absurd, perfectly impossible.

Yet it *had* been him.

Why?

This was too dangerous.

He'd told himself from the very beginning, as they'd entered his cottage and prepared the food. Then again as they'd ventured on foot to this quiet little pasture. Then a third time while they partook of their meal and watched a small herd of sheep on the other side of the wooden fence.

She didn't look dangerous.

Even if she was, he didn't think he could defend himself.

With his back propped against a holm oak tree, Heath watched his sister's abigail brush bread crumbs from her dress. She was talking, always talking. Some sweet little story that made her eyes smile, made a soft laugh escape every so often.

This wouldn't last long, he was sure. Her infatuation with him, her interest and attentions. Her beautiful stories and clumsy explanations. How long before she bored of him?

He wouldn't blame her. The danger was his own choice. Surely, when it ended, it wouldn't hurt so very bad—would it?

"Shall we go and see the sheep?"

At the strange request, he leaned forward. "You want to?"

"Not that I like sheep especially, but it would be rather pleasurable. My father's father was a sheepherder—or so I read in our Bible. Mother writes down accounts of all the family. What was your father's father?"

"I don't really know."

"I already know your papa was a sailor. How very exciting life on the sea must have been, don't you think? Is that what you shall do someday?"

He shook his head as he stood, then reached for her and tugged her up.

"Then what do you wish to be?"

Had anyone ever asked him that? The only one who had ever cared had been the rector—and he already knew. "I want to work for the church."

"A clergyman?"

"Not exactly. Just someone who helps."

She was quiet for a bit, walking beside him close enough that her sleeve bumped his, that he could hear the rustle of her dress—and his body tensed with the dread of what was coming.

But when she spoke, she mumbled nothing of bad decisions or nonsense or regrettable choices. Instead, she entwined her hand with his. "I think that is lovely, Heath Duncan, and I should be very proud of you for such a calling. I daresay, God should be very proud of you too."

Proud? Could she possibly mean such a thing? Why did it make everything different? Warm blood suffused his soul, and he tightened his fingers around hers. *Proud of me.*

She didn't seem to realize what she'd said. As they reached the edge of the fence, she leaned against the wood and laughed when a lamb cried out to a ewe. "Heath, look how that one races for its mother. Did you see how they called to one another? Almost as if they knew. . .as if they knew they belonged together. Isn't it terribly amazing?"

He kept his gaze fixed on the herd and didn't answer.

But his heart whispered, *'Twas amazing, indeed.*

CHAPTER 17

No comfort stirred Gil at the thought of returning home and resuming life as it had been. Nervous dread churned his stomach, sucking his strength more than poison.

Nan sat close to him in the carriage. One of her arms looped through his, and too many times she settled her head against his shoulder. "I do not doubt you are eager to be free of Bletherton Manor," she said. "These last two days have been an eternity."

"That's surprising."

"Why?"

"I should have thought Lord Humphries would have kept you perfectly contented."

"Not with you ill." She yawned. "La, why am I so fatigued?"

"Doubtless from watching after me night and day." He wanted to give her hand a small pat, as he might have done before. He didn't. "Get some rest, Nan. I shall wake you when we reach Dorrington."

She murmured an answer—one too soft to detect amid the creaking carriage wheels—and in moments, her head went limp against him.

What am I going to do? The repeated chant nipped at his sanity. He needed a plan. He couldn't just return home and allow life to go on, allow the camaraderie to continue as if nothing had changed. He needed answers. A way he could fix what he felt like the clock upstairs or put himself back together like Charlotte's theatre.

But as the carriage jostled back through Dorrington's gates, his heart deflated with the truth. There was no answer.

He had no idea what to do.

"Do you like it here?" Nan leaned against one of the stalls while Charlotte grabbed a stool and stood next to her.

Heath glanced at the both of them with a small smile. "Very much."

"That was a silly question anyway, Nan." Charlotte jutted out her chin with a hint of authority on the matter. "He likes it a lot, and he doesn't plan on ever leaving. Do you, Mr. Duncan?"

Now he laughed, tossed the hay from his pitchfork. "I know Golda doesn't plan on leaving. Not with you to take care of her."

"You don't suppose she likes me better than you, do you?"

"Wouldn't be surprised."

A thrilled giggle left Charlotte's lips. "That would be something!" She hurried from the stool. "May I take her for a walk? So she might stretch her legs?"

Heath nodded. A warm, quick smile stayed in place until long after Charlotte had flitted away with the horse.

After all these years, maybe Nan didn't know him. Not like she always had before. But years or not, she knew that smile. Knew it enough to know it was rare but growing more frequent. That it used to be limp and forced but now spread more easily and with greater joy.

Her brother wasn't the only one who'd succumbed to this change.

"She likes you." Nan circled around the stall. "Very much."

"And I her."

"Charlotte is not fond of very many—and even of those, not very often. Indeed, she hardly cares for me most of the time."

"Really?"

"Yes. She is an unpredictable child in every sense. However have you won her?"

"I believe Golda did that."

"Truly?"

A nod.

"And did Golda win Temperance too?"

His pitchfork froze. Color spread to his cheeks just as his eyes made a slow climb to hers. "How do you know that Temperance has been won?"

"That I cannot tell you." She dropped her voice to a whisper. "There are far too many ways I have realized this truth, and all of them you must discover yourself."

Oh, the happy light that brightened his eyes like stars. He thrust his pitchfork back into a pile of hay. "I intend to."

"Well, ye do still live here, don't ye?" Loftus had taken no more than three steps into the kitchen when his gaze slid into hers.

And burned.

Temperance scooted away from the table, gathered up her empty bowl and mug. "If you will excuse me—"

"Wait a minute." With startling speed, he seized her forearm. The earthenware bowl slipped to the ground and rolled. "I want to talk to ye, lass, and ye better not be denyin' me the right."

"You have no right."

"No right, ye say? Almost married you, I did."

"But you didn't, see, and there's really nothing to say."

"Temp—"

"Please, Loftus." She wriggled away from him. "Just leave me alone, won't you? I cannot fathom what you would want with me, and I am certain any such discussion would waste both of our time. Now if we must remain at Dorrington Hall, can we not just forget one another? Or at least, if nothing else, live somewhat amicably?"

Heat discolored his complexion. "Ye wouldn't be so bloody quick to forget me if that blackguard Duncan hadn't come along."

"What could it possibly matter to you?"

"It doesn't." He scowled, cursed, took two steps away. "Doesn't at all. Who would want the likes o' ye anyway? Ye're just a bird-witted fool—and poor pity to the man who gets ye." With one last string of oaths, he kicked the bowl across the room and marched outside.

The study was not so large as it had seemed as a child, when Gilbert had sat in the chair by the hearth and talked to Papa for hours. Sometimes, lectures had forced him here. Other times, he remained more for himself than out of any obligation.

He didn't know why he was here now.

"How are you feeling today?" With one hand still scribbling numbers, Papa broke the stillness. "You appear peaked, which makes me think your mamma was not at all unwise when she said you ought to remain in bed a few days."

"That is unnecessary. I have already assured you and the rest of the house I am well. What must I do to convince everyone? Dance a jig?"

The feather pen lowered. "Must we be so forceful, Son?"

"I am sorry."

"Forgiven."

"I am not myself."

"That I have already noticed." Just as he'd done countless times in years past, Papa lowered his spectacles and peered at Gilbert. Why did it always seem as if the man knew everything?

But he didn't know, of course.

No one knew.

If Gilbert did tell Papa, there would be no words to explain what he didn't understand himself. How to say that he fathomed himself in love with the girl he used to play pirates and gypsies with?

"Dash it all, but I fear I hear Charlotte calling for me." Gilbert rose too quickly to be natural. "I had better go see what she wants—"

"Son?"

At the door, he paused. "Yes?"

"Whatever is troubling you, don't let it win, hmm? And if you can't fight it yourself, I am always up for joining a good battle myself."

Gilbert murmured thanks, then slipped away into a quiet hall. In some ways, the small words infused him with comfort. In other ways, they didn't.

Because the fight ahead was his alone.

And losing was inevitable because Nan would never love him back.

The evening was much the same as any other—with Mr. and Mrs. Stanhope sitting in their usual places, Charlotte sprawled on the floor, playing with chess pieces, and the hearth blazing warm against the faint September chill.

But Gil was different.

Had been ever since they'd returned from Bletherton Manor. Something about his face, his eyes, seemed to beg for relief.

The poison, Nan told herself. The pain, the sickness. All viable reasons his smile should suddenly become so forced, his voice so lacking enthusiasm, his manner so devoid of usual mischief.

Yet it was more than that, and she had a sinking feeling it had something to do with her.

"Nan, what's the horse again?" From flat on her stomach, Charlotte craned her neck back and held out a wooden chess piece.

"The knight."

"That's ridiculous. Horses cannot very well be knights. Will you teach me to play sometime? The real game, I mean?"

"I fear I am not strategic enough to make a winner of you. Perhaps Gil would be a better instructor."

"Will you, Gil? Please?"

From the window, he turned for the first time. His eyes avoided Nan entirely.

Avoided Charlotte too, really, as he slid his glance to the array of messy chess pieces with an odd flicker of annoyance. "Blast it all, Charlotte, must you always badger me about something? You'd never have the patience to master the game anyway. Go and trouble someone else for once." Without so much as an uttered apology, he aimed for the door and left strained silence in his absence.

Mr. and Mrs. Stanhope shared a disconcerted look—one that resonated with the uncomfortable thrum in Nan's chest.

Charlotte's chin puckered. Real tears this time, not the customary ones she produced to gain her way. "Stupid knight." Blinking hard, she knocked over the chess pieces, scrambled to her feet, and raced for the door—

"Oh!" The butler retreated from the doorway and allowed Charlotte her escape. Then, flustered and muttering apologies, he spoke from the doorway. "Miss Duncan? Very sorry to disturb, but a letter just arrived for you."

Nan rose, accepted the letter from the butler's ornate tray, then flipped off the familiarly crested seal. She scanned it, breathed in, then turned.

"Well, my dear?" asked Mr. Stanhope. "Who from?"

"Lord Humphries." She studied on the words this time. "It appears her ladyship is requesting Gilbert and I at once."

"What? Tonight?" Mrs. Stanhope's mouth formed a grim line of protest. "How very presumptuous. Of course you cannot go—"

"I fear I must."

"But—"

"It seems another disaster is upon them, and I doubt they would summon us unless our assistance was greatly needed." With the last words, she focused her eyes on Mr. Stanhope. Dear, kind, steady Mr. Stanhope—who forever understood and responded to Nan's pleas.

He didn't fail her now. "Do as you wish, Nan dear."

"But Fredrick, the hour—"

"The hour, the hour," came his soft rebuke, as if it were hardly relevant to anything. Then a smile tugged at one corner of his lips. "Besides, anyone willing to endure Gilbert's foul company tonight must be very obliged to go, indeed."

"What are you doing here?"

Gilbert didn't know. Out of all the rooms in the house, why should he choose the one room which would inflict him most?

Nevertheless, here he stood—fingers idle on soundless keys, his heart a new wreck at the sound of her voice in the airy music room. Why the deuce had she followed him?

"Fine. Do not answer me if it is too much trouble."

He turned to face her anger head-on. Almost welcomed his own, because at least in argument he was on comfortable ground again. "What do you want?"

"For you to stop acting the bully, for one."

"If you're referring to Charlotte—"

"You made her cry, you know. Not that I suppose that would trouble you deeply, considering she apparently is such great trouble to you."

He should have been chagrined. Should have apologized, sought out his injured little sister, made amends like any good brother would do.

But he had room enough for only so many emotions at once. Right now, he was already filled to the brim.

Nan crossed her arms over her chest. Defiance, annoyance, maybe a bit of worry all made her brows crease. "If there were time, I would demand to know whatever is the matter with you."

"Nothing."

"No?"

He whipped one hand down the keys. Pounded hard on the last note. Said with more force, "No."

"Then you shall have no objection to escorting me to Bletherton Manor. I've already sent word for the carriage to be prepared and—"

"Tonight?"

"Yes."

"I'm not going."

"Another horrible misfortune has occurred, although the letter omitted any details, and I am certain that—"

"And I am certain, Nan, that I am *not* going. Neither are you."

She uncrossed her arms. "Of course I am."

"No, you're not. Lord Humphries can manage difficulties without you. Or is he such the coward that he needs you there to weep on?"

"Why are you being so cruel?"

"I'm not being cruel. I am being frank. And if running off at dark to share the dragon's every pain is your pleasure, go ahead. Just don't involve me."

She stared at him. Child and woman. Confident yet confused. Ordinary while beautiful.

God should have had mercy when He sent Nan Duncan to Dorrington Hall. He must have known this would happen. That they'd be standing here now—separated while still together, lost to each other, doomed from everything they'd taken for granted all these years.

Poor Nan. Innocent, unsuspicious Nan. Would she ever know the truth?

Heaven knew he'd never tell her. Such news would ruin not just him—but her too. Then where would they be? Would she feel obligated to return his affection, even against her heart? Or would she run from him, forsake him, dread every encounter for fear of the awkward exchange?

No, he could never tell her.

Not ever.

"Fine." He couldn't read her expression, and he made certain she couldn't read his. "Forget I inconvenienced you so greatly. I shall give her ladyship your regrets."

He didn't stop her when she left. Much better if their bonds were broken slowly, subtly, without great pain to either of them. He would fade away and make trips and become busy often—anything to dissolve this wretched, torturing attachment.

Surely that was the best plan. The way out he'd been looking for. The battle strategy he could set his mind and heart to.

In the performing of his plan, maybe he would realize the truth—that he didn't love Nan, not the way he thought. That all of this was nothing more than ridiculous infatuation. That in the end, this pain would slip carelessly back into the role of old, fraternal love.

If only that would happen.

He tapped the pianoforte once more, its rich pitch so reminding him of Nan that he knew his hopes were in vain.

He loved her.

In a way he never ever had before.

"I'm glad you came." So much better than being alone, since Gil had refused to accompany her.

Heath sat next to Nan, the reins in his grasp, and answered in the darkness, "Papa has not yet returned. Figured I would work later this evening."

"He's been gone for days."

No answer.

"What if something—"

"Nan." Not unkind, just strong enough to silence her.

She settled back into the padded seat of the gig. "You're not worried at all. Something might have happened to delay his return. Do you even know where he went?"

Just a flick of the reins.

With a frown, Nan followed his lead and decided for silence. Perhaps he was right not to worry. After all, hadn't Papa managed on his own all these years? But why would Heath, his own son, not spare him one conversation's worth of concern?

She didn't try to puzzle it out—no more than she tried to puzzle out Gil's strange behavior. Were all men so unbearably unreasonable?

The ride to Bletherton Manor was slow and chilly. She'd nearly allowed the smooth rocking motion to lure her into sleep when. . .

"Smoke." Heath spoke the word before the smell reached her.

Nan sat straighter, squinted into the moon-brightened sky.

Her stomach dropped. "Heath, look." An orange glow in the distance—too high to be the stable, the carriage house, the sheds or alcoves or gardens. Too high to be anything but Bletherton Manor itself.

Pity circled around her, deepening the chill as their gig drew them closer. Heaven only knew how Lady Julia was enduring this nightmare. How any of them were. How could this keep happening?

Halfway up the cobbled driveway, a cluster of servants halted the gig. A sooty-looking footman, devoid of his wig, approached with two buckets sloshing at his knees. "Who're you?"

"A servant from Dorrington." Heath had already reminded Nan that the role of servant-mistress must be played to perfection—for her own sake. "Bringing Miss Duncan at her ladyship's request."

Some of the footman's wariness eased. "Al' right then, down with the both o' you. Care to offer your hands, fellow? East wing's still in flames."

Heath swung Nan down. "And her ladyship?"

"I shall show Miss Duncan to my mother." This came from behind as a dark-cloaked Lord Somerset dismounted his horse. He whipped the reins at another servant. "Get this bloody gig out of the way along with my mount. Another wagon of water is coming through."

Servants scurried to obey, Heath was loaded with two buckets and whisked away, and Nan was left awaiting Lord Somerset to come through on his promise.

He stared at her through blackened cheeks and wild, moonlit eyes. "My mother has sent for you, has she?"

"Yes."

"How infinitely bored you must become with our trifle affairs." Disdain marked each syllable as he ripped the topper from his head. "Are you so refined, Miss Duncan, that you dare not ask? Come now, I know you too well. You must be oozing madly with curiosity."

"You are in terrible error, I fear. In regards to your first remark, I could never be bored with the heartache of others. As for the latter, you do not know me at all."

"A point we can both be grateful for." He grabbed her forearm with greater force than necessary, then marched her across smooth, symmetrical cobblestones. Every step clomped and clinked, the noise mingling with shouts, flames, and chaos. "Since you are too gracious to inquire, I shall tell you freely. Someone set Bletherton Manor into flames with every intention of crumbling it to ashes."

"There is no way it might have been an accident?"

"Do not be a fool. It is all deliberate and savage—moves of an adversary desperate to meet his goals."

"Which are?"

"If I knew, Miss Duncan, I would not allow it to continue, now would I?"

"I suppose you wouldn't." They passed a flock of servants, all running with empty buckets, as a wagon came rushing to their left. Glancing to his profile in search of a reaction, she dropped her voice. "There *is* one matter that has piqued me though, my lord, which I would breach decorum to address."

"By all means." He tugged her along the driveway's perimeter, out of the way, where they walked in the shadow of tall, endless boxwoods. "The devil with decorum."

"How often do you frequent the Simon and Cat?"

His steps faltered. Eyes snapped to hers. "What are you suggesting?"

"Nothing, my lord. I merely asked you a question."

"An insane one. I have never been there in my life." He picked up his pace again—fast, stiff, his hand tightening on her flesh. "I insist you not repeat the question to anyone else. Understood?"

"Is that a confession?"

A string of choice words left his lips. He lunged her between two boxwoods, behind them, then clamped his hand across her lips. Her heart spiked. "You have taken great liberties, Miss Duncan, and I shall thank you to take them no further."

Fright seeped in, raced the flow of her blood. "Mmm, mmm, mmm—"

"Silence."

"Mmm—"

"Listen." He loosened his grip on her mouth and slid his other hand to her neck. "If I have ever visited the Simon and Cat, it was to meet you. We have met many a night, the location prime choice for the sake of both our reputations. I wonder what Mother would think were she to know Lord Humphries's devoted ladylove first soiled herself with the roguish elder brother?"

"What lies—"

"Lies are more ravishing than truth, aren't they now?"

"What are you saying?"

"I should think it would be obvious."

"Surely your reputation would suffer more greatly than mine at such a tale. . .surely you would not defame yourself with such disgrace."

"A man can resist only so long, can he not?" She shuddered as he leaned closer. "I have denied you endless times for my own brother's sake—but you have pursued me so ardently, how could I withhold?"

"You are vile and despicable."

"An attribute I claim, if not take pride in. Now should you like to talk more of the Simon and Cat?"

"Your involvement there must be heinous, indeed."

"That was not the question."

"Wasn't it?"

He ripped away from her so quickly she stumbled into the soft foliage of a boxwood. His glare cut her through a hundred ways before he forced a grin. "I believe this discussion is finished, Miss Duncan. I am anxious to see if you are going to follow through with this little unnecessary task lacking wisdom." He held out his arm. "Shall we find Mother?"

She didn't want to touch him, to face such proximity again.

But she was too afraid of what he might do if she didn't. Without looking at his face, she folded her arm around his, some of her fear diminishing when they stepped back to the noisy drive. Just before they reached the manor and were prepared to climb the steps, however, he stopped again. He bent close to her ear, his breath against her cheek. "At least I can take comfort in one point."

Her teeth clenched without answer.

"If you do speak of our little secret, I shall take fervent pleasure in watching Lord Humphries get rid of you. That is," he said with a final grin, "something I am very desirous to see."

CHAPTER 18

"Well." The wigless footman, Giles, clapped a wet hand on Heath's shoulder. "Seems e'ery last little flame is out for good, eh?"

Heath tossed out the remaining water in his bucket. He glanced up, studied the damage for the first time in an hour.

The east wing was a ruin. Black, charred walls. Windows already missing their draperies. Beams that were creaking and moaning as if at any moment part of the roof might fall in.

"Thanks be for a windless night." Giles brushed endless ashes from his livery. "With a bit o' a breeze, could've been the whole manor up in flames."

"Any notion how it started?"

"We've all got our notions. Some says it was Cook, idle woman that she be, setting some bit of cloth or such too near the hearth. Others say it was her ladyship, as her quarters are on the east wing, and how like as not, she overturned a candle."

"And you?"

"I only do what I'm told. Not employed to think, you know—but I do know this." The footman's thin, grimy face cocked to one side. "I was planning to sleep in the butler's pantry this night on account her ladyship has been fretting terrible o'er the family silver."

"And?"

"And not minutes 'fore the fire, a strange feeling struck me, so's I went to the window and glanced about. Know what I seen? A man, that's what. Running in the evening dusk, fast as you please."

"See his face?"

"No, too far away. But I couldn't help noticing how he escaped the grounds, how he lunged off into the garden and then was gone."

"Is that so strange?"

"I suppose not. It's just that there's only one way out of Bletherton from the garden, and that be squeezing through the wall by yanking out them four loose stones."

"Maybe he's still there. Maybe he didn't leave at all."

"A'ready thought of that. I combed the whole garden, I did, and know what I found? The gap in the wall, the moved stones. . .and not just any sort of chap would know how to wiggle them loose." Giles's chin moved up and down with certainty. "Had to have been someone who knows Bletherton well, who knew the garden well. . .who'd been through the wall before."

Julia's hands were icy, clammy, her grip so tight that Nan longed to withdraw from the touch and flex her own fingers.

But she didn't. She returned the squeeze every so often and offered small smiles in return for Julia's silent shudders.

"Hmm, let us see." Mr. Goody stood across the parlor—one of the rooms that the fire had left untouched—and seemed to be scribbling notes inside his brain. "The carriage, the gazebo, the magpie, the fire. Have I missed anything, Constable Hearne?"

The short, overly large lawman shrugged.

"The poison," Nan answered instead and met the magistrate's startled gaze, as until now she had remained in silence.

Her ladyship huffed from her chair. "Did I not specifically request young Stanhope to be here tonight?"

"You did, my lady, but he—"

"There is no excuse. I requested him to be here and so he should have been." The dowager turned toward Mr. Goody and Constable Hearne, started to say something, then coughed against the scent of smoke. "Oh, this wretched air. Aylmer, open a window!"

Lord Humphries stepped forward. "But Mother, the air outside is—"

"Never mind. Sit down and keep quiet, won't you?" Back to Mr. Goody, she frowned. "As I was saying, Stanhope would have told you, had he been here, of the shocking events that took place upon his last visit."

"Since he *isn't* here, suppose you be so kind as to recount the event yourself."

Between handkerchief-covered coughs and several unrelated complaints, her ladyship managed to fill in the magistrate and constable on the poison catastrophe. Nan supplied any details left out.

Mr. Goody locked his hands behind his back. "This is all very interesting, I'm sure. Why was the constable not informed before tonight? I should think this would be a matter brought to him after the carriage seat defacement. Do you not value your property, my lady?"

"I certainly do!" Her breast swelled with outrage. "How dare you insinuate I don't."

"Then why have you kept these events secret instead of informing those who could prevent them?"

"And soil my reputation? I would not hear of it."

"I fear everyone shall hear of it now." The magistrate spoke with a slight lift of his lips, as if the whole ordeal were somewhat amusing. "Let us get to business. Who is the culprit in all of this mishap?"

"If I knew that, Mr. Goody, I would not have called for you."

Another hint of a smile. "Well, we shall just have to keep our eyes open, shan't we?"

"Is that all you have to say?"

"For the moment. Anyone else have something of value to add?"

Constable Hearne made his usual quiet shrug.

Lord Humphries and Lord Somerset both shook their heads, while Lady Julia merely wiped her eyes and looked away.

From the other side of the room, a door clicked open. Heath entered with clothes wet and sullied, but at the sight of so many, he colored and started to retreat—

"Wait a moment, fellow." The magistrate's booming tone lured him back into the doorframe. "You're the. . .the. . ." His finger snapped. "The witness in the Coombs's case, of course. Step in, won't you?"

Her ladyship straightened. "I say, who is this anyway? Just because the house is in flames doesn't mean we accept uninvited callers, you know. Are we to lose all semblance of pride in one night?"

Heath bowed, his eyes never once drifting to Nan. "Miss Duncan's escort, my lady. The servants told me I might find her here."

"You might have waited outside the door. Obviously, you have never been taught decent propriety—and my goodness, you are dripping upon my carpet."

Before Heath could answer, the magistrate spoke. "I cannot say it is a pleasure to see you again, fellow, but it does save me a bit of work in finding you later."

Heath turned to face him. "Sir?"

"The letter arrived. You are to appear on January the sixth of the year eighteen hundred fourteen at the Assize Court in Taunton, Somerset, to act as witness. Clear enough?"

"Yes, sir."

"Good, because I never repeat myself." He planted his beaver hat atop his head then, smiled at the dowager, and made a slight bow. "The constable and I will make our farewells. As the night is closing in, I do suggest we all go and find our bedchambers."

Nan took the cue most willingly. With one last bit of pressure to Lady Julia's hand, she stood and whispered, "Do take heart, my lady, and try to get some rest."

The woman nodded without expression. "My bedchamber is gone, you know."

"Never mind, Sister." This came from Lord Humphries, as he neared and took Nan's arm. "We shall find you something more suitable anyway. Miss Duncan, can I drive you home?"

"No, my. . .servant shall do nicely, thank you."

"Very well. Until we meet again." Without warning, he lifted her hand to his lips and pressed hard in a kiss that was surely driven by devotion and passion.

Her soul only sighed as she pulled her hand away. "Good night, my lord." With a quick bow to the dowager and a stiff nod to Lord Somerset, Nan followed the magistrate, the constable, and her brother from the smoke-scented parlor. She couldn't help wishing she'd never have to return, never have to see any of them again—including Lord Humphries.

Which was all wrong, of course.

After all, wasn't she supposed to be falling in love with him?

Cool night air rustled Temperance's dress as she eased down Dorrington's great stone steps in the darkness. "Is that you, Miss Duncan?"

As the gig drew to a stop, moonlight illuminated the two passengers.

And made her heartbeat erratic.

"Yes, Temperance." The voice carried across the night, but she hardly heard. She was too enamored with the way Heath Duncan glanced her way twice, the way he slid from the gig and swung down his sister, the way he came closer when he had every excuse to walk away.

"Did you hear me?"

Temperance started.

Miss Duncan stood next to her on the third step, brows raised, ringlets swaying in the breeze. "I said I do hope no one waited up for me. Have they?"

"Mrs. Stanhope would have. She was frightfully perturbed when she realized Master Gilbert had not accompanied you. Between Mr. Stanhope's coaxing and my insistence that I would wait up for you, she finally retired."

"I am glad. You were kind to wait for me." With a slight smile that seemed more distracted than anything else, Miss Duncan continued up the steps.

Leaving Temperance alone.

With Heath.

She ought not remain in the dark with a man who so altered the pace of her blood flow. But she couldn't have moved if she'd wanted to.

Because Heath was coming closer. He reached the base of the steps and looked up.

"You look very dirty." Why couldn't she let him speak for once? What sort of thing was that to say anyway?

He smiled, rubbed one of his cheeks, glanced back up with a sooty gleam. "You look very pretty."

Never had such a small set of words set her soul to such frenzy. She couldn't say anything. Didn't even know if she wanted to.

Heath must not have expected a response. With one last smile, he walked back to the gig and led it away.

Papa had returned. His presence changed everything—made the cottage walls feel smaller, made the predawn darkness deeper.

Heath was awake. He should have risen and said something to welcome the old man back home. Had it been the rector, wouldn't he have hurried to greet him?

Of course he would have. He would have helped him off with his coat and asked questions. The rector would have answered. He would have prepared something hot to drink. They would have retired to the hearth and sipped in silence that was warm and comforting.

That's the way it had been with the two of them. Always understanding. Always enough. Always contented and at ease—with God, with each other, with everything.

But Papa wasn't the rector.

Nor was he the same man Heath remembered as a little boy. The one who sat with Nan on his lap, humming Gaelic tunes or singing little songs or smiling around his pipe.

That man was gone, lost forever, and buried deep beneath the worn shell of a stooped, bitter old seaman.

Heath couldn't please him. Couldn't love him. Couldn't even be the son Papa expected him to be. How could this happen? How could flesh and blood become such chains to him?

God, help me.

For close to an hour, Papa wandered about the cottage. He muttered to himself, stumbled more than once, cursed in the fading darkness. Finally, with one last thud, the cottage went silent.

Heath rose and found Papa as he'd expected—limp, dirty, passed out at the foot of an untidy cot.

With a grunt, Heath hefted him up. He eased his body onto the cot and pulled a thin coverlet over the unconscious form.

Clasped in the old man's hand was a scratched trinket box. It had belonged to Heath's mother. The madam had kept it in her chamber, filled it with her hairpins and ribbons, forbidden Nan and him to touch it.

Heath tugged it from Papa's limp fingers and opened the tiny lid. A rush of memories attacked him—the day he'd sneaked into the madam's room, how he'd hugged it close and tried to imagine his mother, the prickling fear when Madame Le Sueur caught him and ripped it away. She'd hurt him that day. She'd made him bleed and weep. She'd terrorized the room with her punishing screams.

No good in it. He snapped the lid shut and returned the box to Papa's side. He left and pulled the cottage door shut behind him.

The early morning grass crunched beneath his feet. *No good in trying to bring it all back, Papa.* Why had returning to the Bobber been so important to him? Couldn't he see how pointless it was?

There was no changing what already was.

There would never be room for tomorrow until Papa let go of every yesterday—and all of its hurt.

She was troubled. Gilbert had learned all the signs through the years. He recognized that faint flicker of uncertainty in all of her glances.

Before, he would have followed her. He would have tugged her somewhere quiet, asked all the right questions, done anything to inspire a laugh.

He missed making Nan Duncan laugh. Missed bantering with her. Missed being the recipient of all her happy smiles. How long had it been? An hour, a day?

No, longer than a day—only days weren't making sense anymore. He couldn't remember the moment everything had changed. He only knew it had. He couldn't remember when seeing her changed from contentment to anguish, when eating at the same table banished his hunger, when sleeping became tormented with dreams of her.

He was right to stay away. If she was troubled, he couldn't help her. Couldn't pacify her worries. Couldn't make everything all right as he'd always done before.

He went straight from the breakfast table to the study, straight from the study to the stable. He rode long and hard. Didn't return until he knew dinner would be finished and Nan wouldn't see him slip up the stairs.

Even in his room, he slid the door closed and turned the lock. Alone, so alone—but it had to be this way. *God, why?*

He jerked out his trunk and flung open the lid. Grabbed his clothes, his shoes, a few books he'd never cared to read before. Maybe now he would appreciate literature. Anything to take him out of this dashed house.

A tap sounded on the door. "Gil?"

After all he'd been through to avoid her, he should have been angry at the sound of her voice.

But he wasn't. Couldn't be.

He threw open the door. "Yes?"

She stood hand in hand with Charlotte, the pair of them looking lost, unsure—as if at any moment a beast might sink his teeth into them. Had he really been such a brute?

"Where are you going?" asked Charlotte, who looked unnaturally serious.

He didn't answer. Just stood there.

Nan's eyes held his. "Can we come in?"

"What the deuce for?"

"You can't expect to go anywhere with a trunk like that."

"Why not?"

Nan frowned. "Did you simply throw everything in without any thought at all?" Tugging Charlotte with her, Nan squeezed past Gil and invaded the sanctuary of his private chamber. How quickly her smell filled the air, suffocated him with its sweetness.

"Why are you bringing these?" Of course Charlotte would question the books.

Even Nan raised a brow in question. "What sort of place are you going to? All these fine clothes but not one cravat?"

He approached the trunk, pulled down the lid. "I wasn't finished."

"No?"

"No."

Charlotte plunged onto his bed. "Where are you going?"

He didn't know. London, Bath...maybe one of the balls he had invitations for but hadn't bothered to answer.

"Well?" Charlotte again, twirling her curl. "Where?"

He almost said something sharp, something that might have made her cry again. Instead, he drew in air and walked to the window.

Nan must have sensed his despair. She ushered Charlotte away. The door opened and shut. Nan sighed as she opened the trunk again.

Neither spoke.

She must have folded everything, added all the things he'd forgotten, while Gilbert merely stared into the night.

When he turned, she wouldn't look at him. "That should be everything you need."

Not quite.

"How long will you be gone?"

Forever, if he had the strength. But he didn't. He would always be drawn back. As long as Nan was here.

"Gil, there is something. . ." Lingering off into tears. "Tell me why you won't look at me anymore."

"I do." He was looking at her now. Couldn't she see that?

She glanced away, turned back to the trunk, and fumbled with a lock that was already in place. "I've enough burden without you making me feel as if I've wronged you."

"Wronged me?"

"Isn't that it?"

"No."

"Then—"

"What burdens?" Couldn't help himself, couldn't stay away. Came closer and pried her shaking hands from the lock. Squeezed them tight. "Look up. That's it. What burdens?"

"I'm afraid to speak of them."

"Why?"

"I don't know what is right. I don't know if speaking the truth is my place, especially if that truth can only bring shame."

"Shame?"

"And reproach and dishonor. . .not only to someone of high standing but also to myself. Do you imagine that people could believe in terrible lies?"

He couldn't follow the questions or make sense of them. "I don't know."

"How could you? I don't even know myself."

"If this truth renders such grievous consequences, you must consider it carefully. You must decide what good could come from it and if that good is worth the penalties."

"And if there is no good to come from it?"

"Then that is your answer."

There it was. The trust, the wonder in her eyes, the fond twinkle he'd grown so used to over the years.

Then she did something he wasn't prepared for. She leaned forward and kissed his cheek. Just a faint touch, meaningless by her account.

But it struck the very core of his being. Made his blood race like madness until he got lost betwixt the hot flash of pain and the cool stir of passion.

"Wherever you are going, do not stay long." She smiled like the child she still believed she was to him. "For I shall miss you infinitely."

Not half as much as he'd miss her.

CHAPTER 19

Heath galloped Golda through frigid morning fog, where the road led him to Dorrington's gates. The place felt different now. No longer stones and statues and unapproachable heights. Instead, the grounds welcomed him like the rectory always had with its gardens or the church with its polished pew boxes.

Some days, as he forked straw in the stables or polished harnesses in the carriage house, Nan would visit him. Other times, young Charlotte would appear—pestering, laughing, hiding his tools, or mothering his horse.

Then Temperance. Not a day passed that she didn't come and seem happier than the day before. Sometimes they talked. Other times, they smiled and blushed in silence.

They both knew. How could they not?

The rector had told Heath this would happen. One day, he'd said, there would be a village girl who would be different. He wouldn't be able to ignore her. This one would be new and exciting, and there would be something in her soul that would speak to his.

That made music, the rector had said. That birthed love.

But however sweet and elating were the daytimes, nighttime always fell with dread. He would leave Dorrington Hall and all its comforts. He would return to the broken cottage where a drunken old man waited for him.

There might be shouting, cursing, accusing, other times crying and begging for forgiveness and wailing out to the name of God.

Whichever came, Heath said nothing. Maybe because Papa was right. Heath was a coward. A fool who'd rather forgive than avenge, or pray than fight, or forget than remember.

No matter what Papa thought, the rector would have been proud anyway.

Heath must remember that.

❧

Another letter that wasn't for Nan. How many did that make?

One for each week. Two weeks, then. No, three.

Mr. Stanhope folded it back at the breakfast table, made some laughing remark about how bored Gil must be in life to go traipsing from ball to ball. "At this astounding rate, I should not be surprised at all if our Gilbert misses Christmastide entirely."

"Do not say such things," said Mrs. Stanhope.

"Yes." From the sidebar, Charlotte spoke without turning. "He promised to get me something grand this year, and if he doesn't, I shall be very dismayed."

Nan excused herself before anything more could be said. Of course Gilbert would be back for Christmas. Had there ever been a holiday he had missed?

No.

Never.

He had always returned, as eager for bantering or playing or laughing as she was. Why, he'd always—

"Miss Duncan!" Temperance whisked from an open door, catching Nan before she ascended the steps. "I was on my way to the breakfast room, but here you are. Did someone already tell you?"

"Tell me what?"

"Lord Humphries has arrived. Looking dapper and a bit nervous, he is. Do you suppose he wishes to ask you something?"

"Really, Temperance, do not carry on so."

"I am sorry, Miss Duncan, it's just that he's been coming so much, and I thought perhaps. . ." The sentence faded with Nan's stern look, followed by a quick apology and curtsy. "Forgive me again, Miss Duncan. Excuse me." With a smile she couldn't seem to help, her maid hurried in the other direction.

Her words, however, did not.

They stayed long and thumped hard, like a hammer to an anvil. *Nervous.* The word came back at her. *Lord Humphries. . .nervous. . .ask you something. . .*

Was it possible?

No, not so soon. Not when they hardly knew each other. Not when their laughs were always forced, when every touch still made her itch, when her betraying mind still imagined him as a dragon.

Which he wasn't, of course. And never would be again.

With that resolve, she approached the drawing room. Lord Humphries stood where he always did lately—at the lounge, grinning, practically oozing with all the sweet words he was ready to drip upon her.

If only she enjoyed receiving them as much as he enjoyed giving them.

"My darling. Is that a new gown, or do you make every dress look so exquisite?"

She glanced down at the white muslin. Chuckled, more at the oddity than anything else. "No, my lord. I fear this is just an ordinary morning dress."

"Which you greatly complement. I hope I did not disturb you from letter writing or breakfast?"

"I have just finished the latter."

"Good." A pause, a smile too wide to be natural. Perhaps Temperance had been correct to say he was nervous. "Good, won't you sit?"

For the ninth day in a row, she sat beside him and clasped her hands. Why they could not take carriage rides or walks or *something* was quite beyond her. But it was not a lady's place to suggest the pastime—and if Lord Humphries wanted to sit here day after day, who was she to say otherwise?

He talked of Almack's Club.

She talked of Gil and his long absence.

Then the uncomfortable silence again, as always. Why was it so difficult? Why couldn't they talk without effort, without thought or meaning or purpose?

If Gil were here, it would have been different. They would have chatted about little things. Things that didn't matter. Things they could disagree on or laugh about or solve on their own.

At least they did not have to sit in graceless silence all the time, scrambling for the next intelligent matter to discuss.

Lord Humphries rose. "This is very difficult."

She might have agreed, but something about his manner was too somber to respond to. He crossed the room and pivoted back around.

He stared at her. Long, hard, with passion that made cool sweat dampen her palms. Then he stepped closer, closer again—and she knew what was happening.

"Darling, I—"

"Excuse me, my lord." She jumped to her feet, told herself to sit back down, to apologize, to allow him to propose a marriage.

But she couldn't.

Before he could say another word, she dashed from the room and didn't look back.

No matter how many times Temperance made the short journey from house to stable, the same dancing wings still fluttered in her stomach. She told herself they shouldn't. After all, by this time, shouldn't those dear wings have flown away?

Shouldn't the visits have descended from the celestial to the terrestrial? Shouldn't Heath Duncan have grown tired of her and shrunken away with indifference?

That's how it always was. Her imagination and overly enthused heart were always making matters greater, feelings sharper, life brighter.

Then reality came, like a brutal knight with lance and dagger, slashing through all her illusions. She told herself that. She clung to that and hoped it would somehow be of help when everything fell apart.

But when she strolled to the stables, reality ran and hid. Her enthused heart became a little more enthused. And the wings in her stomach multiplied by hundreds when she found, upon each new afternoon, that Heath Duncan still cared for her.

He never said how much. But if his eyes spoke truth when his gaze met hers, then he cared very much.

Maybe as much as she did. Maybe enough that the care was turning to love.

When she reached the stable doors, she hesitated long enough for her blush to fade. Silly, that. Wouldn't she blush again when he smiled at her?

She pushed her way inside the empty stables. Instead of calling out, she peeked into the carriage house doorway, then the harness room. Both empty. Perhaps Heath had been sent out on an errand or—

"My." Hands enfolded her from behind with an unwelcome and too familiar smell. "Out here a-lookin' for lover boy again, is ye?"

She twisted around and stepped free of his clasp. "Please. . .don't."

"What?"

What was the use of answering? Loftus never listened to her anyway. She turned to leave—

"Tut, tut." He stepped in front of her. "Ye can't leave yet. Ye came out here for romance, didn't ye? Romance ye'll bloody have, then."

"Loftus, please."

"Please what? Ye used to kiss me, ye know. Or don't ye remember that no more?"

"We must both try our best to forget. Now if you will please step out of my way, I will leave you to your duties, which you are currently neglecting, and I will—"

"Shut up for once in yer life." He caught her again, swung her into a shadowed stall. Pressed her against the wall. "Now listen to me, Temp. I ain't goin' to do this no more. That Duncan fellow. . .he's not for ye. I'll not see ye dallyin' around here no more, talkin' to him, smilin' to him and such."

"Loftus—"

"I'm going to marry ye. That's the way it always were, all them years, and no blackguard stranger's goin' to walk in and change that."

Uncommon anger hurdled across her chest. "Release me this moment."

"No."

"I could never ever be prevailed upon to marry you."

"Ye always wanted to before."

"Loftus—"

"But that Duncan fellow, that worm of a rogue. . .he changed everything." His face dipped closer, intensity lifting his brows. "Why, I'm twice the man he is, Temp. I'll prove it to ye. I'll fix that Duncan until ye ne'er want to see him again—"

"Loftus, no!" She pushed against him. "You cannot!"

"I will. Then ye'll know which man ye want, the one who can fight for ye and win."

"No, you cannot. I beg of you. Please!"

But he didn't listen. He backed away from her, muttering nonsense about beating the nose from Duncan's bleeding face.

Then he left.

Temperance couldn't do a thing to stop him.

"Papa, I can't." From the cottage doorway, Nan spoke the words without blinking. "I'm sorry, but I cannot love him."

He sat at the kitchen table, hands folded in front of him, and didn't even rise at her presence. His eyes lanced through her. "You can and you will."

"I fear it is impossible."

"Not so."

"I cannot even enjoy him, let alone marry—"

A wrinkled hand slammed the table, cut off her sentence, disrupted her heartbeat with a hint of fear. Then he rose. "Come here, girl, and stand in front of me."

She hesitated.

"Come on now, Nan. Come closer."

Each step she moved raised her discomfort, like a hard wind rolls the waters into waves. When she finally stood before him, he did no more than pull a small trinket box from his coat.

Mother's. A new emotion stirred. One that brought back so much. The echo of pain, all the childish fears, the sights and smells and agonies of the Bobber.

She wasn't ready when Papa thrust it into her hands. "Here." Rough, raspy voice. "'Tis right that a girl should have something of her mother's."

"I don't want this." She didn't know why. No more than she wanted to stand this close to Papa or marry Lord Humphries the Dragon.

"Only pretty thing she ever had."

"Papa—"

"All her bleedin' life was one disappointment after another, your mother. Never had anything. Never got anything she ever wanted."

Tears moistened Nan's eyes.

"Were she to know about you, she'd want the same things I want. She'd want you to marry that bloke who's winning you. She'd want you to reach out and grasp the kind of life she could only ever dream of."

"But I—"

"Don't forget where you came from, girl." His hand and hook framed her face. "Filthy rags, hunger, God-forsaken poverty. We're nothings, Nan. The both of us. If there's happiness waitin' for you in this cursed world—"

"There is no happiness." A pause. "Papa, there is no happiness waiting for me with a man I don't love."

"Won't love." His hand lowered, squeezed. "You're just like your coward of a brother. You won't fight. You won't try. You just lay down like a bloody fool and let the world beat you around." More words, harsh curses—and his squeeze turned into punishment.

Perhaps she should have fought, flung herself away, and escaped the scorn. But in the end, she only cried. "I—I'm sorry." Trembling, weak. "I'm sorry, Papa. . .I'm sorry."

"Don't do no bloody good unless you fight, unless you do what I tell you, unless you think about your mother and what she would've wanted."

"I—I will."

"Will what?"

"I will try again. . .I shall try to care for him, to love him. . .if it means so much to you."

"It does." The calloused fingers eased away from her face. The anger fled, the warmth returned. How it burned in his liquid eyes and made his voice less menacing. "My girl. You're the one I can be proud of. . .the only thing keeping me alive. You know that, don't you? If you were to disappoint me too, I'd probably end everything. I swear, I'd end everything." He pushed her mother's box against her shuddering chest. "Now get out of here, girl." He fell back into his chair and wrapped his hands around a half-empty bottle. "I don't want to see you again until you're ready to be a bride."

Pain and dread cramped her stomach as she fled from the cottage. Why did the marriage mean so much to him? Why couldn't he just grab her onto his lap, hum the old songs, and be the papa the little girl inside of her still needed?

Dusk came with cold winds and slight flurries of snow. The two gray phaeton geldings, which Heath had been sent to Wydenshire to retrieve, clomped behind Golda with gaits that almost perfectly aligned.

Good breed, these two. Mr. Stanhope would be pleased with the purchase.

Something moved ahead. A man, a horse, too far away to become distinguishable. Then a voice roared out from the center of the road. "Duncan!"

Heath tapped his heel into Golda's side and urged the animals faster. As the distance lessened, the man's face became clear—and so did his wrath.

"Loftus." Heath halted all three horses. Nodded in greeting. "Mr. Caddy was waiting with the geldings when I—"

"Get down."

One of Heath's brows rose.

Loftus swung from his mount and glared up, muscles bunching beneath his brown coat. "Get down now, or I'll yank ye down meself."

"Why?"

"So I can tear into ye and break ye in pieces."

Why? What had he done to so anger the man? "I don't want to fight you."

"Ye're going to."

"I have no reason."

"I do."

Heath shook his head, made a remark about Loftus mounting up and riding home. Then, without response to Loftus's shouts, he eased Golda forward—

"You dog! You coward of a wretched mongrel!" A rock whizzed through the air. Then another—and it struck Heath's shoulder blade with force and pain.

Heath yanked the reins.

Loftus stopped shouting.

Silence and snow swiveled around the air and deepened the cold in Heath's veins. Didn't want to fight, but he dismounted anyway. Didn't want to feel the anger, but it crept up his spine and infested his blood. Didn't want to tie the horses to a tree branch and take those few steps between them, but now there was no choice.

Loftus swung first. His fist smashed Heath's nose, brought blood, then Heath's stroke hurled in return. At first it was back and forth, a blow for a blow. One down, the other up. The other down, the one up.

But every time the knuckles bashed Heath's face, something hot seared his soul. Some raw, unfound rage unleashed. A legion of old fears and long-ago pains and unspeakable hate rose until he couldn't see for the agony of remembering.

"Little rat. . .little mendicant. . ."

Madame Le Sueur's fists, but this time Heath fought back.

"You are a garçon ingrate. . .garçon ingrate. . ."

Pounding, pounding, pounding. Loftus was down, but it didn't matter. Still pounding. Over and over and over again until the madam couldn't hurt him. Couldn't hit him. Couldn't fight back.

God, help me.

A whimper.

Help me stop.

Another faint sound broke from Loftus's bloody lips, with the same pleading and helplessness as when Heath had begged for mercy.

The madam had never given him any.

But Heath would. Because it was right. Because there should always be mercy, just as the rector had told him, just as God would wish it.

With shaking hands, Heath fisted the brown coat and yanked Loftus to his wobbly feet.

The man shook free. "Blackguard." The scowl accompanied a dribble of blood. "A pox on you, you wretched. . .dog."

Heath turned away—

Another rock. It smacked the back of Heath's skull and made his legs give out beneath him.

Then Loftus appeared, dripping blood on Heath's face, starting back a fight that should have been finished. His fists showered down without mercy, without any mercy.

Dear God, I can't. All the bands of forbearance snapped. Heath rolled twice, escaped the blows, pushed to his feet, and lunged.

Then his knuckles made one last throw at Loftus's face. The man crumpled to the ground, hit the rocks. The snow drifted and landed soundlessly upon a face gone still and pale.

Heath wiped his nose, his mouth. Would have turned and walked away but couldn't seem to make himself.

Because the longer he stood looking over top the man's body, the more blood seeped out beneath the back of his head.

And the more Loftus looked like a corpse.

Nan crumpled the seventh letter and tossed the ridiculous thing to the floor. She wiped more tears and reached for another paper, but would it do any good?

She didn't know what to say. *I am sorry, Lord Humphries, for dashing from the room upon realization that you were about to propose?*

His lordship was far too sensitive for such candor.

Forgive me, my lord, for such a hasty departure—I fear I had a most vicious headache?

Gilbert would chide her for that answer. If she were going to give any excuse, she must find a way to do so without resorting to cowardly lies. Then again, why not?

Everything about this, even from the very beginning, was a lie. Her attentions to the dragon. Her smiles to him. Her encouraging gestures. How long could she go on playing this game, pretending she could fall in love with a man she'd only ever been annoyed with?

But Papa was right. Of course he was right. It was the only answer that made sense.

She'd never tried to begin with. She'd gone through countless motions and fulfilled the part without ever whispering love to her heart. Love was a choice, after all. Why not Lord Humphries?

He was handsome, courteous, pleasant, flattering, respected, wealthy.

Everything she could ask for.

Everything Papa wanted for her—expected of her.

She tried not to think of his fingers pressed into her flesh, his rage making her quiver, feeling trapped for the first time in years. She'd do nearly anything not to face that again. She'd try as hard as she knew how. She'd devote herself to Lord Humphries and stop waiting for warm flutters or pulsing heartbeats.

None of that mattered.

Love was more than that, more than feelings or thoughts or preferences—and in the end, she'd realize that all of this must be right.

She dipped her goose ink pen and began letter number eight. Her hand shook when she penned words she didn't mean with endearment that seemed unnatural. More than once, she had to dab away tears, lest they drip onto the letter and leave smearing evidence of her unhappiness—

The door behind banged open.

Nan jumped. "Temperance, what is—"

"It is your brother." The words ricocheted within the bedchamber walls like thunder. Tears swelled in Temperance's eyes as she held her candle higher. "Please come, Miss Duncan. Please come."

All of Nan's emotions numbed, slid to the brink of something she was afraid of. She hurried after her maid through dark halls, down long stairs, through more corridors.

When they reached the foyer, the front entrance was open.

Mr. Stanhope stood along one wall, serious, the reflection of candlelight flickering upon his spectacles. The butler motioned to those outside.

Then footmen came through the doorway.

Carrying a body.

"Is it—"

"Loftus." Temperance choked out the answer before Nan could finish. She reached for Nan's hand and held tight, as if squeezing hard enough would dispel some of the fear.

Then Heath stepped inside. He looked larger, with his blond hair ragged across his forehead and his eyes fixated on the footmen's load. Blood smeared him, evidence of something, but Nan didn't know what.

Temperance must have. "This is all my fault."

No one answered the whispered words. They drifted along the silence and were carried away into the cold night.

Mr. Stanhope stepped forward. "You were right to bring him to the house, son. A servant has been sent for Mr. Puttock. I am certain, with Loftus being as young and strong as he is, that he will recover from this—"

"I wanted to kill him." Heath's eyes lifted to the ceiling, crammed shut. Then the words came again with a trace of tears. "God forgive me, but I wanted to kill him."

Ice stabbed Nan's chest. What was he saying?

Temperance waited until the apothecary had arrived, until the rest of the house was too busy to notice, before she donned her red cloak and slipped outside.

She was certain where to find him.

Nan said he'd probably gone home, but Temperance knew better. She knew he'd be waiting at the stables. She knew where he'd be standing and what look would be marring his face.

But she didn't know why he'd murmured those words.

The ones about killing.

About *wanting* to kill.

Perhaps if there were not a dying man lying in the upstairs of Dorrington Hall, she could have dismissed such a self-accusation.

But there *was* a dying man—and the words spun around her brain and made senseless jabs at her bewildered heart. How could it come to this?

She should have warned Heath. Why hadn't she? Much better to ride into Wydenshire alone, shirking her duties here, than to see a man dead. For the thousandth time in her life, she'd done the wrong thing.

And it was costing her again.

Fingers numb with cold, she entered the stables and approached the farthest stall to the left. Golda's stall. The stall they'd smiled in and laughed in and threw straw in so many times.

He stood with the look of one condemned. His hand made steady strokes—down Golda's neck, across her side, back to the neck again. He didn't glance up. "He is dead?"

"No." Temperance halted at the stall's edge. "Mr. Puttock is with him now."

A nod, more strokes.

"Are you injured? If so, you may as well return to the house and allow the apothecary to—"

"No." Deep, heavy. "I am uninjured."

Except for his eyes. They were wounded in ways she couldn't comprehend, to a degree very strange for one usually so quiet, so calm, so kind.

"Heath. . .I am sorry." Another step toward him. "I beg of you to forgive me, for I should have found you and told you. Loftus had already spoke to me of his plans, see, and I knew he wanted to fight and—"

"Doesn't matter."

"Oh, but it does! It is all my fault, see, because—"

"Temperance, no." In two steps, he was out of the stall, grabbing her, holding her, crushing her in their first embrace. "Nothing is your fault."

How wonderful to be held against him, enclosed in his warmth, his strength—yet it hurt to be so near his pain. Every heartbeat thudded against her. His breath eased in and out of her hair.

"Why did you say it?" Her whisper escaped with tears. "Why did you say such things about killing him? I know you could not have meant it, could not possibly have meant such things."

"It is true."

"No."

"I wanted to. . .when he hit me I just. . ." Silence. Then deeper. "There was one other time."

"What?"

"Years ago, after the rector took me in, there were village boys. They hit me, and I couldn't hold back. I tried to. Heaven knows I tried, but I couldn't."

"What are you saying?"

"I don't know."

"The boys. . .what happened?"

"One had broken bones. The other was unconscious."

"And Loftus?"

The question hung without answer. Then his arms tightened around her, and his murmur came out agonized. "I didn't want to hurt him. Not at first. But the more he hit me, the more I wanted to stop him until next thing I knew he had...he had stopped moving."

"It is not your fault."

"Isn't it?"

"Nan has told me about that place, about the Bobber. I know what you must have been through all those years and how you must have hated—"

"Doesn't matter." He stepped away faster than she was prepared for. "I shouldn't have fought. I wanted to hurt him, and it was wrong." He glanced down at his hands, his red-stained hands. "I'll never fight again."

CHAPTER 20

*G*ilbert took his first glance of Dorrington Hall without the slightest flinch. No ballroom or smiling maidens had made him forget Nan.

He couldn't live without her, which only meant one thing.

His love had to adjust. He needed to retreat through old territory and return to the old fraternal care, the sweet brotherly affection he used to be content with.

No more running. No more avoiding Nan Duncan as if she were shrouded in some sort of plague. He was finished with all of it. He would settle his mind and, in the end, his heart would learn too.

At least he hoped so.

When the carriage pulled to a stop, Gilbert jumped down without waiting for the footman. Those wide, snowy, ornate steps might have been daunting had he not already discovered his plan.

But he knew what to do when he reached the top, when he saw Nan, so there was no room for pitiful trepidation. Brave sort, he was. Wasn't he?

He entered the foyer with snow blowing in with him.

The butler smiled a soundless greeting, then took his hat, gloves, and overcoat. Even for a dull afternoon in winter, the house seemed a bit quieter than normal. Why was Charlotte not running upstairs? Or Nan playing her pianoforte?

The butler said quietly, "They are in the drawing room, Master Stanhope."

"Thank you." He strode to the drawing room doors. One was cracked open, and he caught both the sight and voice of Nan.

She was seated at the lounge. Only her profile was visible, decorated with springy curls, but she spoke with tones quiet and serious. Something about pity, hope of recovery, then something else he couldn't quite catch—

The crack widened. "Why, Gil." Mamma stepped out, eased the door shut, and reached for his cheeks with both hands. "You did not write you would be coming so soon."

"You know me. I am committed to writing letters as seldom as possible."

"Which is a fault, my son, not something you should boast of." She took his arm and guided him away from the drawing room. "Come, let us find another place to sit. I do not wish to disturb them, and I have countless questions to ask of your journey."

"Why should we disturb them?"

Mamma's sigh filled the silence. "Nan and your father are trying to appease poor Temperance. Let us sit with tea before I explain—"

"Mamma." He stopped her in the hall, his hands on both her shoulders. "Please, I should like to know what goes on."

She nodded, dropped her eyes for a second. "It is Loftus, and the news is grave indeed."

"What happened?"

"A fight. An accident, really, for poor Loftus provoked Nan's brother into blows. Heath Duncan's strength must be greater than he realizes because he brought Loftus back unconscious."

"Has he woken?"

"No."

"How long has it been?"

"Four days." She hesitated long enough to make Gil's chest tighten. "And if he doesn't awaken soon, I fear he never shall."

Pity stirred through Nan's chest.

"Who shall tell Heath?" Temperance sat stiff, erect, sadness mottling her face. "He shall never be able to bear this, such a terrible thing. Who shall tell him what he has done?"

"The damage could have been from the rocks," Nan said, "just as likely as Heath's fist."

Temperance nodded, smeared away more tears. "What small comfort that shall be to any of us. And what of Loftus's parents? Who shall tell them that their young son is gone, that he never opened his eyes again—"

"Temperance." Mr. Stanhope shook his head, too kindly to be a rebuke. "We must not carry on this way. I know we have all lived side by side with Loftus since he was a boy, perhaps you more so than the rest of us. But we cannot change the tide of time, and we cannot restore what is broken. Only God can do such things. And as Mr. Puttock said, the boy may well awaken."

"Yes, Mr. Stanhope. You are right of course, and I shall do everything in my power not to behave so unseemly." Her face scrunched with more tears. "If this whole tragedy were not my fault, I might be able to bear it more easily. But it is my fault, see, and though I have long since realized that I do not love Loftus in such a way that I would marry him, I fear I care for him still. Indeed, I feel utterly responsible."

"As do I," said Mr. Stanhope. "That is why, as I made clear in the letter to his parents, we shall not give up hope until the very end."

Temperance rose. "Indeed, you are right again. Excuse me, but I must go sit with Loftus and see if he—"

"Let me go, Temperance." Nan stood as well. "Please, you must rest. I shall sit with him till evening, hmm?" Without waiting for an answer, Nan exited the drawing room. When she entered Loftus's chamber, she stood by his side.

He was unchanged, still, lifeless almost. What a pity one mistake should cost him so greatly, that in one fit of rage he had lost everything. How many days could a man live like this?

Maybe Mr. Puttock was right. Maybe he would yet awaken. Maybe Heath would not have this guilt yoked upon him forever nor Temperance such terrible sadness intermingled with her newfound love.

"He is too warm, you know."

Nan jerked in surprise.

Gil stood nearby. He looked older. His eyes held no mirth, but warmth and ease radiated from him as always. "Just because a man cannot wake up and say so doesn't mean he does not get hot. Who's been feeding that hearth?"

Nan smiled. Not for any reason, just that seeing him brought comfort into the sadness, light into the dark, hope into the despair. Why did he make everything seem all right?

He moved to the side of the bed and pulled down Loftus's bed linens and counterpane. Gently, he reached for a wet cloth and eased it along the pale, sweating face. "Much better, eh, chap? I say, you shall do anything to get out of work, won't you? Have you no scruples, man?"

Silence.

Gil stared, swallowed, drew back the cloth with a faint look of sorrow.

With a shudder, Nan crept to Gilbert's side. She weaved her arms around him as his arm dropped around her shoulder. "Oh, Gil." A murmur. "Is it not terrible?"

"That is the way of it."

"The way of what?"

"Life." He held her tighter. "We are all destined our lot of pain. No matter who we are or what we do to escape it, somehow or other, that pain will find us, and we shall have to live it out."

"Would to heaven it were not that way."

"Would to heaven it were not."

In four days, Temperance had not been to the stables. Not that he blamed her. Not that he expected her to come. But it hurt.

Everything hurt. All through the day, as he'd glance at the manor house, angst and guilt and fear played games with him. How long would it be? Another day? A day after that?

Then he'd hear the news, the horrible news. They'd carry out the coffin. They'd gather together at the church graveyard, and Temperance would be there with tears. How he dreaded any thought of looking at her—of seeing sadness and blame in eyes that still tried to be soft and kind.

He didn't deserve kindness if the man he'd spent his rage on died.

"Pssst." The small sound drew his attention. When he didn't answer, it came again, louder, "Pssst! Guess where I am?"

Charlotte. Dear, playful Charlotte. Didn't she know what he'd done?

A giggle leaked into the air, and a flash of curls peeked out from a stall.

Heath approached. "Am I close?"

Another giggle.

With a smile he couldn't seem to resist, he leaned over the stall wall where she crouched in waiting.

At the sight of him, she laughed again and stood. Her hands landed on her hips. "Do you know how long I have been there?"

"How long?"

"A long time. I have been watching you, and you did not even know it. Isn't that sport?"

He couldn't imagine what could be so amusing about watching him brush horses, but he shrugged in response.

"You never know where I shall be, do you? I can show up anywhere. I'm awfully quiet when I want to be, aren't I?" She sashayed by him and flipped her hair. "Do you mind terribly if I steal Lady of the Bright Stars for a bit?"

"Do you want her saddled?"

"No. I shall just walk her around the grounds. We like to do that, you know." Leading Golda from her stall, Charlotte started away with a hum trailing after her. Halfway to the door, however, she paused. "Oh, and Mr. Duncan?"

"Yes?"

"I suppose, with Loftus gone, you shall be stable master now, don't you think?" Her young features remained unaltered. "Of course, Papa shan't say anything until after poor Loftus is buried, but I am certain you shall get the position. Then you shall likely stay at Dorrington forever." With one last brisk smile, she disappeared.

Her words left the air bitter and choking.

Because Loftus was dead.

Eating breakfast with her was something of a wonder.

Gilbert sat where he always did, in a chair close enough that he could catch her familiar, maidenly scents. Not that he noticed. By George, he was beyond all that. Now his mission was indifference—and indifference it would be, no matter how many times he had to remind himself.

Nan talked of things that didn't matter. He listened with rapt interest as she laughed and ate and smiled at him a hundred times over. When had her face changed? When had that soft look of child dissolved into this softer, finer look of woman?

Better not to question such things. Because as much as she looked the lady, she must always look the child to him. He must train himself, learn to deceive his heart.

When the meal was over, they didn't roam their separate ways, as they might have done before. He should have, but then again, why be the coward?

"Take a ride with me."

Curious eyes lifted to his. "At this time of day? But haven't you work in the study—"

"The devil with my study. Take a ride with me."

She needed no more persuading. Within minutes, she had changed into her riding habit and returned to the bottom of the steps with a look of pleasure. "I had supposed after so many unwritten letters in your absence, you no longer had time for such a forgotten creature as little Nan."

Forgotten?

His chest ached in protest, but he said nothing. They made their way to the stables and mounted without any assistance. Where was that brother of hers, anyway? He didn't know, and it didn't really matter.

With the cool wind in their face, they rode beyond the Dorrington gates and escaped into a world he wasn't prepared for.

Sometimes they rode quickly. Not too fast, as Nan had always feared any reckless speed. But quickly enough that her curls came loose, her cheeks flushed, and her smile became daring and thrilled.

Other times they trotted very close to one another. Too close perhaps. Close enough that if things had been different, he might have reached over and grasped her hand.

"Isn't it ever so lovely?" She studied the land as they reached a valley covered with snow-laden grasses. "Let us get down and walk, shall we?"

"Is this some sort of ploy?"

"Ploy?"

"So that you might attack me with your weapons of snow?"

They dismounted and fell into step beside one another, as she breathed out another frosty laugh. "What mischief you credit me for."

"Then you are innocent?"

"In this matter, yes. We are no longer children, you know."

"I know."

"They were pleasant days, were they not?"

He didn't know how to answer.

"Oh, Gil, look at that hare. Can you see him?"

He was bleeding, and she couldn't even see.

"Watch how he runs away as if we were hunters ready to end him."

But running away didn't help. Gil could have told him that. Nothing helped and nothing saved him and nothing stopped the bleeding.

"Look at his little footprints in the sn—"

"Nan."

Her eyes flew to his and widened as he stopped, faced her.

"Nan." What was he doing? Didn't know. Didn't have control. "What if it hadn't happened this way? What if we weren't here like this, right now?"

"What are you talking about?"

"Twelve years ago. My father. . .when he brought you to Dorrington, when I saw you that first time and all the years after, when we played and argued and pretended. The gypsies and the pirates and the—"

"I don't understand."

He swallowed. Allowed his hands to curl around her arms in a way that plunged the rest of his strength into weakness. "Now." Soft, closer, but she still didn't know. "We could have been strangers. We could have met for the first time right now, and our whole lives could have been so very different."

"Do not say such terrible things." Tears, sudden and glistening. "If not for your father, I would have died in that wretched crate or suffered more years at the Bobber."

"Pretend there was no crate."

"I cannot."

"Pretend you never had to return to the Bobber."

"Gil—"

"Pretend we never knew each other until this moment, and there was nothing behind or before. Can you imagine it?"

The tears slipped free, slid down her cheeks and disappeared. "No, I cannot." She pulled away from him. "Nor would I want to."

He stood without answer as she climbed atop her horse, whipped her riding crop, and galloped away.

Just as she had every right to do. He had acted the fool. They were far too old for pretending anything.

Heath had expected Papa to be here.

God, forgive me. He stood in the cottage doorway, stared into the lifeless room, and almost wished the cruel old man were here to torment him.

But Papa was gone.

Heath was alone.

His hands shook hard with the agony and guilt and wretched disbelief. *Forgive me, God.* Over and over. *Forgive me, I beg of Thee.*

He moved toward the table, collapsed into a rickety chair. Shouldn't be here. Didn't know what he was doing. Why had he left the stables anyway? What would they say when they realized he was missing?

But he couldn't have stayed. Not today. Maybe never again.

Forgive me. He whispered the words, cried them, moaned them. *Forgive me, forgive me, forgive me.* A thousand times over, until the table was wet with his tears and the window turned from light to dark. How would he bear this? The knowledge that he'd taken a life. That his anger had murdered. That he was no better, if not worse, than the madam.

The noise of horse and wheels disturbed the night.

He dragged his arm across wet eyes, banished the tears, lest Papa should see and demean him. Then he approached the door. He swung it open to darkness and watched for the hunched, staggering form of an old man.

But it wasn't Papa who approached. No, the figure was small, willowy, with dainty steps and a wind-stirred cloak.

Then she stood before him, close enough that even the darkness could not conceal her. *Temperance.* Whom he loved but couldn't look at. Whom he needed but dare not touch. Whom he longed for but couldn't bear to be near.

"I had hoped most desperately you would be here." Light, musical voice. Did she imagine she had to hide her sorrow for his sake?

"You should not have come." Not at night, not to a man who had murdered. He motioned back into the darkness. "I shall drive you back—"

"Heath, no." Her hand stopped him. Rested on his chest and stayed, as if the touch were something she couldn't draw away from. "I know you have been under the greatest strain these last few days, and no one can blame you for disappearing so early today. As for me, you must imagine me some sort of unkind, thoughtless creature, as I have not come to the stables in days. It was not that I didn't want to, see, but I just—"

"No need to explain."

"I want to. I could not bear it if I could not explain, for the thought that I might have hurt you renders me much grief." Tears arose in testament to her words. "It was wrong of me to blame you, to think of you—even for a moment—as differently than I know you to be. What happened to Loftus was an accident. 'Twas not your fault. If anyone is to blame, it is I because—"

"You cannot take his death upon your conscience."

Her eyes widened. Her lips parted, at first without words. Then, "His death?"

"You are faultless. It was me. I am the one who hit him, who hurt him, who *wanted* to hurt him until he—"

"Heath, I thought they told you." More tears. "I thought you knew."

"Knew?"

"About today. About Loftus." The hand on his chest finally eased away. "He awoke sometime this evening. He is very confused, doubtless, and keeps falling back into sleep—but the apothecary seems certain he is out of great danger. Isn't it terribly wonderful?"

Wonderful?

Could it be true? Surely there was some mistake, or in her pity she had merely lied—

But no, she was smiling. Smiling with too much joy to be mistaken and too much confidence to be anything but truth. "Oh, Heath." Her hands reached for his face. "My dear, beloved Heath, can you ever forgive me for doubting you? For staying away from you these last horrid days?"

He drew one of her hands to his lips. Soft, cool fingers. What had he ever done to deserve this?

Dear Christ, I thank Thee. Another kiss, then his mouth met hers. Sweet, warm, moist. The reality of her overwhelmed him until he forgot about her question and he forgot about answering. Indeed, he forgot about most everything.

Except that his hands were no longer bloodstained.

And the woman in his arms was overtaking his heart.

Nan scrutinized every last detail of her hair in the full-length mirror and brushed a bit of fuzz from her quilted spencer jacket. There. Perfect. Even her ladyship, with her sharp and criticizing eye, would not be able to find fault.

Temperance hurried into the bedchamber with four baskets in tow. "These are filled, Miss Duncan, with all sorts of lovely things. Shall I show you everything? There are fruits and paper and old ribbons and mittens and—"

"I am certain it shall suffice." Nan strolled to her and accepted half the load. "Although I am still unclear why her ladyship has requested my presence in their visiting of the poor."

"Doubtless it was not her ladyship at all."

"Perhaps." But since Nan had run from his proposal, Lord Humphries had not visited Dorrington Hall. Both of his letters had been short. Was it possible she had doused his interest?

She tried not to imagine what that could mean, what Papa would say, how long it would be until he spoke to her again. All he wanted of his daughter was a profitable marriage. How grave would the consequences be if she failed?

She needn't have worried. When she reached the bottom of the stairs, Lord Humphries was there—grinning in navy tailcoat and flowing cravat, reaching for her baskets, speaking words so flattering she should have blushed over them.

Then he showed her to the waiting carriage, where the dowager marchioness and Lady Julia waited. The former grunted, as if Nan's presence had been unfavorably forced upon her. The latter smiled, albeit barely, then folded her hands in her lap and took her gaze out the window.

For the ride into the village, only Lord Humphries spoke. He told riddles no one understood, complimented his mother's hat twice, and was even so bold as to weave his gloved fingers with Nan's at one point.

She felt his heartbeat through those fingers. She told herself it was a good heartbeat, a pleasant one, a throb she could learn to love. Maybe that's how it worked. Maybe love was not something that simply occurred—but was rather a process. A slow, definite, mathematical process, where a heart learned to analyze everything and appreciate the little things.

Today she would love his heartbeat. Tomorrow, perhaps she could love his voice, or persuade her heart to appreciate his eyes, or nudge her brain to react to his smile.

Yes, she could do this. She wasn't giving up. She could satisfy her own expectations for herself and still meet those of Papa—couldn't she?

Another worry crowded her thoughts. Gil. What was the matter with him, anyway? Asking her to pretend, saying things that made no sense, looking at her as if. . .

Well, of that she didn't know either. But it was vexing, to say the least.

They traveled from worn cottages to indecent hovels, where the three women—escorted by Lord Humphries—would take turns delivering baskets.

"To increase Wydenshire's good opinion," her ladyship explained on the way back through the village. "With all these unfathomable calamities occurring, I shall not allow my pristine character to be defamed. Nothing disgusts me more than the thought of ignorant tongues waggling about my family and our affairs and—" The words broke off as the carriage jarred on uneven cobblestones.

"And what, Mother?" said Julia.

Her ladyship didn't answer. Instead, she pressed herself closer to the window until her rheumy eyes bulged and her thin, wrinkled lips fell open.

"Mother, what is it?"

"Silence, Julia."

"You are so pale—"

"Never mind that." Whatever had garnered her interest must have passed, because she settled back into her seat and left the window alone.

Nan glanced out her own window. Behind, all she could see were drably attired villagers, a throng of street urchins playing in front of an alehouse, and a long-haired dog who yapped at the carriage as it drove away.

"For a moment, I thought I saw someone I knew." Her ladyship frowned. "Someone I used to know a long time ago." Then silence fell upon the carriage, and for the return journey, the dowager said not a word more.

֍

"How long does it take to give away dashed baskets?" Gilbert thrust his fork into crimp cod and oyster sauce. "They ought very well have had her back hours ago."

Mr. Stanhope had long since finished his first course and was working quietly on a piece of roasted fowl. He glanced up without any apparent concern. "That would depend, I suppose, on how many baskets."

"I am serious, Papa."

"So am I."

Gilbert ripped the napkin from his neck. "It is insanity she is permitted to traipse around with a family so plagued by mishap."

"I do not doubt Lord Humphries will see to her protection."

"But who will protect her from him?"

Mr. Stanhope's brows both rose. "From him?" As if the question were baffling, ridiculous, uncalled for.

Mayhap it was.

Gilbert scooted from his chair. "Excuse me, Papa, Mamma. My appetite leaves me." After bending a slight bow, he quit the room and headed straight for the foyer. By George, it was uncommonly late for Nan to still be out, despite his father's apathy. With a brazen enemy of her ladyship's still at large, any number of dangers could easily befall the coach of well-doers—and Nan would be caught in the chaos.

Yet it wasn't the unknown enemy that stirred Gil's concern. It wasn't what made him fidget as he stood in the foyer, as he laid a hand on the door and debated if he should open it. Should he really go after her? And say what?

No, they would think him a fool. Just as Nan had thought when he had lost control on their ride and said things that didn't make sense. Pretend, he'd said. As if such a thing would do any good. As if hoping would really change anything.

Carriage wheels, then the low rumble of voices announced their arrival.

He must have been a coward, because by the time Lord Humphries had escorted her inside, Gilbert was already upstairs in his bedchamber. He stood at the window, watched as the dragon came strutting back out and descended the stone steps.

He walked as a man with purpose, with confidence, with blissful hope. As if he knew, after all these years, he would finally win Nan Duncan.

Maybe already had.

A creaking sound, yet indistinct enough that it lacked the power to draw her from sleep. She was warm, floating, halfway in a dream. Was that the dragon?

Ah yes, he was here too. He had eyes that brimmed with devotion, with boyish adoration and attraction—but someone else loomed behind him. Foggy, so foggy. Why was it so foggy?

Then she recognized the street. Cocksedge Road. How cold ran the blood in her veins as her stomach twisted with hunger she hadn't felt in years. "Pretend," cried a voice, but she didn't want to listen. She didn't want to be here. Didn't want to be alone.

"Gil, no." A whisper in her dream, but it wasn't Gilbert who had spoken to her. Someone else stood in the fog. Someone with hair black as sin, with luminous eyes, with a hideous tongue that lashed out in drunken French.

No, no. She ran, but the madam would catch her. *Please, no, no.* She tripped, smacked cobblestone, but she wasn't fast enough to scramble to her feet before—

A hard hand cupped her mouth. The reality shook her, jostled her from Cocksedge Road to the quiet confines of her bedchamber. She was awake, safe, unharmed.

Only the hand didn't fade away.

God, help. She was too afraid to open her eyes, but they opened anyway. *Papa?*

He hovered inches from her face until his heavy breath crawled along her neck and brought goose bumps. "My little Nan." He reeked of ale, a smell she hadn't known since her days at the Bobber. "Sing to me, Nan? The old songs. The ones we used to sing."

She pried away his hand. She tried to rise, but he wouldn't back away. "Wh–what are you doing here?"

"I come to see you."

"How?" A whisper. "How did you get up here?"

He glanced to the window, where the draperies fluttered around an open window. The night air rushed into the room. Chilling, frightening, enveloping. "Nan, you're going to do it. No more waiting, hear me? You're going to do it."

"Do what?"

"Don't play addled with me, girl. You ain't going to disappoint me too. Not like that worthless, good-for-nothin' brother of yours who should've—"

"Stop it!" She tried to slide out of bed, but his arms came down and trapped her. "Stop it," she said quieter, with a lump swelling at the base of her throat. "I will not hear you talk of Heath this way. He has done nothing worthy of your scorn. Nothing."

"He's a woman."

"No."

"He'd rather feed the church mice than stand up for himself, than stand up for you."

"What are you talking about?"

"The madam. Wouldn't even go back with me. . .wouldn't even make her pay for what she done to you." A hiccup. "Was his job, you know. Lookin' out for you. Instead, I come home to find he let you starve in the bloody streets and let some family I don't even know take you—"

"We had no choice." The lump dissolved into tears. "You left us no choice."

"I did what I had t' do."

"So did Heath. If he hadn't let Mr. Stanhope take me—"

"I bloody well know—and there's opportunity here, so in the end it all turned out." Papa's wide, liquid eyes came closer. "Our chance is now, with Lord Humphries, and you're going to take it."

She didn't answer.

"Hear me?"

She said nothing.

His face turned red. "You're defying me, girl."

"I do not wish to be forced."

"And I don't want t' be disobeyed." He looked as if he might have said more, but in the end he didn't. Instead, he cursed out an ale-scented breath and ambled back to the open window.

Moments later, he was gone.

Nan curled beneath her bed linens and sobbed.

CHAPTER 21

"Are you certain you wish to do this?" Temperance stood beside him, one hand on the doorknob, the other pressed against his arm. "I do not imagine it shall go as well as you think, see, because I fear he—"

"Even so." Heath nodded toward the knob. "It is something I must do."

Heath entered alone, shut the door behind him, and approached the bed, whose curtains were tied to the bedposts.

Loftus must have been asleep. His eyes eased open slowly, lazily—then widened so fast it made him jolt in bed. "You."

Heath swallowed against the accusations in that one syllable. But he nodded and drew closer. Thrust his hands into his pockets. Didn't look away. "How do you fare?"

"Ye almost killed me."

"I am sorry."

"Are ye?"

"Yes." Heath's heartbeat throbbed in his ears. "I am very sorry."

"Some consolation that would o' been if I'd o' been grave-lain by now." Red burned to his cheeks. "And to think it was all over that stupid chit who couldn't hold her blasted tongue if her life depended—"

"I'll ask you to say no more about her."

"Flighty, senseless little body who—"

"I'll ask you"—Heath edged closer—"to say no more."

Something about his tone must have possessed steel, because Loftus frowned and looked away. "I'll be out of this bed within the week, so ye just better be doing yer bleedin' chores at the stables. If I get out o' this bed and find ye ain't been keepin' up, I'll be right tempted to talk with Mr. Stanhope and see ye out o' here."

"There has been no slacking."

"Ye better not."

"I am sorry again you have suffered."

"Humph."

With a parting nod, Heath retreated for the door—

"And Duncan?"

Turning, Heath waited.

"Just so ye know, ye'll have no more fight with me." Sharp words, biting words, but the man's eyes were strange and moist. "She was meant for the likes o' you anyway."

The words nearly knocked him senseless. He smiled, heart skipping, as he pulled the door shut behind him.

Nothing truer had ever been said. Not in all his life.

Gilbert crept behind Nan. She sat so still and concentrated at the sitting room writing table, her head bent over a crisp, neatly written letter. But her curls. How tiny and soft as they drooped down her neck and caught morning sunrays in their spirals. Had she no inkling he was two steps behind her?

In one flashing movement, he swiped the letter from her fingers. "By Jove, what does it say?"

A jump, a small gasp, then she twisted in her seat. "Gil! You are terrible to frighten me so—now give it back!"

He retreated, lifted the letter above him. "I am in great agonies over this. You must appease me. What does it say?"

"Do not be ridiculous. You are as bad as Temperance." She rose and came toward him, then held out her hand as if she imagined he would return the letter to her palm. "Come on, place it here."

"Or what?"

"Or I shall tell Mr. Stanhope his son has gone mad."

"Perhaps he has." The letter raised a little higher when she made a jump for it. "And shall doubtless go madder still if he is not granted permission to see this letter. After all, it took you long enough to read it. I have no doubt but that it is of the greatest interest."

"You are vexing me!" A laugh broke from her lips. How fondly and warmly it spread throughout the room, as she weaved around him and strove for the letter. "I have not time for such childish games. Can you not see I am busy?" Another laugh. She stepped upon a rolled-arm bench and made yet another grasp.

He dangled it out of her reach.

She stretched inches toward him.

And somehow, by some wretched disaster, she lost balance and came tumbling.

Tumbling toward him. Tumbling into his arms. Tumbling against his chest, where those curls he had resolved to only look at now touched him.

This was a mistake. He should not have followed her into the sitting room. He should not have made sport with her and pretended they were children again. He was not the old Gil, and she was not the little Nan. They were changed, irrevocably changed, in ways he wasn't brave enough to face.

Heavens, why didn't she pull away? How long would she stay here, close to him like this? An eternity was already gone, but it'd only been seconds. Impossible, possible. . .he didn't know anything.

His arms were moving up, not away. They were guiding his hands to her face, where his scandalous fingers seeped into the curls. How oddly she looked at him. Not as one frightened, only confused.

If she would step away, he would have control again. He could stop himself. Could end this self-destructive madness.

But she stood still until he dropped his mouth to hers. Hesitated. Breathed. Then pressed—with a passion so alive it sailed him away, tossed him in a storm of wonder and fear.

She tasted of everything he'd ever expected. Sweet gentleness, rich womanhood, tender innocence and—

She flung herself back so quickly he flinched. She took one step. Then two. Then three, until her legs hit that fateful, horrendous bench. Why didn't she say something?

She stared at him as if he'd injured or compromised her. Stared at him with tears so big and confused he wanted to drown in them.

Then she bolted from the room.

Part of him wanted to run after her. The larger part of him couldn't. *God, where is Thy mercy?* He dragged a shaking hand across his mouth, the mouth she had touched. *How long can I endure this?*

As if in answer, he spotted the letter he had stolen from her grasp. He bent down but didn't touch.

My Darling Nan,

Mother wishes that I should invite the Stanhopes and yourself to Bletherton Manor for the twelve days of Christmas. We are to have a ball like no other for Epiphany, and there shall be much gaiety and dancing and food. I do hope everyone can come. All that aside, however, I should wish you to be there for a more intimate reason, a more significant reason. For you see, my darling, there is something I have wished to ask you for a very long time. I was uncertain what your answer might have been before, but feel more confidence now. I have no doubt but that it shall make us both greatly happy.

The letter was signed lovingly by the dragon. The man who was breathing fire upon Gilbert Stanhope and burning him alive.

This couldn't happen. Couldn't. In the name of everything holy, this *could not happen*.

Nan raced as far as shaking legs could carry her, with no care how her half boots splashed mud or how her hem was soiled. Thank mercy there was no one near. There was no gardener around the courtyard walls, or scullery maid by the well, or footman lingering wigless and aimless with a pipe.

There would be no one to see her like this—whatever this was. Numb, maybe. Dully, gruesomely, horror-strickenly numb. How could this happen to her?

Maybe it was all a dream. A terrible dream, just like the other night. She had run from the madam with fear she imagined was real. Hadn't she?

But it wasn't real. There was no fog and no alley and no madam. She had awoken and everything was over. She was safe, unscathed, returned to a life she loved.

Nan could never return from this.

With something between pants of breath and quiet sobs, she reached the tree, whose limbs were wet and frigid. She hoisted herself up. She climbed and slipped and cried, climbed higher and slipped less and cried more—until she reached the highest point she'd ever reached.

Then she sat looking out, tears cold on her cheeks, shaking so hard she fathomed she'd fall. *Why, God?*

The sky was quiet and gray. A cold breeze murmured back sympathies.

Why should Gilbert ever wish to kiss me? She touched her cheeks, touched her lips. How strange they felt, as if a dark, irremediable curse had formed there.

She wanted to imagine such a disaster was an accident. That in one swift moment he had acted on impulse, on meaningless emotion. That the kiss was nothing more than playful gesture.

But she'd tasted agony in his lips. She'd sensed fear and lack of control in his short, warm breaths. She'd felt passion and known hidden secrets when his arms closed around her and couldn't seem to let go.

And she knew.

Perhaps she should have known all along, throughout all these strange days, when his eyes had changed how they looked at her. Then again on the ride, as they stood overlooking the valley, when he'd begged her to pretend. . .how could she not have known?

This cannot be. Her entire body wept with the words. *This cannot be, cannot be.*

In a few days, she would accept Lord Humphries's offer of marriage. She would love him because she had chosen to love him. Everyone would benefit, and Papa would at last be proud.

And Gilbert?

She would be forced to lose him. Her companion, her source of comfort, the man she loved—but in a different way than he loved her.

And that is why she was numb.

She'd never have feeling again.

The evening was much as any other, yet different. Temperance always knew when things were different. Even when everything seemed the same, she had the uncanny ability to predict when life was about to alter.

She always thought so, anyway. Perhaps she only imagined such a fantasy.

There *was* something in the air tonight. She walked hand in hand with Heath Duncan, weaving along a walking path they'd made use of often these last few weeks.

He was quiet. He was always quiet. He was quiet in a way that made her incessant talking feel welcome, not dreaded. Anything she should ever wish to say, nonsense or not, was taken with interest and responded to with kindness.

But that was the way of this man. So much the tall, strong, sublime tower who stood amidst everything, yet alone somehow.

He wasn't alone anymore. She was here—walking beside him, holding his hand, feeling like she was inside his tower instead of far below.

"Are you cold?"

"No." She slipped on the hood of her cloak, lest he think the weather too harsh and decide to turn back. "I am infinitely more familiar with cold weather than hot, because when I was younger, it was my duty to rise before dawn and light all the fires. The mornings were ever so dreadfully cold. It is no small wonder I longed to be a lady's maid."

He smiled, nodded, then silence again.

For a while she was content, and holding her tongue was just as pleasurable as not holding it. But as they rounded the walking path into the shadows of wet trees, she broached a different subject. "Loftus returned to the stables today, did he not?"

"He did."

"Was he horrid to you?"

"No." Another smile. "Not horrid."

Her laugh echoed throughout the trees. "It is most wonderful, Heath Duncan, that you made apologies to him. For despite all of Loftus's shortcomings, he is not a man entirely without heart. I imagine he respects you in a way and that your visit did him much good."

"Not only him."

"What?"

"It did me much good too." Something passed over his face, a shadow of a nightmare. Then, in a lower tone, "Perhaps it is as important to forgive as to ask for it."

"I suppose that is true."

"But it's not easy to forgive someone who has never shown repentance."

"Such as?"

He looked away as if the answer required too much pain.

Temperance squeezed his fingers. "You do not have to tell me, yet I fear I know already. Does she haunt you still?"

His eyes dipped to hers. Sad, lost little boy eyes, with fears and pains too great to understand. "Yes, she haunts me." Deep, husky. "I wish I could forget everything. Wish I could forgive her."

"Why can't you?"

"I don't know."

"Perhaps you already have. Heath, surely you already have! I see no hatred in you, no wicked unforgiveness."

"You forget about Loftus."

"That was his own doing. Besides, I cannot help but think that all these years, you have been forgiving the madam already."

"But would she ever know?"

"She does not have to. She does not deserve to."

"And maybe that's why I must tell her." He paused on the path, where wet leaves made dripping sounds all around, and took her other hand in his. "Maybe it's something I must do."

"When?"

"If I leave now for London, I can return in time for the trial."

"But then I shall not see you for the twelve days of Christmas. Indeed, you shall doubtless have to leave day after tomorrow—Christmas Day, no less."

"I shall be here for Epiphany."

"Only barely."

"Is this to say you shall miss me?" His eyes turned soft and hopeful as his fingers tugged her inches closer.

"Miss you? Can you ask such a question? I shall be forlorn and detached throughout all the festive merriment—and I will likely be thinking you shall forget about me and never come back. Who is to say you shall not find some lovely little girl from your London past who will—"

"Temperance." A rebuke, but so remarkably sweet she trembled. "Do you think I could go anywhere in this world that would make me forget you?"

"Oh, but—"

"And do you think there is any girl who could ever make me not come back to you?"

"I don't know, see, yet I—"

"Marry me."

Silence fell as softly as fluttering wings or as powerfully as bolts of thunder. She stood with every heartbeat out of rhythm, waiting for him to take back the words, as terrorized as she was hopeful. "Marry you?"

"I shall obtain a common license and we can be married at once. Tomorrow." A pause. "Because it is nearly Christmas." A longer pause still, as his shy eyes dropped and lifted. "Please."

"You cannot be certain."

"I am."

"Me. . .you wish to marry me?"

A nod.

"But I am so. . .I mean, I am terribly silly, don't you think? And I talk far too much. Who would want to endure me all of their days—"

"I would." His face drew closer, mere breaths apart. "And I will if you'll let me."

Light gleamed under the study door, just as there had been a light under Nan's door.

But he hadn't knocked when he'd stood outside her bedchamber. He'd just stood outside, listening to her footsteps, wishing he had not been such a fool. Kissing her had ruined everything. Destroyed his plan. Severed their bond of friendship—the only bond they'd ever have.

Gilbert tapped once on the study door, then waited until the soothing voice rose. "Come in."

He entered without his dignity. He entered without his confidence. He entered without any brave smile or feigned happiness or strong countenance. How to say this? Were there words?

Somewhere in his chest, stuck in his throat, there must be words, because he could keep them in no longer.

"You love her." Papa sank deeper into his chair along the bookshelf. His grim expression expressed neither judgment nor understanding. "You love our little Nan."

"I never meant to."

"Yet it has happened."

"Could I end such a curse, I would."

"A curse." Papa uncrossed his knees, snapped shut his book, and sat straighter. Serious, probing eyes pierced Gilbert. "Love is never a curse, my son. Love is life, freedom, and hope."

"Not to me." His fingers curled tighter until his nails punished his palms. "What you have with Mamma may offer you all those things, but this is different. This is chains to me."

"Chains?"

"Of her indifference."

"Does she know?"

"In the name of mercy, I wish she didn't."

"But she does."

"Yes."

"You told her."

"No, I. . ." His lips still stung with the touch, the haunting memory. "I kissed her."

"And Nan?"

"She ran away. I tried to approach her hours later, but she fled again. Then all through dinner she. . .she would not even look at me."

Papa's eyes half closed. "Late this afternoon, when you were off on a ride, Nan visited me too."

"She said nothing of the kiss?"

"No."

"What did she say?"

"That a decision had been made concerning her heart." Papa looked away. "She intends to accept Lord Humphries's proposal of marriage just as soon as he should ask."

Gilbert's stomach sank. He had known all along it would be so. That it would end this way. If not with the dragon, then someone else.

But that didn't stop the groan from building in his chest and wrecking his heart. He was chained to someone who, very soon, would belong to someone else.

"You shall be there, won't you? Of course you shall. Who else should I wish to be close in the greatest moment of my life? And Mr. Stanhope and Mrs. Stanhope and little Miss Charlotte and. . .oh, there are so many people I am fond of. If I could but sweep them all up into my happiness so that they might be as wonderfully content as I am." Temperance spun in a circle without ceasing to chatter. She flounced from mirror to window, from window to writing desk, from writing desk to mirror again. "Shall I wear Nellie's old wedding dress? I think I shall. She has offered it to me twice already, and even for the gown of a chamber maid, I think it rather fetching."

From the other side of the room, Nan sat very still. She tried to pay attention. She even forced a smile and nodded once or twice. But the only thing she could see or hear was the happiness Temperance spoke of. The happiness that even now was spread about her maid's cheeks, and sparked twinkles in her eyes, and threw dance into every step.

The happiness Nan would never have.

Lord Humphries would never have.

Gil would never have.

Without meaning to, Nan had ruined all of their chances. She had hurt herself because she wasn't brave enough to deny her father. She had hurt Lord Humphries because she would never look at him the way Temperance looked upon Heath.

And she had hurt Gil. Hurt him in ways she couldn't understand and had no way to remedy. Hurt him because while he was loving her in new ways, she had loved him in the old. Why should he change? After all these years of such friendship, of such comfortable care, why should it all stop?

She was empty, as if something had been ripped out of her. Something she needed. Something she'd depended on so long she never thought she'd lose it. *Oh, Gil.*

Could she ever look at him the same? What of the way he looked at her? Could she ever bear his eyes, all the while knowing the thoughts of his heart? That they strayed so far from the pattern of her own?

Madness. That's what it was—all of it. He was a fool to ruin them this way. He was a fool to imagine romance. He was a fool to think she might have returned his kiss when he was nothing more than a friend to her. That's all he'd ever been. All he'd ever be.

She was already settled on her match with Lord Humphries. Maybe they weren't in love to the same degree that Heath and Temperance were. But did that make it any less love?

No, of course not. Surely their love would grow every day. Wouldn't it?

"Oh, Miss Duncan." Temperance fell down before her, grasped her hands. "What is the matter? Something is terribly wrong, for you are so quiet and sad."

"Do not let my sadness taint your happiness. Not when tonight is so wonderfully special for you."

"You are not angry I am to marry your brother?"

"I am overjoyed."

"You are not dreading the twelve days of Christmas at Bletherton?"

"I could never dread Christmas."

"Then what? Please tell me the truth. I could never be perfectly happy knowing you are not."

"If you really meant that, Temperance, I fear you would never be happy again."

CHAPTER 22

$\mathcal{T}$he wedding was a blur. Heath faced the vicar with his bride, repeated the vows, and entered the vestry to add marriage lines into the parish register.

Then she was his, this delicate child of sunshine. He held her hand as they waved goodbye to the small group—Mr. Stanhope, Mrs. Stanhope, Charlotte, and Nan—all with smiles or happy tears. No Papa, though. He'd been gone for two days, likely holed up in one of the village taverns.

Didn't matter, though. Not really.

Because today, some of the darkness flitted away. Light was within him, *her* light, driving the shadows of his past away.

Thank You, God. As they climbed into the carriage Mr. Stanhope had lent them. *Thank You.* As they rode through snow-touched countryside. *Thank You.* As they reached the worn, vine-covered cottage and he carried her over the threshold.

He didn't set her back to her feet. She slipped her hand to his cheek, her breathing deep, her eyes turning moist.

"Heath, can this be real?"

Maybe it wasn't.

"Can love be this perfect, or can it feel this right, or can anyone truly be as happy as I am?"

He didn't know what to say, so his lips found hers.

Then she laughed. Wonderful, soothing, beautiful sound—and it scared away every devilish nightmare that had ever plagued him. "We shall have so many children, my sweet Heath. They shall have your eyes and my nose, or my silliness paired with your strength." Her arms wound tight about his neck. "We shall wake up every morning to the sound of those little feet, and every year, these cottage walls will bear more laughter." Her lips pressed his cheek, the corner of his lips, then his lips themselves. "And every year we shall be more happy than the year before. It ought to be that way. Don't you think so?"

"I love you."

"Truly?"

"You doubt?"

"No." She nuzzled closer to him and breathed the next words against his ear. "I cannot doubt such love when I am consumed with it myself."

All he could think was the same prayer his heart had murmured all day long. *Thank You.*

❧

"I want to speak with you." Gilbert caught her alone in the hall, with pinkish morning light filtering in from a window alcove.

She paused. Uncertainty flashed across her face, then fear—then something else more definite. Anger? Resentment?

She continued toward him and resumed tying her white bonnet strings. "I am leaving now with Mrs. Stanhope and Charlotte."

"To Bletherton already?"

"Yes." She closed the distance between them. "You and Mr. Stanhope are taking the second carriage later this morning." Beside him now, the faint scent of her tickled his nose, and the sway of her satin gown—

"Gil, let me go."

Had he grasped her? Ah yes, her elbow. He uncurled his fingers and took a step back, but the shame still burned his cheeks. "Give me a word, Nan."

"No."

"Please."

She looked at him, just a second, but it lasted so long. Then her eyes fell away, with a blush rising to her own cheeks. "I cannot," she murmured, "else the carriage will leave without me. Perhaps later."

Gilbert nodded, swallowed, said nothing more as she continued down the hall and out of sight. Then he slipped back to his bedchamber.

His valet was still hard at work—folding shirtsleeves, tossing pantaloons, forming a pile of different-colored tailcoats. "All these go in one trunk, Mr. Stanhope?"

"Two." Gilbert approached the open one and glanced inside. "Put everything I shall need for twelve days at Bletherton in this trunk."

"And the other?"

"All of my belongings go in the other. It may remain here until after Christmastide."

"What happens after Christmastide, sir? Will you be taking another travel then?"

"Yes." This time, he had no intention of coming back.

❧

Temperance awoke in his arms. She'd never awakened like this before, this close to another person, with her head against a bare and solid chest.

Thump, thump. Against her ear, whispering to her soul. The dearest, most beloved heartbeat she'd ever heard.

Then he stirred and a yawning breath fell upon her head. "It is daylight already." Deep, groggy voice.

She tilted her head to see his face. "I dreamt I was still in my little room at Dorrington. How sad and lonely it was, and I kept looking out the window to see if I might spot you. Did you know I could see the stables from my window?"

"No."

"Well, I can. I mean, I could." She sighed as she lifted her finger and traced it along the cleft of his chin. "Isn't this just divine?"

"What?"

"Your chin. It is as if an angel, when God was fashioning you in the womb, decided you were too special for an ordinary chin—so he swept down and pressed this with his finger."

Heath's laugh was quiet. "Tell me what the angels did to you."

"Oh, they left me alone. They knew I was dreadfully ridiculous and doubtless tried to talk with God about the simple solution of birthing me without tongue."

"I am glad they didn't."

"Are you?"

"I like your voice." He stroked her hair. "And I like the things you say."

"Then I shall go on saying them, and I shall do anything else you wish me to do. I am undyingly at your service, my sweet Heath. You may depend on me always."

He murmured something back, something too quiet to understand—then his lips found hers. Was there anything more exhilarating than his kisses?

All too soon, the moment was over. They arose and broke their fast with a small meal of bread and milk.

Then she stood outside of the little worn cottage, and she hugged her cold arms as Heath tightened Golda's saddle. "Miss Duncan wishes that I should go to Bletherton while you are away. She is sending a carriage for me shortly."

He nodded.

"But I shall return here sometime after Epiphany. It is not so very many days away, is it? And you will not be delayed?"

With one last pull at the saddle, Heath came toward her. His arms folded around her without answer, and his lips pressed twice upon her cold cheek. "Until then." That was all he said, and she was too afraid of tears to whisper more.

With nothing more than a quick smile between them, her husband mounted Golda and rode away.

❧

This was a sanctuary. Among the rosemary, laurel, and bay—with so many guests seated and finishing off the last of their Christmas meal—comfort could be found for Nan.

Because three seats down, she didn't have to look at him. There were enough distractions, enough laughs and conversations and passing of dishes, that she was not forced to acknowledge his presence.

Yet it was the only thing she acknowledged. The only thing she wanted to do. Why had she refused to speak with him today? Yet if he asked her this moment for another word, would she give it to him?

No. She was much too afraid. How terrible it was that the one person she could confide in, the one person who soothed her fears, should suddenly be lost to her. Why had he done this? Why now, when she needed him most—when she was most uncertain about everything?

"Is that any sort of way to eat a Christmas dinner, my darling?" Lord Humphries, who sat beside her, dabbed a napkin at his mouth. "You must eat more heartily if you ever wish to be merry."

She did not wish to be merry. She wished to be left alone, to process this new grief, to let it sour into anger if that would make things easier. Or was she angry already?

For the first time since they had been seated at the Bletherton dinner table, Nan glanced three chairs down.

Gilbert sat stiff in his chair, pretending to listen to the round-faced, red-cheeked gentleman next to him, who had the unfavorable habit of speaking and chewing at the same time.

Poor Gil. If it had been any other day, he would have spared her a glance—an insufferable, half-smirking glance—and when the evening was over and they were alone, they would laugh about the ridiculousness of such an ill-mannered man.

"I say, did you hear?"

Nan forced her attention back to the dragon, who had scooted his chair an inch or two closer. "Forgive me, my lord. My mind must have been elsewhere."

"Apologies are unnecessary, Miss Duncan. I was merely telling Mother how delightful it would be for all present if you were to grace us with a song after dinner."

A flutter of protest soared through her stomach. "I do not think—"

"That will be splendid." From the end of the table, her ladyship spoke loud enough to quiet all other conversations. "Lord Humphries is always telling me of your voice. We shall hear for ourselves if his praise exceeds your skill."

The flutter turned into violent roiling. She glanced around the table—where unfamiliar guests stared at her, and Mr. and Mrs. Stanhope smiled at her, and her ladyship wore a challenging frown.

Only Gil, with eyes that understood her panic, gave a nod to her.

She took courage from his confidence. "Yes." She begged her lips into a small smile as she turned toward her ladyship once more. "I should be happy to sing and play for such a willing audience."

"Marvelous," said Lord Somerset. He had not spoken the length of the evening but now made deliberate attempts to send a disdainful grin Nan's way. "I am most anxious for this, indeed."

The music room was large, high-ceilinged, and grand enough to make the one at Dorrington a quaint little corner. An organ graced one wall, a harp the other, while the glistening pianoforte stood before floor-length windows.

This is where Nan slipped quietly, her cheeks the same color as her pink dress. Even from across the room, Gilbert noted her tremble—and when she played the first notes, they were unsteady and too heavy.

But then the song rescued her. Just as it always did, the melody swept her away into a world beyond him, a world that made her smile. She sang as one of the angels. Rich, clear, loud—yet soft at the same time.

Pride burst within him. Gilbert glanced to every chair, every face, and witnessed the look of sweet enrapture. Even her ladyship, as cynical as she was, seemed to forget that Nan was an unwanted match for her son—and tapped her fingers to the rhythm of the music.

"Charles, is she not everything I ever admired her for?" From somewhere close, Lord Humphries whispered to his brother.

"She is tolerable. Nothing more."

"You are a hopeless critic."

"At least I am not a swooning fool." Lord Somerset must have left then, for the conversation halted and the music room door opened and closed seconds later.

Gilbert moved until he had a clear view of the dragon's face. The man smiled, clapped gloved hands at the end of each song, made praising remarks to those around him.

Perhaps he did care for Nan. Mayhap, in some trivial and boyish way, he fathomed he loved her.

But he did not love her as Gilbert loved her. No one else in this world could do that.

❦

"I smell smoke." Charlotte poked her head through her white bed jacket, then fidgeted as Temperance tied the strings. "Do you smell smoke, Nan?"

"It is normal to suppose the smell would not have left yet. After all"—Nan went to their bed and drew back the soft linens— "it is a wonder they are hosting guests at all, what with so many of their chambers still ruined."

"Is that why I must sleep with you?"

"Yes, now hurry up and hop into bed. Do you know the hour? I should have thought you would have been asleep already."

"I wanted to wait for you." Charlotte lunged onto the bed and thrust her legs beneath the covers. "Besides, I have another toothache."

"That is true, Miss Duncan," said Temperance. "Poor dear, but she has been holding her chin all day and murmuring such dreadful complaints. Why, she would not even eat all of her pie today."

Nan chuckled. "That is grave indeed."

"Do you suppose Mamma remembered to bring our clove essence? It always helps so."

"Knowing your mamma, I do not doubt it. If she would make certain you eat better, you would not have such problems."

"Will you fetch it, Nan? Please?"

Temperance started for the door. "I shall get it—"

"Never mind." Nan went instead and spared them both a smile. "I know the room and will only be a moment." Pulling the door shut behind her, Nan slipped into the blackened hall. Charlotte had been right. The air still carried the dull, foreboding scent of smoke as if to remind the occupants of Bletherton Manor that danger was meant to find them.

She could only pray it didn't. How much more could Lady Julia endure? Even tonight, amid the gaiety and merriment of Christmas Day, she'd been dejected and withdrawn.

"That was quite the performance."

Nan stopped. Even without a candle, she could make out the distinct features of Lord Somerset as he approached her in the darkness. What was he doing here? And dressed in his banyan, no less?

He must have sensed her question, because he answered in kind, "I hope it is not a great disappointment to find me on the same hall as you. I know you think the world over despises me—but surprisingly enough, my mother did invite me for the twelve days of Christmas."

"I see."

"But this does create a situation, does it not?"

"I am certain I do not know what you mean."

"Don't you?"

"No, I don't." Blood pumped to her face. "Now if you will excuse me, I am on my way to Mr. and Mrs. Stanhope's chamber to—"

"Were you, Miss Duncan?" He moved closer. Too close. "Or were you on your way to *my* chamber?"

"You appall me, sir."

"Do I?"

"I will not be taunted."

"Some people are meant to be taunted."

Forget the clove essence. The toothache would be less painful to Charlotte than this humiliation. She turned—

He captured her forearm with a bare hand.

Her blood ran a little colder.

"As I said before, Miss Duncan, that was quite the performance tonight." His white teeth flashed in the darkness. "Maybe my brother was not as senseless as I thought."

She fled away with a heart stuttering out of control.

The road stretched out before Heath, flanked on both sides by wooden fences and mossy stones. The air smelled of winter—that biting, wet, deathly scent that always stung the nose.

He remembered the days when he had hated such a smell. How many nights he'd lain with Nan curled next to him, the both of them shaking, yearning so bad it made them weep for the scents of a hearth.

There'd been countless times his fingers had felt frozen and hardened. Sometimes Nan would rub them. Sometimes he'd rub hers. But it didn't do much good because the cold never went away.

Other times he could scarcely walk, feet too numb, too blistered from cold. But he did it anyway. Fell down but he always got back up because Nan needed him. Who would find bread for her if he couldn't walk?

No one, and he couldn't let them die.

Those were the hard days. The days he didn't think he'd live through. Maybe it was Papa's fault because he left them. Maybe it was the madam's fault because she forced them to run. Maybe it was Heath's fault because he chose life on the streets rather than life at the Bobber.

Or maybe it wasn't anyone's fault. Not really. Maybe it was just the way it was deemed to happen, the way God had planned it all along.

And it was over.

By a hundred different miracles and a thousand different blessings from God, they'd survived. Everything was behind them. Tomorrow—the dear, beloved tomorrow they'd always hoped for—was finally almost here.

God, help me.

In three days, the road Heath traveled would lead him into London. He would find the East End, and he would stand face-to-face with the woman who had injured him beyond forgiveness.

He would forgive her. He needed to forgive her. The rector and God and his wife—they would want him to forgive her. If Heath were ever to be the man he'd vowed to himself he would be, he *must* do this.

Then he would climb atop Golda and leave the Bobber forever. He'd come back home to the bride God had given him.

Then tomorrow could finally begin.

The days at Bletherton Manor dragged by. Mr. and Mrs. Stanhope, on account of poor Charlotte's aching tooth, made apologies to her ladyship and returned home. Whether Gilbert returned with them was yet a mystery to Nan.

Not that she cared. Why should she? In the eight days they'd been here—all through visiting the poor, playing snap-dragon or bullet pudding, and eating overwhelming feasts—Nan had hardly spoken to him.

Except once.

The morning after she played and sang, when there were few occupants in the breakfast room, he had paused as he passed her chair. He'd bent close to her ear. "You baffled the lot of them with your songs, my little Nan."

She'd glanced at his face—his close, flushed face—and felt a pinch of something at her chest. "Thank you."

He'd smiled, nodded, then quit the breakfast room.

But all through the day, the brief encounter swept through her like a whirlwind. Why should it so affect her?

Perhaps because it forced down some of the anger she'd been storing against him. Or perhaps because his words were more than a compliment to her songs. It was almost as if he had whispered surrender in her ear. "My *little* Nan," he'd said—knowing she wasn't little to him anymore but willing to pretend it was so for her sake. Was that the depth of his love?

Deep indeed. Noble and honorable and worthy of endless respect. Worthy of love too, but all she could offer was the same adoration she'd always bestowed him. Why must it happen like this?

They could no longer be friends, and they could never be lovers. They were destined to something she couldn't think of, didn't ever want to think of—

"Miss Duncan?"

Nan snapped her head to the music room doorway, where Lady Julia entered with more color to her cheeks than she'd shown in days. "Oh—do not allow me to disrupt you if you were about to play. Where is Aylmer?"

"I am quite finished." Nan stood from the pianoforte and smiled. "And I believe your brother is enjoying the smoking room with the rest of the men."

"How dull of him to leave you unattended."

"I do not mind."

"Good. Then perhaps you shall join me for a spell of needlepoint in the morning room. I do so tire of sitting there alone all day."

"Certainly, although I cannot own to being much good at needlepoint."

"Neither can I." Arm in arm, the two left the music room, chatting some, laughing a bit, smiling throughout the course of their pleasant conversation. When they reached the morning room, Julia swept in first midway through a sentence—

And halted. Her back arched, both hands lifted to her face, then a scream rent the air.

Nan flung herself forward and tried to hold up the woman's weakening frame.

But it did no good. Julia's body swayed once more, then melted to the ground with a soft, terrible thud.

Nan bent over her and surveyed the room. Yarn on the floor. Needles jabbed into the striped settee. Gashes through the length of the Grecian-style drapes.

And a broken window—where the enemy had climbed in and climbed back out.

Heath was prepared. During the long ride, he had summoned back all the sights he'd tried to forget, he'd recalled the woman he hated, and he'd relived all the horrors of the hardest days.

He thought he'd be calloused by now. Shouldn't he be?

When he caught his first sight of the Bobber, his courage fled. He dismounted, wiped the sweat from his hands, and stood like a child in front of the evening-shrouded building.

Nothing had changed. The walls were a little bleaker, a little grimier. The windows lacked glass, covered instead with dirty boards. The same music spilled outside without tune. Sharp laughter pierced the air. Occasional cheers, followed by the *clink, clink* of those filthy, ale-filled tankards.

Move. The command came once, then twice, then a third time. When he finally did, when he reached the door, sickness stirred his stomach as he pushed the well-known knob.

He entered with every nerve on edge. He almost expected the madam to lunge from the shadows, using her ladle to bash his skull, or her fingers to claw his face, or her fists to pummel his stomach.

I forgive you. The words followed tears as he stepped over creaking boards. *I forgive you.*

From behind the counter, a man in a stained cotton apron turned around, a clay pipe jutting from his lips. "Er, ale ye will 'ave?"

Heath shook his head. He recognized the man—one of the ones the madam had taken to her bedchamber with her—but he hadn't worked the counter in those days.

The fellow yanked out his pipe. "Ye come for one o' the lovelies then, ain't ye?"

Heath followed the man's glance to where two women sat—one with a sweaty, yellow blouse dipping off her shoulder, the other with a shaking tankard at her lips. Both glanced up at him without expression.

"Well, speak up, ye cuif. Which one'll ye 'ave?"

"None."

"Wot?"

"I came for the madam." A pause. "Madame Le Sueur...I need to speak with her."

At this, the man leaned both elbows onto the counter. His yellow eyes squinted, blinked, then he jabbed the clay pipe back into his mouth. He spoke around it. "Ye're a little late."

Heath's temples throbbed. "What do you mean?"

CHAPTER 23

*A*re you well, my lord?"

The constable had come and gone, Lady Julia had been taken to her bedchamber, and her ladyship was finally appeased with smelling salts and her newest cat.

Lord Humphries, however, was anything but appeased. He had stolen Nan away to an empty library, where he stood along a colorful bookshelf and brushed his fingers along the spines. He didn't speak. Didn't glance at her. Didn't attempt to answer her question.

"This has all been terrible." Nan drew closer in the silence. "You barely cope with one disaster, when another befalls you. Can nothing be done?"

"You heard Constable Hearne."

"Yes, but surely whoever has done all this cannot be traceless forever. He is bound to leave some evidence, is he not?"

His eyes rose to hers—half-cautious, half-tearful, sort of hoping and doubting all at the same time.

"What is it, my lord?"

He clamped his lips tighter. She was left staring into his eyes, into their boyish depths. Deep into the heart of him, until she understood him better than she ever had before.

"Please, Nan, let there be games no longer." A pitiful whisper, in the same voice he might have used all these years to coax his mother. "You are far more worrisome to me than any vindictive enemy. Won't you say you shall marry me?"

Tears softened her vision, made the dragon's eager face swim. This was it. Her second chance. Her heartbeat raced against the frail cage of her chest. "Do you love me, my lord? Truly love me?"

"Of course I do! We shall have a grand life together, my darling, with so many balls it shall make you dizzy. We will spend all the seasons in town. I shall introduce you to all the finest company. You will have dresses and jewels and as many carriages as you desire—"

"My lord, please." She didn't want to think of such things, such senseless things. None of it mattered. None of it but his heart...and hers. Oh, why couldn't she know?

He must have sensed something, because the red in his cheeks dipped to a pallor. "My darling, you are not thinking of declining me? I could not bear it if you did. Do you not love me?"

"Yes." It was out before she had a chance to reason it through, or contemplate the truth, or discern her own tangled emotions. She'd said she loved him—so she must. Why else would she have said so?

"I knew you did, darling." Both of his hands took hers. "Now, let us do this once more. Will you marry me?"

"Yes."

His eyes, smile, cheeks—they all burst with life and light and color. "Oh darling, you have made me the happiest creature!" He kissed her knuckles, kissed her cheeks, kissed her lips even when they trembled with uncertainty. "What will Mother say? I cannot wait to tell her. Stay here, my darling, and I shall see if we might see her at once."

She mumbled an answer, then he raced for the door and hurried into the hall. He must have stopped, however, for she heard him speak to someone. "Most wonderful thing...then you must have heard...affianced to the loveliest creature...we shall be so happy."

Someone responded, voice too low to recognize.

Then Lord Humphries's voice again. "Excuse me...yes....I must tell my mother...thank you, Mr. Stanhope."

Nan's very core began to shiver. She leaned into the bookshelf, sick with the realization Gilbert must have overheard, too overwhelmed to imagine how it must have hurt him.

Then he appeared at the door. From across the room, his eyes met hers. Without tears. Without hope. Without life.

Then he shut the door with the faintest thud and was gone.

Epiphany Eve arrived. Hours had long since passed since the men had marched outside with cider and guns and horns, prepared to drive away any evil spirits with a lot of nonsense and noise.

"These traditions," said Lady Julia as she glanced once more out the window. Tiny fires burned in the night. "Are they not preposterous?"

"You would not think so if you were a man." Her ladyship sniffed. "A night with nothing but reveling is good for them. Perhaps it shall make them appreciate the quiet, civilized ways of their opposite sex."

"Or make them long for more Epiphany Eves." Lady Julia glanced at Nan, and something of a smile touched her lips. "Are you always so quiet when the men are not present?"

"It is not that. I am merely fatigued tonight." She rose. "Perhaps I shall retire early—"

"You will do no such thing." Her ladyship motioned to the chair. "Sit down and finish out the evening with us. If you are to be my future daughter, I suppose I shall have to try and tolerate you."

Nan held the narrow eyes, not certain if the words were meant in compliment or insult. Either way, she made a slight curtsy. "I am sorry, my lady. As I said, I am most tired tonight." Without waiting for the dowager's gasp, Nan hurried from the room with her shoulders tight.

One thing was certain. When she became Lord Humphries's wife, she would not bend to her ladyship's every whim and demand like some sort of servant. Nan had more dignity than that. And if the dragon expected—

"You should have thought of that before!" A man's voice. "You are brought to Point Non Plus, my fine fellow, and there is nothing more I can do for you."

A low, sneering response. Lord Somerset?

Against decorum, she padded softly down the black hall until she reached the cracked door. No light brightened the room. Indeed, had the two men not been situated by the moonlit window, she would not have made out their faces at all. Why weren't they outside keeping the fires with the others? Wasn't that Major Sir John Bradford, the guest who had arrived only yesterday?

"Admit it, you well-inlaid miscreant." Lord Somerset's hand reached out, seized the other man's cravat. "Admit what you have been doing to—"

"How dare you!" The major flung back Lord Somerset with one powerful shove. A chair crashed over. Glass shattered. "You've quite run off your own legs, fellow, and your lies are worth less than your purse."

Lord Somerset scrambled back to his feet. He faced the man again, fists balled, wild-eyed enough he might have tried for a blow had the other gentleman not been so superior in height. Then, with a swear, "You shall have it in a fortnight."

"I shall have it tomorrow."

"Go to the devil, man! You might as well kill me now and take my dashed watch fob. That's the only gain you're likely to get in such unmerciful time."

"Three days then." Silence, then the major patted Lord Somerset's cheek. "Three days—and then *you* are the one who shall go to the devil."

The Taunton courtroom was much smaller than Heath had imagined. Spectators, barristers, jurors, and two white-wigged judges all crowded within the four wooden walls. Despite the cold, someone had moved about and opened all the windows, until a fresh breeze stole away some of the bodily stench.

The prisoners moved through in a line. The verdict was announced swiftly, sentence was passed, and a new dingy-faced man was hauled before the court.

Heath rubbed his hands against the cold. How many had been sentenced to hang already? One man was sent to the gallows for the theft of three yards of thread and one shoe buckle, the value of which totaled twenty-two shillings. To be sure, Coombs would not fare well today.

As a corner clock struck the next hour, Coombs strode through the door. His wrists bore the manacles, his clothes the familiar dirt and grime of all the other prisoners—but something was different.

His eyes weren't dazed and sunken. Cheeks weren't hollow, as if from lack of food. Even his countenance held more confidence than the others, less fearful somehow, as the guards placed him before jurors and judges who would likely take his life.

The proceedings began. Heath gave his testimony, the little man in the corner scribbling down the trial report as Coombs offered a mumbled defense. At last the jury leaned their heads together in consultation. "Guilty," said one of the jurors with a nod to the judge.

At first Heath did not comprehend the judge's sentence. He was too busy watching Coombs's face—the way his thin lips sort of eased upward with a smile, the shocking glint to his eye, the way his shoulders lifted proud and unwavering.

Then Heath caught the words. ". . .prisoner will be transported back to HM Shepton Mallet Prison, where he will spend one month before he is fined and discharged. Case closed. Next!"

Didn't make sense. Wasn't possible. That so many men should be sentenced to death in one day—men with petty charges—but that one who was clearly guilty should not be punished.

From across the room, Coombs's gaze snapped to Heath's. He pointed, made a motion with his hands as if he were wringing and breaking a man's neck. Then, as the guards led him away, his gaze locked onto someone else. Someone who made him smile again. Someone who was rising as if prepared to leave.

Heath froze when he caught a flash of the face—a face he knew.

The Honorable Marquess of Somerset.

The day was a terrible blur. Gilbert went through it in step with the rest of them. He stood outside, smiled when the shivering beggars came wassailing. He ate and ate again, though his stomach cramped in protest. He danced and sang and tried to laugh, though the only thing he wanted was to end this agony.

And that's what it was. Agony. Because today, tonight, was all he had.

Then he would leave Bletherton Manor. He'd take the trunk from his bedchamber at Dorrington Hall and say goodbye to every person who meant anything to him.

How can You expect this of me, dear God?

Nan didn't notice. She didn't even understand. It was only by chance, a few swift times, that her eyes met with his.

The rest of the day she was too busy. Lord Humphries, by another great favor of providence, found that ridiculous bean in his cake. Thus, he was king for the night, as tradition would have it—and who should he choose as a partner but Nan?

One of the Onslow daughters discovered the pea. Thank mercy it was the eldest, who was much more content to choose the tall Major Sir John Bradford than a young whelp like Gilbert.

The rest of the guests, in their masks and costumes, finished off their cake—and by and by, all the playactors drifted into the ballroom.

With one motion of her ladyship's hand, the orchestra came to life. When the guests formed together in a square formation, Nan was among them. How long had it been since she'd been so frightened at her coming out?

She'd been so unsure of herself in those days. The slight limp had ebbed away at her confidence, yet now she danced the cotillion with graceful ease.

She was beautiful. She was more refined, more self-assured, so much the lady that he stood in awe.

But he missed the young, blushing Nan of all those years ago. She had needed him then. She had depended on him as if the world would crumble without his presence—and when she had looked at him, there had been such fresh, delightful adoration.

Half of his heart still belonged to that Nan. The other half belonged to the new one.

Tonight was the last he'd have of either of them.

He was stifling her.

For the third time in not so many minutes, Lord Humphries squeezed her hand. Not that he hadn't the right. He did, more so than anyone. But every time, she felt a small kick in the lowest part of her stomach—and next thing she knew, she was slithering away.

At least he didn't seem to notice. He raised his fourth goblet of elderberry wine, sipped noisily, then licked the dark stain from his upper lip. "Darling, must you make me drink alone? Let me fetch you a goblet, hmm? You shall enjoy it."

"No."

His glassy eyes crinkled. "I could order it, you know. I am king for the night, after all. Isn't that fun?"

"Most fun, my lord, but I—"

"Another dance then?"

"No, I—"

"Tut, tut. You are no fun at all, my darling." He feigned a pout, grabbed her hand again. "A kiss then?" Without awaiting her consent, he leaned forward—

And stopped inches from her face. "What?" He turned, the question slurred, and faced a man she hadn't noticed.

Lord Somerset stood complete in his colorful half-face mask and shiny-buttoned tailcoat, with his cravat extending below his chin. For once, he was a welcome sight, scowl and all. "I said Mother told me of the news."

"I suppose you are unhappy." Lord Humphries downed the rest of his wine, then squared his shoulders as if he were prepared for fisticuffs. "You always bullied me into trying to forget her, but I won't listen. And if you have one word to say against the matrimony, I shall—"

"Go to the devil, Aylmer. I don't give a dirty shilling whom you marry." Then his eyes snapped to Nan, where they lingered far too long. "Here, you fool," he said to his brother as he stepped toward her. "Finish off my wine and then have another."

"Where are you going?"

"To acquaint myself with the new member of our family." The marquess opened his white-gloved hand to Nan. "Will you dance?"

Any other moment, she would have refused. But not this time. Not when the drunken dragon was so ready to kiss her. "Very well." With her back stiff, she allowed the marquess to join her in a cotillion.

Not once did he speak. Not once did he smile. If her presence in his family was a source of such disgust to him, why did he feel the need to dance with her?

She favored him as little as he favored her. They were putting up a ridiculous front for no purpose. The sooner she could escape him, the better.

"It is blazing in here," Lord Somerset said just before the dance ended. A round of applause filled the air. The couples bowed. Then the marquess stepped closer and took her arm. "We shall walk outside and get some air."

"I fear I must decline."

"Too afraid of yourself?"

The question hung without answer. She didn't understand what it meant, and she didn't want to. She hurried away without a backward glance and tried not to imagine such a rogue would be her new brother.

The music did something to Temperance, something unearthly. She stood alone in the dark—in a quiet, abandoned hall—and swayed back and forth to the divine sounds. How wonderful it all was. How very much like a dream.

She extended her hand to Heath. He wasn't there, but why shouldn't she pretend? Maybe if she became lost in the dance, caught up in her own imagination, the few hours would be over.

Then she would leave Bletherton Manor. In the sweet night hours, she would find the little cottage and hurry inside.

Perhaps he wouldn't be there. Not yet. But she didn't mind because there were a hundred things she could do. Straightening and dusting and mending—not as an abigail, though. As a wife. *His* wife.

Beauty rang in the sound of it, the thought of it, the reality of it. But was it real?

She couldn't be sure. These last few days, with him in London and her in this lonely manor, the memory of their wedding felt in strange likeness to all her dreams. Faint, soft, misty. Too far away to touch. Too wonderful to forget.

The clock chimed. Another hour gone, as if time itself—in some gallant, benevolent way—had shown pity on her pulsing heart. Did she dare ask to leave?

Temperance left the hallway and slipped through the blackness. The ballroom doors were open wide, with light spilling through, the music much louder and clearer here.

Perhaps it was too early to depart. After all, who would help Miss Duncan out of her dress and stays? But other servants could be found, the night was still young, and surely Miss Duncan would not mind terribly.

She crept closer and peeked into the enormous room. Colors, masks, feather plumes, ivory fans, red-stained goblets, and tall sugar sculptures. How would she ever find Miss Duncan amid all that?

Perhaps never.

Time ticked by. Was Miss Duncan still present? Had she gone upstairs? How could Temperance request to go home if she could not discover her?

"Temperance."

She whirled. "Oh—Master Stanhope. I did not see you."

Gilbert Stanhope pulled the bright mask from his face. "Is something the matter?"

"Oh no. I mean, yes, but I shouldn't think of troubling you with the matter. I am only at sixes and sevens, see, because I cannot seem to find Miss Duncan anywhere."

"Lord Humphries is feeling ill, it seems, and had to retire early. Perhaps Nan has gone to console him."

"Oh, I see."

"Do you need her terribly?"

"I had hoped she might permit me to depart. Heath was due home today, and I so very much wanted to be there with him and—"

"Never mind all that. I shall take you."

"Oh, but I didn't mean that you—"

"I said never mind, Temperance." A muscle tightened in Gilbert's jaw. "I am as eager to be gone from this place as you are."

Nan had been on his arm as he'd stumbled from the ballroom. She'd been next to him as he doubled over and retched on the clean, polished floors. She'd even been with him as the servants escorted him upstairs and eased him onto the bed.

Then she'd stood looking down at him, the laughing dragon, and every part of her wanted to die. Not because he couldn't handle his wine. Not even because he played the fool tonight.

But because of *him*. The way he talked. Everything he said. The way he moved his mouth or tilted his head or brushed a shock of hair from his forehead. His amusements, his passions, his hopes.

All things she should dote on. All things she should love. Oh heavens, what was the matter with her? How could she possibly endure a lifetime with him if she were so afraid of his kiss, so annoyed with the squeeze of his hand?

"Darling, you are angry with me?" A servant moved to one side of his bed, propped a pillow behind his head.

She managed a smile. "No, not angry."

"Splendid. I am most sorry I could not last longer. I fear I imbibed one glass too many, and I shall likely never hear the end of this from Mother."

"I am certain she shall forgive you."

"What good is it to be king if one has to go to bed?" Another laugh, but this time he hiccuped and closed his eyes. "I shall rest a moment. Then I shall return downstairs, hmm?"

She waited until his features went lax and his breathing grew heavy. She tried not to imagine what it would be like to go to sleep to that sound every night, or to wake up next to that face, or to become one with someone who seemed so much the rich, boyish child.

With a grateful nod to the two servants, Nan excused herself. She hurried downstairs but forsook entering the ballroom. She could not bear another moment. She had no wish for lemonade or dancing or making merry with a lot of people who made her uncomfortable.

Before Lord Humphries became ill, he had passed into circulation talk of Nan playing another song. She didn't want to run the risk that her ladyship had heard. The last thing Nan wanted was to entertain.

So she stole through a pair of balcony doors, hurried down the snowy stone steps, and escaped without the notice of anyone.

The sky was big and cloudless, with moonlight and stars brightening her path to the garden. She lingered on the outskirts. Touched a bloomless stem. Sighed and shivered and wondered how much longer until she could return home again.

Dear, sweet, beloved home. How very much she yearned for the simpler days. Before Papa returned, before Gilbert kissed her, before the dragon became a man she was forced to love. Even now, the thought of sitting in the drawing room with Mr. Stanhope's scent of cheroot and Mrs. Stanhope's chatter and Charlotte's nonsense—

"Well."

Nan spun. "Who is there?"

Without answer, a man's shadowy form edged closer. Then the voice came loud enough to recognize. "So you came after all."

Had Lord Somerset followed her out here? Or had he been here already?

She didn't know and hardly cared. She started back toward the manor—

And then a whoosh of air as a body lunged for her. Cold, gloveless hands clamped over her mouth. Her feet lost contact with the ground. He was yanking her backward, deep into the winding garden path, hidden behind boxwoods and bushes and sparse plants.

"I was not here earlier, Miss Duncan, to hear my mother make the announcement." His breath was hot against her neck, reeking of ratafia. "You must be very proud of yourself. Securing so wealthy of a match is a great accomplishment indeed."

She threw back her head, but his hands stayed firm. Fear sliced her chest.

"I told you to leave my brother alone. Did you truly imagine yourself good enough for this family? You, a daughter of uncertain birth, with your pathetic little limp?"

No. She fought, pushed hard against his chest, but it did no good. Her back slammed against a stone wall and pain jolted her spine.

His body crammed closer. "You are nothing." Whispered in her ear. "You are a worthless little child, one hardly worth the effort of ruining."

God, no.

"Maybe that is why I hate you."

Please.

"Why I have always hated you." Closer still, until his punishing hands left her mouth to capture her throat. "Because you tempt me. . .and I want you."

She screamed, but his lips silenced her. Couldn't breathe. Couldn't think. Every muscle fought as she hit him and scratched his face. *God, please. . .please. . .*

He yelped. Only a second, a brief pause, but she darted out of his reach and plunged through scratchy bushes. Plants crushed beneath her feet. A thorny stem whacked her neck. A few more yards and she'd escape the garden—

She doubled over something hard. A bench, maybe. She scrambled back to her feet, but she wasn't fast enough.

Lord Somerset grabbed a fistful of her hair. Ripped at her dress. Exposed her shoulder to his cold, wretched hands.

"Please. . .do not do this." Sobbing, wilting. "Please, my lord. . .please."

"If we had not fashioned such a scandalous little story, perhaps this would not have happened."

"Please—"

"But ever since then, it has been seducing me. That thought." He framed her face again, dipped his lips to her jawline. "You and I. . .and all the intimacy that would be wasted on my brat of a brother."

"Please. . .I'll do anything." More seams ripped. "I'll end the engagement. . .I'll end it, I vow, if you let me go."

"After this, you shall doubtless end it anyway."

"Please."

"No."

"Money then." Her eyes slid shut, teeth gritted as his fingers crawled into her hair. "Any amount. . .any price. . .please, I beg of you."

"You have no money."

"Mr. Stanhope—"

"He would not give it to you."

"He would! I swear he would."

"How much?"

"As much as it takes."

At first he didn't answer. He eased her closer, hovering over her lips with his drunken breath. Then, in a faint whisper, "You are not only tempting, Miss Duncan, but conniving as well."

Her body flung back, toppled over the bench for the second time.

In the darkness, his shadow loomed over her. "Return to Dorrington tonight and secure three thousand pounds. Meet me here before daylight. If you tell a soul, I shall ruin your chances not only with my brother but with any decent man alive. Understood?"

Her answer escaped as a sob as her heart sank. "I understand."

CHAPTER 24

She'd never been so cold in her life. Not even on Cocksedge Road in the filthy little crate. Not even at the Bobber, when they'd slept on the floor and shivered.

This was a different kind of cold. This reached further, until it numbed and inflicted her soul with torturous ice shards.

For the second time, Nan took the first balcony step. She went no further. How could she? Too many chances someone would see. The torn dress. The hair. The shame.

No, she couldn't enter. Without any way to get help or get warm, she had no choice but to return to Dorrington by herself, retrieve the money, and hurry back to the garden as Lord Somerset had demanded.

Both her hands cupped her mouth as she backed away from the steps. She wept with no sound. *God, what do I do?*

The manor windows were aglow, flickering light upon the snow-layered ground. Music resonated through the night. Laughter lifted in between.

God?

No answer. No whisper that she'd be all right, that the nightmare would end, that if she returned to the garden tonight Lord Somerset would not hurt her.

Gil would have said those things. Gil would hold her. He'd make everything all right. He'd know what to do, and he'd help her do it.

She needed him. Needed him more than she'd ever needed anyone, in a way that nearly made her climb those balcony stairs all over again. Because it didn't matter who saw. Didn't matter what they said—just so long as she could find Gil.

Then everything would make sense again. The cold would start to thaw. She'd know comfort in a heart writhing with fear.

Perhaps there *was* a way to fetch him without being seen. She stumbled toward the stables, hugging her ripped bodice, and flung open the creaking doors.

In the light of a dim lamp, a long-haired boy bolted from his workbench. Wide eyes stared her up and down, confused, as if he weren't quite certain if she were a stray ragamuffin or a disheveled guest.

Whatever he thought, when she asked him to hurry to the manor and fetch a Mr. Stanhope, he obeyed without question.

Nan waited for him without moving. Time crawled. How long did it take?

She tried not to imagine what she'd say when Gil came or how she could explain such a horror. Maybe she wouldn't have to. Maybe he'd know already. Maybe one look, one glance at her tears and dress, and he'd understand.

Footsteps approached. She faced the door with more tears. The latch rattled, then a creak.

Gil.

It wasn't him. The long-haired stable boy entered alone, brushing snow from his shoulders, mumbling words that didn't make sense.

"What do you mean?" She shook so hard she nearly buckled. "What do you mean he is not there?"

"Just that. Left a'ready, says someone to me. Hain't there no one else I can fetch?"

No, no one else. No one but Gil.

"Miss?"

"A horse." The cold burned deeper. Much deeper. "I need a horse."

Temperance filled the small carriage with happy chatter. Talk of this and that, of music and pretending, of Heath and marriage vows and wondrous jitters.

Not that Gilbert minded. He listened and he listened hard. He trained his eyes on the eager face and hoped his brain would follow her prattle.

But it lingered back to Bletherton. Lingered close to a woman who didn't realize he'd left because she was next to a man she'd pledged her life to.

A man she didn't love.

A man she wasn't meant to be with.

A man who would never be able to make her happy.

Neither could Gilbert. He was not such a fool as to think Nan could ever feel this way or reach this point or want this thing.

"Master Stanhope?" Temperance asked, her glowing eyes and hushed voice. "Have I annoyed you terribly?"

He shook his head, not certain his voice would work.

"Oh good. I know I have told you far too much already, but I am ever so uncomfortable in perfect silence. Aren't you?"

"I suppose."

"As I was saying, I heard this woman one time tell her husband that—" A pause, in which her profile turned to the window. "Did you hear that?"

"What?"

"I'm not certain. I just fathomed I heard a horse coming up behind us. Do you hear it now?"

As if in testament to her words, the carriage pulled to a stop. Noises outside—the driver calling out, a set of horse hoofs, then a woman's shrill voice.

Nan.

Gilbert burst open the carriage door and lunged out. "Nan?"

The horse drew closer in the darkness until nearness and moonlight made the rider visible. Her hair, wild and untamed, as it fell across her shoulders. Her bare shoulders, where the dress was ruined, hanging open, as if torn away by beastly claws.

He told himself to move, but he couldn't.

She didn't either. Just sat there on a prancing horse, with her eyes seizing his, with terror he hadn't seen on her face since the first day Papa had brought her home.

God, no. He pulled her into his arms.

She melted against him without sound. So cold. Dear mercy, what had happened?

His lips opened. Moved. No words came out because he was too afraid to know. *God, please.*

Then her fists grabbed his coat. "Lord Somerset." His name shook the earth with demon power. "Oh, Gil. . .it was him."

Temperance stood very still until the carriage was out of sight. The cottage called to her with its dimly lit windows and its tiny wisps of smoke rising in the moonlight.

But the magic was gone. There would be no elation in entering her home, in racing into her husband's embrace—because soon enough, she'd have to tell him. What would he say to such cruel news, to such a bitter homecoming?

If only this had not happened. Poor Miss Duncan, with her sweet innocence and gentle spirit. What sort of devil would do such a thing?

Temperance hugged her cloak tighter as she approached the cottage. She was nearly to the door before it came open.

There he stood. Smiling. As eager for that first touch, it seemed, as she had been. She drew to a stop just before him. "How long have you been back?"

He must not have expected the question or else he sensed something amiss, for his smile fell away. "A few hours ago."

She waited, as if to prepare him. For all her experience with words, when she needed them most, they failed her. Why couldn't she tell him?

He ushered her into the house. The warmth enveloped her. Tallow candles in all the windows, a blazing hearth, the sweet scent of a small meal that sat steaming on the table. Had he prepared this for her? For them?

The door came shut. Then his fingers were at her neck, untying her cloak, making her feel as if she were some sort of treasured queen.

"Heath, something has happened. Something concerning your sister."

His fingers faltered, face tightened.

"I could not find her in the ballroom, and Master Stanhope supposed she was with Lord Humphries. We all supposed that, I guess, and that is why we did not say goodbye. He was taking me to see you, then going on himself. . .and that is when Miss Duncan came riding after us."

Fear burned his eyes, burned deep enough it frightened her.

Temperance swallowed. "Lord Somerset. . .he attacked her in the garden. He did not ruin her, did not hurt her terribly, but if she does not return to the garden tonight with a great sum of money—he threatened to see her destroyed."

Heath reached for the door and yanked it open.

"Master Stanhope is with her now. There is nothing you can do. They will keep her safe and—"

"Stay here tonight."

"Where are you going?"

Nothing.

She followed him into the night, into the snow. "What are you going to do?"

Again, no answer.

"Heath?"

He marched toward the barn, shoulders rigid, strides long and fast. They entered the creaking building together, and her stomach cringed as he led Golda from her stall and didn't bother with a saddle.

"You're not thinking. You're going to do something terrible." Outside again. The barn door slammed shut with fury. "Heath, listen to me! I cannot let you go out there like this. You don't know what you're doing!" She latched on to his arm.

And he flung her off. Just a second, a quick glance. She saw rage, white-hot and heinous, but he didn't say a word. He swung atop Golda, dug his heels into her side, and bolted into the darkness.

Temperance's screams lifted. Her throat ached in the cold. Her eyes stung against the snowflakes.

She prayed to heaven he wouldn't do to Lord Somerset what he'd done to Loftus. Or worse.

"She is not going back." Gilbert stood in front of the drawing room hearth, the heat crawling through his clothes and suffocating him. "She is not leaving here."

Mr. Stanhope sat in his chair and tugged a cigar from his pocket. Blast it all, but did he have to smoke at such a time as this?

Mrs. Stanhope seemed strangely calm, as she folded her hands in her lap and remained expressionless.

"I say we prepare the money, and I shall deliver it myself." Gilbert moved to the window, jerked it open. Cold air burst in and bathed his sweating face. "Then both Nan and her reputation will come to no harm."

"And if this happens again?"

Gilbert jerked toward Papa. "I don't see as we have a choice."

"Don't we?"

"What do you propose we do—forget this ever happened, send no money, and let Lord Somerset set a wildfire among all the gossipmongers?"

"I did not say that, Son."

"Then what do you say? If it's the dashed money, I shall pay for it. However much it takes and however long it might take me to pay you back, I will—"

"Gilbert." Mamma spoke for the first time, her reprimand soft but inflicting. "It is not the money, as you very well know. It is Nan we are thinking of."

As if on cue, a noise came from the doorway. Nan entered in a clean muslin gown, her auburn tresses wet and loose, her cheeks rosy and fresh, as if all her tears had been scrubbed away.

"Come here, my little Nan." Mr. Stanhope reached out his hand, and Nan moved next to his chair and grasped him.

A knot eased up Gilbert's throat. His gaze roamed from Nan's moist eyes to Papa's determined ones.

"Gilbert will ride for the constable and magistrate. Nan and I will journey to Bletherton with the torn dress." A pause, as he puffed out smoke and gave Nan's hand another squeeze. "We will explain everything to her ladyship and Lord Humphries and even Lady Julia, if she cares to listen."

"They will not believe us." Gilbert edged closer. "Her ladyship would not dare—"

"I know. None of them will believe." Silence stretched on for a few seconds, as Mr. Stanhope glanced to Nan with a hint of a smile. "But then we shall all go into the garden together, and I should think it would be difficult for even her ladyship to deny our story when her son is there waiting."

"You are out of your heads." Her ladyship stood before them in the anteroom, still dressed in costume, and ripped the mask from her face. "How dare you suggest my son would defame himself with this woman."

This woman. As if Nan were some sort of lightskirt, a degraded predator instead of the victim. Was this how all of Wydenshire would view her from this night forth?

From behind his mother, the dragon met her eyes. The longer he beheld her, the quicker his cheeks and ears burned red—but he made no sign as to whether or not he believed such a tale.

"Show the dress, Nan," said Mr. Stanhope.

She didn't want to. She wanted to clutch it to her chest and run. She wanted to lock herself away and never see sunlight again, until everyone forgot and no one accused her and—

"Nan, show the dress."

With the second command, she forced her fingers to hold it out. The fabric unfolded before them, swished against the floor.

But her ladyship didn't so much as blink. "This proves nothing."

"Mother—"

"Shut up, Aylmer."

"But perhaps Miss Duncan is merely confused as to who attacked her." Lord Humphries stepped around his mother, redder still, and swallowed as he looked to Nan. "That must be what happened. . .is it not, Miss Duncan? After all, it was terribly dark tonight. Wasn't it?"

She wanted to tell him yes, that everything had been a dreadful mistake, that neither she nor his brother had betrayed him.

Mr. Stanhope said instead, "I fear not, my lord. There is no mistake."

"No mistake, he says." Her ladyship sent her mask sailing into the air. "There most certainly is—and you and this she-devil just made it. Do not think I am oblivious to what you are doing. A fine scheme, only I have no intention of handing you over one halfpenny to keep this quiet. My son left many hours ago. He is nowhere near here, and he was nowhere near this woman—now get out of my house."

"No." Mr. Stanhope didn't flinch. Didn't change expressions behind the spectacles. "We are not leaving."

"Well!"

"We are staying right here in this room until Gilbert arrives with Constable Hearne and Mr. Goody. Then we are all going out into the garden together."

"We most certainly are not!"

"But Mother, at least then we would know—"

"Shut up, Aylmer!" Her ladyship smacked her hands together as if to silence everyone. "I already know the innocence of my son. If we *do* go out into that garden, it will be for one purpose."

Nan nearly shriveled beneath such a furious gaze.

"And that will be to expose this chit you almost married, Aylmer. Because when Charles is not in the garden as she claims, this shall cost her greatly. I will see to that myself."

Nervous energy coursed through Gilbert. No one spoke. An eerie stillness filled the air, an intangible dread that hovered about every soul who stood before the garden.

Except for Mr. Goody. He stifled yet another yawn, adjusted his continental hat, and made a stiff remark that whoever was to enter the garden better do so quickly.

"I will." Gilbert stepped forward, but Nan's quick grasp held him back.

"No, Gil. If he sees you, he shall run."

"Not so far I could not catch him."

"Even so, it should be me." How brave she seemed—with her cheeks pale and cold, her eyes tearful, but her heart still willing to go in anyway. "Please."

"If we stand here like this all night, both Lord Somerset and ourselves will die of cold and sleep deprivation." The magistrate motioned toward the entrance. "Go on then, Miss Duncan—and the constable and young Stanhope shall follow behind."

Nan made no remark, nor did she look to anyone for courage. With her back straight, she entered the garden path until the foliage and darkness swallowed her from sight.

After a few long breaths, Gilbert and the constable entered the garden. They walked lightly, kept their heads bent low lest Lord Somerset should spot them, and—

A scream ripped the air. Nan's scream. Blood-chilling and terrorized, until every muscle in Gilbert's body sprang into motion.

God, no. He ripped away leaves. Crashed through growth. Forsook the path and plunged through everything to reach where he'd heard the cry.

Then he stumbled into the open, with the constable gasping behind him.

Nan stood next to a bench, both hands clasping her mouth. Sobs escaped her fingers.

"Nan."

She jumped at the voice, glanced up at him with another frail noise. Then her gaze dropped back to the ground.

A body.

Face down.

With blood seeping into the soil beneath him.

CHAPTER 25

Terror clawed through Nan's stomach. Panicked whispers came from the path as the others came racing for the scene.

Mr. Stanhope burst into the open first, but his fear faded when his eyes found Nan unscathed. Then Mr. Goody, with a mild oath and gasp, and Lord Humphries, with a start of surprise.

Then her ladyship. She strode forth with her shoulders poised, her lips tight, as if she expected Nan to be weeping apologies at the absence of her son.

But with one glance toward the bench, she saw. She didn't scream, hardly changed expressions—just rushed forward and bent next to him. "Charles?" In a voice so different than she'd ever used before. Tenderness rang with a touch of fragility. "Son, stay very still, and I shall get help. Aylmer, ride for the apothecary!"

No one moved.

Her ladyship jerked to her feet, glared at them, shouted again.

Still everyone remained. No one said anything.

"For the love of the saints, someone help him!" But she said the words without conviction, and instead of insisting she was obeyed, she sank next to her son. She overturned him. She pulled his smeared face onto her lap. "Do not worry, Charles. Whoever did this to you shall suffer. . .shall suffer like no other man has suffered in his life. I'll see him punished. I'll see him hanged. Oh Charles. . .my son. . ."

The air became too hard to breathe. Too haunted with the sound of the dowager's moans. Too polluted with the stench of dead plants and flowers and blood. Nan didn't want to be here. Didn't want to stand this close to the body. Who would do such a thing?

Yes, he was a rogue. He was despicable and unkind and frightening. But she'd have rather given him all the money he asked for than to see him like this. Dead and cold. With his white fingers splayed open, blood on the tips. With his face smashed into the dirt.

"You're all right, aren't you, Nan?"

Gilbert. Dear, beloved Gilbert—who stood beside her and held her hand. Were it not for him, close to her like this, could she even bear such a scene?

"Let me take you home, hmm?" Another squeeze. "There is nothing more we can do here tonight, and you shall feel much better when. . .when. . ."

"Gil?"

His eyes were sharp, alert, scanning back and forth as if looking for something.

"Gil, what is the matter?"

"I heard something."

Mr. Goody must have heard too because he stepped forward with raised brows. "I hate to be insensitive, everyone, but I'd wager to say we're not alone here tonight. I say, those bushes—"

Gilbert ripped away from her. Everything happened so fast, a blur—and next thing she knew, he was lunging through the tall bushes.

"Gil, no!"

Noises, grunts, then the sound of running feet.

Dear God, please. She pressed her hands to her mouth, heart stuttering. The man who had slaughtered Lord Somerset was still out there. He was running away from a crime that could cost him everything. He knew the stakes, and he wouldn't be taken down without unleashing terror.

And Gilbert was after him.

Alone.

"Someone. . .help him." Her plea turned on Mr. Stanhope and Mr. Goody, but they were already marching forward.

Constable Hearne followed behind, pistol drawn, though it quivered as he squeezed through the first set of bushes.

Lord Humphries remained where he was. Whether from lack of courage or shock, he stood stock-still, tears trailing his ashen cheeks.

A shot rang throughout the air, so loud it pierced Nan's soul and made her legs nearly buckle.

Then it came again, the pound of feet. The men ploughed through the bushes— Mr. Goody parting the foliage, Constable Hearne coming next with his gun, Gilbert and Mr. Stanhope dragging the killer by both arms. They slung him into the moonlight, to the base of the bench, where he clutched his bleeding arm and looked up.

Nan's stomach clenched. "Heath."

Pain burned through Heath's arm like fire, and every breath stoked fear in the pit of his gut. The night came alive with servants, torches, noises. One man wrenched both of Heath's hands behind his back and tied ropes about his bloody wrists. Another drove him to his knees. Another—the footman called Giles, who was without his wig again—patted down Heath's body.

"No knife," he said, stepping back. "No gun neither, my lady."

The dowager stood illuminated in the torch light, watching as the servants finally emerged from the garden. They carried her son into the open, outside of the garden's perimeter.

"Lay him here." Cool, detached. "Lay him in front of me."

With uncertain glances, the men deposited the body at her feet.

Then silence again, terrible silence. Everyone waited. Everyone stared. From somewhere in the darkness, the marquess's sister came rushing toward the scene—but Nan embraced the woman, hid her face, and tried to quiet the devastated whimpers.

God, please. But it was too late to pray. Heath knew that. *Please.*

The body looked different without the shadows of the garden. Darkness no longer hid the slashes. One gash tore open his neck. Another bloodied his stomach. Two more ripped at his arms until the trickle dripped down to his white palms.

Her ladyship moved forward until she stood glaring down into Heath's face. "You." She had the look of the madam, that wild and demonic rage.

He expected it when her hand buffeted his face. He didn't wince, didn't look away, not even when her spittle landed on his cheek.

"You filthy, miserable dog! What have you to say?"

He didn't answer.

Another smack, then a blow cracked his head from behind. More pain. Circles, blackness, his forehead in the gravel—then rough hands yanked him up again.

Her ladyship hovered closer. Nose to nose. A blur to him. "Why did you do it? Why did you kill him this way?" Wrinkled hands seized his shirt. "In the name of mercy, why?"

"Mother." Lord Humphries reached for her. "Mother, please—"

"Leave me!"

"But Mother—"

She didn't fight when her son's arms engulfed her. He led her away from Heath, away from the body, where the torches no longer lit her face.

Mr. Goody took her place. He motioned to three men, then Heath was forced to his feet. They shoved him toward a waiting wagon, nudged him into the splintery bed, then climbed in next to him with guns and torches.

"Lock him up in the village cage. Bagnell, you stand guard the rest of tonight and all through morning. No visitors. Understood?"

Both men nodded. The constable climbed to the wagon seat and took the reins.

"As for you, Duncan, I'd rather be the blind beggar than face your lot." Mr. Goody smiled, just for a second, as if the thought lightened the darkness of his mood. "Hanging, I've no doubt, will be your greatest anticipation." He started to turn, but another figure appeared next to him from the blackness. "What do you want? Come now, miss, what is it?"

Nan's voice came too quietly to understand, but Mr. Goody answered with a sharp "Very well, but do so quickly" before he turned and marched away.

She crept forward, touched the edge of the wagon, stared up at Heath with little-girl eyes that didn't understand. "Heath?"

Every question came loose when she spoke his name. He wanted to answer. He wanted to make everything better, to soothe away those tears and fears.

But he'd never been good at that. He'd never possessed the power to keep her from harm, no matter how much he'd tried. Why must it always be this way? The two of them hurt. The two of them lost. The two of them never satisfied, never free, never safe—with Nan always afraid and Heath always trying to make it better.

But he couldn't. He couldn't pretend. He couldn't change now any more than he could've changed the Bobber or the cold, lonely streets or the ship that never returned.

"Your arm." Choked. "It needs cleaned and wrapped. I shall beg the magistrate to let me come with you so I can—"

"No."

She blanched. Her fingers tightened on the wood of the wagon until her knuckles were white and bony. Then, in less than a whisper, "What happened?"

He shook his head.

"Heath, please. I must know—"

"There is nothing to know."

"But you didn't kill him." A statement, not a question. Her wet eyes begged him to say it wasn't true, that the blame wasn't his, that he hadn't slaughtered the man who had threatened her.

But he couldn't.

He couldn't say anything.

He only stared at her until the wagon finally jerked away and carried him into the dark.

Morning light streamed within the cottage windows before Temperance heard. A horse, a neigh, approaching footsteps—

The door came open before she could move from her chair. A man entered in loose-hanging clothes, his skin red and wizened, hair strung into his eyes. Heath's papa, Nan's papa—and yet he bore no resemblance to his children.

He stepped further into the room and tossed his hat. "Wake you, did I? When I was young, I'd be hanged before I'd outsleep the dawn."

She rose from her wooden chair, which had occupied her through a long and sleepless night. Only in the last hour, as dawn had mocked her through the window, had her weary vigil slackened into sleep. "You have seen Heath?" she asked.

"They wouldn't let me."

"Let you?"

"High and mighty fools. Have you any breakfast?"

"But who? Oh please, who wouldn't let you? Where is he?"

The man went very still. Something changed in his expression, something strong enough to make his yellow-tinted eyes grow moist. "I figured they bloody well told you already, seeing as how you're his wife."

A cold jolt worked through her. Made her throat close. *No, no.*

"Caught him up in a murder last night. Fool, that boy. Stabbing a marquess like he did, then hanging around to get grabbed."

No.

"Sitting in the village cage right now, and I reckon they'll be sending him off to gaol soon enough. No chance you can see him, though. Wouldn't even let his own papa in, that rotten guard."

She moved without feeling, tore past the old man, stumbled through the door. "Where you be going?"

She ran to the barn, hitched a dirty cart to the only horse, and climbed in. *God, please.* The creaking wheels jarred into motion. *Please, please, please.*

Because he wouldn't do such a thing.

Not Heath.

Not her sweet, quiet, gentle Heath—whom she trusted, whom she'd given her life to. He wouldn't kill a man. He wouldn't forfeit their happiness this way. He wouldn't betray God and disrespect the old rector's memory in one terrible moment of rage.

A sob escaped, nearly doubled her over. "No." A murmur, but she could see it anyway. Loftus's face. His bruised, unconscious face. The face Heath had beaten—almost to death.

He wouldn't do this.

The assurance became a chant, a senseless echo she tried so hard to believe.

When the tiny village cage came into view, flanked by leafless hawthorns, she slowed the cart. Morning fog hovered above the ground, lifted around the four stone walls of the building. She pretended it was empty. She pretended there was a stranger inside. She pretended she was young again, the curious child who used to watch for the constable to escort a thief or poacher to the whipping post.

But pretending did no good, because when she drew closer, her husband was still inside.

"Ye're not gettin' in, lady, so you might as well jus' get back in that cart."

"You do not understand. I am his wife, see, and I have every right to—"

"Ye hain't got no rights, not when Mr. Goody says ye don't."

"All I ask is to speak with my husband. You don't have to use the key or open the door or anything. I'll just stand right there and shall be finished just as quickly. Surely not even Mr. Goody would protest that, would he?"

The man hesitated, readjusted his musket to the other shoulder. Then, half under his breath, "Have yer deuced word, lady. When I get done with my smoke, though, ye better be leavin' in that cart, hear?"

She nodded and waited until the guard had moved away with his clay pipe and gun.

Then she crept to the door with its tiny window and wrapped her fingers around the frozen bars. "Heath?"

Chains clanked inside. "Temperance, go home."

"Come close to me. I must see you. All night I waited, praying there would be no trouble, crying for the thought of what might happen. Heath, can you hear me?"

No answer. No moving of chains.

"Please answer me! I will not move until you come. You didn't kill that man last night. I know you didn't. You couldn't possibly." Tears slipped loose so fast she could taste their salt on her lips. "They say it's so, but they're wrong. They must be wrong because this cannot happen to us. Oh Heath, why won't you answer me?"

Nothing.

"You promised you wouldn't fight again. . .because of Loftus. Remember?" She pushed to her tiptoes, squinted into the dark little room. She couldn't see his face, just the hunched sight of his shoulders in the shadowed corner. "Why won't you look at me? Why won't you tell me it isn't true? Please tell me it isn't true."

Silence.

Silence she hated.

Silence that burned his guilt into the core of her soul. *Dear Christ, I cannot do this.* She stood still, numb, more empty than she'd ever been in her life. What kind of man had she married?

Fool, always a fool. She never did anything right. Never made the right choices. Never saw things or life or people as they were.

She always saw the good. She'd seen the good in Heath. So much goodness, so much gentleness and wonderful kindness. Oh, why couldn't it have been enough?

"You did kill him." The accusation damaged her, slaughtered all her fascinations and dreams and respect. Maybe it damaged him too, because his shoulders stiffened in the darkness.

"A'right, lady." The guard's voice came from behind her. "Run 'long to yer cart now, hear?"

She backed away from the door, from the window, from the man inside she loved.

But it was a love that had lost life. A love that hurt and bled and didn't understand—and had no choice but to shrivel into disappointment and die.

"I wish to see Nan."

"She does not wish to be seen."

Lord Humphries stood in the Dorrington Hall foyer, cheeks pink, looking so intimidated he might have turned and fled. Instead, his shoulders deflated. "You need not worry I shall drag her to church in performance of a wedding ceremony, if that is your fear."

Gilbert frowned. "She still does not wish to be seen. All of this has been a trying. . .ordeal for her."

"Undoubtedly. At least permit me to have my word with you then, and you may relate the news to Nan yourself. Agreed?"

Gilbert nodded, then motioned for the butler to take the lord's hat and coat. "Follow me." Neither spoke until they had entered the drawing room, where Gilbert flipped open Papa's satinwood cigar box. "Smoke?"

"No, thank you."

He snapped it shut with force. "Fine. Why have you come?"

"For many reasons."

"Such as?"

"First, to apologize." The man's cheeks grew redder still. "For my brother."

Gilbert turned, faced the dragon with a small pinch of sympathy. "None of his actions were of your doing. Nan blames no one."

"Even so, as my brother's title falls to me, so falls his shame. I wish to amend all wrongs."

"All?"

"Yes." A pause. "There were others."

"Such as?"

"Gambling, mostly." As he spoke, Lord Humphries crossed his hands behind his back and paced back and forth without glancing to Gilbert. "Major Sir John Bradford approached Mother and me this morning, just as we returned from the burial. It seems my brother has been quite in debt for some time, and the funds he owed the major were extensive."

"You will honor those debts?"

"I already have. Bradford hinted there were more gentlemen to which money was owed—but my brother was a private man. He kept such things to himself."

"I am sorry."

"As we all are. Not only has Charles disgraced our family, but he has shamed poor Nan as well. If he were not deceased, I would have very hostile things to say of him."

Gilbert nodded. "I shall tell Nan your words."

"That is not all I wish you to tell her." The pacing stopped. His hands unclasped. He stood facing Gilbert with a sickened look of dread. "Answer me plainly, Mr. Stanhope, and do not spare the truth. I do not like what I must ask, but I must know."

"Go on."

"I have never heard the name Heath Duncan until they were binding him two days ago in front of my brother's dead body. I admit to seeing him before but supposed him to be a servant."

"He is under my father's employ. He works the stables."

"Yes. A servant who shares the same name as Nan, who lives where she lives—indeed, who attacks and kills the very man who behaves unseemly toward her. Now tell me, Mr. Stanhope. Who is this man and what is he to Nan?"

Gilbert held his eyes. "Her brother."

Lord Humphries took the news without blinking. He nodded, looking away with a heavy breath. "I assumed as much, and for this, I am truly sorry. I do not suppose it would have worked anyway. Not after all that has transpired over these last two days."

Gilbert's chest worked faster. "Am I to understand you are ending the engagement?"

"I have no choice. With my brother's title, I have even greater responsibilities. Such a marriage would be unsuited for both of us." Then he sniffed, bowed. "Good day, Mr. Stanhope. Please tell Nan I am sorry. . .deeply sorry for everything."

Temperance refused to eat.

Not that Nan blamed her. Every bite of her own was hard to swallow and settled like stone in the pit of her stomach. When was the last time they'd slept? How many nights had it been? One, two?

The hours were morphing together like a dreadful dream. They sat lifelessly in Nan's bedchamber and spoke no words of Heath Duncan.

Sometimes, Nan told herself he was innocent. Other times, she knew the truth, the reality neither his wife nor sister wanted to face.

Because they loved him. Maybe they should have seen it before, all the terrible signs. When he'd been young, when the madam would finish another beating, Heath had crawled into a lonely corner and wept. So many times, he'd pounded the floor with his fists. Over and over again. Murmuring things she was too little to understand. "Nan, I want to kill her." The words came back, words she'd nodded to as a child.

She hadn't realized he was telling the truth. That the hurt had birthed such anger. That the anger could murder so easily.

A knock disturbed the quiet.

Temperance stayed in her chair, so Nan rose instead. She pulled the door open. Gilbert stood there with his brown waves partly covering his forehead, his eyes soft, his easy manner soothing. Oh, but she was drawn to him like a spring rushes to the ocean. He was the mountain, she the valley. He was the lifeblood that rushed through her veins, gave her heart the power to go on beating even when it was too weak on its own.

"Take a walk with me?"

She stepped into the hall, closed the door behind her, stayed close to him. "I shouldn't like to leave Temperance."

"Taking it horribly, is she?"

"Yes."

"And you?"

She couldn't answer because she didn't know how. She was too numb, too confused to comprehend anything. Sometimes there was pity for Heath. Other times grief. Then, perhaps more so, came the anger. For doing this to her. For ruining himself. For taking the life of another mortal man—

"Nan, perhaps he is not guilty."

"I wish it were true."

"Perhaps it is. Perhaps someone else—"

"No, you are wrong. There is no one else. I cannot bear such a hope. I cannot pretend he is not a killer, not when I know he...that he..."

"But how do you know?"

"He would have told me were it not. He would have told Temperance." Hurt squeezed her chest. "But he doesn't. He says nothing for himself. Can such a man be innocent?"

"I do not know. Maybe not. Whatever the case, they're transporting him to HM Shepton Mallet with the dawn, and the next trial will not be until April." He looked as if he might say more. Why didn't he?

"There is something else?"

"Yes, but I do not wish to cause you more grief."

"You speak of Lord Humphries?"

"How did you know?"

"I saw him from my window. I supposed he came to say he did not wish to marry me."

The hallway grew quiet. How strangely his eyes searched her face, as if he imagined she would wilt in a wave of anguish. Then his voice, husky and soft, "You are hurt, Nan?"

"No."

He looked as if he didn't believe her, but she had no strength to assure him. Blinking hard, she returned to her quiet bedchamber and pulled the door shut.

Heath squinted against the sun as he jumped from the bed of the wagon. The massive stone walls of the prison towered ahead, with their tiny, barred windows and daunting arched doorway.

"A'right, let me off with them manacles now." The man who had stayed guard on Heath these last few days dug a key from his pocket, while the footman Giles—who had driven the wagon—circled around to Heath's side.

"Eh, anyone taken a look at that arm?"

Heath shook his head, rubbed his wrists as the manacles fell loose.

"Should have seen to this, Bagnell." Giles ripped away some of the fabric. His face scrunched against the smell, but when he'd probed the flesh and flaked away dry blood, he only nodded. "Lucky chap, you are. Just grazed a bit. Here." In one quick flash, he fluttered a handkerchief from his pocket and wrapped it tight about the wound. "Ought to help a bit, that will."

"Thank you."

The footman nodded. He could have walked away, but he studied Heath with something like pity. "For what it's worth, fellow, I can't be bearin' no hard feelin' against you, even if you did stab that marquess. Someone needed to do it, I say.

Back a few years ago, I had a mind to do the same when his lordship kept followin' about the innocent likes o' my pretty cousin—"

"A'right, Giles. Hain't time for all this talk. Besides that, that ol' cousin of yers weren't pretty at all." The guard tossed the manacles into the wagon, barked an order for Giles to water the horses, then nudged Heath for the arched doorway.

The walls closed him in, the sunlight was gone, and the stench became heavy and choking. The man called Bagnell pushed Heath into an open-doored room.

A chair, a desk, a greasy-haired warden with a book of names. "Duncan, eh?" He attempted to spell the word, managed to get a few letters out of order, then rose from behind the desk. "We'll be takin' charge from 'ere, friend. See yourself out."

Bagnell hurried away, doubtless anxious for the fresh air they'd taken for granted moments ago.

"This way, my new friend." The warden's lips opened with a half-rotten smile. "I'm Warden Ord and, in case no one's told you yet, welcome." He grabbed his cudgel and keys, motioned Heath forward, and walked next to him as they navigated deeper into the prison.

Please, God. His heart thudded faster than their footsteps.

The corridors grew dimmer. Doors, so many doors. Sometimes moans lifted at the sound of their approach. Now and again, the warden banged his cudgel into the wall with a shout of warning. "Shut up in there, my little lovelies!"

Then they reached a set of stairs, where the warden grabbed a lantern. They descended, the darkness growing deeper, until the walls felt wet and slimy. *Dear Savior, what have I done?*

At the bottom, Ord grabbed a set of irons from a row of pegs. "Hold out your hands. That's it. What a smart fellow you are." A chuckle, then a mocking pat to the side of Heath's face. "That's my little lovely. I already have orders you're to be treated somethin' special. Seems there's a marchioness somewhere who wants the likes of you taken fine care of, indeed."

How she must hate him, the man who murdered her son. Maybe Nan hated him too. Maybe all of them, every last soul at Dorrington Hall, every last person he had lived with and admired. Did they loathe the man who had brought such reproach on them?

And Temperance. He stayed on her name, wallowed in the glory and misery of it, as the warden shoved him toward a windowless door. Could he bear it if she hated him too?

The key rattled the lock. The hinges creaked. Then the heavy wood swung open to cold, silent blackness.

"In you go." The cudgel nudged his shoulder blade, forced him into the room.

"Have fun with this one, eh, lovelies?"

The door slammed shut.

He was alone in silence, darkness, with irons so heavy they made his wrists ache.

Then a hand, cool and thin, slithered around his neck. Another body pressed close to him. A third whoosh of movement crept in from behind.

"Weel, the coat be mine."

"The shoes mine," came another.

"Och, but can this be a wee handkerchief?" Quick hands pecked at it. "With engravings too."

As his eyes adjusted to the darkness, he made out the forms. Faceless, dim, skeletal creatures. How many were there? Nine, ten? Irons rattled as they slipped closer.

"Now the shirtsleeves, they go to me." Hot, rancid breath against his face, then another man pushed himself forward.

He stood taller than the rest, and the others shrank away as if he bore authority. Then his voice, low and deep. "I heard you were comin', me cove."

Heath's stomach dropped. Coombs?

"Been stayin' upstairs. Private room, you know, until it reached me who be arrivin'." He glanced around, grinned, motioned to one of the men.

A fist smacked Heath's mouth, then a foot drove into his stomach. He doubled over, felt a shower of blows on his back. *God, please.*

Struggled back up, clasped his fists together, and swung. Too dark, too much movement, too many blows to ward off. He fell again. Seams snapped as his coat ripped off in shreds. Then his shirtsleeves.

He threw himself against someone, tackled him to the ground—but another prisoner lunged on Heath's back. Iron chains came around his neck, yanked hard, cut off airflow.

Just as quickly, the chains were gone. He was on his feet, shoving them off again, swinging his clasped fists again with the manacles jangling. They became the madam, and he fought like a man possessed.

For the fourth time, an elbow bashed his face. Blood in his mouth, choking down his throat. On the ground again, shoeless feet kicking his rib cage. He rolled until he hit a wall and couldn't escape.

"That be enough." Coombs's voice came from somewhere overhead. "Pott, go ahead with his shoes."

Cackling, laughing. The shoes were yanked from his feet.

Then Coombs dropped to his knees. He grabbed Heath's hair, lifted his face from the straw and dirt, smeared a bit of blood from off his chin. "Hope you don't be mindin', me cove, but I made a little deal with me friends here."

Fading, everything fading. Too much pain. Couldn't tell if the men were laughing or if the madam were only screaming at him.

"See, they was to 'ave your bleedin' clothes and such." Coombs grinned in the dark. "And I was to 'ave you."

❧

At first it was so strange, and she lacked feeling. Days and nights repeated, but it didn't make sense.

Temperance sat on the edge of her bed. If she strained her neck, she could see the stables through the window in her tiny servant quarters.

But she didn't want to see the stables.

She'd die if she saw the stables.

God, God. A prayer, a murmur, a soft rhythm she rocked back and forth to. Another day. Another night. *God, God, God.*

But He didn't hear her.

Or maybe He did. Maybe He had no wish to help her, to appease the grief, when she had wrought such anguish on herself. How could she not have known? How could she not have seen?

She had married a devil. It didn't make sense. She couldn't understand. Not when it altered everything she knew of him and everything she'd believed him to be.

She'd been wrong. Always wrong. How could she have expected, for once in her life, something to be perfect?

Yet how close it had been. His touches, his smile, the sweet cottage, and all the laughing children they might have had. It had all seemed so real. She might have lived the rest of her life content, if only she could embrace the memories of their few short days together.

But he had tainted their magic. He had broken everything. How much easier it would have been if he had fallen ill, slipped to sleep in her arms, and never awakened.

She could have borne the loss of him. His death would have hurt but would not have destroyed. If nothing else, she would have held on to the wondrous, beloved remembrance of Heath Duncan.

Now she had nothing.

Nothing but the bed, the four walls, and the window she couldn't bear to look out ever again.

CHAPTER 26

Very sorry, Miss Duncan, Miss Stanhope." The ornate entrance door to Bletherton Hall was opened no more than a crack, through which the butler's inexpressive face was visible. "Her ladyship refuses to see either of you."

Charlotte was young enough to sigh her objection, while Nan took the news without comment. After all, hadn't she expected as much?

"Furthermore, she wishes you not intrude upon Bletherton grounds again. I suggest you adhere to her wishes. Am I clear, Miss Duncan?"

"Perfectly." Nan gave Charlotte's hand a slight squeeze, more for her own comfort than anything else. "But do tell her ladyship, no matter what she might think of me, my prayers are with her. I wished to offer condolences."

"With all due respect, I do not imagine she wants them." And thus, the door shut.

"How terribly insufferable—"

"Shhh, Charlotte."

"But to think she would—"

"Never mind." Nan led Charlotte back down the steps, where a footman stood waiting by the open carriage door. It was not until they were both seated and Bletherton far behind that Charlotte spoke again.

"You can be certain *I* shall never go back there to that unforgiving place. How dare she refuse us? It's not as if *we* murdered her ol' son."

"Really, Charlotte. Try to have some empathy."

"What is that?"

"How would you feel if the sister of your son's. . ." The word never came. How quickly her tears were summoned lately. Just a thought, a word, and behold, the tears had returned.

"No one cares what I think." Charlotte picked at a loose thread on the sleeve of her pelisse. "And apparently no one cares for Mr. Duncan, either."

"Charlotte, you do not know a thing about it."

"Yes, I do. I've been hiding about and listening to Papa and Mamma speak of it—and you can scold me if you want. I'm not sorry a bit."

"Let's not discuss it."

"Why not? Everyone else seems to be. Even the servants have been saying awful things of him, that Mr. Duncan would not defend himself to his own wife. Is that true?"

"Yes."

"Temperance thinks he killed that man?"

"Yes."

"Do you think he killed that man?"

A pause, another prick of tears. Then again, softer, "Yes."

Charlotte's eyes rounded at the words as if she had not expected them. A pallor swept across her cheeks, the uncommon strike of solemnity. "You should not say that, Nan."

Nan's eyes drifted to the window. Anywhere to avoid the accusing eyes.

"Mr. Duncan would not kill anyone. No matter what people say or think, I know he would not."

If only they could all have such confidence. But there were things children did not understand. Not all good men were strong enough to resist wicked deeds, and the wrongly accused did not keep silent.

"Nan, look."

The carriage jerked to a stop before she spotted the rider outside her window. Papa? What was he doing here, only minutes from Dorrington's gates?

He dismounted his horse with difficulty, as if aching knees hindered him, and came hobbling for the carriage. He yanked open the door. "Out with you, girl."

"Papa, what are—"

"I said out with you!" He snatched her hand, pulled hard enough that she left the seat.

She braced herself, her foot steeled at the doorway, her free hand pressed against the carriage wall. "Whatever is wrong?"

"Plenty an' more."

"But how did you come to be here?"

"I've been waiting for you, waiting to talk." This time he jerked so hard she stumbled out of the carriage and would have hit her knees had he not held her up. "Now tell the driver to go on without you."

"But—"

"Do as I say. I'll return the likes o' you myself when we're finished."

Nan's pulse quickened under the pressure of his arms. She glanced at Charlotte first—pale on the edge of her seat—then to the driver, who looked as if he might jump down and attack with one nod from Nan.

Which was ridiculous, of course. Why should she need protecting from her own father?

She didn't.

Not at all.

Her fears were senseless, shameful—and as soon as she eased from his arms, she spoke the words without quaver. "Carry on without me. My papa will return me soon."

"But Nan—"

"Do as I say, Charlotte."

The girl frowned, bit the edge of her lip, then pulled the door shut.

The carriage gone, Nan was alone with a pair of bulging, furious eyes. "You weren't going to tell me, were you?"

"Tell you what?"

A slap stung her cheek. "Don't you be disrespecting. I won't take it, hear? Not from you or anybody else." He clasped her arm again, pulled her from the road, shoved her against a stone wall where his horse was waiting.

She told herself she shouldn't be afraid. Dear heavens, he was the one she had loved and prayed for and waited so long to be with again.

"Well?" He pressed next to her. "What do you have to say for yourself?"

She didn't answer fast enough. Another slap. Her panic soared until she felt cold and dizzy.

"You could have had everything."

"Papa—"

"You lied to me. You said you'd try. You promised your ol' papa you'd try for your mother's sake, but you lied."

"Lord Humphries b–broke the engagement, not I."

"You pushed him to it."

"No, I—"

"You only care about yourself. Go to the devil to your ol' papa, ain't that right? I told you what it'd do to me, girl. I told you. All you cared about were that deuced talk of love and high honor and—"

"Papa, you're hurting me." But he didn't listen. He bent her backward until the stones bruised her spine and his wretched hook dug into her shoulder, breaking the skin. "Please—"

"You don't know what you done." Over and over, half crying, cursing with a breath that was foul and drunken. "You're just like *her*. Just the same. Lied to me 'cause you didn't care."

Who was he talking about?

"You're not my daughter." The hook deepened. Cut farther. "You an' that cowardly brother. . .you're just the same. Fools, the both of you. You do shame to the Duncan clan and the bloody homeland."

Please, stop.

"Not my daughter."

Please.

"Selfish, foolish wretch."

Stop. So much pain she almost screamed. She crammed her eyes shut instead, listened, and pretended she heard horse hooves instead of the cursing. *Please—*

"That's enough." It wasn't her father's voice. Someone else, someone she loved. "That's enough, I say." The horse hooves came closer. They weren't imagined.

Then the hook left her shoulder. Papa whirled with both arms wide and open as if prepared for fisticuffs with the man who had intervened.

Gilbert dismounted. "Nan, come here."

"What kind o' man comes 'teen a man and his own blood, eh?"

She wanted to move, but she couldn't. She stayed still whimpering, just the fool and coward he thought her to be. Why couldn't she listen?

But Gilbert understood. He always understood. His eyes held hers, calm, assured—with that faint twinkle that always made her feel as if everything were less serious than everyone always pretended. "What kind of man," he said, shifting his gaze to her father, "makes his own blood afraid?"

"A daughter ought to fear her own papa. 'Tis respect, you bloody whelp."

"Then perhaps you should teach me some."

"Er?"

"Respect, sir. Perhaps you should teach me respect." Gilbert took another step closer. Shed his coat. Tossed it to the ground with the hint of a smile. "Will you oblige?"

"I don't fight with cowardly babes." With another string of curses, Papa hurried for his horse. He was mounted and riding away before Gilbert could get to her.

Then his strong hands framed her cheeks, and his whisper was soft in her face. "Are you hurt?"

Yes, she was hurt. Not only from the bruises and cut, but from the words that had been spoken to her by a papa she only wanted to please.

And Gilbert. He hurt her too, yet with gentleness. Strange, that they should be so near one another, breathing the same air, needing each other like they did—when it was destined they must now be apart.

"Charlotte told me what happened."

He loved her. Again and again came the thought, every day, always chipping away at the stone of their foundation. How they crumbled, the two of them. Maybe they were crumbling now. Why was she crying?

"I came as fast as I could."

She ought to pull away. Heavens, he had no right to caress her cheeks with his thumbs. She should not let him.

"Nan?"

"Please, Gil." Tears blurred his face. "Please let me go."

He obeyed without a change in expression. "Your papa. He was angry at you for something—"

"Lord Humphries, but it does not matter."

"Doesn't it?"

"No."

Silence followed that she should have broken. But she couldn't. Because she was tired of losing him more every day, all the while knowing his love was different.

She wanted to keep him.

Yet it was impossible. Even with Lord Humphries no longer her intended, how could she belong to Gil? How could she love as he loved? How could she forget the years behind, the children they both were inside?

"Here now, no more tears." With the back of his hand, he brushed both cheeks, much as he had done in younger years. "Let me see the shoulder."

She watched his face as he patted away the blood. Smiled a little when he said something silly to make her laugh. Almost wished, for the first time, her heart had changed when his had. How wonderful it might have been. How wonderful to love him.

And she wanted to pretend, just as Gilbert had once asked, that there were no years behind them. She wanted to pretend she was his. Was such a thing even possible?

For the first time, she wanted to believe it was.

Blood covered him, but little Nan was not here to wipe it all away. Darkness cloaked him, but the rector was not near to enter with candle and prayer. Cold and hunger gnawed him, but there was no crate and stolen chunks of bread to relieve him.

Heath was alone. He lay with his bare back against the damp wall, his cheek on a pile of straw, with his eyes swollen and throbbing.

Lord God, if You love me, help me.

Sometimes he couldn't wake up. He tried to. Tried to peel through the unconsciousness and end the spinning and save himself from the madam and her screams.

But even when he woke up, he couldn't be free. Not with the chains. Not with the rats and the stench and the skeletal men who lay next to him.

The blackness ate at him. Why was it always night? His soul hoped for the day, begged for morning that never came.

Sunshine was only a memory. Temperance, his beautiful Temperance. He'd waited his whole life, lived in emptiness so long—and then she came. How easily her joy possessed him. How tenderly she became his, with a touch so soft and loving he would have never known want again.

But he had ruined his own happiness. He had damaged her love.

He was paying the price. Whether it was right or wrong, he didn't know, but it hardly mattered. Temperance was at Dorrington Hall, and he was here. Her life would go on, and his would end.

He had no one to blame. He'd made the choice himself. God forgive him—

From across the room, the large door whined open for the first time in two days. Light spilled in. Chains quivered. The men panted and moaned when bread was scattered among them.

"Take it easy, my little lovelies. Want to make it last, eh, don't you?" The warden motioned another guard in with buckets of water. "That's it, Roadneff. The beasties like their drink, they do." He emptied the rest of his sack of bread, shooed out the guard, and pivoted toward the door—

Then hesitated before whirling to face Heath. He knelt before him with the glowing lantern. "You're the new one, ain't you?"

Heath pushed himself up with one elbow. Nodded.

"Been gettin' any food?"

"Some."

"I can see how much too. Not been 'ere more'n a fortnight and a'ready you're lookin' like a corpse we take to the dead house. Roadneff?"

The guard poked his head back in. "Wot?"

"Get some more bread for our starvin' friend here."

"Yes, sir."

The warden's eyes landed back on Heath. Slowly, amused, his lips upturned. "Coombs does a right fine job, don't he? Lucky for you he stays upstairs, private room—else you'd ne'er make it out of 'ere alive." His grin widened. "Not sayin' you will anyway. Most don't, you know."

Heath squinted hard against the searing light. He didn't expect to live.

"Yes, sir, that Lord Somerset took care of e'erything, he did. Took Coombs under his wing like he was his own son. 'Course I heard the talk like anyone else. It's been said by more'n one fellow that Lord Somerset had Coombs take care o' that little alley murder on account the marquess owed gamblin' debts he couldn't pay."

No wonder the marquess had appeared at the trial. Was his influence so great he could persuade a judge? Was that why Coombs had kept silent and shouldered the blame himself?

Heath mentally shook himself. It hurt too much to think.

The warden brushed his hand against Heath's forehead. "You're a burning like the devil's place. 'Course not my job to worry. No one paying a sparklin' shilling for your care, now is there?" He rose, brushed the straw off his knees, and kicked an old man out of his path. "Nighty night, my lovelies. Like I always say, the rats will eat the likes o' you 'fore you ever eat them."

Then the door slammed, and the darkness returned, and the warden's hoarse laugh faded into silence.

Roadneff never returned with the bread, and by and by, Heath stopped watching for him. Instead, he let the fever come back and steal him away.

He almost prayed he'd never wake up.

Something wasn't right. At first it was just a nagging, faint throb of unsettled remembrance. Only what did Gilbert remember?

He didn't know.

Maybe nothing.

Maybe Nan, with her quiet indifference these last few days, was pushing him to madness. By George, she'd made every effort to stay away from him. He told himself it was because of her papa. The things he'd said to her. The way he'd hurt her—

The cut. Gilbert's memory latched on to her shoulder. He'd torn the dress away enough to wipe the blood, to see the length and depth of her injury.

An injury he'd seen before. Somewhere. On someone else.

This doesn't make sense.

Surely the wide, jagged cut through Nan's shoulder could not be the same slashes on Lord Somerset's neck and arms.

A knife could have done the same. A knife *had* done the same. Heath's knife—the one never found.

In the wee hours of morning, Gilbert stumbled out of bed. He lit a candle. He retrieved a bone-handled knife from his drawer, jerked up his sleeve, and made a small cut.

Then he stared, as the blood came leaking forth. So thin, this line. So straight and clean, the kind of cut any knife would render.

But not a hook. Gilbert sank onto the edge of his bed and smeared away the blood. *Not a hook.*

Nan opened her eyes to someone pounding on her door, but it creaked open before she moved.

"Are you awake?" The door shut again. Then, in the soft lights of morning, Gilbert stood next to her. "I have something I wish to tell you in confidence. Are you listening?"

She pulled the covers up to her neck. How many times had Gilbert inhabited her room? Today felt different. More intimate, as if he shouldn't be here and she didn't want him to be.

"Is it news from Heath?" she asked.

"No, but it concerns him."

"How?"

"I do not think he murdered Lord Somerset."

"Gil, he will not deny—"

"I know all that. I think I understand it too." He ran his fingers through his already messy hair. "Can you trust me?"

Trust him? Was there anyone she trusted more?

"I am leaving this morning to make certain. I shall be back within hours. If I'm right, your brother might have more hope than we thought."

"But who—"

He pressed a finger to her lips. "Don't ask now. Just promise me this." He leaned closer than he should have, swept his hand half into her disheveled curls. "However this turns out, you shall be brave, hmm?"

A warmth pulsated in her heart. Somehow familiar, somehow foreign—but either way, it made her smile. "I promise, of course."

"That's my Nan." He pressed a kiss to her forehead, then hurried from her chamber and shut the door.

But she couldn't help remembering the time his lips had landed somewhere else.

"What are you askin'?" The old man sat still at his crudely built table, his palm downward, hook in the wood. "Stop speaking circles 'round me and say it plain."

"Your son is going to die."

"Eh?"

"Your son. Heath."

"I know his name, you whelp. What you think I can be doin' about it? I don't have power and wealth like that high and mighty marchioness or her haughty son."

"No, you don't. But let's not play games, shall we?"

"See here, get out of my—"

"We both know who killed Lord Somerset." Gilbert took a step closer. "It wasn't Heath."

"'Course it was."

"You're willing to let him hang for it?"

"Fool." He came to his feet so fast his knees nearly buckled, and wiped the sweat off his forehead. "Fool, you are. I don't have any children. They've both forsaken me. I wash my hands of 'em."

"Perhaps it is you, sir, who has done the forsaking."

"What do you want?"

"The truth."

"Then go to the bloody constable."

"I intend to." Gilbert turned. "Good day, sir—"

"Wait." Quiet, strange, powerful enough to make Gilbert face him again. The old man stood trembling. Cheeks sallow, lips half-open in disgust, eyes filling so fast that tears brimmed and overflowed. Was that a hint of Nan's features in these wrinkled, dirty ones?

"I don't know why I done it. I ne'er meant for Heath to take my place. I ne'er meant for it to happen this way. I ne'er even meant to kill the man."

How were so many deathly slashes an accident?

"I'm so sorry. You're right. I have forsaken them. . .my own children. Never should have left all those years ago. Never should have let this happen." More words. Talk of a little Nan and a brave Heath and the cursed madam who had hurt them. Hard to make out his words for all the sobs. "I ne'er meant to do this. Any of it. But some things a man can't be forgettin', has to avenge. You understand, don't you?" He hiccupped another sob. "Forgive me, forgive me. . .you'll forgive an old man, won't you?"

"You had better ask forgiveness from someone who can grant it." Gilbert nodded toward the door. "We had better go."

"Why did I do this? Why does this always happen to me? I ne'er meant to hurt anyone. Ne'er meant to. . .to. . . ." Partway across the floor, his legs buckled. He smacked the ground and seized his chest with his one hand.

Gilbert bent over him. "Mr. Duncan?"

Panting, sobbing, shaking. "Hurts. . .my chest. . ."

"Lie still now. Has this happened before?"

"No. . .not like this." His eyes closed. "Water. . .please."

Water. Gilbert scanned the small cottage, spotted a clay pitcher by a messy bed. He hurried for it, glanced inside. Empty. Maybe there was a well out back he could—

Something smacked the back of Gilbert's head. He fell. Dropped the pitcher. The grimy floorboards scraped in his face.

Then something cool, a blade, sliced through his back.

No. Arched in pain, he tried to stand—

But the hook came into his shoulder blade. Went deep. Ripped hard.

Then he was shoved over. The old man again, only he wasn't clasping his chest and he wasn't crying and his lips weren't blubbering. They were silent.

As he wiped his bloody hook on Gilbert's coat, the rest of the world went black.

Where was he?

Strange, that kiss this morning. Why should it linger there, fastened to her forehead like a button she couldn't rip off if she tried?

Nan didn't know. Gilbert, in some startling and bothersome way, had eroded her good sense. Without ever speaking of it, he had filled her thoughts and heart with the realization of his newfound love.

Everything was changed. She was no longer a little child to him—and he was no longer a boy.

The boy she used to understand, share everything with, play games with, was now a man. Why must life always be changing? How sweet it would be to return to when he had been a pirate and she a gypsy.

"Oh—my dear. I did not think anyone to be in here." Mrs. Stanhope stopped beside her at the window. "What are you watching for?"

"Just Gilbert."

"Still cannot entertain yourself without him, can you? Watching for him shall not make his return any faster. Do come along and play a song for me. My nerves have been terrible, and I'm in need of something soft to soothe me."

Nan smiled and nodded, but glanced once more out the window before she rose. The drive was still empty. What could possibly be taking so long?

"Something has happened."

From behind his desk, Mr. Stanhope lowered his quill and pen knife. "Upon my word, Nan, have you been crying?"

"Something has happened to Gil."

"Nonsense. You know how distracted he gets when he's taking Briar on a gallop."

"He wasn't going for a ride."

"No?"

"He was going after the man who killed Lord Somerset."

Mr. Stanhope came to his feet. "I thought that had all been settled. I thought your brother—"

"I thought so too, but Gil—"

"How long ago did he leave?"

"This morning, just before light."

Mr. Stanhope strode for the door and threw it open. He called for a servant and barked commands at the man. Then, as he grabbed his hat, he said, "Do not worry, my dear. We shall ride after him now, and chances are we shall discover him roaming the countryside in leisure."

If only it were so.

But a sickening rush of dread told her it wasn't.

Cold rushed in the open window and chilled Nan beyond flesh and bone until it reached a landing deep in her soul. *How can You let this happen, God?*

Gilbert was out there somewhere. Someplace not even Mr. Stanhope with all his mounted servants could discover.

But he'd return. He wasn't injured. He wasn't dead like Lord Somerset, with his neck slashed open and his eyes rolled back into his head.

Such a thing could not happen to Gil.

He always returned. Sometimes she had to wait, like the night when he'd been late for her birthday. He had slipped into her bedroom and given her the pendant. He had smiled and laughed and made everything better, just as he always did.

She needed him.

With unsteady hands, she latched the window closed and climbed back into her bed. Her tears did little good, but they came nonetheless, until she cupped her mouth with both hands and fought to breathe. *Please do not let him die, God.*

Because if he didn't return, she could not live.

She had no strength without him.

Temperance awoke to footsteps across her chamber doorway. Then a touch on her shoulder, soft and faint.

"Temperance, are you awake?"

She rolled over beneath her counterpane. "Oh—Miss Duncan." Had she overslept? "Goodness, what are you doing here? Is something the matter? Did I—"

"Nothing is the matter. You must forgive me for disturbing you when it is just light." Miss Duncan's look of angst, the red and swollen eyes, cleared the sleep from Temperance's mind.

She straightened and took Miss Duncan's hands. "Pray, what is it? What is the matter? Oh, never apologize for awakening me. My only pain is that you did not come for me sooner, for I would have spent the night by your bedside if you had but asked."

"Pain is easier spent alone."

"But—"

"Let me finish, I beg of you. I have not dared nor wanted to speak his name between us. Now I must, and if it causes you pain, please forgive me."

A throb started at Temperance's temples. She nodded, too afraid to speak.

"Gilbert told me something yesterday morn, something I hoped against hope was true. He does not think Heath killed—"

"Oh please, do not say it."

"You must let me finish."

"It is no good to pretend he is innocent. Do you not think I have accepted it by now? Do you not think I know the truth of what he has done?"

"You are not listening."

"I cannot bear to."

"I am leaving this morning for the prison. I am going to see him myself, because if what Gilbert told me is true, Heath may be the only one who knows what happened that night."

"He will not tell you."

"Maybe not." Miss Duncan searched her face. "And that is why I wish you to come with me. Maybe if you were to—"

"No." Shaking her head, she climbed out of bed. "I cannot. You cannot expect this of me."

"You must."

"I cannot face him." Temperance hastened to the window, where she could see the stables amid the early morning fog. "I will not go and beg him to tell me he murdered a man. You cannot ask me to."

"I am not asking." Miss Duncan seized her arm, swung her around. "I am commanding. Not for Heath's sake…because I don't know if he is innocent or guilty."

"Then why must you make me face him?"

Miss Duncan beheld her with tears as her grip loosened, then fell. "Because I am afraid. . .for Gilbert, for Heath, even for myself." She glanced out to the window. "I must know the truth."

Nausea swirled in Temperance's stomach. Whether she wanted to go or not, it did not seem she had a choice.

The door never opened twice in one day, but it creaked nonetheless. Faint light spilled in, and Warden Ord swept through the threshold. "Calm down, my beasties. No more bread, if that's what you're a-hopin'. I say, Duncan still alive in here, is he?"

Heath pushed himself off the ground. "Here, sir."

"I see you can stand. Can you make it, fellow?"

The chains nearly pulled him back to the ground, but he grabbed the wall and took a step anyway.

"That's a good boy. Come here, then."

Heath started forward, but a man from the darkness grabbed his ankle. He tumbled, smacked the ground, gritted his teeth against the rise of laughter.

"What a lot of blackguards, you." The warden entered long enough to swing his cudgel into the man's face. A yowl, then the prisoners quieted and shrank back.

The warden seized Heath's arm. "Come on, my little lovely. That's it. Now walk to the door and watch out for any more beasties, eh?"

His feet hurt. Everything hurt. He doubted he could make it to the door, but every time he almost fell, the warden steadied him.

The door slammed and locked. No more room. Just a black and empty corridor, cold enough that his limbs shook and rattled the chains.

"Bet you're a-wonderin' where we be goin', huh?"

What did it matter?

"What would you think if I was to say ol' Coombs wanted another day with you?"

Bile pushed up his throat. He stumbled on. Soon it would all be over.

"Stop here." The warden pointed to a door. He unlocked it, kicked it open, and shoved Heath inside.

No Coombs.

"Just sit tight, and I'll be returnin' soon." A chortle, deep and throaty. "With your *visitor*."

The door slammed shut.

Heath was alone again in a room, quiet and lifeless. He fell into a corner, onto a pile of hay, and kept his eyes trained on the door. Didn't know how to brace himself. Too weak to think, to prepare. Maybe he'd get lucky. Maybe this time

Coombs would hit him hard enough to kill him. Temperance would be spared one last shame, the whispers that her husband had ended on the gallows—

Footsteps approached

Heath's chest worked fast. More nausea, but there was nothing to cast up because he hadn't eaten in too many days. He hoisted himself up, stayed stiff against the darkest wall, curled his grimy hands into fists.

Then the door jerked open. Whoever entered held a lantern that blinded him.

"Five minutes an' no more," said Ord—and as the door shut again, the figure with the lantern crept closer, easing the lantern lower and out of his eyes.

Temperance.

The one person in the world he didn't want to see, whose very face brought more agony than Coombs's clouts. How unfair that she should be here and see him like this.

She stood in something white and clean, with the ringlets he used to touch framing her face. Whatever happened to that sweet glow in her cheeks, the one he had adored so many times?

Now it was gone, just like the adoration, the trust, the love. She stared at him as one beholds a revolting, defeated enemy. Some pity, some sadness, but mostly scorn—and he died beneath the horrors of it.

"Temperance." Her name sounded foreign on his lips. As if he'd never spoken it before. As if he'd never whispered it into her ear. As if she were not his wife at all.

She didn't answer. Strange, that. She always had something to say. Why did she keep silent now?

He took one step toward her—

And she backed up. She feared him, of course. Hadn't she the right?

"You had all of my love." A whisper, faint and detached. Her teary eyes swam with orange lantern light. "We could have been happy. I believed in you."

Pain carved through him. Why couldn't he tell her the truth?

Her lips moved without words. He knew her eyes, understood that she was pleading in silence, begging for him to deny his wicked guilt.

But he turned away instead. Seconds later, the lantern light was gone.

He balled his fists, bashed the wall, tired and sick of praying. His knuckles went bloody and raw, until the white of his bones pushed through, until he collapsed to the ground and wished he'd never get up again.

If You have any mercy, God, let it end.

The warden placed one foot on the bottom step and leaned against the wall with a lopsided grin. "Still can't believe it. The likes o' you, a pretty little damsel, in such close relation to a rogue like Duncan."

Nan grimaced at the scent of his breath. Or did the smell live everywhere in this place?

"Don't get occasion to see many fine ladies, I don't. 'Course we get some strumpets come waltzing in 'ere, claimin' to be sisters and mothers jus' so they can..." He blushed, shrugged. "Well, you know what they do. I can tell you're not that line o' breed, though."

From farther down the hall, the pitter-patter of hurried footsteps resonated. Seconds later, Temperance emerged from the darkness, tears awash on her stricken face.

"Ah, done a'ready, are you?" The warden reached for the lantern. "You ready now, Miss Duncan?"

She ignored him, stopped her maid before she rushed up the steps. "Temperance, did he—"

"I must get out of here." She averted her face, shaking so hard her voice became breathless. "Please, Miss Duncan, let me go."

Nan recoiled. "Warden, will you assist my maid out?"

"Pardon my sayin' so, Miss Duncan, but I'd just as leave assist you." Even so, he sighed and handed her the lantern. "Sixth door to your right. A'ready unlocked. I'll be back in a minute, so make your time count with the beasty."

Nan hurried into the blackness. She counted the doors as she passed. At six, she grasped the knob, wishing the fear would scamper away, wishing she could stop seeing Temperance's face—the pallid cheeks, the disappointed eyes, the quivering lips of a wife who still believed her husband was guilty. Maybe he was.

Nan pushed open the door, entered, and swung her lantern until she spotted a figure. "Heath?"

It couldn't be him.

She stepped closer, until the light better illuminated him, and watched as he struggled to his feet. His chest was shirtless, filthy, and bruised. He had the look again, the same one he'd worn on Cocksedge Road—that hungry, sunken look that made his skin white and his bones more distinct.

But it was his wounds that brought back the nightmares. The festering cuts, the dried blood, the yellow splotches of dying bruises.

"Heath, what have they done to you?" She lowered the lantern, rushed toward him, touched his face, and nearly wept. "You're so cold. So terribly cold."

He covered her hands with his bloodied ones. "You shouldn't have brought her."

"We had to come."

"You should have stayed away. The both of you." He needed her. She could sense the need, just as she always had as a child, and more than anything she wanted to help him.

"There are things I must ask," she whispered.

"I have nothing to say."

"Did you kill him?"

He pulled away, slumped against the wall. "Go, Nan."

"I won't."

"Please."

"Tell me you took a knife and slaughtered Lord Somerset because he attacked me. Then I shall believe you. Then I shall go."

"Nan—"

"Tell me. I must hear you say it."

"I cannot." He glanced up. "But I cannot say I didn't."

"Not even to me?"

"No."

"Not even to your wife?"

"You must go—"

"Yes, I will go." Her chest burned. Every breath made the sob harder to push down. "But you must know you are sacrificing more lives than just your own."

"Temperance will heal."

"I do not speak of Temperance."

"What?"

"Gilbert. He knows who killed Lord Somerset, and he has gone after him, but he has not returned. I fear that. . .that he's been. . ." She pressed her hands to her mouth, lost tears even when she tried to hold them back.

Heath straightened, stepped forward, and faced her, shoulders rigid, eyes holding hers in wretched silence. "It was Papa."

"What?"

"Before the trial, I went to London. . .back to the Bobber. I wanted to face her again. Wanted to let it all be. . .over for me." He paused. "She was already dead when I got there. They said a street robber came at night, slashed open her throat, took nothing but—"

"Mother's trinket box."

He nodded. "When I returned home to the cottage, Papa was there. I confronted him, told him I knew, but he went into a rage. He said if I ever told, you would be ruined, and he'd make carvings in Temperance's face."

Nan's blood drained cold as her heartbeat faltered. "Then?"

"He left. I put it out of my head, pretended it never happened, waited for

Temperance to come home."

"And she told you about Lord Somerset."

"So much had happened. I was angry. . .out of my head. Knew I'd promised never to fight again but didn't care. I went into the garden that night because I wanted fisticuffs with the man who had hurt you."

"And?"

"Papa was already in the garden. Ran when he saw me. . .pulled out some stones from the wall and crawled out. When I found Lord Somerset, he was already dead."

"You should have told the truth. You should have told everything when we found you."

"I couldn't."

"Why?"

"Because Temperance was alone at the cottage. Too many chances he could have gone back and—"

"Please do not say it." Nan framed her face with both hands. "Oh Heath, how could he do this to us? How could he. . .why would he. . ." The sobs came again, too many to keep back, and she slipped her arms around him. "He didn't know about the attack. He couldn't have. He had no reason to harm Lord Somerset. . .no reason at all. . ."

A voice outside the door lifted. "Quite finished in there, Miss Duncan? Brother must go back with the others, you know."

"Nan, promise me something."

"Yes?"

"I don't know if Papa has hurt Gilbert, but you must not go back to the cottage alone. There must be others."

"I promise."

"And Nan?"

"Yes?"

"It may come out. About you and me. . .and Papa. Being a family, I mean. It could ruin any—"

"None of that matters." She withdrew, grabbed his hands once more, pressed them close to her chest. "I wish I could stay. I wish I could wrap your hands and clean the wounds and—"

"Tut, tut, I haven't got all day, my little damsel." The warden threw open the door. "You'll have plenty o' time to see him again before he's hanged, I'll wager."

She forced herself away and grabbed the lantern but paused before she left the room. "Heath?"

He said nothing.

"I shall tell Temperance...I shall tell her everything. Papa cannot hurt us forever."

She couldn't see his face, but there were tears in his voice when he whispered back, "I pray he doesn't."

CHAPTER 27

Mr. Stanhope returned alone. He approached the stone steps of Dorrington Hall, cheeks rosy from cold, spectacles frosted over. Not once did he glance up. Even when he reached Nan, where she stood blocking the entrance door, he said nothing.

She watched his face. "My papa?"

"Gone. The cottage was empty."

"And Gil?"

The silence said everything, every unspoken dread. He looked down, over, up—then tears slid past the spectacles. "Let us all talk inside, Nan."

She didn't have the strength to talk. Couldn't he understand she couldn't bear it?

Gilbert would understand. He understood everything, as if his soul were made of her soul, as if his heart were tangled with hers.

"Come, Nan. Open the door."

She obeyed with a body that was stiff, numb. She passed from the icy outdoors to the warmth of the foyer, yet her mind could no longer tell the difference.

All she saw was Charlotte, dear and young, standing stock-still in the foyer center.

Then Mrs. Stanhope. She slipped beside her daughter so quietly she would not have been noticed, save for the uneven strokes of her breathing.

"Here, take my coat." Mr. Stanhope handed the butler his items—hat, gloves, greatcoat—before glancing up at those who waited. "Into the drawing room, shall we?"

"Tell us here." Mrs. Stanhope never took on that tone. Cold, demanding, sharp as the blade of a smallsword. "Please, Fredrick."

"Very well. The constable and I searched the cottage. Mr. Duncan, it seems, has quite disappeared."

"And my son?"

"Gilbert was nowhere to be found. There was blood on the cottage floor, and

Briar was discovered dead a few miles down the road—"

"No." Charlotte shook her head so hard the curls bounced. "Go again. You have to go look for Gil again. You have to—"

"Shhh, dear." Mrs. Stanhope drew her close. "We shall search until we find him. Oh dear heavens, we must find him."

Mr. Stanhope placed his hand into Charlotte's curls and wrapped an arm around his wife, as their groans and tears overwhelmed the room.

God, this cannot happen. Nan slipped back outside, stumbled down the stone steps, raced into the biting air so fast it stung her face. She found the tree again. The tree she loved. The tree she hated. The tree so hard to climb she wished it had never been planted.

"Pretend we never knew each other until this moment, Nan."

She wanted to, more than anything in the world—but she couldn't. Because she needed him too much. She depended on him too much. She loved him, loved him far too much to pretend away all the happy memories.

Pretend we've always known each other, Gil, and pretend it never has to stop. Her aching arms wrapped around a tree branch. Her face pressed into the cold wood. *Pretend we were together always. Pretend we were together now.*

☙❧

Temperance slipped to Miss Duncan's bedchamber door. Sobs came from the other side, just as there had been the night before and the night before that. Maybe the night before that too. How many had it been?

They were all running together, these days. Sometimes Temperance cried herself to sleep too. Not because her husband was a killer, as she had believed before.

But because he wasn't.

Because he had risked his life to protect her. Because he was innocent, yet strong enough to endure the guilt. Because he was suffering, even now, for a crime committed by someone else.

If they didn't find his papa, maybe he'd die for such a crime. Who would believe him now? What sort of judge would be convinced by Heath, with his sad and quiet eyes, when her ladyship was screeching his guilt?

It was so endlessly terrible. That this should happen to her, who had only ever longed to be happy in the tiny little cottage. Or Heath, who had been buffeted enough throughout his life without more damaging blows. Or Master Stanhope, wherever he was and whatever he was doing, if he were even still alive.

And Miss Duncan.

Temperance knelt outside the bedchamber doorway, tears springing forth at the sound of so much grief. In the name of mercy, why must they wait like this?

If only Master Stanhope could be found.

If only Heath could be set free.

If only the old man—that wretched, despicable old man—had never come for his children and tried to destroy them.

But he had and he was.

The only thing Temperance could do was pray.

Light. Just a circle somewhere above him, somewhat covered with leafless branches and thorns—but it was enough. Gilbert knew he wasn't dead.

Not yet.

As long as there was the hole above him, as long as he could still feel the inch-deep water, he knew something was left of him.

Gilbert Stanhope was alive.

But then the darkness came again. The light was gone, and the water grew colder. Sometimes he shook so hard his wounds scraped the rough stones. Other times he went still, the blackness plunging him deeper, and he lost himself in a void of painless oblivion.

He always came back, though.

To the hole.

To the water.

To being alive again, even when he no longer wanted to be. *God, how many days?*

He knew because he'd counted the light and darkness. Six days, and the sun was rising on the seventh.

He was beyond the torture of hunger. Now it was different. Numbness or something, and he stopped trying to climb out because he hadn't any strength.

He sat very still, his torn shoulder against the stones and his aching body in the water. The freezing water. The water he cupped in shaking hands and lifted to his cold lips.

For the thousandth time in so many days, his eyes shut when he told them not to. Maybe today, the seventh day, he would not wake up. Heaven have mercy, was this the end?

He'd always pictured it differently, his passing. Lying in a four-poster bed somewhere, old and coughing, with people smiling and hovering next to him.

But there was no one to bend over him here. Sometimes he thought he heard Nan's voice in the fog of his unconsciousness or felt the whisper of her breath against his skin. Part of him wanted to stay for her. For his sweet, beautiful Nan with the laugh he loved and the smile he longed for.

But then he remembered. Even if he survived, even if he held out for the laugh and the smile, she would still be lost to him.

And that was a death he couldn't live with. How much easier to drift away now. To die alone.

There was no point in going back. Nan knew and everyone else knew—yet even so, in the chill of another lifeless morning, she returned.

How strange and silent the cottage appeared, with its sinking thatched roof and ivy-covered walls. She dismounted her gig and clenched her hands as all the memories of a different lifetime came back to her.

The days when she used to love Papa. That sweet contentment in his presence. The surge of joy in knowing that, after all these years, he had finally come back for her and tomorrow had come at last.

Now it was gone. Love was too powerful to die, so it shriveled and formed into something new. A kind of hatred. A bitterness that got caught up in the imagery of Gilbert's murdered body and Papa's reddened face.

Please, Christ. She didn't know how to pray anymore. She followed the path and pried open the door, then slipped within the quiet cottage walls.

The cursed bloodstains drew her closer. Why had no one come and scrubbed them away? She couldn't either. She knelt next to them, touched her finger to the dark splotches. *God, I hope there was not pain for him.*

She knew he was dead.

Everyone knew.

That's why Mr. Stanhope wore that look, that lost and tortured despondency, as he'd stumble back home after another search. That's why Mrs. Stanhope couldn't leave her bed and why Charlotte couldn't eat and why everything in the manor seemed cold and empty.

After all, nine days had come and gone.

Nine days without him.

"I knew you'd come, girl."

Every muscle in Nan's body went rigid. She didn't turn, didn't breathe, didn't look up.

Then the hand landed on her shoulder. Old, wrinkled, fragile almost—and it squeezed in a way that was more tender than anything else. "I knew you'd come."

Nan rode with her arms circled around his middle. The horse lunged into a gallop until the motion made her dizzy. Tears sprang again. Maybe in fear because she should have escaped him.

Or maybe because she knew that the man she had her arms wrapped around could set Heath free, could take her to Gilbert. Or his body.

If she closed her eyes, she could imagine away the nightmare. She was nothing more than the little girl—he the humming papa with his pipe—and in their short time apart, they had missed each other.

But that wasn't true.

She didn't know this man. Maybe never had. Had she pretended all along?

"Just a little ways more, girl." Slurred again. Did he only kill when he was drunk, or could he kill just as easily sober? "I been waiting for you to come back...watching every day, I have."

Why were they heading for Bletherton?

"I guess you know what's been happening, eh?" When she didn't answer, he grunted. "I don't blame you none for being angry. What they done to Heath...but it'll all be over soon." The horse veered away from the road, trotted into the white, sparse woods.

Trees hovered above them, their naked branches laden with snow, the slight breeze dusting off snowflakes. She shivered when the horse picked up speed again. The world spun into a blur. Dear heavens, where was he taking her? Had he been hiding in these woods all along?

The trees grew thicker, the air quieter. Then, at the bottom of a small slope, a clearing amid the trees. A small hovel nestled there, flanked on each side with bushes and thicket—and the horse approached as if the dwelling were familiar.

"We're here now, girl." He swung down first, then reached for her. "Not much to look at though, is it?"

"Where are we?"

"Home." He said the word differently, with an odd tone, as he grabbed her arm. "Come inside. See for yourself the pigsty your ol' papa used to live in."

"You?" She approached the building. The rotten timber, the filthy wattle and daub, the sinking woven branches of the roof. "But this is Bletherton grounds. These woods belong to—"

"So they do." Papa kicked open the door, motioned her inside. "Right sorry I am for the cold. Can't be havin' no fire, though. Not with everybody looking for me."

A new sort of terror overwhelmed her when she entered the building. She glanced around at the bare walls. The empty floors. The lifeless scent of a house long left alone.

Then the door shut.

She faced him, perspiration moistening her forehead in spite of the cold. "Where is he?"

"Who?"

"You know."

"I know everything." His eyes glittered, almost amused, as he hobbled over to the one chair in the room. He sank into it. "There's bread in that sack in the corner. You better take your fill now 'cause we'll be leaving come morning—"

"Papa, answer me."

"No, you answer me. Tell me how you like this place." His hand made a vicious swing. "Take a good look, girl. But mind you, there's holes in the walls. Look o'er there in that corner. Rats climb in 'em sometimes, and a body gets so cold he'd like to die."

"I don't understand."

"Servants quarters. For the Bletherton gardener." He stood again. "Poor, stupid Scottish folk don't deserve no better, don't you know? We lived here—my faither and mither and me—from the time I was two years old. That is, until she died one winter. That's what happens when you shiver in a broken-down hovel that gets so cold at night all your fingers turn blue."

She blinked hard. Nothing made sense.

"That weren't the worst part, though. I could stand the cold. Didn't even mind breaking my back helpin' my faither in the garden. But it was the girl. . .that's the thing about it, Nan." Tears flashed, yet they possessed more than sadness. Rage, almost. Years upon years of hatred with no outlet, of injuries without balm—and it made his body tremble. "She'd hang around everywhere I went, smiling at me, telling me to teach her Gaelic songs and such, kissing me when no one was there to see it."

"Papa—"

"You know what she done to me? 'Twas the year I turned seventeen, an' I'd been planning and hoping and waiting for years to ask her. But the very moment I tried to say the words. . .she laughed. You hear me, girl? She laughed at me. Said how I was nothing, not nothing to her. After all those years, all those days o' loving her. . .and all the time she'd been laughing at me." He took one step forward.

Nan took one back. Couldn't look at him. Couldn't bear the red, liquid eyes, the way they cut into her with their fury. "Such things are finished—"

"They're not finished."

"That was years ago. So many years—"

"Not so many I forgot. I'll never forget. The pretty little marchioness may be high and mighty now, but she'll wish to heaven she'd never laughed at me."

Nan stared. Shuffled farther back. Tried to think.

Then everything made sense. The tragedies at Bletherton Manor. The poison. The fires. Lord Somerset and the slashes and—

"You're going with me tonight. They'll let you in because they know you. We could have had everything, everything of hers, if you'd married when I bloody well told you to. But now it's too late. We'll have to take what we can get an' do away with her ladyship and—"

"Papa, no." She backed to the door, but he followed her. Blood raced hot and fast through her veins. "I won't."

"We have to."

"I won't."

"Girl—"

She pivoted to the door, grasped the knob, threw it open. His fingers snatched her dress, but she ripped free and ran. *God, please.* Pumping her legs, she lunged for the horse. She seized the saddle and would have made the jump, but he grabbed a fistful of her hair.

"Why you want to run from me, Nan?" He yanked her to the ground, drove her face into the snow, hovered over her with the heavy scent of ale. "Don't make me hurt you too. So many people dead, but I don't want to hurt *you.*"

"Gilbert." She gasped the name as his hand went to her throat, as his hook lingered next to her cheek. "Please. . .where's Gilbert?"

"Out back. In the well."

Her vision blackened.

"I had to kill him. I'm sorry."

God, no.

"He stayed alive a long time. I thought maybe it could be over soon, and someone would find him after I left. But he died down there a few days ago. I'm sorry. I didn't want to hurt him, not like I did the others. Why does it always happen like this? She shouldn't have laughed at me. She had no right to laugh at me like I was nothing."

"Papa, p–please." The cold metal moved back and forth. Like a caress, only she knew better. "Please let me go. I—I won't stop you."

"Then you'll help me?"

"I cannot."

"What?"

"Her ladyship. . .she hates me too. She won't let me in."

"You're lyin' to me."

"Papa, I swear. It's because of Heath. . .because she thinks he killed her son." A sob escaped as the hook lowered to her neck. The snow burned, burned as deep and cold as her fear and his madness. "Papa. . .please!"

He shook his head, back and forth, and mumbled things she didn't understand. Then he hauled her up. His fingers crept back into her hair, squeezed hard as he yanked her toward the horse. "We're goin' to get what we can get. I'm not leaving Wydenshire with nothing. All your mother ever wanted was pretty things. . .all the pretty things the bloody marchioness always had handed to her."

Nan's body slammed into the horse. "My mother. . .she wouldn't have wanted this."

"Be hanged if she would."

"She wouldn't want her son in prison for what you did."

"Girl—"

"And she never would have wanted you to leave us all those years ago. Why did you have to leave? Why didn't you come back for us. . .all those times we waited?"

No answer, but his hand slipped free of her hair.

She pressed her forehead into the rough hide of his horse. "I prayed every night. I used to climb to the window at the Bobber in the middle of the night, because Heath said you'd come. I believed him. Today or tomorrow, he said. . .and I thought it was true. I watched for you."

More silence.

"But you never came." Her very core began to give way when she finally faced him.

He stood farther back now, a foot away, with both arms dangling at his sides. His cheeks were ashen, his lips slack, his eyes the dull and vacant stare of a man too agonized for expression.

She had more questions, more accusations. They wouldn't come, though. They just hovered in the air between them, silent and lethal, harsh enough that both of their tears came again.

"I never wanted to do wrong by you, Nan."

Her soul ached.

"I always want to do good, to do right. . .but I just can't seem to do it." He took another step back. Slipped his hand to his chest, through the buttons, as if his own heart ached too. "I wanted to make your mother happy. I couldn't do that either. It wasn't being poor she hated so much. . .it was me."

She almost ran to him, held him, promised him he was forgiven for everything.

But there was too much hurt. The past she might have forgotten, had as much as forgiven him for already. But then there was Heath, with his bruises and his chains.

And Gilbert. He stood between them like a universe, the expanse too wide to ever bridge. She had no heart to try. She had no strength.

As if he knew, as if he understood, Papa nodded. He smeared the tears from his red, wrinkled cheeks. He approached and never touched her, only mounted his horse and leaned forward for the reins—

A cry left his lips.

For a second he was still, frozen, doubled over his saddle without sound. Then he toppled forward. He hit the snow with a muffled thump. He turned himself over and tried to lift his head, but another howl came instead.

"Papa?" A cold surge rent through her. She bent next to him, caught his hand from its aimless motion. "Papa, what is the matter? Can you hear me?"

White, so white. Why was he so white?

"Do not try to speak. You must not move. I shall go for help and—"

"No." Choked. Labored. "St–stay."

She drew his hand to her cheek. She shouldn't, but she did because the little girl inside still remembered the man with the pipe.

"Sing something." His eyes shut. His fingers clenched hers so tight pain bruised her. "One of the old songs."

She never wanted to sing again, but she lifted her voice, faint and quivering, with a tune that threw her back in time.

Midway through the song, the calloused fingers lost their grip. The hand fell onto a still chest. The eyes rolled beneath the wrinkled eyelids.

Papa was dead.

CHAPTER 28

She knelt for a long time, with her dress growing damp in the snow, with her hand on Papa's unmoving chest. Then she picked herself up. The world was quiet, surreal, a dream of a place where she existed alone with two dead people.

Have mercy on me, dear Christ. She made her way around the side of the hovel, followed the path so faint she almost couldn't find it for the light layer of snow.

But she found the well.

It stood alone, rough stones half overgrown with briars and branches. She pushed them back. Snapped some of the twigs. Hardly noticed when a thorn scratched her wrist as if to prepare her for the pain.

Then she leaned forward.

The hole reached into the earth, deep and dark—but not dark enough.

Because she saw him. How tiny he looked down there, slumped forward and motionless in the black water.

"Gilbert?"

No answer. She'd never hear his voice again. She'd never have a chance to tell him what Papa had said, or how he'd died, or what it had done to her insides when she'd held his lifeless hand.

She'd never get to tell him something else. Something she wasn't sure of herself. A strange sort of beckoning to a place she'd never desired to go.

But Gilbert had. She had been oblivious, but he had loved her anyway. She had been a child, but he had seen her as a woman. She had been a friend, but he had given her his heart.

She didn't understand love. She couldn't even try. She only knew that whatever it was, hers belonged to Gilbert. Maybe always had. In some beautiful way or another, a part of her had always been his—and a part of him had always been hers.

They were more one than two, her and Gil.

Now she had to live without him.

She didn't look when they lifted Papa into the wagon. So much motion, so many voices and low commands and crunching footsteps in the snow.

Then they walked to the well and despair nearly choked her.

"All right, send him down." Mr. Goody motioned to one of the servants, and the constable disappeared into the hole. Inch by inch, they lowered him into the lifeless abyss.

Mr. Stanhope stood close. "No need for you to stay, Nan."

"I want to." The voice wasn't hers. It belonged to someone else, some other girl who used to live and laugh and be happy. The girl Gilbert used to love. The girl who loved him.

Why did it take so long?

Minutes fled.

Maybe hours.

Maybe a lifetime, only what life did she have left? She had nothing without Gilbert. She had no one without Gilbert. She didn't even have herself, because that was dead too—and the rest of her days she would be trapped in a living body with a lifeless soul.

Then a voice from deep in the well, "Back up!"

She couldn't watch, wasn't strong enough to lose his laughing face to his dead one. She whirled—

Mr. Stanhope caught her arm. Maybe he imagined she should stay, after all. That somehow this would be comfort, healing, a reality she could grab hold of when nothing felt real. Or maybe he needed the touch himself. Whatever the case, he pulled her head into his shoulder and squeezed. They stood wrapped in each other's arms, shaking, as the men pulled the rope up.

The constable surfaced with Gilbert.

She caught a flash of him before the servants sprang to help, grunting and lifting, saying things she couldn't make sense of.

"That's it. To the wagon with him, men." Mr. Goody helped the constable brush off his coat. "I say, let me help you off with this rope, man—"

"Sir!"

Nan's stomach lurched as the men dispersed, left a body sprawled out on the snow. The eyes were closed, sunken, with deep blue circles underneath. The skin was bloodless. The lips purple. The body limp and thin and twisted in a way that made Nan weak.

"Sir what?" Mr. Goody stomped forward. "I said get the body to the wagon. Hurry up!"

"Yes, sir, only..." One of the servants bent next to the body again. Swiped his hand across Gilbert's lips. He sprang back up. "That's the second time I thought...well, I thought I felt him breathe."

Her vision tunneled. *Gil?*

"I want to go in."

"You mustn't."

"I want to be with him."

"I understand." Mrs. Stanhope didn't. No one did. "But Nan, my dear, you must get some rest yourself. It is past midnight already. The apothecary must be allowed his time—"

As if on cue, the door opened. Mr. Puttock ambled out, rolling one shoulder as if to smooth out a kink. Noticing Nan and Mrs. Stanhope, he frowned. "Men expect miracles of doctors and apothecaries, I fear."

Nan's throat tightened. "Gilbert. Is he—"

"I shouldn't imagine he will make it till morning. It is a wonder he has made it as long as he has."

"He will." Nan's gaze fell on the open door, the sliver of Gilbert's face on white bed linens visible beyond. "He *will* live till morning. Beyond morning. He's going to wake up, and he's going to be healed, and he's going to—"

"Nan," Mrs. Stanhope said. "You must know that...whatever happens, we must be brave."

"And accept the inevitable," said Mr. Puttock.

"Because, dear, Gilbert would not want us to despair."

"Or underestimate the circumstances."

"And if he dies, we must go on."

"Because he *will* die. That is my medical opinion, I'm afraid, and it is only a matter of hours before—"

She fled from the blurry forms and distant words. She slammed herself into Gilbert's bedchamber and locked the door when they told her not to.

Then she flung herself next to the bed, next to him, and seized the hand that lay inert and colorless. "We must not listen to them." Close to his face. Closer than she'd ever been except the time he kissed her.

Why had she been so afraid that day? Why had she run?

She stared at him now, every smooth plane and crevasse. How long were the dark lashes that rested on his cheeks. How thick and moist were the lips that could no longer smile, or speak, or laugh.

She pressed her hands to his face. She breathed his air and let him breathe hers. "When all this is over, we can go riding again. Briar is gone, but we'll find a new horse, one you like better perhaps." Her tears dripped onto his cheeks until it seemed as if he cried too. "You are especially fond of the ones most difficult to handle. You always teach them well, though, don't you?"

Silence.

She pressed closer still, until her lips brushed against his, until the taste of him awoke new passion. "Pretend you were awake, Gil." A kiss, then another, but his lips remained like death. "Pretend you knew I loved you. Pretend you weren't going to die. Pretend we had one more chance. . .to be. . .to be together always."

She melted against him with sobs.

Because she knew he couldn't pretend.

Their time together was almost gone.

Temperance stood at the farthest corner of the cottage. How different everything seemed now, with the wool-shrouded body on the table, with the rising scents of death instead of the warm aromas of that one special meal Heath had prepared for her.

Her ladyship stood next to the old man's corpse. Black crepe floated around her face, and her bombazine dress hung on a frame that seemed thinner and more hunched than weeks before. "Would to heaven he would have never come back here."

Mr. Stanhope sighed.

Mr. Goody, who stood on the other side of the table, only crossed his arms and nodded. "Then this is the man?"

"Yes, it is the man."

"And everything Miss Duncan relayed to us was in truth?"

"Yes." Her ladyship blinked hard. She glanced about the room with a frightened look, as if something about the body robbed her composure. Then she sniffed and started away. "Good day, gentlemen—"

"Wait." Temperance took one step forward.

Her ladyship stopped, jerked her head, glared at Temperance as if her delay had better be imperative. "Who are you?"

"She is Nan's abigail, my lady," said Mr. Stanhope. "I believe she wishes to inquire about her husband."

"Husband?"

"Heath," said Temperance. "He is still in prison, see, and no matter what you feel for his father, Heath had nothing at all to do with it. He only took the guilt to spare me, to spare his sister, because if he hadn't—"

"That is quite enough. I understand." Her ladyship's glance swung to Mr. Stanhope, as if Temperance were too below her station to converse with herself. "I shall see to it the young man is released immediately."

"Thank you, my lady." Mr. Stanhope bowed. "We are most grateful."

Temperance echoed her gratitude with tears.

Her ladyship pulled open the cottage door. She took one step out, paused, then glanced back at the occupants of the room. "There is one part of Miss Duncan's story that was not told, gentlemen." Moisture gathered in her eyes when they settled back on the body. "I may have laughed at young Duncan, all those years ago, as such a match was impossible for both of us."

Silence a moment.

"But I cried too. I suppose that is one thing Duncan never knew."

I'll do anything, God. Sometime through the night, in the dim candlelight of his bedchamber, Nan knelt beside the bed. She knew it was almost over. Mr. Puttock had said so. Everyone said so.

Gilbert seemed different now, with his skin a new shade of pallor, with his breathing more shallow and faint.

He was dying.

Right now, with her kneeling here, with her hand intertwined with his. Nothing she could do. Nothing anyone could do.

Except God.

Please. If only she could say more. If only she could know the words. If only everything could make sense, and she could make God know how much she needed him, and touch His pity with her grief and anguish.

But the only word that would come was *please.* With Gilbert's hand pressed to her cheek. With her knees grinding into the hardwood floor. With her eyes crammed shut against the candlelight.

Oh God, You are faithful.

Even if Gilbert died.

You are holy.

No matter what.

Your ways are higher than my ways, and You know what's best.

Every place in her heart came unraveled, exposed before a mighty Savior—and she must have touched His pity because a warm presence settled around her.

But please, if it be Thy will, give me a miracle.

Peace stirred among her fears when she whispered aloud, "Please do not let him die."

Gilbert lived beyond morning, all throughout the day, and into the evening.

He survived another night.

Then another.

Sometimes she just sat beside him, holding his burning hand, murmuring prayers into the quiet, deathlike stillness. Other times she sat on the edge of the bed. She'd lean down and press her head upon his chest, listen to his weak heartbeat, let her tears slide into the fabric of his shirt.

Mr. Stanhope entered with every new hour. He'd walk to the head of the bed, stare down without saying anything, then leave again.

Mrs. Stanhope came more often. She'd bring fresh water. She'd fuss at the bedclothes. She'd adjust the pillows behind Gil's head.

Then Charlotte. She was more timid than the rest—and the first few times she entered, she made it no farther than the foot of his bed.

Now, as the fourth day was upon them, Charlotte crept to Nan's side and stared down at him. "I wish I could give him something."

Nan's arm weaved around the girl's waist. "Your prayers are all he needs."

"But I have been praying."

"I know."

"Why do his fingers move?"

Nan jerked her gaze to his hand. No movement. Her heart sank. "Dear, there was no—"

"See!"

His fingers twitched, stretched, then his lashes fluttered too. Disoriented eyes glanced at her.

"Charlotte, go for your mamma and papa. Hurry!"

The girl fled the room.

Gilbert's eyes closed again as she edged closer, as she held his cheek. "Gil?" Breathless. "Gil, can you hear me?"

At first nothing.

Then they squinted again, hazy, yet they lacked the bright look of fever. "N–Nan?"

"Do not talk. You are not well enough. There is so very much to say, to tell you. . .but not now. Can you hear me still?"

A ghost of a smile crossed his lips. He nodded.

"Are you thirsty? Hungry?"

He nodded again, as if to both.

She rose quickly, crossed the room, and poured cool water into a glass. When she whirled back to the bed, however, his eyes had sunk shut.

But it didn't matter. He had awakened. The fever was behind him.

And God was answering her prayer.

He was giving her a miracle.

Warden Ord held the last door open. The door that led outside. "Come now, my beasty. You want out or don't you?"

How startling, the lack of pressure and weight on his wrists. That first breath of air that wasn't putrid. The blinding streams of sunlight that had him squinting in pain.

He held out his hand to the warden. Maybe he shouldn't have.

Yet the warden met his grasp and shook the proffered hand, and he seemed genuine when he smiled and said, "Kind o' figured I'd be carryin' you out in a box 'stead of this. Nice change, this shakin' hands business."

Heath nodded and passed over the threshold. He hadn't known there'd be a carriage waiting, or that the door would already be open to him, or that the footman would be half smiling as if he knew.

Temperance stood at the carriage door, with a cloak and dress that billowed. Both hands were clasped in front of her. She beheld him in a new way, a different way, a way he hadn't expected. He had hoped that with everything over, she might have forgiven him and returned to the way she used to love him.

But she hadn't. No adoration warmed her stare, no sweet fascination.

He couldn't approach her. Had no heart to bear more coldness, more hurt, the loss of something he couldn't live without.

He waited and braced himself, tried to keep breathing when, inch by inch, she drew closer.

Then she was in front of him, looking up at him, as silent as he'd ever known her. His wife. The only person in the world who belonged to him, who made him brave enough to keep waking up every morning. If he didn't have her love, did he have anything?

He had plodded on after he lost Nan. And the rector. And his life at Dorrington Hall. But how much longer could he keep losing before he lost himself?

He touched her arm. Careful, hesitant, lest she fling herself away.

But she didn't. Oh, why didn't she speak?

Yet the longer he looked, the more he knew. Somewhere in her eyes, in this new and peculiar stare, he sensed everything. Her pain, her fears, her torment.

And it gave him courage to touch her other arm. To pull her closer. To wrap his bruised, aching arms around her shuddering, silent body. Only then, with her face crushed into his shirt, did she speak. "I—I do not expect your forgiveness. I am too afraid to even ask for it."

His forgiveness?

"If anyone should have believed in you, it should have been me. Your wife."

"My fault. Everything was my fault. You must know that."

"No, it was mine. Despite everything, it should have been me who believed in you. I, the one who loves you best and needs you most and understands everything about you. How could I have thought such things, such terrible things? How could I have been so unfaithful and wretchedly untrue to you?"

"I gave you no choice."

"But I should have known."

"I forced your doubt—"

"I was foolish enough to embrace it. Now so much has been altered. I fear you shall never look at me the same. I fear you cannot love me, not as you loved me before, because your faith in me has ended."

"No, Temperance."

"But how can you ever—"

"Do not say such things." He squeezed harder, pressed his face into the sweet smell of her hair. "The trouble is finished now. We need only forget it."

"But I'm so ashamed. And your love—"

"My love has not changed." His chest thudded so fast he could hear little more than the deafening pounds. Sweet comfort raced through every vein. The first breath of relief swept upon him, as if the rector were smiling and God were blessing and all the tortures were finally finished. "It has not changed at all. Except to grow greater."

⚜

For a long time, Gilbert had stayed in the darkness, content to float in the emptiness and rest in the void. Maybe he was still in the hole, but he couldn't see the light. Had he lost count of the days?

Then light. Not far away like the tiny hole, but all around him, bright and familiar.

Nan had touched his face. Must have been a dream again. He'd heard her voice, answered her. The confusion started to ebb away.

Thirsty?

Yes, thirsty. Needed water.

But the darkness had sucked him back. This time it was less comforting. He no longer wanted to remain in this place, this blackness, because Nan was waiting for him.

So he fought. He clawed. He strove against wave after wave of oblivion—then he surfaced more often.

Sometimes Papa stood over him, rubbing his forehead.

Other times Mamma was talking, and he answered with a nod or a smile or a hoarse word.

Then Charlotte, who did little more than stare at him with quizzical looks, as if she feared a wrong action might hurl him back into the blackness.

But always Nan was there. She was here now, as he awoke again to morning light. Did she ever sleep? Or go downstairs for breakfast? Or slip out of doors for a fresh breath of air?

The bed sank a little as she settled on the edge. "Good morning."

A glass of water pressed to his lips, and he waited until he had swallowed it before he answered, "Morning."

"How do you feel?"

"A little less like. . ." He bit back the word *death*. "I feel better."

Charlotte burst in. She rushed to the side of his bed, and must have lost her previous fears, because she launched into a long, excruciating story that took all of his strength to focus on. Good heavens, did it have an end? Or a point, for that matter?

Finally, with a little urging from Nan, Charlotte bent over Gilbert, kissed his cheek, and left the room.

Silence settled around them, warm and soft, as pleasant as a rainbow after hours of rain.

And there had been rain. More of it than he'd ever known. A storm so vicious he never fathomed it would end, or that he'd wake up, or that the pain would go away.

"You are most tired." Nan drew the coverlet against his neck. Her fingers brushed along his forehead, pushed back his hair. Like an endearment. He could almost imagine he were a different man, her husband maybe, and she were bent over him with a wife's ardent love. "I've soup waiting, but I fear you need rest more."

Soup. Rest. None of it he needed like her touch. . .like her hand still sweeping at his face. How unfair this was. To be trapped here, in this bed, with a comfort that would only injure him later. Didn't she know how she hurt him?

Something in her eyes hurt too. She stayed close, breathed deeper, looked at him with tears he hadn't noticed before.

"Nan." He said her name more to keep the darkness from stealing him back than anything else. "Nan. . .what is it?"

"Don't you know?"

He shook his head. He wished his eyes weren't so heavy, didn't try so hard to drift shut.

"I think you do." Closer. "You always know, Gil. Why shouldn't you know this?"

What was she saying? Maybe if the slumber weren't calling him back, he could tell. He could understand. Everything would make sense.

Then her lips touched his. Faint, quick, a touch so light he wondered if he were already asleep. His heart thrummed like madness. What had she done?

CHAPTER 29

Something was different.

Temperance paused in one of the familiar corridors, slipped into a quiet room, and wandered to a window she'd been looking out her whole life.

The same view stared back at her. One she'd seen a thousand times. Why today did it seem so different, so much lovelier despite winter's dull shades of gray and brown?

"There ye be, Miss Temp—er, Mrs. Duncan, I mean." A young maid leaned into the doorway and smiled. "Been lookin' everywhere for ye, I have. Did Miss Duncan tell ye?"

"Tell me what?"

"Five o' her pretty ol' dresses are to be adjusted to yer size. Miss Duncan says ye'll need 'em sure at the rectory."

The rectory. The thought was undoing and baffling. Was it possible? Could it be true that in only five days, she would depart for the place she'd so often heard Heath speak of?

Maybe that was the difference. Maybe Dorrington Hall had fallen under a spell, as if the old walls and stairwells and chambers knew she would be departing forever.

But it was a forever she would be spending with Heath. Her husband. A man who would labor for the church and assist the new rector, just as he'd done before.

How wonderful all of it would be. Could this be real? Could it be true?

Ah yes, it must be. Because every morning when she woke up, Heath was still there. Nothing had changed. Each day was closer to her departure.

She had never been more ready to tell Dorrington Hall goodbye.

They had not spoken of the kiss. With strange mayhem stirring her chest, Nan bustled about him every day—fixing his pillows, handing him white soup, drawing the drapes and closing them again. She told him of Papa. He told her of the well.

But still, they could not speak of it. The kiss. That memory that lingered between them, strained and taunting, like the echo of a dream after one has awakened.

For the first time in days, Nan left him alone in his chamber. So many things to do, to prepare, as Temperance finished the last of her packing. "This dress, Temperance?"

"Oh no, Miss Duncan, it is far too wonderful. Such exquisite white work and—"

"And this one?"

"Yes, but it is so beautiful. I couldn't think of—"

"This too. You have always said you admired the embroidered gold thread on this mull, haven't you?" Nan glanced over with a smile, as her maid took one of the dresses to the full-length mirror, held it against her, and spun.

How perfect Temperance was to behold. Even in her calico, with her hair slightly askew, she possessed a touch of something that made her beautiful. Happiness, perhaps. Unfeigned ecstasy and an inexplicable energy, as if every wish of her heart were finally made true.

But hearts did not always attain their desires, did they?

Nan left Temperance alone with the dresses and returned to Gilbert's bed-chamber. She told herself not to. Why should she? Why should she remain there, close to his side, when nothing was as she had hoped?

She should not have kissed him. She had imagined there would have been a change. That somehow, when her love and his at last collided, a new magic would come to life.

But it hadn't.

At least not for him.

All the hours after and throughout all the days that followed, he had said nothing. Just pretended, it seemed, that they were children. That this, whatever it was, had never happened and that their care for each other had not altered, that they weren't now lost somewhere in the painful in-between. For mercy's sake, what was he doing?

She reached his door and entered. An empty bed stared back at her and she started forward—

"Scold me even once and I shall do far worse than rise from bed."

She pivoted toward the window, where he leaned on the wall and grinned. But it was not a grin without tension and those were not eyes without fervency.

"Must you be so difficult?" She swept to the window and avoided his gaze by staring out the lightly frosted glass instead. "You know what Mr. Puttock said."

"He also said once he heard his pig conversing with his cow."

"A Bansbury tale, I'm sure."

"Indeed, but should one trust such a fellow?"

"Gil—"

"He was either top-heavy with too much gin, unstable in the mind, or is simple enough to imagine such a story could garner anyone's amusement."

"It obviously garnered yours, as you're still talking about it. Does your shoulder hurt terribly?"

"Not terribly."

"And your back?"

"The same."

Quietness. How swiftly it dropped between them like a massive curtain, too heavy to push through even if she tried. But what was there to say?

Deep inside her chest, a wellspring erupted. Every emotion she'd kept careful hold on, tried so hard to repress and ignore, came bubbling forth. How she hated the tears it brought. How she despised the burning blush, the faltering heart...all the things he would see and understand. Why wouldn't he speak to her? Oh heavens, why must he stay in this silence, ignoring the one thing she longed to make known?

Without looking at him, she turned from the window. "You had better return to bed now before you—"

"Nan?"

Her eyes collided with his, so fearful, so ashamed of the tears.

"Do not cry. There is no reason for tears."

"Isn't there?"

"Do not think I am ungrateful for what you have done. But you must know, I have no intention of binding you."

"What have I done?"

He glanced at her lips. Lingered there as faint color rushed to his cheeks. "I was ill and you c–comforted me."

"It was not that. You must know it was not that."

"You don't know what you're saying."

"I—"

"You were upset. I was dying, and you never thought you'd see me again. Can you be blamed for imagining you loved me?"

"But I do." Every part of her, every frail fragment, cast at his feet. "I do not know how. I do not even know when, but if you know me at all, you must know it is true."

"What are you saying?"

"What you have already said but never had words for."

Then silence, precious silence.

For a second he grinned, looked away, glanced back at her with tears. Then he tugged her closer. He placed his hand on her cheek, and with something like wonder, seeped his fingers into her curls. "My Nan."

How familiar were the words, yet they were new. He'd never spoken them like this. With that note of seeming overwhelmed. That musical joy.

Then he laughed. A faint, quiet, happy sound, as his arms folded around her—and all the days of his silence no longer mattered. The sweet way he looked at her was all that mattered. "My little Nan, what would you say to being my wife, hmm?"

His wife? Miss Duncan into Mrs. Gilbert Stanhope?

She stayed on the thought, this foreign ground. His wife meant she would never have to leave him. That she could stay just as she was now, with her head against a chest she loved, in arms that were more of a home than Dorrington Hall.

No more misunderstanding.

No more living together and feeling apart.

No more losing each other more and more and braving the thought that one day they'd have to say goodbye.

Ah yes, she wanted to be his wife. She would have said so too, had she any voice. Instead, she tilted her face to his. Met his lips. Drank of him, this enchanting taste, and lost the remains of her childish love to the love of now.

"I love you." His breath warmed her ear. "Love you so much, by Jove, I almost felt as if I had imagined your kiss. And when I had persuaded myself it was real, I determined you were in error, that you'd made a mistake. . .because I was too frightened to believe, to hope, it might be true."

"And now?" She slipped her arms around his neck. "Need you any more persuading?"

"Just the words. Say them, won't you?"

"I love you."

"Say them again."

"I love you."

"Again."

"I love you, my dear future husband." Her cheek pressed against his, and she closed her eyes as she whispered, "I daresay, I always have."

Heath stood at the carriage door. Sounds echoed all around him—Mr. Stanhope's laughter, Gilbert's voice, Temperance's crying as she gave one last embrace to Nan.

Charlotte was the first to approach him. Little Charlotte, the mischievous imp who had followed him everywhere and played such tricks. Were those tears in her eyes? He couldn't tell. She smiled them away too fast and curtsied.

"Very nice to know you, Mr. Duncan." She hesitated. Then with tears, she pleaded, "Oh, Mr. Duncan, can you not stay? There's plenty to do at our church. I know it. Why must you go to some frightfully faraway place where we shall never see you again?"

He smiled. "We will visit."

"It shall not be the same. And Loftus never lets me do as I wish in the stables, you know. He's a perfect bore."

"But you still have Golda."

"I do?"

He nodded.

"You mean you are leaving her—here? For me?"

"Yours in the fullest." With a small laugh, he pulled her forward and pressed a kiss to the top of her head.

Then Mr. and Mrs. Stanhope appeared, the latter of whom gave his arm a kind pat. "My dear boy, you are welcome at Dorrington always. Never forget."

"I won't. Thank you both."

Mr. Stanhope took Heath's hand, held his eyes, smiled behind the sun-glinting spectacles. "Young Temperance is a whimsical girl, but she is not without fortitude. She will stand by you, Heath. She will make you happy."

"Thank you, sir." Heath's throat closed. "For everything. For Nan...for all those years ago when you—"

"Now, now, son. None of that." Mr. Stanhope chuckled. "Our little Nan is, well, quite a treasure. And I'm convinced, of late, that her brother is of the same breed."

"Thank you, sir."

Then Nan. She moved to Heath, wrapped her arms around his middle, breathed soundless sobs into the wool fabric of his coat. She said nothing at all.

He didn't either.

They held each other, tangled together by all the memories, all the things there were no words for. How close Papa had come to altering them. He had swept into their lives and returned their love with expectations—and in some ways, both had sacrificed parts of themselves to meet those demands.

Nan had nearly married a man she did not love, simply to please her papa.

Heath had given up his promise to service the church in order to take Papa's blame. In the heat of everything and in the bittersweet gladness of having him back, they nearly lost sight of what really mattered.

Not pleasing Papa.

Not making him proud.

Not doing anything—except staying true to themselves. And God. If they had done such all along, perhaps it would not have ended this way.

As if sensing his thoughts, Nan sighed against him. "Is it wrong to say I still miss him?"

"No. It is not wrong." Sweet Nan, his little songbird. Somewhere from the past, he heard her voice again, soft and innocent, asking the same question she always asked.

Today or tomorrow, he'd answer.

They had clung to it, that thought, and survived on little more than its hope. Maybe sometimes along the way they'd stopped believing. So many hurts, so many things that went wrong, so many times it seemed tomorrow would never come.

Maybe it was here.

Right now.

Or maybe it would never come. Maybe there was just today. Nothing more, nothing less. Just the present, with all its pleasures and hurts, with the future just always out of reach. Perhaps tomorrow had never been meant for them at all.

Perhaps tomorrow belonged to God.

Nan slipped from his arms, smiled one last time, and stepped back. Temperance took her place, and together they climbed into the waiting carriage.

The door shut.

Soft goodbyes drifted on the air.

The wheels lurched into motion, and by and by, they exited the wrought iron gates.

"Oh Heath, I'm so wonderfully content—yet it all seems so unreal. I keep imagining us, Mr. and Mrs. Duncan, sitting next to each other in some shiny pew box, and everyone knowing we love each other. And there'll be children too. How many children do you suppose we shall have? Never mind. We shall likely have ten pew boxes before it is over. Yet it doesn't matter greatly so long as we have enough to make all sorts of laughter and—"

His lips joined hers. Oh, but she tasted rich and new and young, like the first scent of spring or the morning's early dew. *God, I thank Thee.*

Temperance sighed, laughed, nuzzled next to him without anything more to say.

And his heart was full.

He was happy.

They walked together on the path they used to run. Soon enough, they reached the tree where he had been a pirate and she a tiny gypsy.

But they did not climb today. He brandished no stick sword and she no clicking wooden spoons. Instead, they stood together beneath the boughs. Quiet, serene, looking more at each other than anywhere else.

"How did this happen to us, Gil?"

"How does anything happen?" Soft and whispered, as if speaking too loudly would disturb the magic. "We do not know how all the spring flowers can bloom at once. . .we are only glad they do."

"Let's not speak of our love as flowers. They are so temporal."

"By George, they are. How about a mountain then?"

"Too rugged and fearful."

"A river?"

"Ah yes, let it be a river. A river that never dries, that runs on forever and ever in its steady course." She laughed, smiled, leaned back against the thick tree. "When shall we tell Mr. Stanhope?"

"I daresay he already knows."

"Truly?"

"He's a keen sort of fellow behind those spectacles, I'll have you know. Seldom does anything escape his notice."

"And he shall be happy?"

"Everyone shall be happy. A bit surprised, perhaps, for some, but happy nonetheless."

"How do you know?"

He leaned closer. Pressed one hand to the tree. Looked at her softly, with the eyes of one satisfied and amazed. "Because love is a sort of miracle, see. It doesn't happen often, and it doesn't happen to everyone."

She smiled again, waited as he drew closer still.

"But when it does happen, the whole world pauses and notices, half in wonderment themselves—and it makes them happy just to see. Do you understand, my little Nan?"

"Yes, indeed. There is just one thing."

"Oh?"

"I am not at all little anymore." Her hands crept to his cheeks, his strong jaw. So fair, so dear to her. "But I am yours. More now than I ever was before."

He breathed a laugh, then leaned closer for a kiss never more tender, never more true.

Somewhere above, the tree shivered in the wind as if in excitement. The earth stilled in respect to the magic. The sun escaped a cloud and leaked its golden rays, in that same happiness Gil had spoken of.

Nestled deep into his arms, Nan's joy sprang to her eyes in tears. For the first time in her life, she did not hunger for tomorrow, with that cold and gnawing need.

She was much too happy in today.

Hannah Linder resides in the beautiful mountains of central West Virginia. Represented by Books & Such, she writes Regency romantic suspense novels. She is a double 2021 Selah Award winner, a 2022 Selah Award finalist, and a member of American Christian Fiction Writers (ACFW). Hannah is a Graphic Design Associates Degree graduate who specializes in professional book cover design. She designs for both traditional publishing houses and individual authors, including *New York Times, USA Today*, and international bestsellers. She is also a local photographer and a self-portrait photographer. When Hannah is not writing, she enjoys playing her instruments—piano, guitar, and ukulele—songwriting, painting still life, walking in the rain, and sitting on the front porch of her 1800s farmhouse. To follow her journey, visit hannahlinderbooks.com.

Other Books by Hannah Linder

Beneath His Silence
Second daughter of a baron—and a little on the
mischievous side—Ella Pemberton is no governess.
But the pretense is a necessity if she ever wishes to
get inside of Wyckhorn Manor and attain the truth
about her sister's death. Lord Sedgewick knows there's
blood on his hands. Lies have been conceived, then
more lies, but the price of truth would be too great.
All he has left is his son and his bitterness. Will Ella,
despite the lingering questions of his guilt, fall in love
with such a man? Or is she falling prey to him—just
as her dead sister?
Paperback / 978-1-63609-436-6

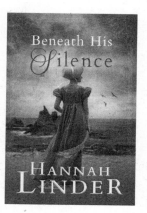

Coming October 2023

Garden of the Midnights
Enjoy another Gothic Style Regency from Hannah
Linder. As the secrets of Rosenleigh Manor unfold
into scandal—and murder—English gentleman
William Kensley's world is tipped into destitution,
leaving him penniless and alone. His only comfort
is in the constant love of Isabella Gresham, but now
her life is in peril. And even if he saves Isabella from
her captors, will he still have to forsake her heart?
Paperback / 978-1-63609-438-0

JOIN US ONLINE!

Christian Fiction for Women

Christian Fiction for Women is your online home for the latest in Christian fiction.

Check us out online for:

- Giveaways
- Recipes
- Info about Upcoming Releases
- Book Trailers
- News and More!

d *Christian Fiction for Women at Your Favorite Social Media Site:*

 Search "Christian Fiction for Women"

 @fictionforwomen